Meeting
Lydia

git

Oswald

Meeting Lydia

Linda MacDonald

Matador
5 Weir Road
Kibworth Beauchamp
Leicester LE8 0LQ, UK
Tel: (+44) 116 279 2299
Fax: (+44) 116 279 2277
Email: books@troubador.co.uk
Web: www.troubador.co.uk/matador

ISBN 978 1848767 126

British Library Cataloguing in Publication Data.
A catalogue record for this book is available from the British Library.

Typeset in 10.5pt Aldine by Troubador Publishing Ltd, Leicester, UK

Matador is an imprint of Troubador Publishing Ltd

Printed in Great Britain by the MPG Books Group, Bodmin and King's Lynn

To Mum and Dad

Acknowledgements

I owe a debt of gratitude to the following friends and colleagues: Marie Carver-Hughes for her critical reading of the first and final drafts and encouragement to continue throughout; Brian Hurn for his commentary, editing, and enthusiasm; Pat Hewitson for her theological input; Elizabeth Brett for Latin consultancy; and Anne Jackson, Sally Nadori, Marion Foster, Steve Tingle, Alan Czarkowski and Robert Bewley, each for their unique contributions.

The following students whom I have had the pleasure of teaching also deserve special thanks: Deyanse Along, Bola Bakare, Ashley Clarke, Elizabeth Dehinbo, James Ferguson, Nancy Freeman, Henry Isamade, Damian Kent, Zibi Nyathe, Miriam Okerejior, Connie Roche, Teresa Sam and my U6 classes of 2010-2011. The chapters depicting students are dedicated to the memory of Jenny Spain.

The Matador team have been invaluable and I would like to thank Amy Cooke and Sarah Taylor in particular for guiding me through the publication and marketing processes so efficiently. Friends and family have also patiently supported me throughout.

I always recognised that the explosion in emailing and the controversies surrounding Friends Reunited and other forms of social networking would inevitably lead to a proliferation of novels and dramas with this as the subject matter. I did not read any of these works until after my manuscript was completed and any similarity of theme is purely coincidental.

Prologue

December 1967

Lydia and Lucy sit on a late eighteenth century settee, primly posing for the photographer.

Lydia, so pretty in pink chiffon, with brown almond-eyes, cute upturned nose and smiling mouth; a rosy-apple blush, confident and self-assured. Lucy is gawky and awkward, pale and drawn despite the greasepaint. A nervous expression and big round saucer-eyes speak of hidden sadness. Lydia and Lucy … aged eleven.

They have never sat so close before, so intimately, and after much anxious thought, the girl who is Lucy ventures to speak.

"Are you excited about tomorrow?"

Lydia nods.

"I'm excited, but scared too …"

"Yes," says Lydia, staring straight ahead.

Lucy tries again. "Mr Russell said it's always better on the night."

"Yes." There is the flicker of a half-smile, but no warmth, no eye-contact, no hint of friendship. If anything, uneasiness.

Lucy sighs and averts her gaze, once more focusing on the man from the local newspaper.

1

August 2001

Searching

Marianne Hayward spent the first seven years of her education at a boys' prep school. Ever since then a hundredweight of baggage had lurked in her shadows like a Moray eel, snapping at emotions when her defences were low. Of course almost everyone who is nearly forty-six has baggage, and it wasn't as if her baggage was particularly special. Indeed it was fairly standard, mass-produced, flat-packed baggage; the sort that comes from being teased mercilessly by school bullies and made to feel worthless. But baggage is baggage, and to each individual concerned it is of limited consolation that others have baggage too.

At forty, she had thought it was time to face her demons, but it turned out not to be simple. She told a few chosen friends about some of the bullying but this had done nothing to lessen the hurt. In any case, the worst moments were still hidden in a locked box, too painful even for her own scrutiny. Sometimes she thought about opening the lid just a fraction and peeking through the tiniest gap to see if perhaps there was nothing alarming in there after all; that it was all a mistake; that she needn't have spent a lifetime of avoidance. But always she faltered, frightened of what she might find, and the box remained shut. Now almost six years later, she wasn't much further on in her quest.

Two weeks ago Holly had breezed in, "Heya, Mum!"

accompanied by the slamming of the front door, the chink of the key as she dropped it in the glass dish on the table in the hall, then the familiar pad, pad, pad, of rubber-soled sandals across the wooden floor. "Where's Dad? Would you like to see the Friends Reunited thing now? Michelle's mum has just found her best friend from Primary and they're going to meet next week. I'm just so jealous … Wish I could lose somebody so I could find them again! It would be so extra! Our generation never will. Not like yours. Not with email and texting. No excuse for losing touch. I've got half an hour before Jodie comes round."

This was what it was like with a whirlwind daughter only a month away from her first term at university and fledging the family home.

Marianne was ironing in the kitchen. She hated ironing. Her mother ironed everything, even knickers. Marianne found folding was a perfectly suitable option for many things. Her mother was from the school of *'clean vests in case of accidents'*. "Your father is playing snooker with Dave." She always said *'your father'* when she was displeased.

"You mean he's at the pub?" Holly's tone was accusing.

Marianne breathed in deeply. "He said snooker." The now-familiar knot in her stomach contracted slightly and reminded her of its presence. If he wasn't playing snooker, then what? Might he be with *her*?

"Snooker … pub … whatever." Holly shook her head and a cascade of dark hair shimmered around her shoulders. She was dressed in the casual uniform of the typical sixth former – flared denim jeans cut low on the hip and a quirky cerise top with an elephant embroidered on the front.

"I do wish you'd stop saying 'whatever'." As Marianne said the words she thought how unlike her they sounded. Perhaps she was turning into her mother. The one thing women say they never will, but often do.

"Friends Reunited, Mum ... Come on!"

Marianne's own dark hair was tied up high in a youthful ponytail and she was also wearing jeans. Like mother; like daughter. "I should really finish this ironing."

"Aw, Mum! You can do that anytime." And Holly pulled the plug on the iron and went upstairs.

Marianne abandoned the pile of clothes and followed her to the guest bedroom that was also an office and housed the family computer in the corner opposite the bed. She pulled up a chair and watched her daughter expertly clicking away until the Friends Reunited website appeared.

"I'll register you so you can browse," said Holly. "Think of a password. Type it in that box ... I won't look."

Marianne suddenly felt very hot. "I hate thinking of passwords." She used the same word that she had for most of her online shopping, but prefixed it with a number.

"What was the name of your secondary school?"

Marianne told her and Holly began to search. *North of England ... Cumbria ... Derwentbridge ... Derwentbridge Grammar School.* She watched intrigued as the page for her school came up on the screen.

"What year did you leave?"

"1975. It was a good year!"

"I thought the seventies were all about miners' strikes, petrol shortages and the Cold War ... And Glam Rock Yuk!" Holly selected the relevant year and a dazzling blue register appeared on a green background. There were about twelve people from Marianne's own year group.

She scanned the list, fascinated as the names from long ago prompted a range of assorted memories and emotions. Danny Froggatt with red hair who fell off a stool when he fainted in a biology lesson during mouse dissection; Josh Casey who was a liability in chemistry practicals ... *Rob*

Tallison! We called him Useless because he couldn't kiss!

"Any old boyfriends here?" asked Holly mischievously.

Marianne ignored the question. "Oh look, there's Sasha Clement!"

"But you're still in touch with her anyway."

"Only just. Christmas cards and the odd email. Pity she married the deadly Graham Simpkins. It's awful when husbands get in the way of friendship."

"What's wrong with him?"

"Little clammy hands. An intellectual bore who thinks he's interesting. And Grandma always says you can never trust a man who wears red jumpers!"

Holly pulled a face. "She was the pretty blonde one wasn't she? Why did she marry him?"

"He had connections in the legal world. She thought he would help to promote her career."

"Did all your friends keep their original names?"

"Sasha was the first. Sasha said adding Simpkins would make her sound like – to use her words – *'one of those anthropomorphised Beatrix Potter characters.'* Not befitting a lawyer, she said. We thought at the time it was very progressive and feminist. Grandma was incensed when I did the same." Marianne peered at the screen.

"That symbol next to the name means information about the person," said Holly. "And, if you want to send someone an email, you'll need to upgrade your registration and pay five pounds. Then just click on the envelope and follow the instructions. Dead simple."

And simple it was.

Now two weeks on, Marianne expertly clicked on the Friends Reunited links and it had become an almost nightly ritual to sit and search for anybody she could remember from the past. It was an addictive pastime for a pub widow in her

4

college holidays. The optional notes that people could add to their listing were interesting to read. Some were funny, some were sad. Most were tediously factual. The insecure waxed lyrical about their rise up the corporate ladder and the millions of pounds for which they were responsible. 'Haven't I done well?' they boasted from the page. 'No need to get in touch with me unless you are similarly successful.' The most amusing were self-effacing and apologetic. 'Don't bother to write unless you have had an equally disastrous life of two divorces and long periods of unemployment.'

It took Marianne three attempts before she decided what to write about herself. At first she wrote a detailed life history. Next, she was more succinct. 'Happily married with one 18-year-old daughter about to study Law at uni. Two cats. Living in Beckenham and teaching psychology at North Kent Sixth Form College.' Then after some thought, she deleted the 'happily' – it sounded smug. In any case she doubted it was still true. If they wanted to know more they could email.

But it wasn't just her secondary school that caught her attention on the Friends Reunited website. What about the boys from the prep school she attended; the boys from Brocklebank Hall? What had happened to them?

The Moray eel peered out from its hiding place and flexed its jaws. *Revenge!*

Barnaby Sproat was a name that sprang to mind and filled her with hostile thoughts. Top of the pecking order, he threw his weight around and made the lives of other boys miserable. And being a girl, the lowest of the low, the boys that he tormented exacted their frustrations on her. Of course she wasn't the only girl in the school, but boys outnumbered girls by about ten to one, and girls were scattered so thinly through the classes that they were never going to provide enough of a force to challenge the mighty Sproat and his minions. Yes, it would be fascinating to know what had become of the bullies.

She clicked through the links but found there was no page for Brocklebank Hall. At first she was relieved, but the eel was restless, a grey shape hidden beneath the rocks, hungry for salvation. She entered the details of the school and sent them off for verification. Once the school was on the site, surely people would rush to add their names. Perhaps *he* would add his name; the one boy in the school who had never been horrible to her.

Edward Harvey.

Even thinking his name made her tingle with half-remembered childlike giddiness. Dear Edward Harvey; the only one from Brocklebank to whom she might write if she found him.

There might be others on the site from later years. First-boyfriend Nick, who called her a *'mad-alcoholic-horsewoman'* on account of her equestrian interests and a bout of giggling after two half lager shandies. Nick, who really liked her and even loved her just a little. She wanted to find him to apologise. To say, 'Hey Nick, I was only sweet sixteen, I didn't know that after you I was going to meet a succession of bastards. If I had known, I wouldn't have treated our romance so casually. Would have given it time to see how it all worked out. I'm sorry Nick. I didn't mean to hurt you. Didn't believe, deep down, that you really cared.'

What if he was married now? Bound to be. Bound to be attached to some competent, not-a-hair-out-of-place woman who could rustle up an impressive supper for unexpected guests without a trace of panic. Someone sophisticated, beautiful and clever, who effortlessly produced a couple of well-behaved children called Charlotte and Annabelle; someone who enjoyed making cup-cakes and ironing shirts. She would take a dim view about her beloved being emailed by some ex- from way back when. It might upset the apple cart and Marianne didn't want that. Didn't want her own apple cart upsetting either for that matter, though some would say the apples were already on the slide.

Edward Harvey, on the other hand, was a safer option as there was no romantic history to cause alarm. Perhaps they might meet again at a Brocklebank reunion?

Marianne had seen tales of school reunions on the TV that brought her baggage to the surface and made her cringe. The quiet and the shy coming face to face once again with the key characters who were still loud and confident and operating as a pack.

'Great to see you after all these years! What are you doing now?' they gushed, full of bonhomie as if their unkind deeds were mere nothings in the life gone by.

I remember when you dragged me backwards across the asphalt of the netball court by my green plastic team-identifying band. Dragged me until I fell disorientated in a humiliating heap and then you laughed in my face.

No matter that Marianne was now an efficient and overtly confident mature woman. Put her back in the same company as them and she was sure to revert to frightened mouse.

She would love to find Sarah Strong from riding school days in the seaside village of Allonby. Sarah did impressions of Tommy Cooper. They had such fun every summer helping out at the stables and being 'pony girls': rounding up the horses, saddling and unsaddling, feeling important under the gaze of the paying customers who watched from the other side of a high whitewashed wall.

The August light was fading fast and Marianne grieved for the passing summer. Soon she would be plunged into the predicable ritual of the academic year. How much time for idle surfing then? She got up to draw the curtains, momentarily glancing at the breeze rustling the trees in the garden and the full moon glinting through the branches. She could sense there was a chill in the air and could almost smell the damp onset of autumn. Holly would be leaving soon; the end of the childhood journey. It made her feel sad.

Then back to the computer.

No luck tonight in the hunt for Nick or Sarah, yet every day it seemed new people were joining as newspaper column centimetres and breakfast chat shows advertised the web site and precipitated a snowball effect. She sighed and typed 'Edward Harvey' into the Name Search box.

Then she felt that heat again: a sudden rush, enveloping most of her body. It had been happening for a week now, every time she was ever so slightly stressed. Waves of warmth the like of which she had never experienced before. Even thinking about getting out of bed in the morning brought it on. Surely she was too young to be going menopausal, but a quick exploration courtesy of Google last evening suggested not. Forty-five to fifty-two was the average age of onset. So if that was it, it was early, but not too early. And her period was late.

Or she was pregnant! God forbid. Did you get hot flushes with pregnancy? More surfing had proved inconclusive. She felt sick. Had she been feeling sick before? With Holly just beginning her degree and a husband who was umbilically attached to the pub these days – never mind her other suspicions – this was no time for a baby. She looked for signs of breast tenderness but there was none.

Edward Harvey. Click *Search,* and wait … There were four of them. That's one more since last week. She scanned the new entry, hoping to see some evidence of familiarity. Edward Harvey: Leeds Grammar School, leaving date 1989. Too young. In any case, Edward – her Edward – had gone from Brocklebank

Hall to Waterside Grammar. She remembered that at least (again the heat).

If she were pregnant it would be a disaster. A mega-disaster. Had any of her friends ever mentioned hot flushes when they were pregnant? She certainly didn't get them with Holly.

She scanned the rest of the Edward Harveys in case she had missed something, but they were all either too old or too young. She checked the Brocklebank page, but there were only about half a dozen names, mostly from before her time; her brother Louis's era. Perhaps she would look at the Waterside page again.

But what year did he leave? Was he older or younger than her? She knew he'd stayed on to Sixth Form because of the Science course in 1974 when she caught a fleeting glimpse that prompted a girlish swoon. She called up the lists for Waterside Grammar School and looked through those spanning the three most likely years. No Edwards and no Harveys. Perhaps there never would be; perhaps Friends Reunited wasn't quite the thing for someone like Edward Harvey.

She checked her watch.

It was past ten and her husband was still not back. He used to phone if he was going to be late. How should she deal with this new development? Twenty years of tranquillity had not prepared her for conflict. The eel popped up from its ocean depths as if wrapped in air-filled polythene pillows. She shuddered. All the loneliness she felt as a young child was breaking through a casing where it had been stored away safely for decades. She could feel it rising through her body, disturbing her viscera, forming itself into an inward scream that reverberated and echoed with all the pains and anxieties of memories of a life tormented by bullies. She tried to suppress it, but was becoming increasingly weak against its insistent progression.

She was nearly forty-six; more than likely past half way. How many more years would she have when it would matter? Didn't she owe it to herself to try to mend the broken pieces of her youth while she still had time to benefit? The cooling of the summer marked yet another year of procrastination. Might the solution lie with a website called Friends Reunited? With a list of schools, a list of names, a search box and a promise of something special?

Might the answer lie in finding Lydia?

2

February 1962

Brocklebank Hall

Mrs Swift is a scary woman with a tight brown perm and constantly pursed lips coloured with dark red lipstick. She has both orange and turquoise mohair cardigans which she wears alternately in the winter months, and she thumps on the old piano in the corner of the classroom in the way that teachers do.

The tables and chairs have been moved against the walls for the first form's music and movement lesson. A dozen prep-school five-year-olds, in tiny grey prep-school uniforms, skip and jig with no embarrassment and no self awareness, just like lambs frolicking on a sunny springtime evening.

Mrs Swift, seated at the piano, claps her hands and the children rush to form a circle. They hold out their arms and shuffle sideways and outwards until they are not quite touching.

"Er, Neville," says Mrs Swift looking sternly over her shoulder. She says 'Er' a lot, usually with enough menace to keep the most recalcitrant child in line without any further elaboration. "Neville … you begin."

Then the thumping on the piano starts, Mrs Swift working the foot pedals with grape-treading vigour.

"In and out the dancing bluebells; in and out the dancing bluebells; in and out the dancing bluebells, who will be my partner?" The children sing as Neville weaves in and out of the circle of classmates, stopping on the last word, behind the nearest child and tapping them with both *hands on the shoulders.* "*Tippy tippy tapper on your shoulder; tippy tippy tapper on your shoulder, tippy tippy tapper on your shoulder, you will be my partner.*" *And now the child in front of Neville leads the weaving in and out and the verse is repeated until there are no dancing bluebells left in the circle, just a long line of children, skipping around the classroom; a conga for the kindergarten!*

Marianne likes these sessions, but not when Pete Glanville is the tapper and he stops behind her and almost batters her into the ground.

Marianne aged five stood quaking fearfully by the breakfast table as her mother buttoned her into her navy-blue gabardine mac. She was aware of a checked tablecloth, of toast crumbs, a box of cornflakes and green-patterned dishes; of her father's kipper bones hanging over the edge of a plate. Familiar things …

She breathed quickly, finding it hard to hold back the tears. Her mother probably sensed the anguish and was especially gentle fastening the belt and running the end through the loops at the front and the side, but she said nothing. Marianne's mother, who was half French and called Daphine, had an Emma Peel flip hairstyle and painted eyebrows. She feigned cheerfulness by smiling.

Slender fingers were eased into grey woollen gloves one at a time and a tasselled blue beret was placed at a jaunty angle on her head. Marianne felt secure at her mother's touch and wished this ritual dressing would go on forever.

"Ready?" called her father, Roger, striding down the stairs and grabbing his worn, black briefcase from behind the door. He was a tall man with piercing dark eyes and a brisk manner. He was an architect by profession and precision was his watchword.

She would never be ready to be taken from these cosy walls.

"Pens, pencils, handkerchief?" He always asked this and she always said yes. It was one of the many routines that made her feel secure.

Then it was out into the chilly winter, white-frost morning, into the car and off to school for another tortuous day.

Brocklebank Hall was a forbidding, Munsterian house perched on the top of a hill on the edge of the small town of Derwentbridge in Cumbria. It was a place of woods and rhododendron bushes; of green playing fields and lawns. It might have been considered an ideal location for a child but for the psychological battles that were played out by some of its inhabitants every day.

Marianne stepped from the car and onto the asphalt and waved to her father. Then she walked towards the heavy oak front door, dragging her feet, pausing before she turned the brass handle and then pushing hard with all her weight.

Behind the door was a spacious hall with parquet flooring, a rag rug and a leather armchair. The Headmaster's yellow Labrador, Alfie, rose from the rug and bounded towards her, wagging his tail. He had a huge, flat wedge-shaped head and a pink nose. She stopped to pat him, remembering that it was best to do so while standing up. Once when she'd been sitting in the armchair, he had wrapped his front paws around her leg and made peculiar jerking movements. He had seemed excited and wild-eyed. She liked dogs, but not when they acted like they were possessed.

A large globe stood on an oval mahogany table by the window. Sometimes when she waited for her mother after school, she would spin the globe and gaze at the names of the countries and the vastness of the oceans. Great Britain seemed an insignificant pink speck tucked away on the edge of everywhere else.

The shelves were stacked with books and piled high with well-read *National Geographic* and *Look and Learn* magazines. On the wall, school photographs hung in their elongated, horizontal black-rimmed frames, full of tidy schoolboys and the occasional girl, caught for a moment in time.

The first form room was behind this wall, a large sunny room with a huge bay window and rows of tiny desks and tiny chairs. A nature table adorned with disused nests and the first spring flowers guarded the wall by a piano, and a model town was laid out on a trestle table in the window overlooking the tennis lawn. The walls were festooned with posters – 'a is for apple' and so on – and white cards on which were big red felt pen dots, set out like the numbers on dice. It was a cheerful room and Marianne felt safe in it.

It was outside where the darkness lay. Outside where the big boys prowled; where the bullies lay in wait to taunt the weak.

Mrs Swift was already there with three boys. She was in the corner where the hula hoops and balls were kept, and was showing them how to tie their shoelaces using wooden boards with two rows of holes in them and brightly coloured strings threaded through. Marianne went to her desk with a superior air. She had been able to tie her laces since she was four.

She looked around for Alice, but Alice wasn't there. Then she remembered. Today Alice was off having investigations on her eyes. She shuddered nervously at the thought of a day without Alice.

Alice Waugh was the only other girl in the first form, but she might as well have been a boy for she loved to get involved in the rough and tumble of the typical five-year-old. She had blonde wavy hair and glasses with one lens covered with sticking plaster. She was Marianne's only playmate and she lived in the country in a white manor house with so many staircases that Marianne had been frightened of getting lost when she went to visit.

When break time came, Marianne hung back inside the

classroom as the boys rushed out to get their milk from the dining room and then to play outside.

Mrs Swift shooed her out in front of her. "Er … Run along Marianne. There's a good girl. Fresh air will do you good."

Grown-ups are always saying this about fresh air, thought Marianne, wondering why Mrs Swift didn't go out with them and instead tottered on small heels down the narrow corridor to the staffroom.

Marianne avoided the bottled milk in the dining room because it made her feel sick, and instead slunk outside where older boys from other classes ran and pushed and yowled and yelped.

The frost had thawed, but there was still a fearsome Cumbrian chill in the air against which bare knees didn't stand a chance. Almost immediately the shivering began.

Her mother always told her to put on her coat when she went outside, but the boys had called her a sissy and she didn't like that. Yet even without her coat, they called her names. She tried to remain unseen and crept behind the enormous yew hedge that bordered most of the front of the school house, camouflaging the dustbins.

"Oi, you!" yelled a boy of about six with a thick brown fringe and an entourage of minions close behind.

Marianne froze.

"Where's yer little speccy-four-eyes friend? D'you wanna come an' play with us?" The boy, a second former called Barnaby Sproat, put his hands on his hips and grinned at his friends, tossing his fringe.

For an instant Marianne was grateful. Her face lost its worried frown and she moved towards them.

But Barnaby Sproat was only joking – scoring points, leading the pack – and as soon as she came close he and his friends turned and ran shouting: "Get lost, girl! Who'd want to play with a weed like you?"

Marianne looked bemused standing out in the open in the

middle of the asphalt, a fragile scrap of a thing, hair in two little dark brown plaits. This time she sought cover through the rhododendron arch that led into the woods. There she stood among the trees and started to cry.

She had never played with boys of her own age before and didn't know how to start. Her brother Louis was seven years older. These little boys were an alien race, often noisy and rough, and they seemed always to be involved in games of chase that were anathema to her.

The woods were a dangerous place for a small child to be alone. A gang of Teddy-boys sometimes lurked there, slicked-back hair, long checked jackets and pointy shoes, strangely incongruous among the shrubbery. Marianne didn't understand the perilous nature of her escape route. For her the branches were comforting arms against the enemy without.

Minutes passed, but to Marianne it seemed like an hour before the bell rang to signify the end of break. She rubbed her hand across her face, spreading the tears, but still she sobbed and sniffed; still she shivered.

Thankfully lessons offered some respite from the traumatic world beyond the classroom and once back at her desk, she began to calm down. She loved to learn. In the few weeks since she had started school, she had developed a taste for all the basics and was racing through the *Janet and John* books as if she had been born being able to read. She devoured Mrs Swift's work cards of mathematical calculations, and the exercises in *Ronald Ridout's English Workbooks*. Perhaps it was being bright that caused all the problems. It made her different from the others. She thought too much and tried to intellectualise when merely being would have helped her to relate to other children.

The only older girls in the school at that time inhabited the fourth form and were aged about ten. Almost adults in the eyes of Marianne.

"*Frightfully mature,*" her mother had said with a touch of sarcasm when two of the girls had helped to show them round the school the previous year.

They wore blue stretchy hairbands and had relinquished the top part of their pinafores.

Fiona Pattinson was small, dark and serious-faced. Amanda Oglethorpe exuded composure and grace and had a ballerina walk. Marianne wished she was like Amanda and sometimes followed her around until the day when Amanda noticed and scowled with such ferocity that Marianne never followed her again. Caroline Farrow, or Carrie as her friends called her, always said hello to Marianne and clearly liked little children. She had a mane of hair in waves of red-brown curls and was Neville's elder sister. Then there was Oriel Pimblott who was pretty, plump and giggly and had a crush on Jamie Russell, the Headmaster's son. She had a perm that went wrong and sent her hair skywards in lopsided peaks like a fir tree blown by the wind.

In the afternoon of the day that Alice was away, Marianne stayed in the dining room long after the nauseating lunch of spam fritters and semolina pudding was finished and everyone else had gone. She remained sitting alone on a pine bench in a trance-like state until one of the cooks came in to wipe down the tables and coaxed her from the room. She hung around in the hall, spinning the globe and patting Alfie until one of the fifth form prefects appeared from the passage.

"Outside!" he commanded. "Or I'll give you fifty lines!" The boy was known as Blockhead and had thick rimmed glasses and hair like the back of a scottie dog.

Fifty lines of what? thought Marianne. She wasn't sure what being given lines meant, but judging by his tone of voice, they didn't sound very pleasant, so she fled through the front door and onto the asphalt, bare knees in the cold once again. A group of boys from her form were playing chase. When she approached them, Pete Glanville who was enormous, pointed to her and yelled, "You're *It*," and then ran off with his gang around the side of the house.

She knew that being *It* meant she had to try to catch them so she ran as fast as she could, but with little success. For a while they seemed amused in trying to avoid her grasp and they slowed down until they were almost within reach before running away with whoops and mocking laughter. Marianne was unused to playing and had no idea of strategy. She kept running in circles as they weaved and dodged, eventually putting her foot in a pothole and falling on the asphalt.

She felt the pain in her knee as if a knife had twisted into the flesh. At first she was too shocked to cry. She sat up and dusted her hands on her skirt, specks of gravel embedded in her palms. Blood was trickling from the cut in a bright red stream to the top of her grey sock. Only once before had she grazed her knee this badly. She looked around for help. All the boys had magically disappeared. She felt sick and dizzy but picked herself up and limped towards the back of the Hut where the bigger girls often gathered.

She overheard Oriel speaking: "Mrs Swift is an old bag …"

Marianne wondered why her teacher should be compared to such a receptacle and she visualised a creased brown shopping-bag with a tight brown perm.

Fiona spotted her first. "Shhh!" she commanded. "It's your shadow, Amanda."

"Uh-ho, let's scram."

But Carrie recognised straight away that Marianne needed help. Carrie was kind; Carrie had a heart.

"We better find Mrs Russell," she said, taking Marianne by the hand and leading her back towards the school house. Oriel grabbed her other hand and the other two girls followed behind, now looking concerned and wanting to help.

Mrs Russell was the Headmaster's wife and also the school's Matron and she roamed the upstairs dormitories with piles of sheets in her arms. She had grey-streaked black hair and in later years Marianne would think of her as looking like Virginia Wade.

Marianne expected to be told off, but Mrs Russell was very understanding and bathed the wound. A bell rang in the background. Soon Marianne was sporting a large white dressing over her knee, held in place by pieces of plaster.

Carrie took her back to the classroom where afternoon lessons had already begun.

"Er, Marianne, what have you to say for yourself, coming in late like this?" Mrs Swift pounced, pursed her lips, took her by the elbow and marched her rather roughly to her seat. "Sit yourself down, and not a peep out of you till quarter to four. We will have words. We can't have you running off like this."

Carrie began trying to explain what had happened, but Mrs Swift wasn't listening.

"We've been worried to death. We searched outside ... Not a sign ... And with those Teddy-boys about ... She must learn she can't just disappear like that. Do I make myself clear, Marianne? Do you understand?"

Marianne felt the words stinging just like the pain in her knee and heat began burning her cheeks.

"Shut up you old bag!" she said.

This was to be a rare moment of courage in Marianne's young life and she would always remember the look of stunned disbelief on Mrs Swift's face and the smile of approval from Carrie. But for most of the time she kept quiet, a child alone and often scared, who could never tell anyone how she felt because she didn't have the vocabulary. She hated coming to school because of what happened outside lesson time and she longed for the day when she would be old enough to do what she wanted, to make her own decisions and be free. But for now, she was in this dark and often joyless world, little knowing that before it got better, it would get a whole lot worse.

3

Second Best

Beckenham lay on the edge of south-east London, a leafy, suburban jewel with a village green and several parks. On the downside, the high street was gradually being devoured by restaurants and coffee shops. With a postal address in Kent, Marianne's northern friends thought she lived among hop-fields and orchards and were surprised to discover her proximity to Catford, Sydenham and Penge.

Beechview Close was a cul-de-sac of semi-detached houses off one of the roads leading out towards Bromley. *'A spacious three-bedroom dwelling,'* the young estate agent had said with more than a touch of hyperbole when Marianne first went to look round. But it had French windows and a south-facing back garden with established fruit trees, and Marianne had thought anything was spacious compared with the flat they had been in for the first five years of their marriage. Now it had been home for some fifteen years, it was as familiar to her as an old friend, but today she had a feeling of dread as she came through the front door with her shopping.

"Have you seen my tennis racket, Mum?" yelled Holly from upstairs.

"Give me a chance to get in."

She struggled through to the kitchen, shaking her head. That was another of her mother's phrases. What was happening to her? She was boiling hot and even though it was still August, this was a heat with a difference, coming on suddenly and spreading in waves from her knees to her head. There was still no tell-tale sign that all was well and she was spending hours of tortuous brain chatter playing the scenario of discovering she was pregnant. What would she do? Whom would she tell? What were the options? And the more she thought, the sicker she felt and the doubts crept in.

"I'm packing for college," shouted the voice from upstairs.

"You're not going for another three weeks!" Marianne shouted back, playing for time. She knew she had put the racket somewhere safe after Holly's predictable annual Wimbledon-inspired, Tim-inspired, midsummer obsession with the game. But where? She couldn't think. She began unpacking the groceries, unaware that she put the sugar in the fridge.

Her mind wandered. She couldn't be. Surely not. *Please, please. Not this …*

She had surfed and searched endlessly for information. The web was full of contradictions about symptoms and signs; full of answers to every question but the one that was keeping her awake at night.

And her best friend Taryn wasn't much use, pulling a face and backing away with her arms in a cross-shape in front of her.

There was the sound of several pairs of galloping feet on the stairs and then teenage voices making plans for an evening clubbing; then laughter and the front door shutting.

Holly appeared in the doorway. How lovely she looked, simply dressed in jeans and a sleeveless vest, with her dark hair up in a braided plait, standing there on the threshold of the kitchen, on the threshold of a whole new life in the big grown-up world of university with all its joys and tears and wonderful friends and challenges.

"Jodie and Paul," said Holly by way of explanation.

"Back together?" asked Marianne, placing a pot of basil on the window sill.

"Just friends. Paul says he doesn't want ties when he goes to Warwick."

"Probably wise. And what about you and Lee?"

"Oh, we're finished and he *doesn't* want to be friends."

"Are you okay?"

"It's cool."

Marianne continued unpacking vegetables: *beetroot, lettuce, cress, celeriac, fennel, beansprouts, red and yellow peppers, aubergine, courgettes, tomatoes, broccoli, carrots, cauliflower, garlic, ginger, mushrooms and chives.* She murmured their names to herself like a mantra as if desperate to be distracted.

"Mum?"

"Yes darling."

"Why has Dad gone away without you?"

"He's gone specifically for a few days walking. There's been another coastal collapse somewhere in Devon. He's looking for fossils. He wouldn't want me tagging along."

"But you haven't had a holiday together this year. You usually do."

For a few moments there was an uncomfortable silence, each knowing that the bagged cat was struggling to be let out, but both scared of what they would find if they confronted it.

"We just never got round to it, that's all." Marianne couldn't tell her the real reason; that they decided not to go because of all the rows; because of *her*.

Holly decided to change the subject. "Any luck with Friends Reunited yet?"

"Had an email from Phil."

"Who's Phil?"

Marianne told Holly a censored version of the Phil story.

Phil Ackton had led a fascinating life as a young teenager. He was from Newcastle and Marianne used to meet him annually during their summer holidays in Allonby where they both used to help out at the riding school. At first the horses were the prime focus and they took little notice of each other. However, when they hit puberty, Phil's activities attracted attention because although he wasn't particularly handsome, he had an unbelievably successful technique with girls. Perhaps it was the money he used to flash around (his father had a lucrative haulage business), but as Marianne wasn't impressed by that, she found it hard to understand that it would be of interest to any typical fifteen-year-old. Phil and his sidekick Kevin would go on the hunt for potential talent lurking in the chalet parks or on the caravan sites; pretty girls looking bored and too sophisticated for the bucket-and-spade beach holiday on which they had unwillingly been dragged by their parents. The large white riding school buildings dominated the centre of the village and were one of the favourite haunts of Phil and Kevin, largely because of the hordes of young girls hanging about the stables. One year Marianne watched fascinated as Phil went through his routine.

Two newcomers to the village were sitting on the low wall that surrounded the house, watching keenly as Marianne took charge of one of the ponies used for short rides on the banks. No doubt they hoped that eventually they would be asked to do the same. God knows why they were all so keen to help. It was slave labour, often involving hours of lifting sticky toddlers into the saddle, dodging their ice cream covered hands and sandy feet.

"Feet, uggh!" Sarah Strong would whisper under her breath and grimace as she guided them into the stirrup leathers.

Then miles of walking and jogging round and round until they were exhausted. If they were lucky, they might be given a bag of chips at the end of the day.

The two new girls were about sixteen – a shade older than most of the others and both blonde and pretty. Dee, the quiet one, was more than pretty. She was stunningly naturally beautiful. Needless to say, she was the one who Phil homed in on with his active radar and instructions to Kevin, looking none too pleased, that he was to entertain Caitlin, whose nose was just a shade too large for perfection. Marianne watched the pantomime.

Phil went and sat beside Dee, casually picking up a handful of sand and scattering it at his feet. "D'you like horses, then?" he asked, not looking at her.

"Yes," she said, quietly through her hair.

"Can you ride?" enquired Phil, casting his best line and waiting for the fish to bite.

"Yes," she said again, equally shyly.

Phil was not one to waste time. "How about we go this afternoon on the three-fifteen? All four of us? My treat." He jingled the money in his pocket. The owner of the stables called him 'Money Bags Phil' and it suited him fine.

"We couldn't—" began Dee.

"Yes you can. No problem. Kevin'll pay for your friend, won't you Kev?"

Kevin shrugged, then nodded. He had been talking to Caitlin about where they were staying; playing the dutiful friend. But he was displeased at being lumbered with the less pretty one, something that always happened and would lead to arguments in the future. And Caitlin, even though she had a good deal in that Kev was better looking, picked up on his displeasure and went into a sulk.

A year or two later, it dawned on Marianne that next to her attractive friend Sasha Clement, she was the reject, she was the one that would always be second best. But she didn't tell this part of the tale to Holly, nor the part that involved Phil pursuing her friend Sasha during a trip to stay with Sasha's aunt in Newcastle, and bringing with him his friend Nick to keep Marianne company. Holly would not be impressed. There had only ever been one important man in her mother's life as far as she was concerned, and that was her dad.

They had gone to a Ten Years After concert at the City Hall. Nick was a lovely guy. Good-looking too, with long, straight black hair parted in the centre and a wide smile. He and Marianne really hit it off in the gloom of the auditorium. There was lots of flirtatious teasing, and that was when he first called her a mad-alcoholic-horsewoman. It was her first visit to a proper concert and she was high on the atmosphere of teenage energy and incense, and Alvin Lee on stage with his mane of fair hair shaken this way and that as he rocked them through the night.

This was the Nick she was looking for on Friends Reunited.

She had been amazed when he wanted to see her again. But he really liked her. Said she looked like a pre-Raphaelite too – not the regular type of chat-up line from a 1970s seventeen-year-old. Years of feeling less than beautiful had eroded her confidence so much that she couldn't accept that he saw her like this. Whenever she looked in the mirror, she didn't notice that she was slowly turning into an attractive young woman. Instead she saw the gawky kid that everyone made fun of, and when after several months of long-distance letters and occasional weekend visits, Nick declared love, she had backed away in disbelief.

No, she could never tell Holly the truth, the whole truth. She couldn't tell anyone. These were her secrets, carefully boxed and stacked away from prying eyes. Since she'd been married, the secrets had been largely undisturbed, but she knew that the box was gradually disintegrating; that the onset of midlife fears and concerns about her marriage were wearing down the barriers that had kept her safe throughout her adult life. The Moray eel thrashed within. Now the secrets were quietly eating their way through her soul and her confidence and she knew that she should face them.

But it was harder than she thought. How do you face the demons of a childhood spent being ridiculed about the way you looked? Here lay the problem that was to haunt her for thirty-three long years; until she met Lydia again.

4

The Hut

Marianne notices the new boy straight away on the first day of term. She sees him sitting alone at a desk at the front by the window, small, bespectacled and dark-haired, with his head in a book, both hands over his ears, seeming to shut himself off from the mayhem that as usual is erupting between lessons as they wait for the teacher. Marianne immediately feels some empathy and even compassion. He looks so lost and lonely. She wants to say hello, but she knows that this will cause him problems with Sproat and Colquhoun who sit at the back of the class, orchestrating the action, and waiting to pounce on any sign of weakness.

The new boy's name is Edward Harvey ...

The Hut lay to the side of the Brocklebank schoolhouse with the cricket field beyond. It was little more than an enormous shed with bare floorboards and a dusty, damp atmosphere, best suited to practical activities such as woodwork or gardening. It was sectioned into three by two zigzag partitions that folded up against the walls. At one end, there was a tiny stage from which the Headmaster, Mr Russell, took assembly every morning. In the middle there was the third form room and at the far end, backing on to the rhododendron-bordered drive, the slightly larger fourth form. There were small windows on either side, but with the main school building looming large and grey close by, it always seemed a gloomy place. The double desks were wooden and old, with lifting lids, their polished surfaces gouged by generations of schoolboys, each adding their name for posterity.

Marianne was in the third form now and she sat on her own at a desk in front of the teacher's.

"Is that yer geography homework?" said Pete Glanville. He sat behind her, a shambling giant, twice the size of most of the boys in width as well as length, and if he slumped down in his seat during lessons, he could kick the back of her chair or scuff his muddy shoes against her blazer.

Her geography exercise book, with its pale green cover, lay open in front of her on the desk; on the page, a carefully drawn map of Europe with coloured pencil shading and the key towns and cities marked with red dots, the names written in beside. She froze and said nothing.

"Bit tidy, isn't it?" mocked sneaky-faced Lanigan, seated next to Glanville.

Marianne did not turn round.

"Swot ... swot ... swot ..." they chanted.

Here we go, she thought. *Something is going to happen; something unpleasant.* And she braced herself, shoulders tensed, for whatever might follow.

Glanville then took his fountain pen, angled himself to one side and flicked it towards her work, covering the pristine pages with a shower of blue droplets. "Ooh, not so pretty now!" The two boys laughed and looked over their shoulders to check that others had seen what they'd done.

"Get lost," said Marianne, her heart quickening lest this response caused even more trouble.

"Leave her alone, commanded Barnaby Sproat from the back of the room, not because he wouldn't have done the same himself, but because he was King Cockerel and Glanville and Lanigan must be subservient to him. Sproat had sharp blue eyes that constantly scanned his territory like a radar beam, checking that everyone minded their place, quick to reprimand those who took liberties. Willie Colquhoun sat beside him, repeating commands, following orders; his henchman.

Later, when the homework came back graded, there were red biro circles around every one of the ink splatters, and a comment about the importance of presentation. As usual Marianne said nothing to her teacher, feeling the injustice but scared of making things worse.

This was what it was like in a world away from the cosy confines of forms one and two, with Mrs Swift and her tight perm and mohair cardigans banging on the piano, or leading the chanting of the times-tables, or reading them a story about the mischievous dog called Pooky.

Away from the main schoolhouse, Marianne was easy prey for the bullies. Spittle-coated paper pellets frequently stung her cheek, having been propelled through the shaft of an empty biro. She dreaded the hiatus between one lesson and the next when the chaos would unleash automatically and the 'thut-thut' of the peashooters would punctuate the din.

Occularly-disadvantaged Alice had gone to some far-flung boarding school and left Marianne on her own. Now she was the only girl in the class. When Alice had been there the two of them had sat conspiratorially at the far side and taken no notice of the boys. Marianne thought if she stayed out of their way, they would forget her and if they forgot her, they wouldn't taunt her with name-calling. It had worked when Alice was there, but not any more.

Name-calling had haunted her since the beginning, since she was five. It was what happened to the weak and frightened, and once it started, it became your identity. That was who you were; no longer Marianne Hayward. And it cut her to shreds every time she heard it, and even now, even at the age of forty-five she has never told a soul.

During moments of self-doubt, she hears that name again, is that person again. But of course to most of her adult world she has always been Marianne. They would never know.

She wasn't the only one. Pete Glanville was Jake but she didn't know why. Timothy Hopkins was Bunny and Jeremy Lanigan was Titch. There was Yackie and Fattie, Dracula and Snotty Gash. This was the world of prep school where nicknames were the way it was and if unlucky enough to be saddled with one of the cruellest, then it would haunt the owner all their lives. Such is the privileged world of private education.

She tried to tell her father about the bullying.

He had been to prep school and public school and had heard it all before.

Knowing what had worked for him, he taught her a dog Latin rhyme: *'Caesar ad sum iam forte, Pompeii aderat, Caesar sic in omnibus, Pompeii sic in at.'* She had smiled indulgently at the time.

But Glanville and Lanigan didn't like Latin and they were too dim to understand why the rhyme was funny. That day they took her satchel off the back of her chair and started throwing it between them, spilling the contents all over the floor until Timothy Hopkins on watch by the window shouted, "kef, kef" (at least that is what it sounded like to Marianne), and there was a sudden scampering into seats and opening of books so that by the time the teacher strode in, all he saw were angelic faces thirsting to be filled with knowledge and Marianne kneeling on the floor, hurriedly scooping up the contents of her bag. Didn't the teachers know what was going on? Didn't they care?

She told her father that his plan hadn't worked. He decided that more heavyweight tactics were required and taught her the rude words to 'Colonel Bogey'. "They'll be impressed by that," he said. "Tell them that; they'll leave you alone."

She didn't know what the words meant, and although she had heard of Hitler, she didn't know Himmler, Goering and Goebbels.

She didn't know what balls were either – except to throw and catch – but one day when the frost was hard on the ground and the windows were still icy from the freezing night, she told the rhyme to the gathered rowdy throng. Certainly her rendition left them speechless, but it did little else. This time they stole her French text book, tossing it above their heads from boy to boy until it found its way into the hands of Barnaby 'Bas' Sproat.

"D'you want it?" he taunted, waving it at her, calling her name, *that* name, and shaking his thick brown fringe with a flick of his head.

"Yes," she said, falling into the trap.

"Come and get it then," he held it out to her, then when she was just within reach, he snatched it away, smirked and put it carefully into his desk.

Marianne went back to her seat, her brain racing with a mixture of hatred and anxiety. When Mr Jenks came in, she was the only one without a text book. "I've left it at home," she lied when questioned.

"It's no use there, is it," said Jenky, kindly. "Remember it tomorrow."

She breathed a sigh of relief.

Marianne was younger than everyone else. Not just a little bit, but a whole year younger than most of the class. This was a place where the brightest were fast-tracked through the system, which was fine during lessons, but didn't take account of social skills. Or lack of them. No wonder she was lost. She still had no idea how to get on with boys and with no friend to talk to, she watched instead.

That's how she came to notice so much about Edward Harvey.

Edward Benjamin Harvey, with his slight build and glasses, and newly arrived from a Lakeland village, was not like the rest. Apart from having an intellect substantially more impressive than anyone else she had come across in school to date and that she knew she respected even at age nine, he never called her by her degrading nickname – in fact he never called her anything in the whole time they were at school; never stole her satchel or her Bible or maths equipment. Indeed as far as Marianne could see, Edward Harvey never did anything that most of the other boys did at least some of the time.

She watched him sitting quietly, reading, ignored by the others in the class and wondered if, somewhere out in the playground or late in the evening when the boarders were enjoying some free time before they went to bed, he was bullied too.

Once she was sitting in the brown leather armchair in the hall, waiting to be taken home by the school taxi service – a minibus known affectionately as The Tank – and Mrs Russell was showing Edward Harvey's parents out of the building. Voices were concerned, and hushed, but that made Marianne listen all the harder. She heard words like "nightmares" and "sleepwalking", surmised that they were talking about Edward, and next time she saw him sitting reading on his own in the classroom, she thought perhaps he had a tortured soul like her.

Did he suffer as she did? Certainly he seemed lost in those first few months in the third form. If only they could talk and share the burdens of their plights. But that could never be. At least she had an ally of a sort, albeit a silent one, and with his academic performance way ahead of most of the rest, here was someone with whom to compete in tests and exams. The cries of 'swot' no longer hurt so much for she didn't feel so different any more.

Years later it would always be 'me and Edward Harvey' when she told the tales of the Latin lessons and the demonic teacher Mr Wallis. But she never thought their paths would cross again and his name was confined to a memory store along with other mythical beings.

5

Memories

Marianne was scurrying around the kitchen putting together a packed lunch to take to her first day back to work at the college. Late afternoon summer sunshine glanced through the trees in the garden and cast lemon-drop patterns on the draining board. The pungent smell of tinned salmon drifted in the air.

"When will Dad be back?" asked Holly, absently drying dishes. She was wearing her hair in two plaits tied with blue ribbons and looked girlish in a short denim skirt, pink vest and trainers.

"Later this evening, he said. He's stopping off on The Isle of Purbeck."

"Why there?"

"One of the best places for fossils. Don't you remember? We went there for a holiday when you were eight. Stayed in a farmhouse near Worth Matravers."

"Oh yeah … And Dad said we were going to find a dinosaur! I believed him too!"

Marianne smiled, remembering happy days watching Holly running along the cliff paths or scraping about in the shingle below. Without a brother or sister, they always tried extra hard to entertain her, to keep her from being lonely.

What if I am pregnant? What if the brother or sister is within me now?

She swallowed as panic and nausea gripped her stomach.

"Mum? You're not going to get divorced, are you?"

"Heavens no!" She was shocked at the very mention of the word. *Surely not.*

Holly continued: "He's always somewhere else ... off walking ... or at the pub ... even in bed? I've hardly seen him this summer."

Perhaps she wants reassurance before she goes away?

"He'll be fine when he starts work again." Marianne tried to sound upbeat, but in truth, she wasn't convinced.

"You will say if things get worse, won't you? You won't suddenly tell me when it's a *fait accompli* – like Jodie's Mum did?" Knives and spoons jingled as Holly flung them one after the other into the drawer.

"All couples have arguments," said Marianne.

"You should go out with him, Mum."

"I haven't time."

"Of course you have. You've time to surf Friends Reunited."

"That's your fault! You started me on that!"

"Who are you looking for anyway?"

Marianne wondered what Holly was thinking. "Oh, no-one in particular."

"C'mon Ma ...I've seen you searching and searching. Tell me! Old boyfriends?"

She felt herself going hot again, but she wasn't sure whether she was blushing. She had looked in the mirror a few such times, but had seen no tinges of pink to give the game away.

Please be the lesser of the evils ...

"I do wish you wouldn't put the fish slice in with the cutlery. I can never find it when you've been drying."

"Mum," persisted Holly. "Who? You've been on that site every night. Don't think I haven't noticed."

"Just alleviating the boredom when you're with your friends and your father's out. And it was you who said what an 'extra' thing it was to do."

"So who, then?"

"Oh, someone I knew at Brocklebank Hall. Edward Harvey."

35

It was safer to mention him than ex-boyfriend Nick.

"Is he in those old photos?"

"Probably." Marianne knew that he was in two of them and possibly three.

"Show me."

Marianne finished wrapping her salmon sandwiches, complete with bones for added calcium, and went rummaging about in a drawer in the living room.

It was an elongated black and white photograph which she extracted from a tight roll. It persisted in returning to shape and resisted any attempts to flatten it.

Holly looked on, expectantly, tea-towel over her shoulder.

"Here, you hold this end," said Marianne.

Between them, they unravelled the roll and laid it down on the table by the window. Holly anchored her end with a fruit bowl and scanned the black and white rows of uniformed schoolchildren lined up against the backdrop of the rhododendron bushes on the Brocklebank drive. There were fixed expressions on most of the faces – some smiling nervously, others stony-faced as if resigned to their fate. Some were neat and tidy with hair slicked down and blazers buttoned. One or two were a little dishevelled with ties awry and collars crumpled.

"Oh, there you are! Bless! You don't look very happy. How old were you?"

"About ten." Marianne stared at the rows of pupils, mostly boys, and her throat tightened as she remembered.

"Which one is Edward then?"

"The intellectual-looking one."

"There?" Holly spotted him immediately. "Oh my ... Harry Potter! He could've made a fortune in the films. And he's better looking than – what's-his-name."

"D'you think so?" Marianne smiled.

"Yeah. Finer features. Did you fancy him?"

"Holly!"

Holly grinned and made a whooping noise, removing the bowl from the photo which sprang back into a roll against Marianne's fingers.

"Wonder what he's like now. Pierce Brosnan with glasses!"

"Don't be daft." Marianne felt the heat again.

"He could be."

"Or he could be bald and have a rampant beer-gut."

"Does it matter?"

"It shouldn't matter."

"But does it?"

"I don't know. Anyway, this is all hypothetical as he's not on the site and there's virtually no chance of us ever seeing each other again. And we were very young. Hardly ever spoke to each other."

"So why him? Why are you looking for him? What about the others?"

Marianne paused and wondered that very question. "Because I thought he had hidden depths. I thought we would have had things to say. I wanted to talk to him, but I never did."

"Why not?"

"It was never the right time. Then we went our separate ways and it was too late."

"But if you never spoke, why did you think you would have got on?"

"I saw him with others. I heard what he had to say in the lessons. I felt he understood—" She stopped abruptly, on the verge of saying more than she intended. "He was clever, and even though we weren't friends, he was never horrible to me."

"So it wasn't just because he looked cute?"

"At the time I didn't think he was particularly cute. Not standard cute, anyway. I admired his mind!"

"And you were ten?"

"Nine, ten, eleven."

"He sounds nice."

"Yes, he was."

"So you'll keep on looking?"

"Maybe."

"Will you mail him, if you find him?"

"I'd like to know what happened to him, that's all. I'd like to know if he's doing wonderful things – fulfilling the promise – unlike me. If he writes some notes by his name, that will tell me all I need to know."

That night when Holly was out with friends and her husband had still not returned from his mini-break, she went back to the Brocklebank photograph and gazed again at the young Edward Harvey, touching his hair and feeling it clean and boyishly soft. Then she trawled again through the pages of faceless names on Friends Reunited.

Memories were strange things: paper fragments, some black with jagged edges and some softly curving and brightly coloured. Edward Harvey was one of the latter. Edward Harvey was nice at a time when boys were anything but.

When she closed down the computer, she took out her journal with its plum cover and gold stitching. She went downstairs, slipped off her sandals, collapsed on the sofa and began to write.

Still no sign of Edward Harvey on FR. He's probably not the FR type. But now I've started, I really want to know what's become of him. Showed Holly the old photo of us. It was so long ago, but that frightened girl is still within me. I hearing her crying sometimes; I feel her pain when they call her names.

And her mind drifted back to the Latin lessons in the third form …

6

Tacite Patiuntur

It is half past eight in the morning and having left her coat in the main schoolhouse, Marianne climbs the steps into the Hut. Her breathing is fast and shallow and her eyes are anxious. This week it is her turn on the sweeping rota. She is partnered with Edward Harvey and together they are responsible for cleaning the classroom floor. She is relieved not to be paired with one of the bullies, but even so, since the beginning of term she has dreaded this week, fearing that the task will be left up to her, or that Edward will be embarrassed, or that he may start treating her like the others do.

Yesterday in maths they were cutting out shapes from graph paper for an activity on symmetry. At the end of the lesson, Mr Russell commented on the state of the floor, now covered with clippings.

"Who's sweeping this week?" he said, marching over to the rota that was pinned on the notice board. "Hayward and Harvey …" He had looked at Marianne and Edward. "Can we do something about this before school tomorrow?"

Marianne spent a restless night worrying about where the cleaning equipment was kept and whom she should ask.

But today she can hear the sounds of furniture being moved and when she enters the classroom, she sees Edward wielding a brush. She hovers uncertainly. He will think she is completely useless.

"What shall I do?" asks Marianne, dropping her satchel by the partition.

"Put the chairs on the desks," he instructs, looking up momentarily before continuing brushing. It is the first time he has spoken directly to her since arriving in the school.

Marianne follows him round the room, lifting chairs on and off desks as indicated while Edward brushes beneath. He is fully focused on the task in hand, paying particular attention to the corners of the room.

"Dustpan," he says, gesturing towards an old metal object on the teacher's desk. Marianne dutifully holds it on the floor while he sweeps the debris into it. The process is repeated two or three times until all the dust and fragments of paper are gathered and emptied into the waste bin. The job is completed in no time.

"Thank you," says Edward before disappearing with the equipment to the main building.

Marianne is relieved and all her anxieties drain away. She should have known better; should have had more faith in him. Only Edward would have taken so calmly the fact that he had to complete the task with a girl.

Among other things, Edward Harvey was very good at Latin, and so was Marianne. Edward and she tussled with the more difficult parts of the translations in their orange-backed reader *Civis Romanus*, while their peers sat back in their chairs.

Mr Wallis was a teacher of the old-school type. Reptilian, humourless and strict, there was something almost extra-terrestrial about him. His hair was greasy, sparse and black in colour and he wore the same expression almost all the time, neither smiling nor frowning, but blandly self-satisfied behind wire-rimmed glasses. He looked rather like a gecko as he stealthily paced the floorboards of the Hut with Bible, history book or Latin text, firing questions directly at particular individuals and not letting them get away with silence.

When he approached Marianne's space and leaned across to pass judgement on her work, she noticed the damp pallor of his skin and the whiteness of his knuckles as he gripped his red pen with fingers and thumb circling close to the point, ready to score the page with a tick or scathing 'rubbish'. There was a faintly sour smell about him and his proximity made her shiver.

One winter's morning, he was in a particularly bad mood and refused to help them with a piece of Latin to English translation.

"Yes, Marianne," he said, nodding at her in his supercilious way, expectant of an answer. She tried and failed.

"Any thoughts, Harvey?" he looked at Edward, usually so reliable, but his effort was also dismissed. Mr Wallis scanned the rest of the class without much hope and one or two answers were attempted and shot down with a disdainful shake of his head.

The bell went and the children began to shift in their seats and gather up their books and pens.

"We're not going," said Mr Wallis in a calm but menacing voice. "Not until we've finished this paragraph." He seemed to be taking some sadistic pleasure in their discomfort.

Even then Marianne sensed the injustice of it. They hadn't misbehaved. They'd done their homework and tried their best.

All through the break Edward and Marianne tried and tried to find the answer with no help from Wally, and the rest waiting helplessly.

Marianne felt Pete Glanville's foot kicking the underside of her chair. She daren't turn round.

Barnaby Sproat hissed through his teeth, "C'mon Harvey," and scowled as if it was Edward's fault that the class were being punished.

Marianne couldn't understand where they were going wrong. They had tried every option. Why wouldn't Mr Wallis help them?

They were brought back at lunchtime as well, but still they couldn't get it right. It crossed Marianne's mind that they might be coming back for days, stuck on this same sentence among the orange covers of *Civis Romanus*, along with Romulus and Remus, Tarquinius Superbus and the Trojan Horse. Minutes dragged by, playtime lost, and gradually Edward and Marianne became silent as all their efforts failed. Still Wally refused to back down, insisting they return to the Hut after games at the end of the day.

Tired from running about on the hockey field, the class gathered once more. The skies were darkening and Marianne was worried about missing her lift home in The Tank. There seemed no hope of achieving the desired result, and none of the children spoke despite Mr Wallis's attempts to extract an answer. In desperation, he had no choice but to help them and the class breathed a sigh of relief.

But Marianne was puzzled. It seemed that the correct answer was one they had already tried – tried more than once. But no one would ever dare to question Wally, and the class dispersed.

It wasn't the only time that Mr Wallis had shown a streak of cruelty.

An incident with one of the boys was permanently branded on her mind. It was an unremarkable day in many ways when Timothy Hopkins did something, or said something, undetectable to the rest of the class, that sent Mr Wallis into a rage the like of which Marianne had never seen. First there was a loud bark of: "You boy!" An explosion that made the children jump in their seats and look with disbelief at the scene unfolding in front of them. Mr Wallis sprang like a hare from his position in front of the blackboard and over to Timothy's desk. There were growls and unintelligible mumblings and curses coming from between his clenched teeth while he lashed out at Timothy, boxing his ears relentlessly. The punishment seemed to go on for ages while the other children looked on in mute horror, and Timothy became redder and redder in the face and started to cry.

When at last the beating stopped, Mr Wallis stood up straight, lowered his shoulders, picked up the text book from which he had been reading, turned his back on Timothy and calmly resumed the lesson as if nothing had happened.

Marianne was shocked into silence for the rest of the lesson, even feeling sorry for Timothy as he tried to quell the tears. And ever after, the class were wary and guarded; Glanville and Lanigan keeping their feet under control and even Barnaby Sproat resisting his *sotto voce* jibes at lower-ranked pupils.

"Each cigarette cuts fourteen minutes off a person's life," said Wally during one registration session, fulfilling his pastoral role as form teacher with a little health education.

Marianne was disturbed by this piece of propaganda. Too young to question its validity, and with two parents who smoked, she began a series of complex mathematical calculations, firstly estimating the age at which her parents might die without having smoked, and then calculating the number of minutes she would have to subtract. It was a complicated process full of divisions by sixty, then twenty-four, then seven, then four, then twelve. Time and again she lost track and had to go back to the beginning. Much later she wondered if Mr Wallis knew the impact of such information on someone so young and impressionable. If it was designed to stop her from smoking, the thought had never crossed her mind. All it did was to create an anxiety that lasted for years.

Yes, Mr Wallis was unforgettable and unforgivable, and it is in some ways surprising that Edward and Marianne learned so much in such a climate. But although lacking in compassion, Wally was good at imparting knowledge.

Edward and Marianne were at an age when information percolated effortlessly into their brains like rain on rocks made of limestone. They vied for the top position both in Latin and in the form as a whole. The first term that they were together, the form prize went to Marianne. She was top in Latin, French and maths and second in English and scripture. Her teachers wrote glowing comments on her report which was vastly improved on those for the previous year when she had been embarrassed into underperforming by the relentless taunts every time she did well. She was once again showing the promise of her first two years with Mrs Swift; again enjoying her work and the healthy competition of being tested.

The position was repeated the following term, but by the end of term three, perhaps inevitably, Edward took the glory and although Marianne was disappointed for herself, she felt it was deserved. And after that he never looked back. Here was a young chap going somewhere, and in years to come she would ever be proud that she had held her own in his company and that they had spurred each other on to greater things during what was undoubtedly a crucial time in their intellectual development.

Marianne thought she might have had a crush on Edward Harvey. It was very innocent and born out of respect for his mind and the fact that he never treated her unkindly.

7

Marianne

Marianne was a Sun sign Capricorn with an Aries Ascendant and a Libran Moon. Astrology guru Linda Goodman said there are two sorts of Capricorn: the tethered goat content to nibble around a stake in the ground, and the wild mountain goat leaping from rock to rock and scaling the heights. Marianne was the first of these, but had dreams of breaking the chain and leaping up the hill.

Brocklebank Hall was the chain; a chain thus far too thick for her to crack.

Marianne remembered Holly's observation about the photograph of Edward Harvey, then realised she was smiling and went all hot again.

Pierce Brosnan indeed!

This heat business was getting her down. There was definitely something amiss. The thought of being pregnant made her scream inside. A long, empty howling noise, like wolves in the moonlight; an assault on the ears; a cry of desperate pain.

If it was the other business ... the M word ... Well, she wasn't ready for that yet. Wasn't expecting it until she was nearer fifty. It was the slippery slope of decay. In the animal world, only human females lived significantly beyond their reproductive years. They never used to. The price to pay was bits dropping off. *Not yet, please.* Now was far too soon.

I will have to start wearing layers ... Wearing cardigans! Oh God!

She was home alone again, cooling off after playing a game

of tennis in the park with her friend Taryn. She could have asked Taryn back for supper, but Taryn, as flighty as ever, was going out with some man.

In the back garden, under the fruit trees heavy with ripening apples, she sat on a wooden seat with her journal. Sometimes she bit on the end of her pencil and sometimes she drummed her fingers on her cheek.

I wonder what Edward Harvey's like now. I wonder if he's doing great things … What happened to my great things?

She began to write.

"She went to a boys' prep school, you know."

"Did she now! That tells us a thing or two. Gives us some insight; throws some light."

"She lived on the outside of the action until she was ten. They said she was the only girl in the class for a year and that she was bullied."

"Poor kid … Prep school has been known to fuck up the best, never mind a girl in a world of boys."

"She was deeply affected, or so they said, but she hid it well. If you met her in later years, you'd never have known. She didn't even know it herself until she was almost forty-six."

"But she didn't continue in the private sector, did she?"

"After the prep school, she went to the local Grammar. They called her a posh bird at first – or some such – but eventually she had friends and boyfriends. She survived."

"It must've been like a holiday camp after what she'd been through."

"By the time she went to Sheffield she was just like the rest. Not a trace of lah-di-dah."

"Blah," said Marianne out loud.

"She read psychology, yeah? Psychology, the seventies pseudo-subject for posers and the mad …"

"That's a trifle unkind."

"… And the do-gooding fraternity. We mustn't forget them."

"You're not overly fond of psychologists then?"

"We managed without them for hundreds of years …"

"After the degree, she became a teacher. Went down to the London Institute and trained in Secondary English."

"Why would a school phobic want to go back to the classroom?"

"One of the treatments for phobias is 'flooding', so I understand. Maybe she was subconsciously looking for the cure."

"Or maybe she's a masochist."

"Of course, her family didn't approve. They had her all lined up for a career in the law like her brother."

"I didn't know she had a brother."

"Louis is seven years older. He went to Brocklebank too, but left as she arrived."

"Louis and Marianne …"

"Their maternal grandmother was French."

"So why didn't she go into law?"

"Rumour said it was lack of confidence."

"When I met her at the college in 1999 she seemed perfectly confident."

"It was all a veneer."

"Miss Efficiency, I would have called her."

"On the surface, yes, but a bundle of neuroses within. I think deep down, she was frightened of criticism; frightened of failure."

"Focused and organised, they said. Stones were never left unturned by Marianne."

"But you have to agree, she wasn't ambitious."

"I have to agree."

"So she started out teaching English in a school in Chislehurst and later in an FE college in Bromley."

"During which time Holly was born and she worked part-time, gradually picking up the psychology teaching as her hours increased."

"And then in 1998 she began working as a full-time teacher of psychology at North Kent Sixth Form College in Beckenham."

Then Marianne thought *who is this* 'she'? *Is she me or my alter ego?* She put down her pencil and closed the journal. She was aware of birds twittering and of one of her tabby cats in pouncing pose beneath a rose bush.

The journal was something she started when her world began to unravel earlier in the year. Journals are dangerous things, but how else can one hold the thoughts of a moment; thoughts that float like soap-bubbles and evaporate into nothing if they're not written down? She had always liked to write; to scribble her musings for future reference. Sometimes she wrote short stories and sometimes poems. When she was young, she wrote diaries, but she threw them away when she was thirty because she didn't want anyone to see her childish ramblings after she was gone.

She would really like to write a book: a novel about bullying inspired by Brocklebank Hall. But she didn't know where to start. She had no plot. All she could do for now was jot down odd disjointed thoughts and dialogue when the inspiration struck. One day, she hoped, the mists would clear and she would put it all together. In the meantime there was a new term starting and her mind kept flitting to teaching, lesson planning and the avoidance of negative residuals.

Negative residuals happened when results were less than those predicted by students' previous exam success. They were the new buzzwords at work along with differentiation, baseline grades, targets setting, and benchmarks. If you really wanted to impress, you would reel them all off in the same sentence. They were what Ofsted inspectors fussed about and Principals agonised over, herding their Heads of Department toward a common belief that failure was no longer just an unclassified grade, but a negative residual as well. Of course it was all of questionable validity, but senior management teams throughout the land were now being driven by statistics and this message cascaded down to the teachers, the classroom and the students.

Marianne went back inside the house. Still no sign of husband or daughter; still no text messages or phone calls. What a pity Taryn was otherwise engaged.

She fixed herself some pasta with a pancetta, onion, and tomato sauce. Soon the smell of garlic and oregano drifted appetisingly in the air. *Tagliatelle Cavalli* was christened after a friend who gave her the recipe. She added the pasta to the sauce, tipped the result into a shallow bowl, grated some Parmesan cheese on top and took it out into the garden with a novel that she kept behind one of the cushions on her chair in the living room. She sat with fork in one hand and book in the other.

This particular novel, she read only in times of solitude. Her husband didn't approve of any fiction unless it was worthy of critical acclaim. He was a reader of Dickens and Tolstoy; of Louis de Bernières and Iris Murdoch. He told Marianne that anything less than the erudite or memorable was not worth the time and effort. Consequently a string of classics and Booker Prize winners graced her bedside table, while she became a closet reader of blockbusters, hidden in various locations around the house. If she heard his key in the lock while she was immersed in some fantasy romp, she would deposit it under the sofa and grab a copy of *The Times*.

Her husband would have been surprised at her deception. Even more so if he discovered that this was only one of several things he didn't know about his wife.

8

The Worst and the Best of Times

On Tuesday and Thursday afternoons throughout the winter months in the third form, Marianne is usually dressed in a navy blue divided skirt, pale blue Aertex shirt and red socks – the Osprays house colours. Carrying her boots and shin pads, she makes her way from the upstairs changing room in the main building, down the central staircase and to the back door. She is with two other girls, Abi and Janice.

Abi Ross is a new girl, with copper-coloured hair. She is a year older than Marianne and in Form Four. She is funny and clever and Marianne and she have quickly become friends. For the first time since arriving in the school aged five, Marianne has a friend she would have chosen if she had ever had the choice; no longer making do with whoever happened to be there. Now she feels less out of synchrony with her peers.

All three girls carry hockey sticks. Outside the door, they sit on the step and put on their boots and pads, glancing at the sky to see if rain might curtail their games. Then they hobble on the path past the tennis court and through the hedge that leads to the playing-fields. The older girls look relaxed as they part company with Marianne and head off towards the larger of the two sports fields on the hill overlooking the town of Derwentbridge.

The younger members of the school are gathering on the nearer, smaller field and with a final glance at her friends, Marianne joins them. It is grey and misty and the ground is like a swamp from the November rains. Every step sinks in with a squelching noise and splatters muddy droplets up her legs. The field slopes slightly towards one of the goalposts and a pool of water is beginning to accumulate. Marianne is pleased she *is playing in a wing position where she can stay out of the way of the wet.*

Jeremy Lanigan and Pete Glanville are practising bullying-off using a fir cone that has fallen from one of the pines at the edge of the field. Lanigan swipes his stick in the direction of Glanville's ankles, missing the fir cone deliberately. Other boys run about shouting and playing chase. Barnaby Sproat and Willie Colquhoun are limbering up by racing each other between the goalpost and the field boundary. Both excel at sport and take games lessons seriously. Cries of "Well done Bas," will soon be heard echoing across the field in the damp, wintry air. Marianne thinks it is so unfair that excellence in sport is revered by peers while academic success is scorned. She lurks by the sidelines, hoping not to be noticed, but soon she is spotted by Lanigan who looks at Glanville and nods in her direction.

A furtive glance down the track towards the school to see if Mr Wallis is approaching and then they swagger up to Marianne, each hooking a hockey stick around one of her ankles and pulling in opposite directions until she sits down in the mud.

It hurts a bit, but more than that she feels humiliated. The boys saunter off laughing and waving their sticks, glancing across the pitch to check that their action has been noted by King Cockerel Sproat, then looking at her over their shoulders and spitting on the grass.

Marianne looks down and sighs. She is angry but feels helpless. Whenever this happens – and it happens nearly every hockey session, twice a week – she wants to lash out, but fears the consequences. Who would come to her rescue if they attacked her?

Such incidents and others like them were to fester in the depths of Marianne's consciousness throughout the rest of her schooldays, her college days and her working life. Prep school has a culture where bullying is accepted as the norm and laughed about in later years as something that is 'character building'. What about the muffled tears under bedclothes in the dormitories; the nightmares, the bedwetting, the degradation and humiliation? What sort of character does that build?

When she was older, Marianne questioned the wisdom of her parents at sending her there.

"Your grandmother's decision," said her mother in a clipped tone that suggested she had little say in the matter. This was her paternal grandmother, and not the one who lived in France. "Your grandmother thought the state option would be too rough for you."

How ironic.

Sometimes Marianne wished she had spoken up; made more of a fuss, but there were good things she would have missed if she had been elsewhere. And elsewhere might have been just as bad or worse. If she had gone elsewhere, she wouldn't have known Abi or had the experience of a teacher like Mr Jenks.

Mr Jenks – or 'Jenky' as he was affectionately called – taught French, art and English and was always dreaming up some entertaining lessons that promoted creativity and imbued knowledge almost without the children realising. He was a tall man with large feet and curly hair. Marianne remembered his brown leather shoes and green socks and the way he said "Attagirl" to her and no one else. She didn't know what it meant exactly, but knew it was a sign of praise and encouragement. Lessons with Jenky always passed quickly and were sometimes quite extraordinary.

In the winter in the art lessons, he organised the class into painting murals on the top halves of the zig-zag partitions in the Hut. On one side, half the group created a night time harbour scene with blue-black skies and boats. On the other side, rolling hills and a green landscape with dry-stone walls and sheep. Jenky, who was clearly a talented artist, sketched the outline and later added the details while the children daubed larger blocks of colour into the background.

Marianne and Edward were each assigned areas of sky at the top of the harbour mural. This required standing on desks and balancing precariously to fill their brushes with paint, trying not to shower the rest of the team who were working on various bits below. On the other side of the room, Barnaby Sproat and his gang attacked their landscape with gusto and it wasn't long before paint was being flicked and faces were freckled with green. A sharp word from Jenky was needed to calm them down.

In spring, Mr Jenks breezed into the classroom in his sports jacket, heavy dark-framed glasses on his nose and looked excitedly at the children as if he was up to something.

"Good morning, everybody."

It was an English lesson, but without any further word, he drew what looked like an outline map on the blackboard. He turned to the class who were now sitting expectantly, some a little red-faced and short of breath from the game of tag that had been going on around the desks just minutes before. They were used to surprises from Jenky.

"This is the as yet undiscovered island of Wynlandia. It consists of two parts." He turned back to the map and drew an irregular line down the middle. "On the left is the territory of Brockleland, and on the right is Banquaroon … You, my friends," he continued, with a wide sweep of his arm, "are the Brockleonians, and the fourth formers next door are the Banquese."

The class were smiling broadly, wondering what was coming next.

Mr Jenks continued: "We need to add some detail to the map." He took some coloured chalk and began expertly drawing in a mountain range and a lake from which rivers flowed in all directions to the sea. Around the coastline he shaded blue, and then placed a large white cross offshore to the east.

"These are the Grand Banques," he smiled and paused. Marianne understood the joke and she glanced at Edward. They'd been studying Canada in geography.

"Excellent fishing grounds for the inhabitants of these little towns along the coast." He chalked a string of dots irregularly spaced down the side of the island.

"Brockleland's coastal waters are full of dangerous rocks and are not good for sailing or fishing. The Brockleonians therefore buy their fish from the Banquese. But! Guess what this is? Brockleland has a large forest in the middle." Mr Jenks turned to sketch in some fir trees. What can you do with fir trees Colquhoun?

"Christmas trees, Sir," said Willie, proudly.

"Yes Colquhoun, possibly, but it wasn't quite what I had in mind … Harvey?"

"Timber, Sir."

"Excellent!"

"Now, what shall we call this forest?" He looked around the class. "How about the Forest of Colquhoun?"

Willie Colquhoun looked pleased and Barnaby Sproat shrugged in a don't-mind-me type of way. Jenky noticed at once.

"The Forest of Sproat doesn't have the same ring to it, Sproat, does it? But you will see that the River Sproat is the largest river running across the central plain, and a major highway for the logging industry." He looked at Barnaby Sproat over the top of his glasses then pushed them back up his nose. "Does this river remind you of anything – Marianne?"

"The St. Lawrence Seaway."

"Attagirl! The Sproat is fed by many tributaries which we'll come back to in a minute. During the rainy season, the river floods for a short while and deposits alluvium. Do you know what that is?"

Edward put up his hand again. "Earth from the river, Sir."

"Very good, Harvey. Yes, when the river floods it leaves earth on the surrounding land. This is called an alluvial plain. The fields are very fertile. Excellent for agriculture. There are farms here, and here and here … What shall we call them?"

The children now understood the game they were playing and suggestions for the farms and towns soon came forth by the dozen. Jenky encouraged them to use corruptions of the names of the class members and of their local area. Glan Ville was a town on the coast, and there was Hayward Farm and the Great Lake Lanigan.

For the next few weeks during double English on Wednesdays, the partition between the third and fourth forms was opened and the two classes – representing the inhabitants of the two countries on the island of Wynlandia – engaged in a type of trading.

Marianne was a corn merchant, and she bought from the arable farmers and sold to the miller in Banquaroon and the chicken farmer in Brockleland. Edward was a timber merchant in charge of the forest, while Pete Glanville ran the sawmill. There were all kinds of exchanges going on and although issued with cheque books, there was also scope for bartering. Abi and Waverley Grossett in the fourth form had an export and import business and it was their job to act as the middle persons between the indigenous Wynlandia population and the rest of the world.

Monsieur 'Jenques' ran the general grocery store and the Bank and Post Office on Brockleland and as he claimed his English was very poor, the pupils had to speak French to him whenever they went to buy household provisions, post a letter or cash a cheque.

Effortlessly, painlessly, the Brocklebank pupils were being

educated in all manner of things, yet they thought it was just a game. Piaget would have been delighted! The school was way ahead of its time in promoting such a diverse range of cross-curricular links.

It was an ambitious project which had the potential to go far. But it took up a significant amount of curriculum time and as the exams approached in the summer term, the island life was abandoned in favour of revision.

Marianne had been doing exams since she was five and she wondered why the early part of the brief northern summer should be spoiled for children every single year. It wasn't that she much minded revising, but it was all added stress and she would have preferred to be doing something else. Each day following the exams, the children would scan the notice board in the classroom for the list of results for each subject. Marianne and Edward were usually top or second in most subjects, but it was a source of little pleasure to her because of the scathing comments from the others. Whenever people said that schooldays were the happiest days of life, she thought about the bullying and the exams and wondered whether her optimistic hopes that her future would be different were just crazy, unrealistic dreams.

Despite all this, when Abi and Marianne were together, they had a wonderful time. Abi was socially skilled and confident in ways that Marianne was only just beginning to learn, but they shared similar interests and had the same zany sense of humour. Laughter was never far away and by summer, they had become firm friends.

One lunchtime, they were sitting on the little bank by the tennis lawn absently making daisy chains and chatting about girly things.

"François is looking nice today," said Abi. François was the visiting French student, tall and mature and aged about twenty, but he wore his hair short and tidy and was rather too conventional for Marianne's developing tastes.

She gazed over her shoulder at the rippling green cornfield on the other side of the wire fence. "He's okay," she said tactfully. Still Edward was the only person from school who deserved any sort of admiration, but she hadn't yet confessed this to Abi for fear of criticism.

"Nearly as nice as Napoleon," continued Abi. Napoleon Solo, played by Robert Vaughan, being one of the men from UNCLE in the cult TV show.

"And he's much nicer than Ilya," said Abi with deliberate provocation.

"No-he-is-not!" said Marianne defensively, the more mysterious and enigmatic secret agent being much more to her liking.

"Yes he is!"

"Isn't!"

"Is!" Abi sprang forward and grabbed at Marianne's daisy chain, breaking it in two. Then they chased each other round the tennis net throwing handfuls of grass and daisies and buttercups until their hair was full of green fronds and flowers.

They collapsed laughing and panting on the bank.

"Look, there he is!" Marianne spotted François emerging from between the Hut and the house and heading up onto the cricket field where the team was having a practice session under the guidance of Mr Russell.

The two girls skipped across the tennis court, over the rockery and began following him. When François stopped to watch the game by the edge of the field, they lurked behind him under the shade of a silver birch tree, managing to remain undetected for some minutes, until Abi stifled a sneeze. François turned. He was used to them doing this and he beamed at them benevolently.

"'Ello girls," he said, with a heavy French accent.

"Bonjour, François," said Abi.

"Bonjour Mesdemoiselles. Comment allez-vous?"

"Très bien merci, Monsieur," said Abi, boldly.

"Show off!" whispered Marianne.

The two girls burst into fits of giggles and François blushed. He may have been flattered by their attention, but was far too mature to take them seriously.

"You play cricket, non?" said François.

"We play tennis instead," said Abi. "Come and have a game. You against both of us."

François smiled again and Abi melted. "You girls would win, I think. Tennis, I am not good."

On the other side of the field, Marianne spotted Edward diving on a ball then throwing it to Barnaby Sproat who was keeping wicket. Perhaps they would be allowed to watch the match against Netherby House that afternoon.

The girls bounded back to their sunny place on the bank and Abi continued musing. "In your form, Edward Harvey seems nice … but too young for me …"

Now it was Marianne's turn to blush.

Later in the afternoon, Mr Wallis said they could finish the history lesson early and join the gathering of people in deckchairs on the boundary of the cricket field. Marianne loved to hear the sound of bat on ball and the evocative spattering of clapping out of unison after a shot well struck, or a ball well bowled, and she didn't have a care in the world as she sat beside her best friend in the late afternoon sun, cheering the team and especially Edward.

But something happened in the intervening years between Brocklebank and being a grown-up. She forgot the good times there; forgot the fun she had with Abi and just remembered always feeling isolated, marginalised, bullied and downtrodden. It was a fact of life that repeated itself over and over: one little negative outweighing all the positives like an unbalanced see-saw. The lesson was to learn perspective, but she hadn't learnt it yet.

9

The M Word

Almost to the day when the heat episodes started, Marianne felt as if someone had flipped a switch inside. Along with the heat came a complete loss of sensual feeling and topsy-turvy emotions that had her laughing one minute, and close to tears the next. These were all signs of the dreaded M word and she was filled with an inescapable sense of finality and that 'it' was all over. The 'it' was the stuff that made life enjoyable and she mourned the loss.

Or she was pregnant. Once she would have been overjoyed. Now, the thought filled her with complete horror.

She couldn't cope with the idea of telling anyone her fears because speaking them aloud would make them real. And she certainly couldn't tell her husband. Things had been bad enough recently and this would be the last straw. She was terrified of not feeling sexy any more; not being desirable. If only she had married someone who didn't compare her all the time to other women. He never used to. Only this past year or so. Only since the drink had become such a significant part of his life. Before that he had been an unwavering diplomat and kept his thoughts to himself.

The surgery was small, but brightened by having a big window opposite the door, and cream walls. Marianne sat in a chair to the side of Dr Curren who looked like Sebastian Coe with a beard. All counselling types arranged their furniture this way nowadays. Supposed to be more empathic and less confrontational. She hated being here among the faintly antiseptic smell and the ominous bed behind the cream curtain.

Dr Curren was a man of few words, and he looked at her expectantly.

"I'd like you to have another look at that mole of mine, please," she said. She had been paranoid about moles ever since Valerie at work had a chunk taken out of her thigh just in case the mole she'd had since childhood might turn malignant. Valerie's mother had died two years earlier from skin cancer and Valerie wasn't going to take any chances. Her doctor had said there was no need to be alarmed. Said to beware of moles that change colour, of moles that move, moles that itch or weep and of satellite moles. He also said that the inside of the thigh was a very unlikely place for a malignant mole. But Valerie insisted, and the offending mole was duly removed and found to be perfectly safe. Valerie was surprised by the size of the dent in her leg and wondered if perhaps she had been over-cautious.

Marianne remembered it well and had surveyed her own moles regularly ever since. 'Mole-mapping', she called it. She had already been to see Dr Curren a couple of times about the one by her hip bone that had appeared one winter after a summer of intense sunbathing at a time when the dangers of such had not been established. Slowly the mole was getting bigger. He had told her it was a seborrhoeic keratosis and innocent. She didn't think that anything called a seborrhoeic keratosis could possibly be innocent and she watched it suspiciously for any of the signs that Valerie's doctor told her.

Again she showed it to Dr Curren and again he said it was fine, though he did add that there was some fairly simple procedure he could perform on it involving local anaesthetic, a needle and some scraping.

Marianne thought she detected a gleam in his eye as if he

might relish the chance of performing minor surgery.

She leaned forward, taking the weight onto the balls of her feet, ready to spring from the chair and leave as fast as possible. But then she paused, sat back and took a deep breath.

"I'm not sure if you need to know this for your records, but I think I'm going menopausal ... hot flushes, and that sort of thing ... Lots ... Didn't expect it so soon. Didn't think it would happen for a few years yet. But there you go ... On the other hand, could I be pregnant?" She'd said it. It was out in the open. Real. No going back.

Marianne hoped for some sympathy, but Dr Curren seemed unphased by the news.

He asked questions about the likelihood of contraception failure.

She said she couldn't recall any.

He asked her to describe her hot flushes and other symptoms.

She did.

He said that the onset of peri-menopause was the most likely explanation, then tapped on his keyboard, took her blood pressure and said she should come back if there were any problems, in which case they could discuss HRT.

She raced from the surgery and headed for the supermarket.

As if she wasn't feeling bad enough already, on the fish counter it took some time before the young man in a white coat and with the face of a bulldog, noticed she was there, and even then he was barely polite as she asked him to search for a piece of haddock that wasn't the size of a shark.

Then on the checkout, a woman of a certain age who should have known better, carried on a conversation with the young blonde girl at the next till, laughing about some stroppy member of staff.

I am here, thought Marianne. *I should like to have your full attention as you pass my broccoli and turnip across the bar-code scanner.*

Then it was, "Would you like help packing, dear?" and "Thank you love," and Marianne thought *don't you 'dear' and 'love' me. Don't make me feel like an inconsequential ancient person not a million miles from taking ages rooting through my purse to find the exact change.*

So that was it, she was officially invisible. But it wasn't like that when she went shopping after work. Oh no. With her make-up on and her high-heeled shoes, there was none of this 'dear' and 'love' and none of the lack of acknowledgement from whichever acne'd youth was on the fish counter. Hmm.

Now she sat at the computer in the upstairs office clutching a hot water bottle. At least she now knew for certain that she wasn't pregnant. She'd always known, really, but it was a relief to be sure. Her brow was furrowed. Hesitantly, she typed the M word into Google's search engine box.

She wanted to do it differently from the paper-flapping bunch at work who seemed to have lost their sense of joy and lost their dreams. She wanted to do it without the scary, controversial, contradictory HRT. She was alarmed at the speed with which Dr Curren had suggested this.

An array of options presented themselves on her computer screen: *Guaranteed Menopause Mood Swing Stabiliser.* Momentarily she visualised herself riding one of those old-fashioned children's bicycles with thick white tyres and two extra tiny little wheels sprouting from either side at the back.

It was true that her moods were all over the place, but she was rather enjoying the roller-coaster ride reminiscent of teenage years. Without the capability of plunging to the depths of despair, there can be no highs; no sweet sensations of euphoric joy.

Herbs for Menopausal Symptoms; Symptoms of the Menopause;

Sex and the Menopause. (She sneaked a quick look at this last one and found it to be about vaginal dryness, bladder weakness, loss of libido, infections and the risks of pregnancy. All cheery stuff!)

Menopause: a New Beginning ... Now this looked interesting. She found the web page and scanned the information. It was all about ancient civilisations revering the post-menopausal as Wise Women. It was the modern western world that looked upon it with dread and loathing. *Loathing, now there's a word,* thought Marianne, thinking of her husband's possible reaction.

Then *Male Menopause: Myth or Magic* caught her eye. Maybe that was what was wrong. Maybe that was the cause of the drinking. Perhaps it wasn't her at all, but him. She printed off a few sheets for future reference and was about to switch off the machine when she thought she would have another peek at Friends Reunited.

It was now mid-September and so far her searching had led to a communication with an old grammar school classmate and two exchanges with university friends. It had been interesting hearing about how lives had panned out. Neurotic Angela now with three children, married to an artist, and seemingly calm, whereas tranquil Sheila, once so placid, sounded extremely anxious and onto her second husband. Steve – always a little off the rails in his youth – settled into farming in Wales. One could never predict what would happen to people.

But there was still no sign of the three she most sought, Sarah Strong, Nick and Edward, and she was beginning to lose hope.

10

The Blond Adonis

There is an uncommon enthusiasm about Marianne this morning as she says good bye to her father and steps from the car onto the asphalt in front of Brocklebank Hall.

"Pens-pencils-handkerchief?" he calls towards receding heels.

She runs toward the Hut, wondering if he's there yet. Not that he will speak to her if he is, but she can enjoy the propinquity and live in hope.

She turns the handle of the door and steps inside …

After three terms of her penance as the solitary girl in the class, Marianne was moved up to the fourth form to join Abi and a new girl, Willie Colquhoun's elder sister Susannah. What joy! Abi and Marianne were already inseparable, and Susannah was a great source of fun and wouldn't stand any nonsense from the boys, least of all her brother. Even Barnaby Sproat kept silent when Susannah was nearby and Marianne felt like she had two personal bodyguards. When they went on walks in the low-lying hills around the town during games lessons, Abi and Suzannah kept Marianne between them and the worst of the bullying stopped. She watched how the older girls parried the insults from the boys and began to do the same, growing in confidence as the weeks went by and at last feeling safe.

It is probable that these were the happiest days she had at Brocklebank. She had friends to talk to in between lessons and no longer whiled away the minutes anxiously watching everyone else and wishing for the teacher to arrive.

And as well as Abi and Susannah, the fourth form brought someone else who was to have a significant impact on her Brocklebank life and even the life beyond.

He arrived with the Indian summer weather as the most beautiful vision of boyhood the girls had ever seen. He had thick straight flaxen hair the colour of the mane of the perfect palomino, worn in Beatles' style and daringly long compared to everyone else. As a dayboy he could get away with this. No doubt the boarders were regularly subjected to a visit from the most ruthless of barbers! He possessed all the self-assured confidence of one who has been told from a very young age that he would break many hearts, and he strutted and preened and entertained in the most beguiling manner. The girls were smitten. Marianne hadn't known what smitten was until Sam Rycroft appeared on the scene. His very presence made her heart skip and her stomach turn over although at the age of ten, she didn't really know why it did this. She looked forward to going to school in a way that she never had before.

Of course Sam Rycroft pretended not to notice the glances of adoration. Sam was nearly twelve. The girls weren't in his league in the pecking order of significance, and although he occasionally passed a joke or two with Susannah, it was purely platonic. His romantic inclinations were exercised publicly as he flirted with Penelope Castle, the temporary geography teacher who was only about eighteen and wore very short skirts with opaque black tights and black polo neck jumpers. She had kohl-rimmed eyes and a thrusting chest. Sometimes Sam managed to make her blush and become flustered, but it was all good humoured and you could tell she thought he was adorable too.

Throughout the winter it became the thing for the girls to watch the school football matches even in the most inclement of weather conditions. They stood by the touchline, wrapped in woolly scarves, shouting for their hero Sam who was every bit as charismatic as David Beckham, and with a talent that was streets ahead of the average eleven- or twelve-year-old playing prep school football in west Cumbria.

He wore the shortest shorts of anyone on the field – his red shirt almost hiding them from view, like Georgie Best. And he knew how to play the crowd; knew all eyes were on him as he scored the goal that took the team to victory. How he was cheered in the fading wintry light, as the teams were clapped off the pitch.

Dear Edward was forgotten.

Some four years later, Sam was to reappear in Marianne's life when he turned up at the local grammar school, two years ahead of her, still having the same impact on the female population. Now the flirtations were of an altogether more serious nature. He and his friends would stand on one side of the playground and Marianne and hers on the other. It was like a giant aquarium with side-viewing access. When anyone dared to walk across the yard all eyes were on them, taking them apart, making comparisons. Marianne and her fellow third formers watched the fifth and sixth formers with awe, wondering if they would ever be so old and sophisticated; wondering if they would get away with wearing a skirt so short with legs like theirs.

When they were about fifteen and began going to parties of a more adult nature, they watched the procession up and down the stairs to the bedrooms with some curiosity and just a little trepidation. The unspoken question was what exactly was going on up there among the maxi coats and the Afghans piled on the beds? Suspecting the worst and labelling as 'loose' the predictable group of girls who always partnered one or other of the 'key' blokes, they wondered whether there would come a time when they would take the plunge and be revered by the younger girls.

'Was Sam with anyone?' This was the question often asked the day after such events. Sam Rycroft could have had any girl he wanted and often emerged from a darkened room, adjusting his t-shirt, then running his hand through his thick, long, but now darkening flaxen hair. Just sometimes, he would date the chosen one for a few times afterwards. But not for long. *Playing the field* was a phrase well used when referring to Sam Rycroft!

By now Marianne's hormones were running rampant and her crush of Brocklebank days had taken on a whole new dimension. Of course she knew he would never look at her. In any case she was far too immature at that time to compete with the willing throng of party groupies, and even had she been old enough, she wasn't that type of girl. But that didn't stop her fantasising. Sometimes he would nod at her when he passed her at school; an unspoken acknowledgement that they had both been to Brocklebank. It gained her a kind of kudos with her friends: the fact that she knew heart-throb Sam Rycroft.

Time raced on as it does through the teenage years, and Marianne and her friends began to understand the complex rituals of courtship. When they entered the fifth form and Sam the upper sixth, Marianne noticed him looking their way quite often as they sat on one of the wooden seats in the playground. But it was not at her he looked, but at her pretty friend Sasha. At first the notion that he might fancy Sasha hit Marianne like a slap across the face. In the evenings when her girls' gang had taken to stalking his gang in the park, sometimes they would all get talking and it was because of Sasha, pouting and sultry Sasha who had a touch of the Bardot about her and who had looked good in hot pants even at the age of twelve, that they were tolerated by such notables.

They all talked of progressive rock music and the latest

albums in the fading light, trying to say the right thing and using words like 'epic' as often as they could. 'Epic' was the Cumbrian 'cool' of the late 1970s. Marianne remembered once enjoying herself so much that she lost track of time and 'forgot' to go home by the ridiculously early curfew imposed by her parents.

"There's Daddy, Marianne!" said Sam in mocking tones, and she turned to see her father with the dog and had to take her leave feeling about as embarrassed as any teenage girl possibly could. What would they think of her? No wonder she stood no chance with them. She was just a kid by comparison. A kid who in addition to not being sexy and beautiful, wasn't allowed out past eight o'clock without a major incident occurring.

Her parents thought it was common to hang around the park. It probably was, but there was nowhere else to go and if her friends were going to hang there, then she was going to hang there too. Parents never seem to understand the importance of fitting in, and to Marianne – who had only discovered the capacity for such in recent years, it was torture to be made to feel like an outsider all over again.

It would be only a matter of time before Sam asked Sasha out and Marianne would have to pretend not to care, say that she didn't mind because she didn't have a chance anyway.

It happened one afternoon break in the spring term when Marianne was in their fifth form room extracting the enormous physics book from her locker by the open window. Sam ambled across the playground in a nonchalant kind of way and leaned on the window frame, smoothing his long hair, probably fully aware that there were many eyes watching him both from the playground and from inside the room.

"Hiya Marianne. Sasha about?"

Marianne knew this was the moment she had been dreading.

She called to Sasha who was sitting by the blackboard deep in conversation with the boy they called Charles Bannerman. His real name was Andy Endercott, but he looked like a student called Charles Bannerman who had been on University Challenge the previous year.

Sasha was the epitome of cool and was already familiar with the concept of dating. Although she had a fair idea of what Sam was going to ask her, she kept him waiting for a couple of minutes while she finished her conversation with Charles Bannerman. Meanwhile Marianne talked to Sam about some youth club that had opened in town, trying to appear bright and cheerful when inside a gloom was descending. When Sasha joined them, she tactfully left them to converse alone.

Sam asked if Sasha would go out with him that weekend. Later that night Marianne wrestled with her loyalties and shed a tear or two and wished and wished that she had been pretty enough to attract his attentions.

But she and Sasha were good friends and she was not going to let this come between them. She would be pleased for them; she would cease to think of Sam in that kind of way. In any case, she was at this time in the middle of her long-distance romance with Nick from Newcastle. And Nick thought she was wonderful. Just that week he had sent her a card of the Waterhouse painting: *The Lady of Shallot*. On the back he had written, '*This reminds me of you!*' The only problem with Nick was that he lived so far away. Their fortnightly letters and occasional meetings did not qualify him for the role of day to day fantasy object.

For this she transferred her affections to Sam's friend, Johnny, who was equally out of her league but seemed to like her. He lived in a road near her street and once when he was walking home from school on his own, he caught up with her and they talked until they reached her house. He offered to tape Pink Floyd's *Obscured by Clouds* for her later that evening, and it was with heady, dizzy, crazy teenage feelings that she took her tape recorder round to his place, and then sat in his bedroom showing him how to work the machine.

"Say something please," she said, thrusting the microphone in his direction, and gazing adoringly at his long brown hair.

"Such as," he said. "Such as, such as, such as, such as."

She flipped the tape over for the recording to be made, and later, when she had both machine and recorded tape safely back in her possession, she searched for his voice on the other side of the tape and played it again and again and again, often blushing even though she was alone. Johnny Ingleton had the sexiest voice in the world!

After that evening he always acknowledged her when they passed at school. And he had the sweetest smile …

She even managed to secure his old geography textbook and changed the way she wrote number sevens to continental style. Even her 'I's became loopy because of Johnny Ingleton. There is nothing like the obsession of a teenage girl!

But he was two years older and just as beyond reach as Sam. Once she was talking to him at a party; trying to cheer him up after he'd had a row with Cassie, his glamorous girlfriend. Cassie saw them chatting on the patio; saw Marianne putting her hippy-headband on his head and saw him smiling and flirting back. Cassie flounced off. The following week at school, Marianne and her friends were sitting at the same dinner table as Cassie when she said to her friend in a deliberately sarcastic and loud voice: "Did you see that kid with Johnny on Saturday night? God, with competition like that around, I don't really stand much chance." And Marianne flushed with embarrassment and hid her gaze, little realising that in the past few months she had begun to lose the gawkiness of her youth and had acquired some curves. She was beginning to look a little like her French grandmother and when heads turned towards her, it was no longer to jeer, but to appreciate.

But Marianne still felt insignificant and young and didn't wait to find out if Johnny might really be interested in her.

It was some seven years later that she met him again in London at one of Sasha's parties.

"There's something crawling up your leg," he said to attract her attention. She was wearing seamed stockings – an attempt at eighties sophistication.

She laughed. *Still the same old Johnny.*

He was really pleased to see her and they chatted for an hour about everything and nothing, oblivious to all others. When he kissed her with some tenderness, she began to believe that there might be something more than friendship going on. Things had changed. They were equal now.

And two years after that they were married and all the mystery of the unattainable had gone. And now? Now he drinks too much and for several months they have inhabited that world of middle-aged relationship angst.

11

Johnny

Johnny's sweetest smile had not been much in evidence recently and the angst had only occurred since *she* came on the scene.

It was ten past midnight when Marianne heard the front door slam and the grinding squeak of the bolt. She wondered what state he would be in this time. She didn't want a row. Perhaps she would pretend to be asleep. She listened for the footfall on the stairs, but instead she heard him open the living room door.

Soon there was a blast of music from the TV. It sounded like some late night show with Jools Holland. She hoped it wouldn't wake Holly. Ten minutes later and he was making noisy progress up the stairs, fumbling with the door handle then collapsing fully clothed on the bed. He didn't even speak to her, or try to see if she was still awake. In seconds he seemed to be asleep on his back, a throaty rattle punctuating his exhalations. There was the smell of beer and sweat and smoke and Marianne felt sick.

She turned her back, eyes wide, hot and restless, staring into the gloom.

Johnny Ingleton had been christened John by his parents and had acquired the Johnny tag from his football team mates soon after starting junior school. At secondary school they called him Jing and at college he reverted to Johnny. Only a few months earlier when he was forty-seven, did he announce to Marianne that he wanted to be called John again.

"I'm damned if I'll ever call you John! I've never known you as John," Marianne had protested. "John is too sensible and conservative for you."

"Perhaps it's time I became more sensible and conservative."

So Marianne had tried it for a while to show willing, but *John* didn't sit comfortably in her mouth and after a week or two she gave up and reverted to Johnny.

It hadn't always been difficult between them. They had been the envy of their friends for many a year. When the women got together to have a moan about their spouses, Marianne was the one to sit in an almost embarrassed silence, once again an outcast; not 'one of the club'. There wasn't much gossip mileage in a husband who was sexy and charming and made her laugh every day. And Johnny often used to tell her that when his mates started talking in disparaging tones about 'her at home', he would shrug and nod sympathetically and be glad that his wife wasn't nagging, hypercritical and unadventurous in the bedroom.

It helped that they talked. At least Johnny talked and Marianne willingly listened. She knew what was beating in his soul because he externalised his thoughts, hoping she would miraculously solve his problems with suggestions or solutions.

"Wait twenty-four hours," she would often say. "In twenty-four hours you will feel differently. What seems big now will be small in twenty-four hours. You will be rational. You will make the right decision."

She was calm and measured; a counterweight to his hotheadedness. She knew he loved her for it.

He was the ideal husband and father while Holly was growing up. He cooked and cleaned without being asked. And as well as flowers, he would buy other little gifts and sometimes hide them around the house for Marianne to find whenever. He wrote her poetry, played his guitar and sang to her, took time when making love and phoned her often to say he was thinking about her.

Time and again he told her he thought she was beautiful and Marianne would smile, but never believe it. Inside she was still the scrawny kid that boys made fun of, but if it didn't matter to Johnny, then she was happy enough.

Of course the intensity of the early years subsided as it always does, but even after Holly was born, they managed to keep a glittering thread of romance running through their relationship.

When he wasn't being domesticated, or working, or having cosy chats in front of the fire, he was out in the wild outdoors, on mountain slopes, surveying panoramic vistas of rugged outcrops, lakes and forests, or walking the coast. He often disappeared alone for a day in the country where he would trek for miles until he was exhausted, eventually returning home late in the evening to a hot bath, supper and languid sex with Marianne.

As Holly grew more self-sufficient, some of the habits of their early years together began to creep back into their routines: candles and incense, aromatherapy oils and relaxing massage. While Johnny was out, Marianne enjoyed preparing for his return, soaking in a bath of scented bubbles and taking time to do all the personal maintenance things that benefited from privacy and time.

Where had it all gone? Now when she looked at him, the once open book was closed and her measured calm was lost. Since January, the glittering thread had snagged and seemed to be unravelling, and the candles, the oils and the incense had remained in their box.

Marianne remembered to the day, when the boat began to rock, coming back from work to find this vision of feminine loveliness sitting in the kitchen having a cup of tea with Johnny;

sitting on the stool by the table, mug between both hands, legs crossed, short skirt riding up above her knees and with an air of someone who did this every day.

"Oh!" Marianne had said, surprised to the point of forgetting her manners and standing gawping, conscious of how dishevelled she was by comparison.

"This is Charmaine, love," said Johnny without concern. "She's covering Rosie's maternity leave."

Johnny was Head of Geography and Geology at Cedarwood Secondary School. Although not far from where they lived, this was the first time he had brought anyone home unexpectedly.

Marianne had tried to smile, but her head was spinning and her stomach churned as if possessed by snakes.

Charmaine was just the sort of woman you didn't want to find your husband alone with – even if all they were having was a cup of tea. She was about thirty, blonde and curvaceous and heavily made up. Marianne was thinking *tarty cow*, which was a trifle unfair, but she knew that this was just the look that men couldn't help acting on. It was the look that turned their heads and had them driving into lampposts. *No wedding ring either, and this woman was going to be working with her husband for six months!*

Johnny was still a very attractive man. He was lean and rangy and hadn't acquired the almost requisite beer-gut of the over forties. He kept in shape with his walking and weekly games of badminton and although he never made a show about being interested in clothes, he was always well-pressed and co-ordinated. He had a certain *je ne sais quoi* together with a sense of humour that made women flock to be in his company. His hair was slightly less luxuriant than it had been, but it was still charmingly longer than the current popular style, and gave him a continental, cavalier air that made him stand out in a crowd.

More than this, his intense blue eyes and captivating smile still shone just as they had done when he was at school. Marianne believed there was no question that Ms Rosie-Replacement would be impressed and in seconds the bindweed of jealousy began to twist and wind around her heart.

She quickly composed herself, used to giving the pretence of being in charge of a situation. She put her files down on the work surface, took off her coat and smoothed her skirt.

"You're very brave taking on the kids of Cedarwood."

"They seem nice so far." Charmaine smiled, exposing a row of rather obvious crowns.

"Do you live locally?"

"About two miles away. Not too far."

Not next door then, thought Marianne with some relief.

"Has Johnny offered you something to eat? I'm always ravenous after teaching." She went to the bread bin and began making a honey sandwich with thick slices of wholemeal bread.

"Not for me thanks," said Charmaine breezily. "I should be going." She turned to Johnny. "Thanks for looking after me today, John. Appreciate it." She placed her mug on the work-surface, bright pink nails manicured to perfection, gleaming in the light.

John! Hmph! thought Marianne. She had watched their every move and glance, looking for tell-tale signs of attraction. A more securely confident woman might have thought little of it, but all the hurt and inadequacies from her childhood and teenage years – largely under wraps during her marriage thus far – resurfaced with a clarion call loud enough to shake her usual composure.

Later that evening she couldn't help saying, "I wish you hadn't invited that woman here without asking me?"

"Charmaine? Why?"

"You're too nice sometimes, Johnny. People take advantage."

"She's only just moved into the area and doesn't know anyone round here. No big deal. Thought I'd make her feel welcome."

"Exactly."

"Exactly what?"

"She doesn't know people. She'll get dependent."

"Mari … I don't think so."

"You wait. I know women like that."

"You don't know her at all. She's nice—"

"Typical man. All you see is 'blonde' and 'chest' and you come over all chivalrous."

"Where's all this coming from, Mari? You're not usually like this."

She wasn't. Usually. For over twenty years she hadn't been jealous or felt threatened. It must be her age. Even if Johnny thought she was beautiful when she was young, he wouldn't think so as she got older. And rather than creeping up on her slowly, all she had to do was take the lid off her Brocklebank experience and unleash the monster that was her early-life inadequacies.

Johnny had reached out to touch her arm as he often did in rare times of tension, but she pulled away, her eyes pricking with tears from long ago. And later that night when he tried to cuddle her, she uncharacteristically turned away.

After this, their once idyllic marriage took a turn towards that dark place of self-destruction. This was when she started writing her journal again, detailing events of emotional significance so she could remember what he said and how it was and how she felt. Whenever she confronted him, he said she was over-reacting, but the evidence lay between the covers of her journal.

The mention of Charmaine's name sent Marianne into hedgehog mode and Johnny, who plainly didn't believe that he was doing anything wrong, returned from his weekend excursions and sought solace at the pub. Since getting married, he never used to drink much at all, but she knew things had changed by his manner when he came home. Even during the week he began to have a pint or two after work, and when he didn't go out, a bottle of wine was all it took to render him tactless.

It was Charmaine this and Charmaine that and Marianne wanted to say, 'fuck Charmaine', although not meaning it exactly. But she kept quiet and merely sighed.

Now it was September and outside the sun still shone but inside there was a grim game being played.

Transactional analysts might have called the game *The Goddess*. Transactional analysts would say that when the husband makes advances to his wife and is rejected for reasons he cannot fathom, he designs a strategy to justify this in order not to feel humiliated. The game might involve talking about a perfect woman as if she exists somewhere out there, and intimating that his wife doesn't measure up. He can then interpret rejection as being a result of his belittling comments rather than due to a reason he cannot understand.

Marianne knew that because she had reached an age where she felt less worthy of love, she felt threatened by another woman entering her husband's life. Every time she went spiky at the mention of Charmaine, Johnny misbehaved all the more. They were playing the roles of parent and child, preventing any form of reasonable adult discussion and resolution of the issue.

Transactional analysts know a thing or two about relationship games. They even know how to solve the problems. Trouble is, even though Marianne knew all the theory, she was far too immersed in the problem to act rationally and take a different path.

In the morning, she was up and dressed before Johnny – still in his clothes – began to stir.

He stretched and grimaced and wandered bleary-eyed to the bathroom where he was soon heard showering.

Marianne was shaking the duvet and plumping the pillows when he came back into the room naked. She couldn't help but notice and appreciate, but there was sadness in her eyes.

"You were late last night," she said, trying not to accuse, but knowing that was how it would sound.

"I popped in for a quick pint on the way home. There were a few mates from school. Rosie's not coming back and Charmaine has been offered a permanent contract."

So that means Charmaine was in the pub. Marianne paused, leaning over the bed, glad that he couldn't see the expression of despondency on her face.

"Oh, that's nice," was all she could manage, knowing she didn't sound convincing and sure that after all she had said about Charmaine, Johnny wouldn't believe her.

By the time Johnny had dressed and left the room, her head was spinning. All she could think of was Johnny and Charmaine together – at work, in the pub, in her kitchen – Charmaine calling him 'John' … There was no escape now. The assumption that everything would return to normal when the maternity leave ended had, in a few short words, been upturned, and the ghosts of Brocklebank Hall were ready to wreak havoc once again.

12

Lydia

Marianne and Edward wait side by side on the miniature stage at the end of the Hut. For years this has been the preserve of the teachers during assembly and it is strangely empowering being so elevated. They are each clutching paperback booklets and looking earnestly at Mr Russell, the Headmaster, standing on the floor below them.

Beyond a nod of acknowledgement, there is no communication between them, but nor are there any hints of the hostility that crackles in the air when she is with many of the other boys. Marianne trusts Edward completely and knows that even if she makes a mistake, he won't use this as ammunition to taunt her at a later date as some of the others might. She also knows that he will be able to do whatever is asked of him and all she has to do is try to match his excellence in the scene they share.

Mr Russell is directing the action, telling them where to move and where to place emphasis in delivering the complicated language of a bygone age.

"Now Edward," he says. He is a kindly man and saves the surname tags only for the classroom. "If you sit there on what will be a proper eighteenth century style seat when we do the real performance," he gestures to the two classroom chairs that are in the middle of the stage, "and look as if you are reading ... that's right ... Marianne comes rushing in with a pile of books. She's been to the library ... She's breathless ... She comes across the stage to here and turns. Edward, that's when you close the book, put it on the seat and get up. Each book that Marianne gives to you, look at it dismissively and drop it on the seat. We'll go from the beginning." He points to the wings and Marianne

skips offstage with her copy of the play and a pile of imaginary books.
  "Action!"

The children were now in the fifth form and had moved back into a room in the main school building. Marianne was almost eleven and a prefect with responsibility for supervising the younger forms during wet breaks, and for ringing the bell at lesson changeovers every third Friday. She could even give lines to misbehaving pupils, though she never did.

Sadly, Abi and Susannah – and Sam Rycroft too – had left Brocklebank at the end of the previous school year. Abi had gone to Africa with her parents and although she and Marianne communicated endlessly via pages and pages of tissue thin airmail paper, it wasn't the same as being able to pretend to be The Seekers – standing on beds in long nightdresses with hairbrush microphones performing 'The Carnival is Over'; or giggling over the latest escapades of Ilya and Napoleon and arguing over who was the most fanciable secret agent; or singing at the tops of their voices in Abi's mum's little white Daf as they motored round the country lanes between their respective homes. Marianne missed her terribly.

She missed Susannah's zany and infectious humour too and her no-nonsense attitude with the boys. But for the arrival of Sally Mainsford, she would once again have been the only girl in the class. Sally had shiny brown hair and a quietly mysterious aura. Now it was Marianne's turn to make decisions and lead the way.

When Mr Russell announced at assembly that there was going to be another school play – Sheridan's melodramatic comedy, *The Rivals* – and read out a list of fourth and fifth formers who should report to the Hut for auditions that afternoon, Marianne was enthusiastic. She liked reading aloud in class and thought this might be something she would enjoy.

Abi and Susannah had left her with some confidence and she was no longer afraid to speak up for herself.

The choice of play was an ambitious undertaking for a group of eleven- and twelve-year-olds, and with due concern for their tender age, several abridgements had been made and many of the longer speeches pruned.

There were four female parts in the play: Mrs Malaprop and her niece, Lydia; Lydia's cousin, Julia; and Lydia's maid, Lucy. Marianne thought that with only two girls asked to go to the auditions, there was a high probability that she would soon be treading the boards.

Lydia Languish devoured masses of the equivalent of today's bed-hopping, corset-busting blockbusters and played tortuous games with her suitor in the hope of being loved to madness. In her teenage years Marianne was to become like Lydia – empty headed when it came to matters of love, as stuffed full of romantic nonsense from watching black and white movies as Lydia was from reading trashy fiction.

The upshot of the auditions was that Marianne was the only girl to be given a female role: that of Lucy. Ian Dangerfield, small of stature and with an aptitude for English was, perhaps ironically, to be Mrs Malaprop, while Richard Zammit, freckled and red-haired, would be Cousin Julia. And Lydia? The charming and beautiful Lydia was to be played by Edward Harvey.

Edward, who Marianne had almost forgotten existed since the arrival of Sam Rycroft.

She hadn't noticed how self-assured he had become, and how while still keeping a wide berth from involvement with the likes of Barnaby Sproat and Billy Colquhoun, he certainly wasn't short of friends. Waverley Grossett in particular, was a gentle and friendly boy who had arrived in the fourth form at the same time as Abi, and thought nothing of chatting enthusiastically to the girls in between lessons, ignoring the disparaging glances from many of the others.

The rehearsals took place during the end-of-day games lessons and because the abridgements had cut completely the first scene of the original play, at first it was only Edward and Marianne attending as they shared the first part of scene two alone together.

And how Marianne looked forward to those sessions.

Not only was anything preferable to scampering about on a hockey pitch in the cold, damp air of a northern winter late afternoon, but she took to acting like the proverbial duck to water. And then there was the added bonus of Edward, who day by day began to resume a position of favour in her eyes. But not in the same way as Sam had been.

Drooling over Sam the previous year had been bubble-gum pink, frivolous and fun. With Edward it was the same innocent admiration as before but with a touch more intensity. It was a feeling of respect, of trust; of intuitive understanding.

When it came to acting, he was supremely competent for someone so young. Like Marianne, he learnt his words quickly such that real progress could be made as they were unencumbered by books – except for Lydia's.

When those playing female parts were summoned to try on their costumes by the Headmaster's mother, known to all affectionately as Grandma, they met in the sanctity of the Russells' drawing room, with its imposing high ceiling and ornate cornice. Now it was taken over by wigs, fabrics, dresses and 18th century costumes hired from a local theatre. Red jackets with gold buttons were strewn around over the furniture, and the floor by the wall was lined with long black boots and square-toed shoes with clumpy heels and silver shining buckles.

Marianne had changed in the staff cloakroom next door and

was now wearing a pale blue full-length pinafore dress with three-quarter length white puffed sleeves. Mrs Russell was attempting to tie a crisp white apron around her tiny waist.

"What you need is a mop cap," said Mrs Russell. "And we could have a strand of hair sticking out of the front in a corkscrew curl."

Marianne didn't understand about mop caps or corkscrew curls and remained unblinking and silent. Her hair had always been very reluctant to wave or curl and she doubted even Mrs Russell's ability in persuading it to be anything other than straighter than straight.

Grandma was fussing around Edward, pinning him into a voluminous mass of pink chiffon, cunningly gathered to imply a bosom. Ian Dangerfield and Richard Zammit were still in their grey school uniforms and looked on with more than a little apprehension.

"Oh my!" Mrs Russell looked up from tying the apron bow. "Edward, you look magnificent! And once we add the wig, no-one will ever guess." She rubbed her hands together in obvious delight.

Ian Dangerfield fluttered Mrs Malaprop's fan, eyes glinting mischievously, but Edward remained impassive as if dressing in a frock was merely another of life's interesting challenges that he would rise to with alacrity.

Marianne had never looked at him properly without his glasses before – despite the fact that he never wore them on the games field – and she was immediately struck by his beautiful brown eyes. They were eyes that drew her into unfathomable depths, and beyond to a kaleidoscope soul.

Dear Edward … when she remembered how their lives had touched at that special time, and yet they never talked. If she could turn back time, if she could have been as forthcoming as she became in later years, she would have made more effort to speak; to find the common ground she knew was there.

On the day of the dress rehearsal, a dark brown wig with the hair in a ponytail, and the addition of stage make-up, completed Edward's transformation. Marianne was awestruck. He looked so ... pretty! Gone was the boyish intellectual, and in his place, achieved with cool confidence, was, unquestionably, Lydia.

They performed their dress rehearsal in the afternoon in front of the rest of the school. Mr Jenks's creativity and talent with the paintbrush had transformed the stage from bare and spartan into something resembling a theatrical backdrop. Four steps had been constructed in the middle leading down to the main floor, and small extensions had been built out on either side. The dusty old floorboards were painted in a chequerboard of brown and cream, and a false wall at the back depicted panelling and windows with long blue curtains hanging down. Flats had been added, decorated with a painted stonework design and 1723 written on one of the bricks.

It was a little chaotic without Mr Russell guiding the action from the front. Mrs Malaprop was taken to task afterwards for chewing gum in his opening scenes and for nibbling the ends of his fan when others were delivering their lines. The curtain got stuck at the beginning of Act 2 and Captain Absolute almost fell backwards off the stage during the sword fight.

"It'll be all right tomorrow night," said Mr Russell optimistically at the end.

All afternoon Marianne felt strangely at ease with so much 'female' companionship. Afterwards, when the man from the local newspaper came to take photographs, she tried to talk to Lydia.

But Edward responded with a shrug, seeming puzzled by her friendliness.

The photographer looked like an owl and was so surprised

to discover that Lydia was not a girl that he singled out Lydia and Lucy to be pictured on the settee.

The two children sat side by side and Marianne tried again to talk to Edward. All she achieved were monosyllabic replies.

Why won't he talk to me? She thought. We have things to say, I know we have. We could be friends …

"The caption could read '*Guess who's the Real Girl*'," said the owl to Mrs Russell who was acting as chaperone. "It-is-remarkable!"

Perhaps that's why Edward seems cross, mused Marianne.

Clearly the photographer thought better of his idea because the only picture to appear in the paper was one of the whole cast.

On the night of the performance – the only performance in front of an adult audience – the atmosphere about the corridors of Brocklebank was hot with excitement and nerves. The day pupils stayed on for supper and it was as if they were being offered a privileged view of the usually private and more intimate world that existed after four o'clock.

Edward and Marianne were first into make-up and they sat in their form room in the main building being decorated with greasepaint by an ex-movie actress who was a friend of Mrs Russell's.

"Darlings you look wonderful," she said in a deep dramatic voice, surveying her handiwork. She was the same age as Marianne's mother, but had a modern very short hair-cut and wore masses of black eye-shadow and eye-liner. "Break a leg," she added, as they got up to leave the room. Marianne thought this was a very strange thing to say before such an important performance.

Then it was out into the wintry night across the passage that separated the schoolhouse from the Hut, through the wooden door and up the steps at the side of the stage.

Edward and Marianne hovered in the wings. The curtain was down and they could hear the audience murmuring beyond. They were shaking with fear and excitement, mouthing their words, breathing ever so slightly faster than usual. Marianne's throat felt dry. What if she forgot her lines? What if she let Edward down? No, it would be fine, she hadn't forgotten them during any of the rehearsals so why would she now? Yet still she fretted.

Edward looked at her over his shoulder. "Time to go!"

"Good luck," said Marianne.

It was too late for a last look at the script. Edward as Lydia had taken position on the dainty little settee and was languishing – literally – and apparently reading a novel.

Mr Russell said a few words to the audience at the front of the curtain, Tom Sowerby began pulling the curtain ropes, and slowly, gradually, the bright lights came up onto the stage and Marianne knew this was her cue to enter.

She rushed from the wings, clutching her pile of books, past the seated Lydia, turned and, remembering to address her words outwards so the audience could hear, she breathlessly began.

LUCY: Indeed Ma'am, I traversed half the town in search of it: I don't believe there's a circulating library in Bath I ha'n't been at.

LYDIA: And could not you get *The Reward of Constancy?*

LUCY: No, indeed, Ma'am.

LYDIA: Nor *The Fatal Connection?*

LUCY: No, indeed, Ma'am.

LYDIA: Nor *The Mistakes of the Heart?*

There was a ripple of appreciative and encouraging laughter from the dark depths of the Hut. Edward was really laying it on.

LUCY: Ma'am, as ill luck would have it, Mr Bull said Miss Sukey Saunter had just fetched it away.

More giggles and a guffaw from the back. It was the first time Marianne felt the thrill of making an audience laugh and the feeling would stay with her always.

LYDIA: Well, child, what have you brought me?

And here Lucy went through each one of the pile of books she was carrying, handing them to Lydia, who glanced at them dismissively and dropped them on the settee. As each one fell, the audience laughed. It was going well; it was fun; it was just the best thing Marianne had ever done.

And for the next hour and a half the little stage witnessed one of those watershed events in the lives of those who cavorted and gestured and swooned and twirled.

At the end of it all, the cast lined up for the curtain call and held hands. Edward next to Marianne didn't make a fuss about this, and they all walked to the front of the stage and bowed. The clapping echoed loudly in the Hut and when the lights came on, happy, smiling faces of adoring parents beamed at their offspring with pride and affection.

In her father's car on the way home after the performance, Marianne sat in the back with her grandmother, her head in a whirl of excitement, the lines and the applause reverberating, and her heart dancing with a passion of the sort that only eleven-year-old girls can know.

"I cannot get over Ian Dangerfield. His Mrs Malaprop was superb," her mother was saying.

"Clearly an exponent of the language of the fan," said her father.

"Those gestures! Incredible for such a young boy. Must have an old crotchety aunt."

"Comic timing down to a tee," said her grandmother.

"And Clarissa's son was very good as Captain what's-his-name, though his feet did look rather big in those boots."

And what about Lydia? Thought Marianne. Say something about Lydia. Wonderful, wonderful Edward! She was still wearing full make-up, but with her school uniform, and the smell of the greasepaint filled the car.

"We've got plenty of cold cream at home," her mother had said to Mrs Russell who had seemed none too pleased at Marianne being hurriedly whisked away. It wasn't the done thing apparently, but Marianne's parents didn't care about done things when it came to escaping the discomfort of small hard chairs.

And Marianne was none too pleased either for she wanted to savour the glory with her peers and spend a little more time in the company of Edward. For once some sense of camaraderie reigned between her and the boys, and even Barnaby Sproat had complimented her on her performance and treated her with something bordering on respect.

But what about Lydia? Edward had been astonishing in his portrayal of the flirtatious young woman – especially during the heart-stopping moment when he had been unable to free the clasp on the necklace and had angrily torn it from around his neck, flinging it at Captain Absolute with all the conviction of having practised the move at rehearsal. Beads went everywhere, but with true professionalism, Edward carried on delivering his lines. What a hero he was!

"Raymond Salkeld was a scream," continued her mother.

"But were the lines he was saying, the lines in the play?" said her father.

"When he said '*I forgot me words!*'"

"Priceless!"

"And Lydia was good too, don't you think?" Marianne chirped from the back.

"Lydia? Oh yes … The Harvey boy … Yes. Totally convincing; very clear. Heard every word," said her father.

"That dress was a dream," said her mother.

"He was the best, I thought," said her grandmother, perceptively.

Marianne settled back in her seat, satisfied.

But now, thirty-three years later, half a lifetime of passions since then, Marianne sat by her computer, such joys long forgotten, her life in disarray, the Friends Reunited search facility open on the screen, sobbing for the girl she once was and the woman she might have been but for the dark days of Brocklebank that haunted her still.

13

Never Enough

Last September ... He loved me then, thought Marianne. *What changes a year can bring ... Now I am totally alone with the shortening days and the flat grey skies ... and memories ...*

A persistent drizzle misted the windscreen of Johnny's car causing the wipers to squeak irritatingly. Holly had just been dropped off at Sussex University to begin her law degree and Marianne and Johnny sat stony-faced on the journey back home, Johnny driving because he nearly always did when there were two of them, and Marianne in charge of the map, her thoughts in disarray.

Although settled back into their respective routines of the academic year, the atmosphere between them was less than convivial. Johnny had continued drinking more than he should, and Marianne wondered if it was her fault for being cranky, or if there was something more sinister behind his eagerness to escape to the pub or to reach for the bottle.

She was still hot and she hadn't told him yet.

Johnny's eyes were glassy and he had been very quiet since they waved goodbye to Holly. Marianne knew what a wrench it was for him to lose his darling, precious, beautiful daughter to that world of ebullient youth. It had been bad enough when he could meet and vet her boyfriends, but to live in ignorance of whom she was choosing to spend time with, was something he would find extremely difficult.

That was the problem with being male. Men knew what it was like to have a young man's thoughts and fantasies and reckless urgency towards the act of copulation. Knowing his dear daughter might be on the receiving end of this frantic pursuit of pleasure would be just too much to bear.

Seeing Holly bouncing off gleefully to join the other freshers had been both reassuring and heart wringing at the same time. She was sociable and well-adjusted; popular and pretty. Young men and women would flock to share her company. She would be fine. She didn't need them any more.

For Marianne herself, she was losing a friend, a confidante in recent weeks, someone to shop with and tell you with utmost honesty that the pink, skin-tight, sparkly t-shirt from the trendy high street store was far too 'young' for you but that the style was okay, it was the fabric that wasn't and that if you could find the same thing from a more up-market store, then that would be fine.

She would miss Holly's increasingly competent efforts to cook supper and her help with the minutiae of life like the washing-up and the cats and the laundry and the rubbish.

How empty the house would feel without the trail of teenagers wanting food and sometimes an extra bed. No more 'could you collect me' phone calls from parties in the dead of night. No more heated discussions about whether she could do this or that. Not that Holly had tried to push the boundaries farther than she was allowed.

Someone at work once said to Marianne that there were two children in her destiny. The woman called Maggie had firmly taken her hand one day when her guard was dropped, and had read the intricate pattern of lines and grooves that tell the story of a life and of lives created.

"We've just Holly," Marianne had said, puzzled all the same.

"Are you sure?" asked Maggie, furrowing her brow and shaking her wild red curls until her gold chandelier earrings tinkled and chimed. "Are you sure? There's definitely two ᵢ₁ere. I can see two as clear as day or my name's not Maggie."

And Marianne turned her head away, hoping those who were gathered watching with the curiosity of a group of cows wouldn't see the pain, for she never spoke of the time when she thought just maybe …

When Holly was three and delightful, with ribbons in her hair and sunny giggles, always dancing, twirling; when every day was a rainbow of chatter and discovery; that was when she thought just maybe … when she felt something different. There was the slightest change about herself … hard to explain … but something not quite usual.

She hadn't told Johnny … wouldn't tell Johnny until she was sure.

Then just nine days later, there was the pain. Excruciating pain. She had almost screamed at the traffic lights, begging them to change to green so she could rush home to her bed to hide. Such pain in her belly and in her heart, knowing somehow that this was the last chance and that if not now, then never.

"There's definitely two," said the woman called Maggie who was Celtic and fey and picked up the slightest things from out of the ether. "Is there something you haven't told us, Marianne?"

Marianne shook her head, blinking back the tears, knowing that Maggie was right.

After that moment, that precious painful moment that Johnny would never know, she went back to working full-time, and five years passed and Johnny said perhaps they should accept it just wasn't going to happen, that Holly was everything; Holly was enough. They were happy, weren't they? Now was not the time to start again with the nappies and the sleepless nights and the never-ending tiredness.

Marianne agreed, and back they went to the days of their youth; to being careful, just in case.

Now Holly was gone, and Marianne's world seemed dark

and all the hundreds of 'what might have beens' tumbled around in her brain.

"It's just us now, Mari," said Johnny, his eyes on the grey road ahead.

'Just us' hadn't seemed so bad this time last year, but now it meant emptiness, loneliness, loss. She had no answer; she was too choked with holding back the tears.

The following week, still unused to the quietness, Marianne decided to make an effort to be less frosty. "You're home early," she said to Johnny, giving him a hug and a smile. She was in the kitchen washing and chopping vegetables for a stir-fry.

"Postponed the meeting till tomorrow. Charmaine had forgotten and made an appointment."

"That's a nuisance."

"These things happen."

Normally Johnny complained furiously if plans had to be changed; if the staff in his department hadn't read the school calendar and meticulously put all the meetings into their diaries or Year Planners. Marianne sniffed. No doubt Charmaine had thrust her ample bosom in his face when she told him. *Tarty cow.*

"We did say we'd go out for a meal tomorrow … Now Holly's gone," said Marianne. How alien and empty those words sounded.

"We can do that anytime. We could do it tonight!" Johnny was the impulsive one.

Marianne waved her knife over the chopped onion and the bowl of sliced chicken and Johnny shrugged.

There was a pause. Marianne continued chopping and Johnny went to hang his jacket over a chair in the living room, calling as he did so, "I thought we might invite Charmaine round for supper one evening."

"Are you serious?" Marianne had been counting the weeks

till Charmaine's departure and now not only was she a permanent fixture at Cedarwood, working in the same department as her husband, but she was even supposed to befriend her and invite her round for supper.

"Er, yes."

"I don't think so."

"Why not?" asked Johnny, returning to the kitchen and sitting on a stool, the very same stool on which Charmaine had sat in secretarial pose with legs crossed seductively, when Marianne first discovered her existence.

"You know why not."

"No. I don't. Tell me. What is the problem with Charmaine? You'd like her if you got to know her properly. She's really nice; an interesting person; good fun; great sense of humour."

Suddenly the good intentions of just seconds earlier began to slip away and the light welcoming mood began to turn. Marianne could feel it trickling down through her body and into the floor, but she was powerless to stop it. Her mouth opened as if controlled by puppeteers and words came forth that good sense would have kept inside. "I suppose she laughs at your jokes?"

"So?" Johnny helped himself to a piece of carrot and bit on it with a loud crunching sound.

"You're so dense sometimes." Yet more words from the bag of tricks.

"Christ, Mari!" he snapped. "*You* laugh at my jokes."

"And she calls you '*John*'."

Johnny gave Marianne one of his long, lingering blue-eyed stares of incredulity, and in his tone she thought she heard a touch of a sneer. "Is it because she's young and pretty? Is that the problem? Is Mari feeling a tad insecure?"

Marianne winced and stopped chopping. "What do you think?"

"I think you're crazy! D'you think I might have an affair

with her? Is that it? D'you think she's a threat?"

"No … yes … maybe."

"And why would I?"

"Because …"

"Because what?"

Marianne wanted to say *because I'm hot and crabby and plummeting towards the menopause, towards over-the-hill, towards unattractive in comparison to the likes of Charmaine,* but instead she said, "Just because. That's all. You should know."

"Well I don't know. I've never given you any reason to doubt me. I don't understand what's going on. Thought I understood women. Thought I understood you – but it appears I don't." Johnny shook his head.

Marianne returned to slicing carrots into meticulous julienne strips. She tried to hide her face from him. She could feel her eyes brimming.

"Tell me Mari. What is it? What's up?" he asked with no trace of sympathy.

"Nothing."

"Oh come on."

"You're out all the time. Drinking."

"Sometimes I need to unwind after work."

"You can unwind here."

"Like now, you mean?" His tone was more than a shade sarcastic.

"Touché." She shuddered.

"If you carry on like this, I'm going out."

Marianne put down the knife and turned to face him, her temper rising and the manipulator tweaking the strings once again. "That's your solution to everything these days. Pub … booze … It's affecting your judgement; it's affecting us."

"Complete bollocks," said Johnny. "I've not been drinking today … Yet!"

"You're not listening to me about Charmaine. You're not taking on board what I'm saying."

"But what you're saying is ridiculous. You're making mountains out of molehills."

Marianne turned on him, her voice raised. "They're mountains to me! I need you to try to understand. You may not agree with me, but you could accept that I might see things differently from you."

"How many fucking times do I have to tell you, there's nothing to see?" Johnny began to shout. "I've told you not to worry. Are you saying you don't trust me? After all this time? That's a bloody insult."

Marianne was incensed. She could almost see the red mist and her head felt like her brain was fighting with itself. "Don't try and make out it's my fault. Why are you speaking to me like this? All I want you to do is listen to my opinion and validate it. If I feel something, I feel it. It may not be what you think I should feel, but you could acknowledge it."

"What the hell d'you mean, *validate*? Don't start being all psychological with me."

"Psychological! It's my job. This is who I am. There's no need to be personal. Just stop … Stop before you say something you regret."

"You are too analytical. Always making things so complicated. It makes my head hurt."

Marianne began to feel the familiarity of something from long ago when the Brocklebank bullies closed in. "That's one of the reasons you married me. Because I understood you; helped you sort things out. How can you throw that back at me now? Just stop!"

But Johnny didn't seem as if he had any intention of stopping. "With you everything has to be dissected. Everything! No wonder you see things that aren't there. You're mad …"

Marianne backed away from her chopping board and covered her head. His words felt like physical battering, each one touching an old wound from when she was young.

"Stop … please stop this."

Johnny waved his arms at her, mimicking. "What's with all this fucking drama queen nonsense? Eh, Mari?"

She backed further into the hall. "You never shout at me like this. This isn't you. We don't do this. I don't want to row."

"Bit fucking late for that now! Sort yourself out. I'm off!"

Johnny pushed past her, grabbed his jacket from the living room chair and left.

Later, Marianne sat on the bed, red eyed, surveying their room and all its familiar objects; her cluttered dressing table and the chair on which Johnny layered his discarded clothes until he couldn't find anything and was forced to tidy up.

She had never told him about the Brocklebank demons, so he was not to know why she went all prickly about Charmaine. When she was younger she managed to hide her insecurities. Now she felt that she could never match up, no matter what.

And with the resurgence of all the angst from the past came a feeling that her earlier happy married life had been one long game where she had acted a part rather than been herself. It was all a charade, a play in which she trod the boards of domesticity and spoke the words of a dutiful wife. She couldn't be herself because herself was flawed and damaged from a long-lost time when the bullies reigned.

No one knew how different she felt from the human race. She saw other women with their husbands and children doing the family thing as if it was the most natural way to be. But for her it had always felt strange; it was pretence. She was a fraud masquerading as wife and mother when she was undeserving of the role. And Johnny didn't know all this. Didn't know about the early pain and insecurity that was rooted in a time so long ago, and that he had been living with an imposter for over twenty years.

She had never told him how unworthy she felt of his love. How she didn't understand why he thought she was beautiful and why now that she was getting old, undeniably old, all the doubts that had been containable until now, resurfaced and fuelled her jealousy.

How do you take away the pain of a lifetime? How do you stop feeling invisible and becoming ever more so with the M word hovering like a spectre? Long gone days of never being good enough were flickering through a cobweb curtain casting shadows on the here and now. She had forgotten about Abi and Susannah and Edward and *The Rivals* and the times later on when she was confident and secure. Only the hurt remained, snapping away under cavernous rocks in the deep. She knew it was this that was behind the crisis they were having, and it was time to face it; to tell him; to be free from it all. But she didn't know how to begin.

14

Missing Lydia

Marianne walks into the form five classroom in Brocklebank's main house, hoping to see Edward. It is the first day of the new academic year. The September sun is shining through the window and for once the wooden desks with all their criss-cross etchings look welcoming.

The drama of The Rivals *has long since passed, but she hasn't lost completely that sense of awe and total admiration that she feels for he who was Lydia.*

He would never guess, for she keeps it under wraps, making no approaches beyond an occasional 'hello'. It is enough that he is there, an intellectual yardstick against which she measures her performance.

Although everything at Brocklebank is familiar now and she has little of the dread of old, she is still somewhat apprehensive on this particular morning because Sally Mainsford has left and she wonders if she will once again be the only girl in the form.

Seeing Edward again will keep some sense of continuity.

But as the morning wears on and the little classroom fills with old familiar faces, and a new girl too, there is still no sign of Edward. At first she is concerned that he is ill, but soon discovers he has gone forever. And she never said good bye.

Edward had moved up to Waterside Grammar School some thirteen miles away, following the footsteps of many ex-Broklebankians, including Sam Rycroft and Susannah Colquhoun.

Marianne had spent her whole school career to date perpetually losing people who mattered. She had forged relationships with one friend after another only to find that a year or two later, they would be off into the world beyond Brocklebank and she would be left to make the effort all over again. It was a fact of her life. Indeed she thought perhaps this was the way things were – would always be – and each time it happened, she learned to keep a bit more of herself back in self-protection.

She shed no tears at the loss of Edward – carrying on with the business of getting to know Christine Trapp who already had breasts and attracted the attentions of the boys in ways unfamiliar to Marianne. But Edward would never be forgotten and somewhere in the deepest recesses of her heart there would always be a place reserved for him.

A new teacher contributed to making it a year of exciting educational challenges. Mr Ottoway taught them Greek myths once a week in Latin lessons, produced a fortnightly school magazine, *Narrat,* and wrote a play in French called *Le Trésor de la Pont de Derwent* for them to perform out of doors in various locations in front of a mobile audience. Although very young, he had all the makings of a fine teacher and was some compensation as a replacement for Jenky who had left at the end of the previous year.

Meanwhile Mr Russell – who was always full of ways to make maths relevant and interesting – organised the bi-annual traffic census down on the main road, the fifth formers working in one hour shifts in pairs, sitting among the long summer grasses on the verge. He also masterminded a decimal currency survey throughout the town, requiring pupils to deliver questionnaires door-to-door and then collect them the following day. Both provided a mountain of data to use in lessons, in addition to making the pupils feel important and giving them a sense of responsibility.

Marianne taught Christine how to make Hawiian *leis* with

fallen rhododendron flowers, and in June they walked the grounds garlanded with pink, purple and magenta blossoms, showing off in front of the boys. It was a time far removed from those early years of fear.

Towards the end of the summer term, Marianne was even chosen to play tennis for the Ospreys in the school house matches. She was drawn against Ian Dangerfield of Falcon House and Mrs Malaprop fame. Edward had been a Falcon. Perhaps if he had still been there, she might have played against him.

Boys gathered on the upstairs balcony outside one of the dormitories that overlooked the court, Barnaby Sproat among them acting as umpire. Ian Dangerfield stood on the baseline on the side of the net by the rockery and with the cricket field beyond, yellow hair and glasses shining in the sunlight. Although quite small, he was very sporty and was expected to annihilate Marianne in two straight sets. An air of confident nonchalance seemed to emanate from him as he took position to serve.

But tennis was Marianne's game. She may have struggled against the boys in hockey and athletics, but she had been honing her tennis skills since the age of five when she and Alice tried to keep the ball alive for as long as possible on the small concrete square next to the main court. When she graduated to the grass, she quickly adapted to the surface. She had a natural double-handed backhand long before such was made acceptable by Bjorn Borg and Jimmy Connors. It made the ball spin low over the net and brought gasps of disbelief from those watching.

Against all expectations, she took the first set from Ian Dangerfield.

The watching Falcons started to jeer and hiss and Ian Dangerfield woke up to the fact that he was being beaten by a girl, raised his game and just managed to secure the second set despite Marianne having two match points.

In baking sunshine the third set was played out to a balcony that was full of schoolboys, crammed together in an impossibly small space like baby swallows just before they leave the nest. Each game was closely contested and several of the rallies went into double figures.

"Come on Hayward!" half of them shouted. It was strange listening to them urging her on, calling her by her proper name for a change, even if they couldn't quite manage 'Marianne'.

Teachers began to show interest, popping out of the main schoolhouse and hovering by the sidelines. This was to be Marianne's downfall. Suddenly more self-conscious, she started making errors. The serves were less well placed; the low backhands became less accurate and in the end Ian Dangerfield squeaked a win. But Marianne had won a personal battle and gained respect. Barnaby Sproat congratulated her on such a close match and asked if she would umpire his game against Richard Zammit.

In this more positive atmosphere she thrived and was top of the class again. But Edward wasn't there to share it all and sometimes she would glance wistfully over to the desk where he once sat, wishing him still there.

Then she too left this fortress of early education, and for the next thirty-two years the good times were lost as she somehow got stuck in the dark memories of the third form with the bullying and the name-calling and the hockey and being cold, and the ghastly dinners and being last in the races except for the fat boy.

It wasn't until 1974 that she had her next brush with Edward, and not much of a brush at that. While in the lower sixth, she and two of her friends signed up for a residential science course at Waterside Grammar School.

Edward Harvey was just a name on the programme; a participant on the course in the geography and geology section while Marianne and her friends were chemistry and biology. Marianne would have quite liked to find him; to say *'look at me now, Edward, I'm not quite the shy retiring violet I once was. I'm ever so trendy and cool in my long flowing skirt with t-shirt, beads and hippy-hairstyle.'* But she was back to worshipping the likes of the blond Adonis (or at least his friend Johnny), and she had a feeling that Edward would be very conventional and conservative and would not be impressed by her pseudo-rebellion. Also, her teenage passions for Sam and Johnny were hormonally charged with thoughts of love and sex and a world away from the innocent admiration she had once felt for Edward. So motivation was not with her to the extent that she was going to put herself out to find him, and some residual shyness still lurked.

On the last day the whole conference gathered in the hall. There was a buzz of anticipation and shafts of dusty sunlight filled the air. Marianne was sitting in between her friends Sasha and Jane and behind a group of girls wearing the Waterside uniform.

Feeling uncommonly brave, Marianne tapped one of them on the shoulder.

"Excuse me. You wouldn't know Edward Harvey, would you? I mean is he in here? I used to go to school with him years ago."

A girl with long brown hair turned round and smiled. "Edward? Yeah …" she scanned the hall. "Yeah, that's him over there in the middle, longish dark hair, in a blazer … That's him getting up now."

As she spoke, the person she said was Edward started walking across the hall towards the exit. Marianne wouldn't have recognised him. He was taller than she anticipated and unexpectedly attractive; no longer little Edward and with an air of ease and confidence. But it was a fleeting glimpse, a side-on view that she still remembers all these years later. She momentarily thought about getting up and running after him, but the conference speaker was about to take the stage and she would have had to clamber across half a dozen young people. He would be gone by the time she reached the door – and what would she say, anyway. There wasn't time.

After that non-event, Edward Harvey was consigned to the history file; Marianne was to be cast adrift in a world without him and never in her wildest dreams did she expect to see him again. Indeed, their meeting again was so unlikely that it never crossed her mind. But she never forgot him completely, and although years would pass without him appearing in her consciousness, whenever she was reminded of Latin lessons, she remembered his awesome brainpower, his resolute determination and the fact that he never called her by her nick-name in all the time she knew him.

15

The Perfect Woman

"Mentally you're the perfect woman for me," said Johnny to Marianne after another evening in the pub, supposedly with colleagues after an Open Evening at his school. He was now back home, sitting slumped in his favourite armchair, legs outstretched, fingers clasped behind his head, a half finished glass of beer on the table beside him, and on the floor a plate smeared with the lurid red-brown leftovers of a Chicken Madras takeaway.

The room was softly lit to flatter with an uplighter and table lamp. Marianne was opposite him on the sofa, legs tucked under her comfortably as she had been for most of the evening. *Newsnight* was on the television, with Jeremy Paxman in heated debate with Ken Livingstone, but the sound was switched off. She froze. Immediately she began to wonder if he thought she was letting herself go.

"Thanks," she said, narrowing her eyes and giving him a hard stare. A year ago he would never have made a remark like this. Perhaps (*oh scary thought!*) she had unknowingly made that transitional jump between relative youth and the beginning of the decline towards the grey perm and the shopping trolley.

Since the row when Johnny had been so hostile, they had both been walking on eggshells, avoiding provocative comments. Conversation had been functional and cool. Neither had raised the Charmaine topic again, though they were both aware of it skulking under the surface. Neither had apologised.

"At least you're mentally perfect when you talk to me," continued Johnny.

"Are you trying to make some point? If so, I'm missing it."
She shifted her weight and grounded her feet like a plane
lowering its undercarriage. She was aware on the TV, of
Jeremy's animated expression, his coat-hanger shoulders and
Ken's benign grin as he delivered some no-doubt unsavoury
fact about congestion charging.

"There you go making assumptions. It's a compliment,"
said Johnny.

"It's a funny sort of compliment."

"What if I met a woman that had your brains, your mind,
and was blonde and curvaceous?"

"Are you saying blonde and curvaceous is your idea of
perfection?"

"I'm talking stereotypes. Just saying, 'what if?' Not
necessarily what I think."

"Have you met a woman like me plus the blonde and
curvaceous?" She was thinking of Charmaine.

"Perhaps."

"You're trying to provoke me."

"So easy ... So easy to reel you in!"

"Why are you doing this?"

"We were talking about wife-swapping."

"Leave it, Johnny, go to bed."

"You shouldn't be so easy to wind up."

"There is no such thing as the perfect woman. She is a
myth."

"Somewhere, there must be the whole package."

"If there was, she wouldn't give you a second glance."

"Ouch ... No need for that!"

"So you can insult me and I can't do the same?"

"I didn't insult you, I just implied that you weren't blonde
and curvaceous – which is a fact, not an insult. I didn't say I
wanted blonde and curvaceous, or that I wished you were any

different from what you are." He breathed out audibly and his voice softened. "You know I think you're beautiful, even …"

Marianne finished the sentence in her head. *Even though you're not.* Out loud she said, "Even what?"

"Even though you don't realise it."

"Hm," she wasn't convinced.

"Let's go to bed," said Johnny, "and have wild, passionate sex, like we used to do. No children in the house to interrupt. No one to have to set a good example to. Just us. C'mon Mari."

She wondered if this was his attempt at making amends, but she was feeling hot again and sex was the last thing on her mind. She began to think of the bits that weren't as toned as they once had been.

"This is your idea of foreplay, is it?"

What had happened to the long, slow rituals of their younger days? Frolicking on the rug in front of the fire, sharing a bath, or being taken unawares in the kitchen? Holly had happened, that's what. Holly, and taxing jobs, and age and familiarity. Was it all past now? All that lust and excitement? Were the next few years to be full of excuses, avoidance and headaches until Johnny, discouraged by rejection, resigned himself to magazines – or to the likes of Charmaine?

"We can foreplay upstairs," continued Johnny teasingly.

"You've been drinking."

"But not a lot."

"Hm."

"Really."

"You know what it says in Macbeth."

"I'm fine, honestly."

Marianne wondered if being with Charmaine had promoted the desire, leaving her to conjure up a performance.

Johnny leapt from his chair and sat close to her on the sofa, head on her shoulder, blue eyes twinkling and a silly grin on his face. This was Johnny being nice, being charming. The Johnny she fell for all those years ago.

Marianne so badly wanted things to be normal again and she knew that sex would be a quick way to smooth the ruffles. If she pulled away now, it might be days before there was another chance.

"I didn't mean to upset you. It's been a long, hard, day. C'mon Mari? How about it? You know you want to really?"

At last she met his gaze, relaxed a little and grinned.

He traced a line down her cheek. "I've only ever wanted you."

How could she resist?

Afterwards, they lay entwined like otters, Johnny fast asleep contented, and Marianne, eyes open, still wondering if a woman other than herself had been the prelude to this union.

16

Friends Reunited

Friends Reunited seemed a strange world in 2001 before the launch of the other famous social networking sites. It had its own chat room of faceless voices spewing out the daily drudgery of kids' misdemeanours and late night pizzas, weekend drinking and Sunday morning hangovers, and the husband who's always watching soccer, and the wife who doesn't care any more and slobs around the house in a shapeless t-shirt and leggings. Vacuous chatter, taking up where they left off yesterday; an exclusive club, suspicious of newcomers. *'Hello, how are you? Went shopping this morning … Marni was sick last night … Must go and put the supper on … Sons squabbling … Hubby watching Manchester United … Hi; bye; till tomorrow darlin'!'*

Perhaps those who inhabit this world are bored with the predictability and mundanity of life. Harmless but lonely souls wanting to share a word or two between the frenzied moments of bustling twenty-first century existence.

'Think you'll have more kids?'
'Too late, husband's a Jaffa.'
'What's a Jaffa?'
'Vasectomy … Seedless! Ha!'
'ROFLOL!'

And occasionally, the innuendo, the hope for something bordering on cybersex. Men lurking, looking for relationships as recompense for their isolated lives spent in front of the computer. They may be old or ugly, or just downright strange; low down in the pecking order when it came to choosing a mate. Or they may simply be sad and disillusioned as their dreams have gone unfulfilled and they hurtle toward retirement with no hope of recapturing the *joie de vivre* ever again.

Middle aged spouses who have long since stopped trying to please. Roof over head, sperm provided, children begat, job done. Men wondering where their 'can't get enough of them' wife has gone. No more high heels and lipstick, perfume and tantalising underwear. Who is this woman in the slippers, with the Bridget Jones knickers? Retreat to the snooker hall, the golf club, the wine bar, the sofa. *'I ain't doin' nothin' for her no more!'* Taken for granted; start picking, wanting something better, something more, something impossible.

Marianne sighed. She sighed a lot these days. Sighs exemplifying a thousand disappointments, a thousand concerns for a life that seemed to be stretching into an abyss. She had good reason to sigh. Yesterday, something happened that seemed to justify her paranoia.

It was now early November and she and Johnny were getting used to life without Holly. There was an emptiness in the house; a quietness that they both felt but dare not speak of lest it was taken as criticism. It hadn't taken much to spark a disagreement this past year, but since Holly had flown, disagreement seemed to be all there was. There was no more idle chatter and laughter from the throng of optimistic teenagers coming and going and phoning and texting, filling the house with an energy that only the young possess. Now the focus was on him and her; their every move, their every word, scrutinised for hidden meaning.

"It's like living with a crocodile," said Johnny two nights ago when she made some derogatory remark about him flicking through the channels while she was watching a wildlife programme.

She didn't speak to him for the rest of the evening, breaking yet again her long-kept rule that one never should go to bed on an argument.

And what happened yesterday? It was almost too hurtful to contemplate. Marianne had finished college early and thought to surprise Johnny, to try to heal the crack before it became a chasm, and to meet him from school and go for a meal together, somewhere more exotic than The Lotus Blossom down the road.

Cedarwood was a large red brick 1950s building surrounded by London plane trees with their grey patchy bark that peeled naturally and shed the sooty damage that was caused by pollution. In summer the trees burst forth magnanimously with their thick green canopy, but now the leaves had almost fallen, just a few still hanging on to the twigs as the shrivelled elderly cling to existence in a nursing-home.

Nowadays the school was ring-fenced with wrought iron and as she approached the gates, she caught sight of Johnny coming out of the side doors and she began to smile and was just about to shout and wave when he turned back to look over his shoulder. She saw his lips move, but was too far away to hear what he said. Then he held the door and *she* had come out. All smiles and energy in a dark brown leather trouser suit, blonde waves cascading down her back and a pink beaded bag slung over her shoulder.

Marianne's stomach had somersaulted and she froze on the pavement, watching her husband offer a helping hand to Charmaine as she negotiated the step on three-inch heels. They were giggling like school kids, sharing a joke, no eyes for anyone but each other, in a space of their own. They didn't see Marianne gazing through the bars of the fence as they walked down the path, through the car park and out of the side gates. Charmaine tossed her hair coquettishly, and Johnny seemed to be drawn along in her wake. They looked like lovers on a date as they strolled down the road that would take them to The Duck and Bull.

Marianne had turned away to go back home, her head hanging and her feet dragging. She blew her nose and wiped her eyes, and hoped that no one had seen her humiliation.

And instead of dinner with Johnny and some attempt to bridge the gap between them, she put a meal for one in the microwave and turned on the computer.

More and more she found herself trawling the Friends Reunited files, knowing she was becoming addicted, but sure it was just a phase that she would tire of eventually. Why was she doing this? Why was she spending a Friday afternoon eavesdropping on these lonely souls in the chat room? Was it because she was lonely too? Holly gone, Johnny down at the pub, too tired to work or speak to friends?

It stopped her from thinking. For an hour or so it stopped her brain chattering on uncontrollably about insecurities, the M word and the possibility that Johnny may be having an affair.

She had tried to find Susannah a couple of times before. Perhaps she was spelling Colquhoun incorrectly. She could try looking at the page for Waterside, the school she went to after Brocklebank. Finding her way round was second nature now.

Find school. *Click.*

Find area. *Click.*

Letter of the alphabet. *Click.*

Click on the name of the school.

Two different addresses. Hmm. Click the one in Main Street.

Year of leaving?

1974. Susannah was older. *Click.*

The list of names appeared before her eyes. Blue writing on a green background. Strange and unfamiliar names of unknown people who had lived unknown and different lives not many miles away from her own.

But it wasn't Susannah Colquhoun that immediately caught her eye, but Ted Harvey.

Marianne paused, emotions beginning to bubble. Ted ... Ted? ... Edward ... Ted Harvey ... Edward Harvey ... Lydia. '... *But I have lost him Julia ... put myself in a violent passion and vowed I'd never see him more.*'

Lydia ... Lydia ... Memory flashbacks to the good-natured, bespectacled boy in the third form who had an impressive brain, who excelled at Latin, who touched her heart. Could this be him? Could it be her Edward at last? Her first crush? But her Edward wasn't Ted. She couldn't imagine him as Ted. It didn't suit him at all. But who else could it be? Surely there wouldn't be two Edward Harveys in the same year at the same school?

She looked for the information sign that would confirm identity, but there wasn't one. This Ted Harvey was being mysterious; if she wanted to know if it really was Edward and what he was doing, she would have to send him an email.

Big decision.

She didn't want to intrude. After all, they were never friends. Mere acquaintances in the prep school soup. Ted Harvey would be living his life – whatever that may be – with never a thought of her. Probably with wife and kids and a whole host of friends, and he might not want to be found by her. And she would never have contacted him by any other means. Even if she had known where he was, she wouldn't have sent a letter or picked up the phone. Friends Reunited offered a way to legitimate communication that would never have been possible before.

She would wait, think, sleep, dream ...

When Johnny came home she didn't say a word about going to meet him or seeing him with Charmaine, and for most of the evening they barely spoke. Johnny collapsed in front of the TV with a bottle of red wine and Marianne sat in the dining room marking essays, stopping periodically to muse about contacting Edward.

Next afternoon, when Johnny was off walking, she called up Friends Reunited again. What if this Ted Harvey had disappeared off the site overnight like her old friend Tom? What then? She should have taken her chance while she had it.

But no, he was still there, his name beckoning; a thousand memories hidden in those few letters. A wave of heat engulfed her as she clicked on the envelope and watched the box open up and fill her screen invitingly.

If you are who I think you are, then I knew you as Edward and also as Lydia Languish, she wrote in the blank white space. That would deter any imposters! *I remember once in the third form at Brocklebank, you stood next to a map of Scandinavia and when asked to point out the capital of Finland, said, 'Oh hell, where's Sinki?' The class thought it so funny.* She smiled at the memory of the reaction to the joke and Edward looking surprised. *It's been such a long time. I saw you when a few of us were at Waterside attending a science conference in the sixth form, but was too shy to say hello.*

What would justify her writing? She couldn't tell him of her childish admiration. That would scare him away.

I was looking for Susannah Colquhoun when I spotted your name on the site. I am curious to know what has happened to us all and am hoping to lay a few ghosts to rest. This was true at least. *I remember you were very good at Latin and a fierce competitor for the form prize. After the dress rehearsal of* The Rivals, *I tried to have a girlie chat with you and wondered why you didn't respond!*

Still in touch with Abi Ross. She is now into alternative therapies and is a qualified homeopath. We went to take a look at Brocklebank a few years ago. It is now a hotel and conference centre and the Hut is a glorified chalet!

After a degree in psychology at Sheffield, I became a teacher and now work in a Sixth Form College in northern Kent – more civilized than a school! Have dreams of writing a novel, but so far it remains a series of half-formed thoughts and scribblings.

Married to Johnny and one daughter, Holly, at uni studying law. Would love to know what has happened to you over the years.

Best wishes,

Marianne.

That would do for now. Just in case is wasn't him; she didn't want to waste time writing screeds of memories.

She hesitated over the send button. To send or not to send?

How often in one's life does the tiniest decision have the most enormous consequences? A link in a chain, but for which there would be no job, no house, no friend, no lover.

She hesitated, and hesitated again. What if it wasn't him? What if it was and he didn't reply? What if, what if … And the image of Johnny holding out his hand to the leather-clad Charmaine persisted in her brain. She needed distracting.

Rain flung itself at the windows like rice tinkling on the glass, and a wind began to howl. She shivered.

In truth, it didn't matter if it wasn't him. There was nothing to lose. If he didn't reply, surely she wouldn't take it personally. Not from Edward.

The heat bathed her whole being as she clicked on *Send*.

Then she heard the front door open and in came Johnny, his hair blown tousled in the way she loved.

17

Phonecall

Once the email was sent, Marianne resolved to give it little thought. Some of her efforts to contact friends had taken weeks before yielding a reply. Edward Harvey might not reply at all. It wasn't as if they'd known each other very well; just two children sharing an education for three years. The sweeping rota, spelling tests and Latin; rivals in more than one sense; mirror fragments reflecting memories of long ago; glittering on the one hand, yet the legacy, a shattered image, a shattered self.

There were no other boys from that class that she would write to. Thoughts of the worst of the bullies still inflamed her. She was angry at their disregard for her emotions; bitter that a chunk of life had been tarnished and that all these years later their actions were still festering and working their malice. How could she forgive?

Edward was the only one that she felt positive towards. In mailing him she could confront the ghosts in safety. Yet she feared to place too much importance on it lest she be disappointed.

"Are you in this evening?" she asked Johnny who had quickly settled onto the sofa, and was watching the sports results on Grandstand. She had hoped he might offer to do the supper like he used to do most Saturdays. But more and more he was reverting to the traditional male stereotype; coming and going when he pleased, leaving the cooking and all the other domestic stuff to her, expecting things to be done for him from shopping to washing to cleaning. *Selfish pig*, she thought, but with so much tension in the atmosphere, she didn't want to provoke an argument about something as trivial as cooking supper.

"Would you like me to be in?" He looked up at her questioningly. There was a touch of ice in his tone.

"You know I would."

"Then I will be. What are you cooking?"

"Roast chicken."

"And roast parsnips?"

"Of course!"

She busied herself in the kitchen preparing vegetables, slicing with the expertise of a chef. She liked cooking so long as it wasn't for an army of people. Any more than four and she went to pieces, near-disasters usually finding their way out of the oven.

Then the phone rang in the hall.

"Johnny ... phone."

It continued ringing.

Marianne wiped her hands on a tea towel and went to answer it.

"Hello? ... Yes ..." Her heart sank. "Yes he is ... I'll get him ... Hang on."

Johnny was pretending to be asleep. "*John*," she said with emphasis, touching his shoulder. "It's Charmaine."

Johnny started and faked a yawn. "What does she want?"

"No idea."

She returned to the kitchen making sure she left the door open. Her chopping took on a quieter sound as she listened intently. Visions of the leather-clad woman accompanying her husband out of Cedarwood swam before her eyes.

"Hello," he said, and Marianne could hear the smile in the word. "What can I do for you?"

There was a long pause during which Marianne bristled with indignation.

"But of course you must … No problem at all … I'll start them off. In fact Mick's free first thing …

"You'll need to take out a second mortgage," he laughed.

Marianne wondered what they were talking about and how easily he had slipped into being Mr Charming when all she had from him so far today was grouch, grumble and curse.

"Will it be a gold one? … Yes … Beware pineapple juice – anything acidic – for the first week or two after. I got electric shocks when I had mine done.

"Complete rip-off … Don't know how they can justify it … Could buy that guitar I was telling you about …"

What guitar? thought Marianne. Yes, he sometimes still strummed away on his old acoustic, but she knew nothing of any desire to upgrade it. Surely his old rock-star fantasy wasn't resurfacing?

"Did you hear the gossip about Andy Erikson? … No? … Caught *in flagrante* in a broom cupboard with Erin-the-art-student! Disrobed is an understatement.

"Did he now? … Randy old sod! … Hope you told him where to get off …

"He says he's a qualified hypnotherapist, so watch out. Used to lodge with Gwyneth and she reckons he's into the black arts … Something about a pentacle on the carpet …

"No … pentacle … A five-pointed star … you know … mysticism and devil worship … mumbo-jumbo if you ask me …"

Marianne had ceased chopping altogether and was listening intently from behind the open door. Johnny used to tell her all the goings-on at Cedarwood, but not this piece of gossip. Was she no longer his confidante? Did he tell Charmaine what he once told her? Jealousy swished its tail and she felt sick and faint.

"Surely you don't believe it? A sane woman like you?

"Gemini! … What does that mean? … Yes, that sounds just

like me … Ha, you flatterer! What about the bad bits? … You'll make a convert out of me yet …

"And are we compatible then?"

Marianne froze, anger building. *How dare he give that woman time of day on astrology when he dismissed it outright if she mentioned it.*

"Well that's good to know!"

She heard the phone ping as it disconnected, and click as he replaced it in the cradle. She couldn't stop herself from following him back into the living room. Johnny was lowering himself back onto the sofa, running a hand through his hair. Marianne thought he looked pleased with himself.

"What did she want?"

The smile faded and Johnny lowered his gaze. "Oh, she's got a dental appointment. She'll be late in on Monday. Crown, by the sound of it. Nasty."

The puppeteers began to gather again.

"She shouldn't bother you at home."

"Why not? It's easier to prepare if I know."

"Told you she'd get dependent."

"Mari … she's a friend. Just because you refuse to invite her over …"

"I didn't refuse."

"No?"

"I don't trust women like that."

"Like what? How can you say that? Please don't start all that again. Stop being so possessive." Johnny got up from the sofa again and turned off the television.

"And what was all that stuff about star-signs? You never take any notice if I mention them."

"She's an Aquarian – apparently we get on …"

"Bastard."

"What? … Mari …"

Marianne flounced out, eyes brimming, and bolted up the

stairs. What was the matter with her? She was losing it big time. Her mouth opened and words came out where once she would have kept diplomatically silent. Immediate regrets, but too late. *And she wouldn't say sorry – couldn't say sorry – because it wasn't her fault, was it? It was that damned woman with her magazine glamour and her fluffy charm; and her damned husband being led astray when once he had been so loyal. Bastard!*

And it wasn't her fault that the fall-out from the Brocklebank bullying was being revived more than thirty years on. She had become a victim again and she crawled onto the bed and howled and barely heard the front door bang as Johnny once more left her agonising alone.

Half an hour later, calm now, she lay on top of the duvet, looking at the ceiling, thinking. It was so quiet without Holly. Dearest Holly … She missed her. Holly's presence meant disagreements didn't fester for too long. And Johnny would never get away with such domestic laziness if Holly was around. Holly was Libran. 'Fair' was her middle name. Law would suit her.

A feeling of panic had settled in her stomach the day she met Charmaine sitting on her kitchen stool, and she was used to it now. It was a kind of sickness creating brittle moods and loss of joy. Tears were never far away, and her breathing was shallow and fast. Now she tried to steady herself, to breathe normally and deeply. It was an effort.

One person cannot be responsible for another's happiness, she thought, but when that person is so bound up in your life and things go wrong, the joy goes too. Every day she scanned her life for trouble, much as a searchlight scans the shadows for intruders. Now the alarm bells were constantly ringing.

For over twenty years Johnny had shared her day-to-day troubles and soothed her. Now he was the trouble and the soothing had stopped.

18

Dear Lydia

'Edward Harvey', announced the sender of the new message in her inbox.

Edward Harvey!

She stared at the letters in their bold black type as one might gaze upon Egyptian hieroglyphs, noting their individuality, searching for meaning. Never had two words on her computer stirred so much expectant emotion. Here was an email from an Edward Harvey, inviting, beckoning, wanting to be read.

Marianne blinked. She adjusted the height of her chair and sat back, surveying the screen. This was too soon, surely? Not two hours since she had mailed him. No one from Friends Reunited had replied this soon. But there it was … Edward Harvey … Could it be him? Could it be Lydia?

The chicken was now hissing and spitting in the oven and Johnny was probably ensconced with a pint in the local, or maybe even with *her,* his departmental side-kick, his floozy, his – and she hesitated even to think the word – *mistress.* She had calmed herself as best she could in these difficult circumstances and completed the supper preparation, despite feeling thoroughly sick. She had returned to the computer merely to send an email to her brother Louis. Finding a reply from Edward winging its way into her inbox was the last thing she expected.

The mythical Edward Harvey … She read his name over and over. What would he say? Edward Harvey, who had once, long ago, intrigued her with his extraordinary eloquence and gentleness and difference. What was he now? Where was he now? She hardly dared look.

She blew her nose again and brushed the dried tears from her cheek. Her spirits began to lift, peripheral noises dimmed into the background and the world seemed a friendlier place again. For a few seconds she paused with her hand hovering an inch above the mouse. Then she opened the mail.

To: Marianne Hayward
From: Edward Harvey
Date: 08 November 2001, 18.44
Subject: Re: Contact from Friendsreunited – Marianne Hayward

Hi Marianne,
What a surprise! What a blast from the past! Yes, I prefer Edward, but regrettably Ted seems to have stuck, and as for Lydia, she is almost forgotten though the photographs are somewhere in the attic. Do you remember Waverley Grossett? We still keep in touch at Christmas. And Susannah Colquhoun: she was at Waterside with me. Do you have news of anyone else? Glad to hear you have a novel gestating!
What was that science course? I don't remember …
Married to Felicity and living in Broadclyst, Devon, with four children, two spaniels – Clint and Gryke (Clint after Eastwood, and Gryke after Clint!) – a cat, a rabbit and three hens. Archaeology Lecturer at the University of Devon for past twenty-odd years.
Coincidentally in reminiscent mood as we're having a 70s revival party. Just picked up your mail when printing the quiz! Who was the first woman to read the news in 1978?

Thank you for writing. Must dash – see if I can fit into
the flares!
Best wishes,
Lydia

Marianne smiled to herself. So he had a sense of humour at
least. And he'd asked her questions. Never ask questions if you
don't want a reply!

She always knew Edward would do something intellectual
and significant. She didn't know much about archaeology
although she often watched documentaries on the television,
fascinated by the mysteries of the past as they were unravelled,
and impressed by the ingenuity of the people who lived at a
time when problems had to be solved without the aid of
modern technology. The building of Stonehenge or the
construction of the trebuchet; massive undertakings requiring
vision and strength and cooperation beyond anything she could
imagine.

Edward had always been good at history so it was no surprise
that this was his chosen field. She had been hopeless; her one
academic weakness at Brocklebank that no one could explain.
Of course now she understood that when she was propelled
into the third form at such a young age, she lacked the maturity
to fully appreciate the idea of dates and time, so she had lost
interest and drifted.

She was relieved he was married too; that he hadn't
metamorphosed into an intellectual weirdo with no social skills
and a fear of the female sex.

Edward Harvey. She savoured his name again, re-
acquainting herself with its sound and flavour. Edward-the-
archaeologist Harvey. Edward Benjamin Harvey, if she
remembered correctly. Now she knew it was definitely him,
she could write a little more. But not yet. She would wait until

the following day; wait until she had time to digest what had already been written.

When Johnny eventually came home later, much later, Marianne had eaten a little supper alone and gone to bed. She heard him crashing about downstairs in the kitchen; the familiar sounds of drawers and cupboards being opened and shut; the dull thud of the fridge and the rattle of the cutlery drawer. She followed his movements in her head. So much for his beloved roast parsnips. They would be dried up and leathery by now. *Good!*

She feigned sleep when he came upstairs, full of thoughts of what she would write to Edward, not wanting to argue with Johnny about where he'd been, or her insecurities, and definitely not wanting sex. He made so much noise in the bedroom, he would know she couldn't possibly be asleep. He even said, "Mari, for fuck's sake Mari ..." And still she ignored him.

He'd gone too far with his deprecating comments, his alcohol-driven thoughtlessness. And to see him flirting on the school steps with that fluffy trollop was just too much. The camel's back had been broken and she had begun the process of self-protection.

The next morning, while Johnny was having a lie in, she turned on the computer, a sense of anticipation growing as she summoned Outlook Express.

She tried to think of something interesting to put in the Subject box. Something pertinent and more creative than 'Hello'. She and her friend Taryn sometimes played games involving who could write the most attention-grabbing email subject headers. In the end she put 'Lydia'.

Dear Lydia ... she began. Then she wrote of *The Rivals* and of teachers – the good and the bad; of the bullies and the Hut and the Headmaster's dog Alfie that shagged anything that moved. She reminded him about the science conference, added that she thought Angela Rippon was the newsreader, asked where he went after Waterside, said his home sounded like he had the beginnings of a farm, and clicked on *Send*.

And Edward Harvey wrote back at lunchtime, tired from the late-finishing revivalist party, bemoaning the fact that he no longer bounced back quickly from such events. He echoed many of her thoughts and added a few things that she had forgotten about a boy called Raymond Salkeld, Sports day, games lessons and an elderly gentleman who came to the school every year to deliver a lecture about wildlife. He said that he recalled the proclivities of the headmaster's dog, that he was amazed by the detail with which she remembered things, that after Waterside he read Archaeology at UCL, and that the newsreader was Anna Ford.

Marianne wasn't so sure about this latter fact. She might have been the first on ITV, but surely even that was earlier than 1978. She thought about challenging him, but what did it matter? It wasn't like a spelling test or an end of year exam. They weren't at school now!

She threw off her cardigan and a smile hovered round her lips.

This was fun!

When she went to bed that night, instead of thinking about Johnny, his drinking and Charmaine, she again pondered the next email to Edward.

"You're lovely and warm," said Johnny, snuggling closer, tentatively, hopefully. They had hardly said a word to each other all day, Johnny disappearing again for another walk in the countryside – or so he said – and Marianne marking essays and catching up with the dreaded ironing.

"I like to be warm," said Marianne, mimicking the tortoise from the *Creature Comforts* electricity advertisements, her hostility dissipating, welcoming Johnny into her space. She thought she might ask Edward if he remembered the time when someone fell off the corrugated shed and smashed their arm. She couldn't remember his name …

"Are we speaking again?" asked Johnny.

"I guess so." She couldn't be bothered to accuse and blame. Hadn't the energy for mind-games when there were now too many other interesting things to contemplate.

They lay close for a while, cuddling with the habit and familiarity that comes from a couple of decades together, but when Johnny began to move closer still, she pulled away.

"Not speaking as much as I thought," said Johnny. "Sorry I misunderstood." And he turned away from her, restoring the wedge.

Marianne continued the email in her head and wondered whether to ask Edward some more about his family.

To: Edward Harvey
From: Marianne Hayward
Date: 12th November 2001, 21.15
Subject: Echoes

Hi Edward,
I had forgotten about Raymond Salkeld reacting like a madman when people blew through the pages of books! When we were in the fifth form, he used to chase us girls, egged on by Barnaby Sproat et al. He was probably harmless, but I always made sure there was a desk between us. He had a wild glint in his eye!
I can't remember the name of that guy who gave us the lectures, but I do remember him bringing in skulls of badgers and foxes … and loads of antlers! At some point in the talk he used to make a loud animal noise

that gave us a fright. A very gifted speaker, pitching it just right for our age group …

Do you remember when someone fell off the roof of that corrugated shed by the rhododendron bushes at the end of the Hut? There was much gnashing of teeth and 'thou shalt not' the day after. Can you remember who it was?

Do tell me more of your family. What are your children called? Have they hit the awkward teens yet?

It has been fun reminiscing these past two days and I hope we can exchange a few more memories before disappearing for another thirty-three years.

Goodnight and best wishes,

Marianne

To: Marianne Hayward
From: Edward Harvey
Date: 14th November 2001, 22.47
Subject: Re: Echoes

Hi Marianne,

Yes I do vaguely remember the shed incident, but not who it was. Possibly Richard Zammit, but I can't be sure.

Kids are James – sixteen, not awkward yet and deeply immersed in sport. Then Rachel who's sensible, Harriet who isn't and Christopher – eight and already skilled in getting his own way.

Very busy day tomorrow lecturing in Manchester.

Time to get the children to bed …

Sorry this is so brief.

Edward

Now decisions. To write straight back might seem too much,

yet leave it too long and the moment might be lost.

Wait two days. She wrote again, elaborating some of her horror stories of her time in the third form; reminding him that she was the only girl in the class for a year and once again reminiscing about their wonderful experience together in *The Rivals*. She asked him about his wife and what his job involved.

To: Marianne Hayward
From: Edward Harvey
Date: 19th November 2001, 21.32
Subject: Re: More Pieces of the Jigsaw

Hi Marianne,
I was oblivious to what was going on in the third form and can't remember you being the only girl. 'The Rivals' left me with leanings towards a theatrical career, but it's an unpredictable life.
In addition to teaching students and the usual admin and research, the job involves a lot of travelling to conferences around the world – presenting papers and so on. Am also often invited to give lectures.
Felicity is an administrator at the University. She is my rock and gladly allows me freedom to do all the things that my work involves. She is fanatical about organic produce (we are almost self-sufficient in vegetables!) and would like to own a restaurant eventually, but while the children are so demanding and I am so busy, this is impossible.
Best wishes,
Edward

Marianne was impressed. Perhaps some of what he wrote was on the internet. She typed 'Edward Harvey Archaeology' into

Google and hundreds of links appeared. *Oh my*, she thought. Most of them referred to him; her Edward Harvey. Typical of him to be so modest, just like the Edward she knew all those years ago. One day she might take a closer look, but just now she felt guilty; felt like a voyeur – as if she had found something she shouldn't.

This discovery almost stopped her from writing to him. He was important – certainly in the world of archaeology. He was no longer merely Edward Harvey, but *Dr Edward Harvey*. Then she remembered that she had beaten him twice for the prize in the third form; that she might not be his intellectual equal, but she was not far behind; that it was what you were that mattered, not what you did.

To: Edward Harvey
From: Marianne Hayward
Date: 23rd November 2001, 16.34
Subject: Still More Pieces of the Jig-Saw

Hi Edward,
I imagine lecturing gives you many opportunities to fulfil your acting ambitions!
'The Rivals' was enormously confidence-boosting – but I didn't appreciate it at the time.
When you were at Brocklebank, what did you do in the evenings? Was it prep and early nights or did you escape to do things that gangs of boys are reputed to do?
I can't imagine how Felicity copes with four children and a job (and you!!). I found it difficult enough with one (child) despite Johnny helping a lot when Holly was young.
Best wishes,
Marianne

Something strange began to happen as Marianne mentally revisited the world of Brocklebank Hall and tapped out her memories to Edward. For all of her adult life so far she had entered the rooms as a child and they looked so huge and unwelcoming from her lowly perspective. But now, she had grown and the rooms had shrunk. The child with all the fears and dreads in the world – the child who cried in the woods or sat in the mud on the hockey field – was a person no longer inhabiting her psyche to weigh her down whenever she was undermined. The hall with its parquet floor; Mrs Swift's classroom with piano, model village, nature table and bay window; the dining room with its long pine tables – even the Hut – all had become proportionate in size to the adult she was now.

This is the cure, she thought. *This is what I've been chasing for so long, but never been able to find.* She hardly dared hope.

To: Marianne Hayward
From: Edward Harvey
Date: 23rd November 2001, 20.05
Subject: Holiday

Hi Marianne,
Four children entertain each other; with one you
probably felt you had to fill this role yourselves.
Not sure exactly what you mean by what gangs of boys
are reputed to do! But we did have a den in the woods!

(*Peeing up trees,* thought Marianne. *And worse!* If this was the case, then she was glad he hadn't mentioned it.)

We all go off to Australia, Pitcairn Island and New

Zealand at the beginning of December. Am missing the
end of term, but first part of trip for me is working as
am giving series of lectures at Sydney University in an
exchange arrangement with Prof. Brad Herringbone – an
expert on patterns of biological variation in south
eastern Aus. Will be away for a month. It's the trip of a
lifetime while the children are still all at home! Friends
and neighbours looking after animals!
Dashing!
Best wishes,
Edward

Dear, sweet Edward … What was he really like? What kind of
man had the boy become? Did he sit at his computer with his
dark hair now greying, the distinguished archaeologist? Perhaps
he had a shaggy beard and a ponytail, but she doubted it. He
seemed enthusiastic about his work and loved his family, of
that she was sure. There was something indefinably contented
about the way he wrote about his life. He was safe. Not one of
those men to cyberchat their way into your knickers.

For a moment she envied him. Yet that was what she had
had until a year ago; until *she* had arrived. *That woman; that tarty
cow.* But Edward must never guess that she was troubled about
her marriage.

To: Edward Harvey
From: Marianne Hayward
Date: 26th November 2001, 21.11
Subject: Re: Holiday

Edward, I have really appreciated sharing memories with
you this past couple of weeks and have found it very
cathartic. The psychologist is healing herself as they say,

with a little help from you as 'listener'. I have been burying the Brocklebank ghosts for thirty-three years. That's a long time for them to fester and grow and create havoc. Now I realise there were many good times too. I had forgotten them, caught up in the darkness of bullying and isolation.

Mailing you was initially a case of 'carpe diem'. I'm glad I did. But I entered your life uninvited and would not wish to outstay my welcome. That said, it is interesting unravelling the new you as we reflect upon the old and it would be good to hear from you again when you return from holiday.

I hope you all have a fabulous time and that it lives up to your expectations.

Best wishes,

Marianne

To: Marianne Hayward
From: Edward Harvey
Date: 27th November 2001, 22.34
Subject: Re: Holiday

Hi Marianne,

I don't feel as though I've been any help at all, but I'm glad you feel better.

Counselling is something I've thought of – as a career change!

We are all looking forward to our trip and in a state of complete chaos here as we prepare to leave. Hard to believe we will be on the other side of the world at Christmas! When we return, perhaps we should meet.

Best wishes,

Edward

Perhaps we should meet!

The words jangled and somersaulted in her mind, caught in a dance with the partying soup of hormones that were having their last fling before their final farewell.

19

The Minds of Men

"Jealousy is one of the most significant factors in the break-up of relationships," said Marianne, addressing her class of upper sixth psychology students. Relationships was one of the topics on the specification and as such matters are a preoccupation of most teenagers, they sat in eager anticipation of what was to follow.

"But what is jealousy? Most of us know what it feels like: ravaging your heart, obsessing your thoughts like a kind of madness. It can start as early as primary school when you feel jealous that your best friend is talking to someone else and you're frightened of losing them.

"These early experiences have a bearing on your later life. They are templates for adult romantic relationships. Anyone not know what I'm talking about?"

Silence.

Eighteen pairs of eyes looked up, pens poised. They sat behind grey tables arranged in a horseshoe shape with Marianne sitting on a wooden desk in the opening at the front. A scent of warm, wet dogs hung in the air and the windows were misting. Outside it had been drizzling all morning and puddles gathered on the flat roofs of the art department below.

She continued: "I'm going to ask you a question about your feelings of jealousy and I want you to close your eyes – to increase validity and for privacy. Have any of you experienced jealousy over the past week? No peeking!"

Seven girls and two boys put up their hands – roughly half the class.

"Sorry to interrupt you Miss, but is it only in the last week, or ever at all?" This was Jason, polite, articulate and an excellent contributor to discussions.

"Well let me ask you 'ever at all' as well. You can keep your eyes open for this."

Almost all the students raised their hands and there was a burst of laughter which rippled around the classroom.

"One who hasn't," said Marianne, addressing Obi, a smiling boy on her right. "So you don't know what we're talking about then?"

"I don't really get jealous." He tossed his head and shrugged. "If a person's really confident in themselves, then I dunno ... I don't get jealous ..."

"Interesting," continued Marianne. "Eysenck 1990 (and, yes, before you ask, you should know a few names and dates) – he quotes a study where over half the students asked, admitted to being currently jealous. Note I said 'students' – we'll come back to that later. "When I asked you about 'currently' it was about half too.

"Jasmine, please, get that can of orange off the desk – we don't want any more stains on the carpet – and the phone out of sight, switched off ... Honestly, how many times ...

"Now where was I?"

"Half the students said they were jealous, Miss."

"Thank you Obi. In fact in males it was over sixty percent. Does that surprise you? Men being more jealous than women?"

Hands shot up around the room and Marianne nodded to them, one at a time.

Cate said, "I thought it would be the other way round because girls know how other girls can be so I think they're more likely to be possessive."

"You could say that about boys as well 'cos we know how other boys can be," said Obi, the confident one.

Ellen said, "But girls suffer more from lower self-esteem issues. Image is everywhere. There's a lot more to live up to, so I think they'll be more insecure and therefore more jealous." Ellen was one of the clever quiet students with an abundance of wavy auburn hair.

"I think girls are more jealous 'cos we tend to display our jealousy more; like boys are jealous – but they won't say it, where as with us, we'll admit it," said Chantelle who was festooned with shiny jewellery, from enormous round silver earrings to an array of jangly bangles shimmering on each wrist.

Marianne stepped in. "Some very good thoughts there. Interestingly, when I asked you about current jealousy, it was about four to one girls to boys. Difficult to say whether this is significant. Clearly both sexes experience jealousy, but why? Firstly, why are men jealous?"

"'Cos, like Obi said, they know what other men are like," said Stanley who sat by the windows, and whose jet black hair was tamed by an intricate arrangement of small plaits.

"Yes, but is that the only reason? Think beyond your age group," said Marianne.

"Are you meaning evolution things?" asked Sean who played rugby and took up so much space he had to sit at a desk on his own. "I think you want to pass your genes on to the next generation—"

"You want to make sure your woman's kids is yours," interjected Stanley.

"Exactly," said Marianne. "And what about women? Why are they jealous? Obi?"

"Insurance, yeah, because if you've got a big strong man protecting you, you're gonna feel secure."

"Another woman might take away the family's means of survival. Food, shelter – resources," added Ellen.

"Yes," said Marianne. "Good … So there's a vested interest in the woman keeping the man for security – hence jealousy. Evolutionary principles again."

"If it was only to do with that, jealousy would be decreasing as the generations went on. Because now you can test to see if the child is yours …" said Obi.

Stanley interrupted with some sarcasm. "Oh yeah – 'I want to be sure this baby's mine' – you can't tell your wife that!"

"Some people do – if they're worried," said Marianne, placating. "So how does what Stanley and Ellen have said, equate with Buss's finding that males are more upset by sexual infidelity and females by emotional infidelity?"

Silence.

Marianne continued: "Stanley said men are jealous about paternity – you don't want to think someone else may be sowing seeds – as it were – in your territory, leaving you to bring up someone else's kids. Consequently men would be more likely to be upset by sexual infidelity. Yes Ayesha?"

Ayesha fiddled with her long, golden-brown hair extensions. "So women, yeah, think they might lose their man if he's in love with someone else – emotional in– what you said."

"Infidelity."

"Yeah. Emotional infidelity. So they would be left alone to bring up the kids, innit."

"That's right, making jealousy understandable, normal, natural. Yet we see it as a character flaw; something to be ashamed of. We feel obliged to fight it. We read self-help books; even go to counselling. We know it causes problems …"

Chantelle shook her head. "You know, I think … I think in some relationships yeah, if you're not jealous it can also cause a bit of a problem 'cos if the boy was flirting with another girl and you're like, '*whatever – doesn't really matter*', the boy will think '*why are you not jealous? What's going on?*'"

"Interesting point Chantelle. So you're saying it functions in keeping people together? It's possible. It's true we all need to be valued. But getting the balance right is the difficult bit. The problems usually arise when one partner feels insecure. Insecurity leads to the type of jealousy that can get out of hand. This jealousy invariably leads to further rejection because it's not seen as an attractive trait, and this leads to even greater insecurity and loss of self-esteem. So the fear of loss of love often ends up destroying that love. Therefore jealousy is a major destructive factor in the dissolution of relationships, and interestingly, an imagined rival can be just as threatening as a real one."

"Oh you are joking!" interjected Sean. "What do you mean 'imagined'?"

"I mean that there's no reason to be jealous … no hard evidence. And this is where the internet has become significant. However, that's for next time."

She should practise what she preached, thought Marianne at the end of the session as she closed her file and rubbed a duster across the whiteboard. The class were chatting animatedly as they left the room, so young and full of hope and optimism for the future. Marianne was impressed by their wide-ranging and astute views.

How could you get to forty-something, with a wealth of theoretical knowledge of psychology, and still make basic mistakes about relationships? Mistakes that inflamed situations rather than making things better. *'Those that can't do, teach,'* she thought, gathering up a pile of essays, and easing them into a plastic wallet.

It was time for a different approach. Being cranky and jealous about Charmaine was just driving Johnny to spending more and more time with her. Why would he want to stay at home with a nagging and suspicious wife? She should be thankful that he was quite open about visiting the pub after work with another woman. There was no sneaking about and no proof that there was anything more to the relationship than a couple of colleagues having a chat.

But he was a man, after all, and her experience of men was that you needed to keep them occupied or they got up to mischief. She was certainly failing in this department. In the last few months, she often put obstacles in the way of intimacy. She didn't want him to notice that he was in bed with a furnace, so she avoided getting close. This, together with her angst, would be the very thing to drive him into something clandestine.

Yet almost overnight – at least in the space of little more than two weeks – her mind set had changed. Since mailing Edward, the ghosts of the past were on the run and with them, the insecurities of a lifetime. She felt light-headed and happy and even the threat of the M word didn't hold quite the same horrors.

She walked and talked with a new confidence. She went shopping and bought some bright new clothes and a pair of black high-heeled shoes. She even bought a set of tasteful but sexy underwear that Johnny would like. She would not turn into one of those women of a certain age who cut off their hair and became sensible. If she had to have cardigans to cope with temperature changes, then they would be modern, fitted, snappy cardigans and not the shapeless, sagging type that were good for nothing except hiding in.

All it had taken to precipitate this transformation was two weeks of fairly intensive emailing with an old classmate. She had been in therapy and it hadn't cost her a penny.

20

Letters Not Written

"Is she going with you to Ardnamurchan?" Marianne was helping Johnny to pack in preparation for the annual geology field trip. She was an expert in getting the maximum amount into the smallest space and was flattening and folding and neatly layering into a rucksack. If Johnny had done it himself, he would have stuffed things in as they came to hand.

"By 'she', you mean Charmaine?"

"Indeed."

"No."

"Why not?"

"Someone has to look after the department."

"What about Mick?"

"Mick is sick." Johnny grinned.

"So who's going with you? You have to have a woman, don't you?"

"Yvonne from PE."

"Ah."

"Does that meet with your approval?"

"No opinion, either way."

Johnny raised a quizzical eyebrow.

"Really."

"I thought you'd be pleased Charmaine wasn't coming."

Marianne shrugged, thinking about the high heels and the varnished nails. "I don't suppose she's exactly an all purpose, all-terrain type of woman."

"And you are!"

"Excuse me; I'll have you know I climbed over 1400 feet in Lahore in 1978!"

Johnny fastened up his rucksack and hoisted it off the bed and onto the floor. "Well, I never knew that! I shall look at you in a totally different light."

Marianne wasn't sure if he was being sarcastic but decided to let it pass. "By the way," she continued, shaking the quilt and avoiding eye contact, "I found someone from Brocklebank Hall on Friends Reunited. We've exchanged a few emails …" Now that Edward was safely on the other side of the world, and it was possible their cyber re-acquaintance was over, it seemed like a good time to tell Johnny. Mailing without his knowledge had seemed a shade illicit.

"Anyone I've heard of?"

"Doubt it."

"What's her name?"

Marianne hesitated. She thought about saying 'Lydia', but decided that would complicate matters. "Edward."

The atmosphere became suddenly charged with unspoken thoughts zipping back and forth and crackling. Johnny hovered in the doorway, his arm raised as he ran his hand through his hair. "Edward?"

Marianne continued, smoothing the pillows. "Edward … Yeah, Edward. Edward Harvey. He was at school with Sam after Brocklebank."

"I forgot Sam was at Brocklebank with you. Wonder what he's doing these days? It's years since we've spoken. I must look him up next time we're in Cumbria … So, what's with this Edward, then?"

"We've been sharing a few memories about the old place."

"You never said."

"You weren't in – I kept forgetting to say. It's no big deal. We didn't know each other very well. But he was in the same class

143

as me for about three years and in the play. In *The Rivals*. He was Lydia Languish; I was his maid Lucy. I must've shown you the photos sometime."

Johnny was back inside the room now, standing by the window, his arms folded. "I don't think you've mentioned him before."

"No? I usually mention him along with the memories of Latin. We used to do all the difficult bits!"

"No. No recollection. So what's he up to now?"

"Archaeology lecturer at Devon uni."

"Ah… clever, then?"

"Yes, very …"

"Does he remember you?"

"Not very well – but it's been useful reminiscing."

"How so?"

"You haven't time for this now." Marianne wondered why Johnny was suddenly so interested.

"You brought up the subject."

She sat on the bed and played with the ends of her hair, scanning the room and noting the sinister triangular shape of a large dark brown moth beside the top of the curtain. "You know I hated being there – at Brocklebank. I'm sure I must've told you that. The bullies gave me a hard time. I've never been able to forget it. But now I've been mailing Edward – and been reminded of the good times – I feel better. It's weird."

"You said it was no big deal. Sounds pretty big to me. And, no, you didn't tell me."

"Finding Edward in particular is no big deal," she lied, "but the Brocklebank angst is or was."

"Why couldn't you tell me?" said Johnny, looking hurt. "You're so difficult to reach these days. You never used to be."

The words stung. *Difficult to reach.* So that's what he thought of her. "It's hard saying some of the things. They've been bottled up for years." She flashed him a sideways glance. "I still can't tell you here, in the cold light of day. Too embarrassing. It's different writing emails when there's no one to see your expression. Different writing to someone when it doesn't really matter what they think. Anyway, I didn't need to tell Edward. He already knew. He was there. That was enough. Knowing he knew."

"Unless, of course, he'd forgotten," said Johnny, unkindly. "It was a long time ago. I can't remember much from that far back. Especially about other people."

"Doesn't matter if he had forgotten. Even telling a cat can be therapeutic. But there are some things Edward would still remember. That's enough."

Johnny gave a slight nod of understanding, but she knew she had wounded him. Good! It wouldn't do to get too soft and sentimental now she was resolved in her new way of being.

While Edward was on the other side of the world, Marianne conversed with him in her head. In between the serious business of teaching her voracious and demanding students, and her domestic rituals at home, her mind wandered to the man that was inadvertently changing her life. Unknowingly and unintentionally, Edward had become her confidante – even her therapist – and she found she could tell him anything during the brain chatter of consciousness, for he would never judge. She wanted to tell him everything in reality, but of course that would have been unwise.

Sometimes she would converse in the supermarket car park as she pushed the trolley from the store, wondering too why she always picked one with dodgy wheels that needed to be coaxed crab-like, tiring her arms in an effort not to run into the rows of cars. And sometimes the off-loading occurred while she waited at traffic lights, or when walking through the endless corridors at college.

Once, all her thoughts would have been first reserved for Johnny, but he was still in Ardnamurchan and in any case, she didn't feel he deserved to hear them any more; at least not for now. In her journal she wrote down her feelings so she could monitor the change and be reminded of progress when the doubts resurfaced as they surely would. She also wondered tentatively whether this cyber re-acquaintance might be the vehicle she could use one day to write the book about the Brocklebank experience: the book she had always known was there, but couldn't find a way to express. Keeping the feelings in the journal would serve as a catalogue of ideas should the time come when she was distanced enough from the drama to feel she could tell the story.

Dear Lydia,

I saw a novel today in Smith's about school reunions. Everyone is jumping on the bandwagon now. Friends Reunited has spawned a whole new genre of twenty-first century literature. Reuniting will be done to death in books, on the radio, on TV and in films. For a whole generation, FR will be part of common parlance and while there will be the success stories charting tearful discoveries of lost friends and relatives, it will be the damning tales of marriage breakdown and betrayal that will command the most column inches in the tabloid press.

Then it will stop. Today's youth won't lose each other like we did. I remember writing to several friends during my time at college, but then work began, new friends came on the scene and there just wasn't time to keep so many balls in the air at once. So some contacts were lost and then regretted years later when they were remembered but beyond reach.

There was Hesta who made me scrambled eggs and marmite on toast when I had 'flu; Jenny from Chorleywood who was mad about Bryan Ferry and wanted to be a spy; Freda who introduced me to Portobello

Market and avocado pears; Mandy, kind and reliable and an expert in maths. What lives did they find after college? What paths beckoned? Perhaps Friends Reunited will throw up the answers or maybe I'll never know.

Now, advanced communication systems make it easy to keep in touch with more people at once; even acquaintances. A text message now and then might be enough. Gone will be the vast separations spanning thirty-three years and more.

Oh Lydia, I cannot begin to tell you how I miss you at the moment. I miss writing to you and you replying. Crazy! Totally, utterly, crazy when we have only been exchanging mail for two weeks. Finding you was one of those frontier moments when the life before and the life after are never the same.

But I know that I mustn't take up too much of your precious time, or seem too needy or seem to care too much. In any case, how can I care too much when I don't know you? One meeting and all the silly bubbles will burst, I am sure. But I think that left behind would be something worthwhile, something friendly and sincere and respectful.

I think of you in an idealised way, heaping upon you all the traits that I admire and dismissing any thought that you are flawed. Not for you the moods and foibles of ordinary mortals! Not for you inconsideration, impatience and incapability with an iron! Until we meet, you are airbrushed to perfection in my fantasy world and I know that this could never be the real you. I am not under any illusions. This is all a game. Nothing makes sense. These are the ramblings of a hormonally imbalanced woman. Forgive me.

Hi Edward,

If we meet will it be as easy as it has been in cyberspace? Will we have things to talk about beyond the memories of yesteryear and the trials of life at Brocklebank? Will you see me as an equal and not the downtrodden girl I once was? Will there be just enough attraction for us to want to be friends, but not so much as to make it complicated?

147

I wish I could tell you about the M word! Perhaps you would understand, but it's just not the kind of thing you discuss with men. Makes men feel uncomfortable. A few of us women were talking about hot flushes in the staffroom the other day, and the man beside us went silent, then escaped … You don't want to know about the early waking and the lying for hours unable to sleep. And how bad I feel some mornings – hardly able to prise myself from bed, and when I do, the lethargy …

Sometimes there's so much going on in my head, I can't focus. Information overload with neurons firing off in all directions, like a pyrotechnic display. And each time I try to grab a coherent thread, the image blurs. Thinking this; thinking that. What is that lesson I have to teach tomorrow? Is the filling that's gone sensitive to hot and cold a sign of something worse? And Johnny …

Then there are the moods that dip down into a pit of despair like I have never known, only to bounce back without warning to an extreme of happiness. This is bungee jumping for the psyche and I've never been much of a thrill seeker.

I wonder for how long this will be; if it will get worse; if it will ever stop. Sometimes I feel so gloomy at the thought of being no longer young, but finding you has at least reminded me of my inner potential. I hope it's not too late.

Do you have midlife fears, Edward? Most people do. It is natural, normal and potentially productive as we reassess and subtly shift the way we do things. If we met face to face would we be able to talk about these things, or would you shy away like the man in the staffroom?

Someone wrote a book once about travelling backwards through life – being raised from the dead and gradually getting younger… With the certainty of incapacity, helplessness and the sure knowledge of exactly when this would happen, culminating in a most painful departure from the outside world, this would be an even more frightening prospect than the chronology as we know it.

Hi Edward,

In the winter months I am a bear. I would happily stay at home in my cave through the dark days. We are not programmed to get up in the pitch blackness of a December morn, working through until it is dark again. It is not natural. No wonder we suffer from SAD. Why can't we go back to a time when we synchronise with the seasons? I'm sure we'd be much happier.

In 1984, I stayed on British Summer Time after the clocks went back. People thought I was mad. Johnny thought it was slightly batty, but those were the days when he loved me for it. I thought it was utterly sensible! I rose at my seven thirty instead of six thirty, and went to bed at my eleven. So much better for an owl like me. Are you an owl, Edward, or a lark? I bet you're a lark. Tapping out research papers on your computer before breakfast while the world sleeps … You are so productive it makes my head spin.

Edward,

Why do we worry about leaving things for posterity? Children, books, inventions …

All will be gone sometime when the world ends. And this may be sooner than we think. The erratic climate could soon make the earth uninhabitable. And we sit alone in our cars and say, 'you can't ask me to catch a bus when I've been driving all my life.'

And we say that wind farms destroy the scenic beauty of the moorland and the seas, but soon there may be no scenic beauty left to destroy.

I want to write a book about my Brocklebank memories; a book for all those tortured souls who have been burdened all their life by the bullies from their youth. But who's going to read it when the world ends?

Dear Edward,

You appeared in my dreams last night, young and dark and lithe from a long lost time when I never knew you. And I am young too, teenage or twenty perhaps, and we have that easy familiarity that comes from a lifetime of knowing, which is strange when it is a lifetime of knowing we have missed.

And when I woke, I woke with a feeling of loss and I missed you.

But if you come back from Australia and we never write again, it won't make any difference. I will be sad of course; sad that you only re-entered my life for such a short time. But that time has been so special. Like the rocket boosters that send a spacecraft on its journey to the stars, you have given me impetus to face the rest of my life. You have reminded me of who I was and what I could be; re-ignited a motivation and ambition that I thought I no longer needed. I will never lose it now. I owe it to you to do things differently from now on.

And just for an hour or two as the day took hold and the watery light of dawn became the assured light of day, I longed for that precious sleep again when I might find you and be young and happy again. I wonder at the oddness of it all. How can I feel this way when you and I have shared nothing but a classroom, a hockey field, a stage?

Am I losing my rational sense? I know that this manufactured image of you is anything but real. It's what I hope you could be, yet cannot be; the recipe for the perfect man. But we all know he doesn't exist. It is my defence against cynicism at a time when my life is full of fears and doubts and disappointments; the frailty of the human condition; the human male; Johnny …

But is it any different for him? While I want so much love and romance and certainty forever, perhaps I am a disappointment to him as I age and lose vitality and youth?

The old fox in the copse at the back of the college has found a young vixen to bear his young this year. I swear I saw a spring in his step and a new gleam to his coat. I wonder what happened to his previous wife?

All the things she might've wanted to say but never did; all the conversations they never had – perhaps never would. It was like he wanted to listen now where once he had been unsure;

like he'd given her permission to speak and this had opened the floodgates of her outpouring.

So Edward became a fantasy object; a distraction from the mundanities of life. How he would have laughed if he had known – far too modest to imagine such a thing. In saner moments, Marianne considered the real picture, but this was much less fun and while her hormones were spinning, she decided to enjoy it. She knew she was thinking the ridiculous thoughts of an adolescent, but there were two ways to approach this obstacle in her life: either become depressed at the thought of losing her youth, or embrace it wholeheartedly as an opportunity – even an excuse – to be silly again.

21

New Tactics

Johnny came back from Ardnamurchan, windblown and healthy-looking with designer stubble, wild hair and a fresh, cold country smell on his outdoor clothes.

"Marianne!" he shouted as he came through the door, dropping his rucksack in the hallway. "Mari! I'm back!" An icy blast of approaching winter accompanied him, together with a few dried-up leaves from the maple in the garden.

It was late on Friday afternoon. Marianne saved the work that she was doing on the computer and hurried downstairs to greet him. In her heart, she was really pleased he was home, but her head said *don't forget his pursuit of the fluffy trollop.* She didn't want to overdo the enthusiasm. He would pay a price for his thoughtlessness this past year.

She gave him a hug and a kiss on the cheek, then released him quickly. She ran her fingers gently over his beard then turned away. "You're looking very well … Good time?"

"Exhausting, freezing cold, but yes." He unzipped his padded jacket and slung it over the end of the banister rail. "We counted them out and we counted them back! Yvonne put her foot down a rabbit hole and twisted her knee, but apart from that, no problems … I brought you this," he added, producing something from out of his jacket pocket. Close your eyes!"

Marianne shut her eyes and held out her hand, apprehensive lest it was something alive or slimy. But it was hard and smooth and cold. "It feels like a stone."

"It is a stone. Ardnamurchan granite!"

She grinned. "Thank you! We can use it as a doorstop."

This was a glimmer of the old Johnny; the Johnny who knew that little things given with thought are more important than big things given without it.

Johnny walked into the kitchen and took a long drink of water from a bottle on the counter. "What've you been up to?" He held out his free hand to her, grasping her fingertips, making an effort.

"This and that; the usual weekly grind." Marianne let him squeeze her hand briefly, then withdrew it.

"Have you heard from Holly?"

"An email saying she was making lots of friends and enjoying the lectures. She's joined the riding club. Seems to have settled in well. Sounds very happy. It's been very quiet without you both." Marianne thought he looked so sexy in his rough Arran jumper that she was finding it difficult to restrain herself. Two days earlier, she had noticed fewer hot flushes and a feeling of being alive again. It was as if the switch had been turned back on, and she wanted him again. *Hold back,* she said to herself. *Wait, then wait a little bit more. Let him come to you.* "How about a leisurely bath before we eat?"

"Will you come and scrub my back?" He twinkled.

"I might," she teased.

Later when they lay flat on their backs on the bed after a steamy session of sex, initiated by Johnny and evoking memories of a long lost time, Marianne decided to tell him about the M word. Catch him while the mood was right; while he was sober; while he thought her desirable and was basking in the afterglow.

"Johnny …"

"Zzzzz!"

"Johnny! Don't you dare go to sleep on me!"

"Zzzzz …"

"Johnny!"

"Yes, Mari …"

"I need to tell you something."

"Oh God, here we go. I knew this was too good to be true." She frowned.

There was a long pause. Johnny's eyes were wide open now.

"I'm going – this is difficult."

"To leave me?" offered Johnny, half-jokingly.

"Menopausal." She blurted it out through clenched teeth. It was so hard saying the word, but there it was, in the open, swooping around, hard to catch. It could never be put back in the bottle again.

"It's a bit soon, isn't it?"

"Early, but not too early."

"What does this mean?"

"It means I am emotional and cranky like a teenager, but when you're thirteen, you don't understand what's going on, but suspect things will get better. Now you do understand, and fear they'll get worse. So it means I need sympathy and compassion because it's hard feeling that it's all slipping away. It's a very odd experience. All the things that people have said are true. You do become absent minded: sugar in the fridge; keys left in the boot of the car. Keys left everywhere. Forgetting names of people you know really well. Forgetting the simplest facts."

Johnny turned to face her, looking concerned. "I don't know what to say."

"You don't have to say anything."

"I wondered if there was something wrong."

"Well now you know." Marianne sat up for a moment, the duvet slipping and revealing her nakedness.

Now it was his turn. She lay back down again and waited. He could apologise; perhaps say that it was all his fault. He could tell her if he was having a crisis too.

Nothing.

"Don't go yet," Johnny reached over and put a warm hand on her shoulder.

"Things to do," she said. "If you want to eat. But you can stay and have a snooze. Catch up on some sleep. I'll call you when supper's ready." And with that she got up and back into her clothes, ran a comb through her hair and went downstairs feeling pleased.

She was redressing the power-balance and leaving him wanting more.

As the days went by, Marianne continued her new policy of being non-judgemental about pub-visits and ceased to grumble if Johnny drank too much. She stopped rising to any swipes that were aimed to tease and taunt, and ignored any references to other women. She also became much more available for sex, though careful to let him make most of the advances. She was newly confident about her allure and decided to enjoy it while the switch was back on.

And day by day, little by little, Johnny returned to his former attentive self. He spent fewer and fewer evenings at the pub, and when he did go, he drank less and came home earlier.

But Marianne was a long way from forgiving him yet. She still couldn't forget the image of him laughing with Charmaine on the steps of the school. She remembered the sinking feeling in the pit of her stomach and how she had felt she might lose him.

Then Holly came back for the Christmas vacation. Marianne marvelled at how she had changed in the short three months since being away. There was a touch of the rebel about her dress and she had crimson streaks in her luscious dark hair that matched the blood-red lipstick she was habitually wearing. She sounded different – using long words and wanting to talk endlessly about everything and nothing, in the way that students do; in the way that Marianne had once, long ago, in a faraway room in a students' hall of residence, when she thought that she had been put on this planet to make a difference and change the world.

Oh to be so young again, she thought, but then remembered all the insecurities that being young entailed. Perhaps it was easier being hot and forty-something. And she wouldn't want to go back to a time when the Brocklebank horrors scourged her waking life from dawn to dusk.

"Mum …" said Holly when they sat one morning after breakfast. "Can I call you Marianne?" My friend Thalia calls her mum 'Helen' – 'Mum' makes you seem old, and you're not."

"I'd rather you didn't," said Marianne, taken aback as she said the words because they were spoken in the same disapproving tone used by her own mother. Her mother would have said 'no'. Was that how she really felt? Her mother got really uppity when some slip of a girl barely out of school called her Daphine instead of Mrs Hayward. But did it really matter what you were called? In any case, it would be just another adolescent phase that wouldn't last.

"Thalia's parents live in Christchurch and have a yacht at Keyhaven. They go sailing round the coast in the summer holidays. She said I could go with them."

"How nice." Marianne tried to be enthusiastic, but the more she heard about Thalia, the more she thought she was the kind of girl to lead her daughter astray. But what could you do? Her own mother had thought that about Sasha at first, especially when Sasha embroidered an upward pointing arrow on the leg of her jeans. It was all misjudgement and misunderstanding of the times. Sasha was a fund of knowledge at a time when a little knowledge was a dangerous thing. And Marianne had made her own decisions. She had been her own person, and no doubt Holly would be too.

It was snowing outside. Not the kind of snow that turns everything Christmas card white in a matter of hours, but wet flakes mixed with rain that melted as soon as they touched the ground. *Sad snow*, Marianne called it. Not the kind of snow to get excited about. Marianne always felt nostalgic in the snow: memories of carol-singing, mistletoe and bright burning fires. Snow at Brocklebank brought out the toboggans, and attempts to create a sledge run in the lane on the other side of the fence by the cricket field.

"You and Dad seem better." Holly interrupted her reverie. "I haven't heard you arguing since I got back."

Marianne smiled. "You notice everything. You should be studying psychology."

"Is he still spending a lot of time at the pub?"

"Much less now."

"Did you ever find anyone you were looking for on Friends Reunited?"

"I found Edward." Marianne began, feeling the heat as soon as she spoke his name. "And a couple of people found me."

"Edward?"

"Edward Harvey from Brocklebank Hall. Except he's called Ted now."

"Oh, Harry Potter! Yeah?"

"So you said!"

"And?"

"And nothing."

"What is he now?"

"An archaeologist."

"Wow, cool! Will you meet?"

"He's in Australia … Or New Zealand or Pitcairn Island."

"Living?"

"Holiday … He may not write again …" Marianne thought

as she said the words that this might be true. He may not write again. She may be abandoned with her precious gift of the cure and have no way of ever letting him know the true extent of what he had done for her. For an instant she felt the loss as a pain in her soul.

"But if he does, will you meet? That would be so extra!"

"Maybe one day."

"Cool."

"I wish you'd stop saying that." (Her mother again!)

"Is he like you expected?"

"Hard to say by email, but there was nothing unexpected about him."

With Holly home, Johnny was happy again; wanting to hear everything and being told very little. Holly and Marianne conspired to keep the most unsettling facts of her student existence just between themselves. She'd met a young man called Dylan and it was clear she was in the first throes of love and thought that everyone else should be too. Used to her father's suspicions and interrogation, Holly told her mother when they were alone and Marianne provided Johnny with an edited underplayed version. *There was someone called Dylan – another law student – who sounded very charming – but it wasn't anything serious. You know what it's like at uni, Johnny …* Now that he was behaving better she didn't want him to start fretting about Holly.

"You don't think she's sleeping with the guy, do you?" he said.

"They've only known each other a few weeks."

"A few weeks in that intense atmosphere is equivalent to a year anywhere else."

"She's sensible."

"By sensible, do you mean on the pill and adept with condoms?"

"I don't like to pry."

"I hope he's not one of these serial womanisers."

"Don't assume the worst."

"Dylan, what kind of a name is that?"

"His parents were probably children in the flower-power generation … a bit like us."

"At least we didn't call Holly after a rabbit."

"More likely that he's called after Bob."

And Johnny was silenced, but Marianne could almost hear the cogwheels of his consciousness battling with irrational feelings of jealousy and over-protection.

She wrote in her journal: *Holly has met a Dylan and is madly in love; I have met an Edward and he has made me sing again.*

Johnny is being sensitive and kind again, but he hasn't said sorry …

For the first time in twenty years, or maybe for the first time ever, I am looking after me.

22

Edward

Is it impossible for men and women to be just friends? Heterosexual men and women, that is. Friends without even a hint of the untoward? When men meet women, the dance goes on however surreptitiously; however under the surface. But when there is no sex, and never likely to be, does it need attraction from at least one of the parties in order to make it sustainable?

Christmas and New Year had been and gone with all the usual fuss and razzmatazz of drinks parties and extravagance, family visits, excesses of food and endless glitzy television shows.

Holly was now back in Sussex and Johnny and Marianne were going through the separation trauma yet again, but less painfully, knowing that they had coped before and realising that they were slowly coming to terms with being alone together.

All was calm in Beechview Close.

It was cold and bleak with dark days of driving rain from heavy clouds. There was a January rawness to the breeze that northerners called a 'lazy wind' because it goes straight through. Johnny and Marianne typically spent their winter Sunday afternoons preparing for the week ahead. When Marianne was using the computer, she frequently sneaked a look at her emails, wondering if Edward was back yet, and if he were, would he let her know, and would they continue their re-acquaintance from where they left off?

But this Sunday, Johnny was painting the spare bedroom upstairs and the smell of *Sea White* drifted through the house. This had been on his list of things to do for about four years. Marianne was sick of mentioning it. It was only when she threatened to do it herself and even went to Homebase and bought the paint that he decided he would make a start. She knew he thought he would do it better. This may well have been true. Certainly he would do it faster. She also knew that this great sacrifice on his part would mean that he wouldn't do anything else for at least another year and she would be expected to balance his effort by caring for his every need. It was a Mars/Venus thing.

She checked her emails again. Nothing …

Johnny had always been suspicious when Marianne claimed a new male friend. New male friends made his antlers grow; made him hoof the ground, toss his head in the long grass and bellow. There was Ashley with whom she used to work, who gave the most wonderful hugs, and had a wife called Imogen who was always busily involved in some high-powered job flitting across to Europe every couple of weeks. When Imogen was out of town, Ashley played the single man. When he invited Marianne to the theatre, Johnny raised an eyebrow. "I don't trust him," he said. "I know men like Ashley. Oh they're very nice and all that, but give him half a chance …" So Marianne thought of some excuse to refuse the invitation, Ashley asked no more, and the hugs became a thing of the past.

Then there was Jean-Paul from Marseilles, who was on an exchange visit teaching maths. He had a wild black beard, a nervous wife and three sons. Marianne tried to be hospitable and invited them for dinner, but his wife couldn't come because she had to look after the children. Johnny watched them like a hawk from avocado cocktail though to Jamie Oliver's *Aunt Sheila's Pudding*. Jean-Paul flirted and complimented and

Johnny's expression said, 'this man thinks he's Casanova', and afterwards he gave Marianne chapter and verse.

Marianne said he was French, that they all behaved like that and he shouldn't read anything into it.

Johnny said French or no, if he left them alone together he would like to bet that Jean-Paul would try it on. "I know what men are like," he said, "I've been one for a long time."

Marianne pretended to take no notice, but when Jean-Paul and his family moved back to France, he sent her a postcard with saucy undertones about *The Last Tango in Paris* and she began to think that Johnny might be right.

There had been other male friends throughout her life, but always something had happened to spoil everything. At school in the sixth form, twice it happened that they suddenly declared feelings that she'd never suspected. Once it was alcohol induced, after a sneaked kiss on the floor by a vegetable rack in a kitchen at a party. And once on the day of her A level results after a split with her boyfriend. Both times she had been shocked. Suspicions were aroused. Was this what they'd wanted all along? Was the friendship false – just a means to get close? Defence mechanisms were raised with the impenetrability of the Thames Barrier and in each case the friendship withered.

Sometimes the problem lay outside the friendship – a jealous girlfriend wanting exclusive female access to her partner's thoughts.

But Johnny didn't know Edward. Johnny had never known Edward, so there was nothing he could say to scupper that acquaintance – assuming Edward wrote to her again and assuming she told Johnny that he had. In any case, she could tell Edward wasn't the philandering type, and nothing, absolutely nothing that Johnny could say would alter her opinion about that.

To: Marianne Hayward
From: Edward Harvey
Date: 17th January 2002, 07.34
Subject: The Return of the Natives

Hi Marianne,
Happy New Year!
We are back safely after a wonderful trip. 'Down Under'
was everything and more … NZ – breathtaking scenery
every which way … The children want to live in Sydney
now!
Shock to be back in the cold and the wet …
Hope all well with you.
Much to do.
Best wishes,
Ted

Ted? Edward just wasn't Ted and never would be Ted to her.
Ted was carpet slippers and baggy green cardigans with leather
buttons. Ted was comfortably dozing in front of the fire with
the TV still on and a mug of cocoa on the mantelpiece.

Names were such important things. Teachers know all
about names. Michelle was sweet faced and quiet; Wayne was
loud and aggressive; Elizabeth was staid and well-behaved,
while Eunice was matronly and may have a lilac rinse. Hugo
and Oliver still talked of Mummy and Daddy even when they
were thirty-five, and Jake would always woo the girls. Even
the spelling variants, abbreviations and level of popularity cast
a tone and led to pre-conceived ideas about attitude and
lifestyle. Mandi and Sandi were young and trendy, possibly
hairdressers and drinkers of alco-pops; Steven and Garry
worked on a building site while Theo and Peregrine organised
lavish parties for twenty-somethings.

To: Edward Harvey
From: Marianne Hayward
Date: 18th January 2002, 17.42
Subject: Re: Return of the Natives

Hi Ted???
So you like Hardy too!?
Is Ted what you would prefer to be called? It doesn't
seem like you but I will if you want.
Good to hear you're back safely and that you've had an
enjoyable holiday. We have had a typically family-based
Christmas with Holly at home. She has a boyfriend, Dylan!
Johnny has taken an instant dislike just because of his
name (and because nobody will ever be good enough for
Holly!) Just about got used to her being here again and
then she was off for another term. Such joys still to come
for you.
I have been thinking about the Brocklebank meals …
Were they as ghastly as I remember or is it just that my
dislike of milk puddings, cooked cheese, solid custard,
lumpy mashed potato and butterbeans has coloured my
image of the whole picture!? And the sausage! D'you
remember it floating about in a dishful of grease? Abi
used to give it to the dog! I did enjoy the cottage pie
and the various jam sponges, though – particularly the
roly-poly!
Question for you … What is the odd one out between
log, saw, axe and shovel?
Happy New Year too!
Marianne

A low key reply, but her heart was smiling. He was back; he had written again. What next? Perhaps they could be friends one day; simply friends. Perhaps they could make the impossible, possible. It was what she had wanted at the age of ten, even before Lydia. Those missing years of adolescence, when love and lust and hormones reigned, might be their salvation. No memory of sexual passion to complicate. Only the innocent adoration of a schoolgirl crush.

But if men and women are so different – and they are – an innocent e-relationship was going to need careful orchestration. They would have to find common ground without venturing into the danger zones of the big three risky topics. Would they have enough to say when the Brocklebank memories were exhausted?

Already Marianne was noticing the differences in their styles. She often wrote laboriously and he wrote in sound-bites. Yet in Edward's snippets there was a plethora of information and many unanswered questions. Marianne wanted to know so much more than she was ever told. Wanted to sit down with the man and exhaust a topic before they moved onto the next. She wanted to ask him how he met his wife Felicity and whether the children were like him or her. She wanted to understand what had happened between Brocklebank and university, when they had grown through their teenage years only a few miles apart from each other, yet a few miles that were even further in spirit than the distance they now shared. She wondered why she was so curious; indeed perhaps it was his very lack of information that aroused her interest, and perhaps she was revealing too much and he would soon get bored.

One of Holly's emails told her she needed a different technique to snail letters, but she was resistant to change. She wasn't a teenager and didn't want to start writing like one. She wondered whether the schools of the future would teach email and texting protocol in English lessons in the way they currently taught how to compose business letters.

Few of Marianne's generation used emoticons when they wrote. Somehow putting smiley faces at the end of sentences didn't seem fitting for a middle-aged woman with a grown-up child. No wonder there were so many misunderstandings. She didn't use fasgrolia either. In fact she didn't know what fasgrolia was until she came across the term in a psychology textbook and there discovered that LOL did not mean lots of love.

To: Marianne Hayward
From: Edward Harvey
Date: 21tst January 2002, 22.17
Subject: Re: Return of the Natives

Hi Marianne,
Prefer Edward, but easily slip into what's usually expected ... Sorry!
I don't look forward to the day when Rachel leaves home. She already has a boyfriend of sorts, but I've been told (by Felicity) not to worry or to make any comments.
Remember Brocklebank food well!!
Waverley was in touch at Christmas and says he remembers you.
Probably wrong; saw ... because it is the only one that spells a word backwards??
Dashing as usual ...
Edward

To: Edward Harvey
From: Marianne Hayward
Date: 22nd January 2002, 20.45
Subject: Saws, shovels and uneducated Russian peasants

Hi Edward,
It was part of an IQ test used to illustrate cultural bias. The correct answer is apparently log because all the others are tools. But uneducated Russian peasants answer shovel because the log can be cut up by the axe and the saw. Our students are divided between log and shovel. No one has yet suggested saw – but I shall now use this as a further example of bias as it is a perfectly valid answer!
Is Waverley the person in glasses sitting next to Mrs Swift in the 1968 photograph?
Felicity is right!
Best wishes,
Marianne

To: Marianne Hayward
From: Edward Harvey
Date: 22nd January 2002, 22.50
Subject: Re: Saws, shovels and uneducated Russian peasants

Hi Marianne,
Interesting! Never even noticed that the log was not a tool!
Have just dug out the old school photographs! It is Waverley next to Mrs S … Well remembered! My children didn't recognise me! Haven't worn glasses since I was twenty …
Too busy to think …
Edward

Always busy, thought Marianne. *Like Rabbit in Winnie the Pooh scuttling about writing notices! And fancy not wearing glasses any more.* She would have to reformulate her visual image of him now.

"Edward is back from Australia," said Marianne casually to Johnny.

"Who's Edward?" Johnny was making supper, and there was a pungent aroma of spring onions, ginger and soy sauce. In fact since coming back from Ardnamurchan, the pub had ceased to be his second home and since New Year, he was hardly drinking at all.

"Edward is the guy I found on Friends Reunited. The person I was at Brocklebank Hall with as a child. You know. He went to Waterside with Sam."

"Ah." Johnny barely paused in his quartering of the pak choi.

"I did tell you … *The Rivals*. Lydia …"

She waited for him to say something disapproving, almost hearing his brain clicking.

But he went back to his stir-fry, adding an enormous handful of bean sprouts from a bowl of water by the cooker.

To: Edward Harvey
From: Marianne Hayward
Date: 27th[th] January 2002, 20.16
Subject: Re: Saws, shovels and uneducated Russian peasants

Hi Edward,
Had been imagining you with glasses so that was a surprise! Last week I mistook a purple motorbike tank (on a wall) for a duck so it won't be long before I pay a visit to the opticians!
Told a class today about you saying the 'saw' was the

odd one, and why. I said that the person who said it was
really very clever – excellent at Latin when we were
kids – and one of the bright sparks said that it was
because you were good at languages that you had
focused on looking for differences in the words
themselves.
In haste,
Marianne

To: Marianne Hayward
From: Edward Harvey
Date: 28th January 2002, 18.32
Subject: Re: Saws, shovels and uneducated Russian peasants

Not so good at Latin at Waterside – bored perhaps
after having don eso much at Brocklebak!
Just back fron lecturing inLondon.New York next week.
Edward

Clearly in a rush, thought Marianne! She took this mention of
London as an excuse to remind him of his suggestion before he
went away.

To: Edward Harvey
From: Marianne Hayward
Date: 30th January 2002, 19.11
Subject: Re: Saws, shovels and uneducated Russian peasants

When you come to London, do you ever have any spare
time so we might meet?
Marianne

Now that Edward was back and there was the possibility of

further developing their re-acquaintance, she wondered more and more about the real person on the other end of their cyber exchanges. To whom was she talking? What had Edward become? Did it matter whether he was hunky or not? And did he have the same questions about her?

"He's a man, of course he will," said Robin Hamilton, a male colleague who was following the story with interest and with whom she shared the occasional cup of tea and exchange of confidences.

"But I don't think he's *that* kind of man," she said.

"Do you think I'm that kind of man?"

"No."

"I rest my case."

She began to generate images, possibilities, in the way that a computer ages those suspected of past crimes. It was difficult imagining him without glasses. Perhaps greying hair, perhaps average build, perhaps average-looking. But what if he wasn't like this? He could have become like a bloated and Hush Puppied politician. Would she like to have been pouring out her Brocklebank angst – her very soul – to someone like that? Or worse, what if he resembled an axe murderer – hollow eyed and bearded with a menacing expression? She had seen some very strange archaeologists on the TV. None of these things should matter, yet they did. Or at least they did during these first few months of reuniting.

Although he had mentioned meeting before going to Australia, maybe meeting would disappoint, would break the spell.

If he really did look like Pierce Brosnan, then that would be dire too. She didn't want to be totally bowled over. She just wanted him to be B rather than C; B rather than Gruffit. A was dangerous. A's thought they were God's gift and wanted trophy girlfriends. But Gruffit would shatter the illusion. Gruffits were prone to dribbling baked beans down their beards or being malodorous or having stained fingers or rotten teeth. It would be hard to be friends with a Gruffit.

Marianne castigated herself for thinking this way, but she couldn't help it. The packaging matters. It affects the way people are perceived. It creates pre-conceived ideas. A lot can be deduced from a person's style and the way they speak. But is this right? Should these things matter at all? Marianne's whole life had been blighted by early judgements on packaging. She shouldn't care. She should shout loud from the rooftops that *Looksism* was destructive and damaging to psyches and to relationships; it was responsible for breaking spirits and shattering self-esteem.

Deep down she knew this would be a futile gesture for behind the media influence and social learning were genetic blueprints from thousands of years of evolution. *What is beautiful is good* was a well-known phenomenon in psychology and whatever the accuracy of the judgements, people continued to assess others using such doubtful criteria. Beauty equalled fitness for propagation of the species and no matter what the rights and wrongs of the attraction game, looks would always count for more than anything else in those whirling seconds of initial information exchange when a man and woman meet.

Perhaps meeting Edward would be a mistake.

23

Anticipation

Even before the date had been set, even before there was any certainty that a meeting would ever happen, Marianne felt anticipation that was probably greater than for any other encounter she had ever had in her life. It was a mixture of fear and curiosity, both enormous, but instead of cancelling each other out, their combined sum generated a mass of emotional energy that made her brain hurt.

There's a huge difference between email and face-to-face. What if they had nothing to say? They'd already done Brocklebank and in any case, if all they had to say was in the past, then there would be no future. What if they just didn't get on? What if the dance was out of time as it is with some people and you can't say why. What if all the mailing, the weeks of thinking, of reminiscing, turned out to be a wasted investment?

Marianne played the meeting a hundred different ways in her head, but she couldn't know. It was so long ago that they had shared a classroom, or a hockey pitch. Half a lifetime had passed since they sat together on the stage in the Hut at Brocklebank being photographed for the *Times and Star*, Marianne trying to have a girly chat, but Lydia being distant and monosyllabic. How often had they spoken before? Hardly at all; except exchanging lines in *The Rivals*, and perhaps when they were on the sweeping rota together.

Why did it matter so? Why did he matter more than any of the other men in her cyberspace? Was it because they had never properly known each other? They didn't know if they could be friends; it had never had a chance. She wasn't sure. She had arrived at a point where even without Lydia, the Brocklebank ghosts would no longer haunt her like they once did. She thought perhaps they could be friends. Friends who have shared a past are special. They know where you come from and what you were. There is no room for pretence, and true friends are so rare.

Then there was Johnny. If the contact with Edward were gone, would she be once again plunged into that world of negativity and jealousy? Would the new-found spark of confidence and second-youth vanish before the patterns had been set? The whole business of finding Lydia distracted her, and her preoccupation with something other than Johnny's drinking seemed to have changed his way of being.

But beyond all the logic, it mattered for reasons she could not say and did not know. It mattered because it always had and she didn't know why.

Johnny was still being nice and attentive like he used to be before Charmaine came on the scene. He seemed to love her again, but Marianne's thoughts were often elsewhere. Sometimes she caught him looking at her, concerned, but he said nothing and nor did she. On the surface they were getting on better than they had done for ages. The rows had stopped and bed was fun again.

To: Marianne Hayward
From: Edward Harvey
Date: 11th February 2002, 21.12
Subject: Re: Saws, shovels and uneducated Russian peasants

I sometimes do have spare time. Will let you know…
Edward.

Marianne read this and her green eyes turned misty-bright and dewy. The winter had not yet released its grasp and yesterday the snow transformed her world into an arctic white-out. She imagined meeting Edward on such a day. Being muffled up against the cold in long black coat and multicoloured scarf, with melting snowflakes in her hair and eyes sparkling with emotion for a long-lost time where together in the world of the Hut, they had embarked upon their academic life journey.

Should they meet on a railway station like in *Brief Encounter* but without the bubbling passion? It seemed like a good idea. Outside Boots' the Chemist, or W H Smith's; or by the information point, or at the entrance to Platform 5; or top of the escalator from the Tube. There are lots of very specific possibilities on stations.

She might tell him she would keep her hair loose, as that would make her more noticeable and that it was shoulder length and darkish brown – perhaps with flecks of grey depending upon whether she had dyed it lately. Should she carry a newspaper? Maybe a book to read in case she was early. Maybe a copy of *The Rivals!*

She'd never done anything like this before. Like a blind date, but not.

What would he tell her? Carrying a sign in big letters saying 'Lydia' would be appropriate. Nicely ambiguous to passers-by!

He'd be wearing a suit like hundreds of others, so that would be no good. He wouldn't look like the Edward in her head and he wouldn't be wearing glasses.

Or maybe she would meet him at one of the London colleges; slotted in between academic meetings with Professor this and Doctor that.

Would they greet each other like long lost friends with a hug and a continental two cheek kiss, or a formal handshake with British reserve? Marianne pondered this one morning as she was putting on her make-up to face her working day.

Perhaps she should offer both hands? Warmer than one, but allowing for distance, in their not-quite-there friendship. A formal peck on the cheek might follow if he looked approachable.

'Hi Edward,' she might say. Or was that too cyber?

She played with 'hello' and the Cumbrian 'hiya marrah' as she dragged mascara through her eyelashes, laughing to herself at the ridiculousness of it all. A lot could be gleaned from a mere hello.

'Hello, how lovely to meet you at last!' She blew a kiss at the mirror and brushed blusher on her cheeks. Very Roedean; very up-town girl!

'Hello, Edward,' was the most likely option, but what about emphasis? Should she be calm and formal, or excited and girlish? She would like to be warm yet sophisticated, but this just wasn't her way. She was as likely to trip over and land in a heap at his feet. Or worse, approach someone who wasn't even him!

Or what about simply, 'Edward!'

How brain tangling the confusion of alternative acceptable rituals in this twenty-first century world. It was too much. Far too much. She was overfull of sentiment and she would never keep it together. It would be a disaster and the end of everything.

In an instant there would be tone of voice, nuance, gesture and those deep dark eyes, Lydia's eyes, that had once drawn her in ever-so-briefly to catch a glimpse of his soul. There would be three dimensions, clothes, the touch of palms, imperceptible scents, a soup of pheromones that may govern whether their friendship chemistry was right. They might stare at each other, embarrassed to do so yet compelled as they searched for some recognisable features from the past.

He would be super cool and composed. She would be just another meeting in a line of many. He would be brisk. No time for soft sentimentality when there were important archaeological discussions before and after. And he wouldn't be sitting now as she was, looking at his face and thinking that thirty-three years of living had etched patterns that would shock someone who last saw you when you were eleven.

She would be all over the place in her head. Any sign of coolness would be mere pretence. But she did it every day at work. Convinced most of the world that she was calm and under control and not dancing on a knife edge between composure and chaos.

Just thinking these thoughts brought tears to her eyes. *"Mad, menopausal woman,"* she muttered. Then, *"Hey, what the hell!"*

Here she was, placing all the chess pieces on her own. White then black; move then counter move; Lucy and Lydia … But what if the white queen was taken unawares and she lost control?

Check mate.

Later that evening, after a busy day chasing up last minute pieces of coursework, she composed another email to Edward but decided not to mention anything about meeting. The ball was in his court now.

24

The Manic Life

It was a rare spring day despite February being barely half way through. In south-east London there was a sense of optimism. Magpies pursued each other with flashes of black and white wings and serious intent, and squirrels played chase along the fence tops. Coats had been left at home and workers walked lightly to the office unburdened by layers and all the trappings of scarf and gloves and hat.

The psychology room at North Kent College had half a wall of south-facing windows through which the sun gleamed with such intensity that blinds and curtains were drawn.

Marianne was pacing by the whiteboard, marker pen in hand, dressed in nothing more than a skimpy red t-shirt and black cotton skirt. But on the back of her swivel chair were a cardigan and a jacket, just in case. She was on form today. The teaching was going well. Students were interested in what she had to say.

"Electronic friendship is a comparatively new area of research for psychologists," she addressed the upper sixth group that were covering the relationships module. "What do we mean by electronic friendship?"

Several hands shot into the air. She nodded at Ruth, a normally quiet girl with a long blonde plait, sitting halfway down one side of the horseshoe arrangement of desks.

Ruth cleared her throat. "Texting, email, chatrooms."

"Yes … And also usernets," added Marianne.

"What are they?" asked Sean.

"Star Wars Fans!" interjected Dwayne and the class giggled.

"Absolutely," said Marianne. "Specialist groups who chat on the net. I'm sure you use these things more than me – well I don't chat at all, except by email …"

The class smiled indulgently.

"In this computer-driven world, we can't study relationships without giving some consideration to the people we meet online … So what is the key difference between face to face and electronic communication? Jason?"

"There's a big difference. You can meet a girl face to face … drop one or two compliments and you can see her reaction, know what I mean?" Jason grinned exposing two rows of perfect white teeth. His eyes crinkled and two of the girls opposite started preening their hair.

Stanley added, "There's only a certain extent a relationship over the internet or text messaging or on the phone can go, but personal face to face relationships …" He paused and the class looked at him expectantly, hoping for something scurrilous so that they could assess Marianne's reaction and heighten their entertainment. He shrugged, refusing to be drawn further.

"But it's good 'cos you can think about what you're saying before you write it," said Cate. "Just, say, you told them the most embarrassing secret of your life. It's good you can't see their reaction …"

"I don't agree," said Sean. "If I'm going to tell them a secret, I wanna see how they respond, yeah."

Marianne continued: "What you're saying is the body language is missing. Sometimes it's good and sometime it's a disadvantage. Non-verbal signals – or paralanguage – are often more important than the words themselves. If someone says you look nice to your face, you see their eyes and have an idea whether or not it's genuine. Without the non-verbals, people can cheat … you can never be sure …"

"I hate that," said Cate. "People lying … I had a friend once … When we were shopping and trying things on, she always said I looked nice, even when I knew it was so hideous. Now she's an ex-friend!"

"How do you know if someone really likes you?" said Marianne.

"They tell you?" suggested Jason.

"Well, they might, but only if they know you quite well. You don't usually say 'hey, I really like you,' when you've only just met someone, because that scares them. People don't want to lose face. You don't want to take the risk that they'll think you're being too 'full-on'. Usually if we like someone, we first try to engage them in conversation, and then we look for signals – nonverbal signals – to see if they feel the same way about us.

"And if they don't look at us much; if they don't meet our gaze … perhaps turn slightly away … like this … or talk to you while constantly checking the environment in case someone more interesting turns up …" Marianne demonstrated by addressing Dwayne close by, but turning away, flicking glances this way and that in exaggerated movements.

The class began to giggle.

"Yes, obvious, isn't it?" continued Marianne. "So we know we shouldn't waste our time on that relationship! Best to sneak away quietly!

"Little kids haven't learnt these rules. At primary school they'll say 'do you want to be my friend?' When we get older we realise that in-your-face-rejection is tough. So we resort to subtle ways of finding out.

"This applies to friendships of all kinds, but is even more important in formation of more intimate relationships.

"So consequently, if you remove the visible person from the equation there's room for misunderstanding. Even with phone conversations there is the opportunity to detect a certain amount of feeling from the tone of voice. But with email there is nothing."

Even as she was saying this, Marianne thought of Edward. Her picture of him was still so very hazy and his voice no more than an ever-changing echo. So much was missing, but perhaps not for much longer.

She continued: "The sender may write in one tone, while the receiver may read in another. This is how problems can occur – particularly if the level of communication is more complex, or if there are attempts at humour …

"With internet communication, one of the ways of solving this problem is to use emoticons and fasgrolia? Shows you are 'one of them', like being in an exclusive club."

Marianne turned to the whiteboard and drew a series of four emoticons.

:-))

"Happy," the class chorused.

Marianne wrote Very Happy beside it.

"What's that second one, Miss?"

:-o

"Surprised," said Ellen.

:-#)

"Swear word!" said Sean.

"Looks like someone with a moustache."

"That's right," said Marianne.

"That's not an emotion!" said Stanley.

"Where did you get these from, Miss?"

"*Carol Vorderman's guide to the Internet*. I've researched this, y'know, it's been done properly."

*-)

"Black eye … shiner," said Dwayne.

Marianne wrote 'drunk' on the board and the class collapsed into shrieks of laughter.

"There's more common ones than that," said Stanley.

"I'm purposely showing you the less common ones, because I know you know the common ones."

"What was that other word you said Miss?"

"Fasgrolia … Fast-growing language of the internet using initialisms and acronyms."

There were some groans and murmurings of "What?" and "Will you write that on the board?"

Marianne obliged. "I'm going to show you some examples in a moment … People I know … if I used this technique, they'd think *oh dear*, because my generation tends not to use them – unless they're heavily into computers.

"FYI," she continued, "IMHO, and FWIW, fasgrolia may avoid offending people, but it's … well … it's …" she paused, conscious that she might upset or offend someone in the class.

Naomi came to her rescue. "Geeky!"

There was a sudden chatter of agreement and disagreement and Marianne had to calm them down before she could continue.

Cate said, "When I talk to my friends on msn messenger, they say something funny and I put LOL, but I don't really laugh. It's just something you put as a response."

"To maintain good relations," suggested Marianne.

"Yeah, like a smile."

Marianne continued: "So what kinds of people are more likely to form relationships in this way?"

"Sad ones!" said Dwayne.

"People who haven't got families," said Ayisha.

"It's true that you need to have time," said Marianne. "But what about the socially anxious and lonely? It's one way of meeting people; expressing your real self which you might find difficult in face to face encounters."

"Yeah, *sad*, like I said." Dwayne grinned.

"Also teenagers," said Ellen. "Because you may not have freedom to go out. If parents are too strict."

"Some researchers have found that if people have an internet relationship first, they like each other more when they meet for real. This is because you get to know the real person without being distracted by peripherals. Appearance is such a key factor when we first meet that you might not give someone a chance to get to know you."

"I don't agree," said Cate. "You get a picture in your head and then, you know, you meet up and it's not the same. This happened to me. When we met, I thought *noooo … No way*. Couldn't believe it; never spoke to him again. Just not my type."

"You told me this morning it was because he was fat!" said Sharna.

More riotous laughter.

"If you have an idealised picture of somebody, and you meet them, you're gonna be disappointed," said Obi.

Ellen said: "Like when you read a book and then you've got the characters in your head, and you go and see the film of it and it's like, really weird 'cos they're not the same."

Again, Marianne thought of Edward and the awful possibility that a meeting would herald the end.

"So what you're saying," said Marianne, "is that the research is wrong. You don't necessarily like someone more just because you first met them on the net? You might be right. Perhaps it can work either way."

Afterwards Marianne contemplated the fun that her students were having with this topic. It was great for discussions, but would they remember the theory, the research, the heavy stuff? She was also amazed by their general knowledge about relationships, sure that she hadn't been so wise at the age of seventeen.

Driving home late in the early evening after four one-to-one interview sessions with her tutees followed by a departmental meeting, Marianne sat waiting at traffic lights. She was surreptitiously eating a honey sandwich whenever she was stuck at the lights – snatching mouthfuls and hoping no police cars were about. Only last week a woman had been stopped for eating an apple at the wheel. Marianne reasoned that she wasn't doing anything dangerous and that her plummeting blood sugar levels were much more of a serious risk.

Dear Edward,

What is it with me? I am so emotional this week. There is sun on my skin and the city is waking from its winter sleep. Everything makes me want to cry with a kind of poignant happiness. I see the world through new eyes now and want to have time to appreciate it; to make a better go of things than I have so far.

I am too judgemental; too impatient. Underneath I have always had a soft and sentimental heart, but it has been encased in layers of stone for so long, maybe for always. Now that stone is being chipped away and whole lumps are falling off. I feel I am acquiring a capacity for something that I never had before. But I'm not sure what it is; not sure what to call it. Maybe it's a heightened sense of compassion; maybe it is love. Now I want to love people more. Yes, that's it … I was afraid of loving before, but I feel I can cope now. Before I couldn't bear the thought of loss so I needed the shell.

Oh Edward, what have you done for me and why am I telling you all this? You are my analyst and that is why. If I did write you this email, you might think I am unhinged, but you wouldn't run away … You wouldn't, would you Edward? I could tell you anything and everything and you wouldn't run away like most men do …

But commonsense prevailed and she didn't write it. Instead she decided to cook a treat for Johnny and she went to the supermarket and bought some clams. He liked clams, but would never cook them himself. He was squeamish about cooking anything that was alive.

She enjoyed shopping for food and wondered if there was some primeval explanation. The option of on-line shopping from supermarkets didn't seem natural. She liked to make some gesture towards catching her prey.

How would the lion feel if the wildebeest was delivered to his lair? she mused. It would be just like being in a zoo.

It was gone seven when Johnny came home, apologising furiously and muttering about an unexpected meeting with parents about a disruptive pupil.

Marianne made sympathetic noises but didn't make any comment, where three months earlier his remark would have received a cold and suspicious stare and a frosty greeting.

"I did try to phone you. Didn't want you to think I was down the pub ... Charmaine said you probably think I go out too much."

She was chopping garlic, red chilli and small shallots which she scraped into a pan to which she had added olive oil. "Humph." *How dare she presume to know what I think!* It was tempting to say it, but she tried to keep calm.

"Looks interesting," said Johnny, breaking her thoughts, nodding at the gathering pile of finely chopped ingredients.

"Clams with linguine," she said, smiling, allowing him to give her a hug from behind.

"Where are they?" He peeked under the damp cloth that covered a bowl by the sink. He pulled a face.

"You know you like them really."

"I don't like thinking about what they are and what you're going to do to them."

"If you're going to get sentimental over shellfish, then you should become a vegetarian."

"They've got a nervous system; they will feel pain," said Johnny with furrowed brow.

"So have cows, but this doesn't seem to put you off steak."

"That's different … You wouldn't kill a cow."

"No, I wouldn't. I couldn't kill anything with a face."

"Yet you happily kill clams."

"Clams haven't got a face."

"I can hear them screaming when you put them in the pan!"

Marianne gave him an incredulous look. "Oh please! If you're not prepared to kill something yourself – or at least condone the killing – then you shouldn't eat it."

Johnny grinned. "I shall look forward to them but I'm not watching the grisly deed. I'll just catch the rest of the news."

Marianne sloshed some white wine into the pan and turned up the heat.

Dear Edward,

I've never asked you if you're a vegetarian. I don't suppose you are. Cumbria didn't spawn many vegetarians in our era – especially not men. Johnny isn't one, but he won't kill anything himself no matter how insignificant. I don't know if you smoke, either. I imagine not; I hope not! All that wild outdoors … And I haven't talked to you about politics, religion or sex, because they're risky areas at the best of times: potential dynamite when you can't hear the other person's response. If we were friends, we would know about all these things. They are conversations-in-waiting, but will we ever have the place or time?

Oh Edward, when I'm talking to the classes about relationships, I sound as if I've got it all sussed. And they look at me in awe and wonder, hanging on to every word. If only they knew how hard it is – that the theory is one thing, but the practice is another; that no matter how old you are, or how much experience you've got, it doesn't take much to pull the rug and send you spinning. Sometimes it's only one misplaced word, or a mistuned tone and the calm and tranquil can become the stressed and turbulent.

Johnny thought the clams were delicious.

"Seafood is very good for the sex drive," he said, hopefully.

"As if you need it!" said Marianne.

Johnny basked in the compliment and Marianne smiled. Perhaps they would have an early night so the clams could work their magic.

25

Accusation

Since Edward had returned from his holiday, Marianne was in a glass half full kind of mood.

I am not pregnant.

I am not fifty … yet!

I am alive.

She felt content and at peace with the world. Not so many hot flushes and more energy. Also, after over a year of almost constant worry, now when she scanned the horizon there seemed so much to look forward to. Day by day she was rebuilding a harmonious relationship with Johnny, she was getting used to being without Holly, and Edward would soon suggest a meeting. Of that she was sure.

She wrote in her journal:

These are things that make me smile:-

Beach pebbles left shiny and wet by foaming waves

Cumulus clouds changing shape in a fierce wind

Wild baby rabbits

Crushed velvet

Chopin's 'Minute Waltz'

Dark chocolate digestive biscuits

Lupins

The sweet-sour taste of the first raspberry as it bursts on the tongue

Giraffes (or should that be giraffe?)

Country church bells

The scent of lilac in the early morning

And honeysuckle as the sun goes down

Tangled otter moments after sex
She wondered what Edward's list would be.
Or Johnny's.
She must ask him sometime …

The next day, she was driving home from work when she became aware that a four-by-four was veering erratically in front of her. It was dark, but she could see the driver was holding a mobile phone. *Prat!*

He hit the brakes sharply to lean out of the window and shout something to a be-denimed youth on the other side of the road. Marianne noted a mass of curly hair bunched in a ponytail and just stopped in time. She hung back, annoyed, and mouthed a few expletives, thinking about aggression and road rage and how it felt safe shouting abuse when protected by the body of her car. She had heard stories of those on the receiving end of such, stopping their cars and going on the attack, wrenching the driver's door open and punching them in the face.

Mad fools.

But there was a lot of madness about these days. There were knives. Unthinkable things happened. She didn't want to appear as an item on News 24.

As the four-by-four carried on up the road she noticed a retriever in the passenger seat, looking important and occasionally sticking its nose out of the window. He couldn't be all bad if he had a beautiful dog like that.

She decided to turn off the main road to get out of his way and she indicated to turn right down a back route that led along the tree-lined roads near Cedarwood School and past The Duck and Bull, the pub where the teachers often went after work.

Where Johnny and Charmaine sometimes pass the early evening hour!

The road was newly humped and she slowed right down. Traffic calming measures were anything but calming to drivers. Progress by hiccupping along. Tootling down the road at twenty miles an hour like Great Uncle Isaac in the nineteen-seventies, creating a tailback of embarrassing proportions.

'What's the delay?'

'Some old geezer in a mini.'

And Marianne aged seventeen, trying not to blush, in the school minibus with her peers on the way back from a geography field trip, disowning her elderly relative for fear of being uncool. Except uncool wasn't the word in the nineteen seventies, the word was … God, what was it? Square or spare or …

Hiccup!

What did this do for the liver and the suspension?

But it was preferable to following the lunatic with the dog.

Then through the semi-darkness as she neared the pub, she saw a man who looked like Johnny standing on the pavement, caught in the glow of a streetlamp, except it couldn't be him because … because he would be home by now, wouldn't he, and he wouldn't be letting a woman other than herself touch him *like that!*

She slowed down even more.

It was Johnny, and the woman was Charmaine and she was touching his face; *how dare she touch his face, only I'm allowed to touch his face;* and although Johnny wasn't doing anything incriminating, he was looking at this woman with the golden hair down her back, and she was standing close, looking into his eyes with, it seemed, her hand on his cheek. He didn't appear to see the silver hatchback almost drawing to a standstill beside them. Didn't see the woman with dark shoulder length hair and wild eyes glaring at his back through the window. Marianne was incensed to a point where she almost ran into the kerb.

She thought about hooting or stopping, but she needed time to think what to say, and she would rather tackle Johnny on his own than with Charmaine hovering in the background. In an instant the snakes had returned to her stomach.

She drove on, glancing in her rear-view mirror, hoping she was mistaken. But she wasn't.

The tarty minx!

Idiot, idiot husband!

Later, as soon as Johnny walked through the door, Marianne forgot all her new resolve. She forgot that they had been nice to each other for over a month and that she was beginning to feel happy again. The house of cards that had been so carefully constructed since he came back from Ardnamurchan came tumbling down as if the floor beneath had been shaken by an earthquake.

It was time for accusations and she didn't wait to think of the consequences. For weeks and weeks she had wanted something concrete to throw at him and now at last she had it. She had evidence. The pressure cooker was about to explode and he had barely closed the front door when she started.

"What were you doing with that damned woman ... with Charmaine?" Marianne leapt from her chair and greeted him with hands on hips and flashing eyes.

"What are you talking about?" He dropped his briefcase in the hall and walked past her into the kitchen. "What am I supposed to have done now?"

One by one the cards fell. She could feel them fluttering and spiralling from their pyramid and landing on the floor. "I saw you ... *I – saw – you!* I passed you on the way home; bad traffic; had to take side roads. Had to detour near Cedarwood – past The Duck and Bull ... Saw *her* and you canoodling on the pavement ..."

"Canoodling? God, Mari … what are you talking about? It was nothing of the sort!" He began to fill the kettle.

"I saw you … no good denying it. She was touching your face. All very cosy, I'm sure."

"Mari …"

"Don't *Mari* me. I told you she wasn't to be trusted and now I know I was right."

"Believe me, I haven't done anything …" He calmly took a mug from out of the cupboard and a tea-bag from the container on the shelf.

"You let her touch you like that. That's more than nothing. More than just friendly."

"I had something in my eye."

"Bullshit." Now she had started, she wasn't going to stop.

"Honestly."

"*That* is a flirty line, and you know it."

"But I did. It was a fly or something."

"You should have blown your nose hard."

"She offered to have a look." The kettle steamed and clicked off and Johnny began pouring the water into the mug.

"Some chance of seeing a fly under a streetlamp! Which means she fancies you."

"Okay, perhaps she does like me … but I swear … honestly … there's nothing more to it." He stopped pouring the kettle and turned to look at her. "Mari, I wouldn't."

"You admit she's been coming on to you?"

"Well … maybe …"

"Absolute cow!" The cards continued to fall; clubs and spades, diamonds and hearts, Kings and Queens and aces, falling, falling, falling …

"I told you months ago that you should be careful. But you always dismissed it as nonsense. My paranoia. Why didn't you listen to me?"

"Because there was nothing for you to worry about."

"How can you say that? Of course I'm going to worry if someone as gorgeous as her starts flirting."

"She means nothing to me."

"And what about what you might mean to her? You're leading her on …"

"Mari … What can I do? I work with her. I'll stop seeing her outside school, if that's what you want."

"Too right you will."

"She's not a bad person – she's confused."

"I've been suspicious of her intentions for months, and you kept saying I was being unreasonable. What are you saying now?"

"Okay … okay …" Johnny threw up his hands. "You're right. I'm wrong. I should have been more careful."

Marianne looked at him hard, trying to see under any veneer of pretence. Words fell over themselves in her head and she was unable to speak. She opened her mouth and then closed it; shrugged then turned away, aware of all her resolve now being in ruins, that it was too late to backtrack now and that she would have to start rebuilding all over again.

A week later and following several more heated discussions about Charmaine's real intentions, the cold war had set in once again in Beechview Close. Marianne phoned her friend Taryn.

"Well, he denied everything at first. Said I'd no evidence … Evidence! This isn't exactly Agatha Christie!

"Eventually he did admit that he'd noticed she was coming on to him, but he said that he hadn't thought anything of it because of some bloke she has – I mean!! That's men for you. She was touching his face, for God's sake! He said he had a fly in his eye. Well maybe he did, but she didn't have to be so all-over him. Dammit, how obvious do you have to get? Would he have noticed if she'd tried to get into his pants? Hmph!"

"Johnny is a babe-magnet," said Taryn in her deep and sexy voice.

"That's no excuse," said Marianne. "Anyway, I went into a mood because I knew I was right and that at last he'd realised. I only intended to be cross for a couple of days, but now he's gone back into booze-mode, I've undone all the good of the past few weeks and I'm afraid I may have lost him again."

Taryn told Marianne to get back to her new strategy. That if she'd done it before, she could do it again. That there was no such thing as a quick fix to relationship issues. A new way of being takes time, she said; well-practised patterns are etched as deep as sheep-trails in the bracken and it is never easy keeping off the well-trodden paths. Only when the new ways are familiar – when they have made a visible mark on the land – only then is it safe to say that a change is complete. "Remember Edward Harvey," added Taryn. "Get back to your distraction."

Marianne told Taryn that she should have been a psychologist and they arranged to see each other soon for an update.

26

The Certain Age

Who are we, the people of a certain age, the forty-fives to fifties? The forgotten age, too old to feel appropriate in mini skirts, too young for Saga holidays, but not long now!

Marianne was in Bromley, ostensibly to buy a bathroom carpet, but she had other things on her mind when she walked through the glass double doors of the bustling store and headed for the escalator to the basement.

Dear Edward

We people of a certain age are misplaced in a world of 'whatever, innit, yeah-right, and sooo-everything'. We reflect on what was, worry about what will be and hide our heads in fear under the feathery pillow of what is. We people of a certain age, whose chemical balance is on the gentle downward gradient, glance across the hairpin bend of life since adolescence, remembering just a little way up the hill when last we were full of wild emotion and feelings and doubts and … oh so much that I cannot bear to say. The nostalgia for that time is laced with rosy streaks, recalling the excitement and forgetting the fears. The parties when I was an innocent fledgling … Watching all the goings-on … an interested observer… curious, fearful …

Hand-in-hand, they went up the stairs to the darkened room with pink-glowing lights and seductive, liquid melodies of Nights in White Satin *booming from the stereo … And couples on the floor among the cushions, awakening passions, perhaps for the first time … I used to think, when would it be me?*

It was a time of hope for better things to come and a time to wonder about what life would hold.

I never thought too hard about what job I would do, or who I might marry. I drifted along with no long-term plan, making decisions as situations presented themselves. After university there were some hollow times of what seemed like endless searching for the so-called right person. It was a time of failed relationships, lone partying, hoping for that magic link, those eyes across a crowded room. But they were never there and the music seemed to play in mournful minor keys. I remember feeling cold, empty and lonely and not worthy of the life that other people had.

I dreamed that one day it would all be right, that the dark legacy of Brocklebank would be a thing of the past. When Johnny and I met again quite by chance, bells rang and the sun came out for him as well as me. Then I found the right job and the joys of motherhood with Holly. But that was long ago, when England's summers were full of butterflies and daisies under a clear blue sky and Johnny and I were so full of passion for each other that the hurts and pains of childhood seemed permanently buried. They didn't count any more – or so I thought. How was I to know that the effects of the bullying would stay just under the surface, just out of reach until the Certain Age, until Charmaine? Now the summers seem fickle and the passion has died. Where has the joy gone, Edward, the joy of life with him?

Sometimes I see it still on the other side of a wispy curtain and it is so clear that I think I could touch it. But when I reach out, it skips from my grasp; tantalisingly close; laughing at me just like they did all those years ago. Barnaby Sproat and Pete Glanville … mocking, gloating … Who do you think you are, Marianne, to be loved to madness now you are a Certain Age? You're on the slide, girl, on the slide to invisibility and then oblivion.

Oh Edward, I hope this is just a blip; that I can soon recapture what I grasped when I first found you again …

Marianne was in the carpet section of the store now, idly

running her hand over the samples in one of the books. She wrinkled her nose at a particularly hideous mustard-coloured one and wondered why anyone would want such a shade in their house. A man with designer stubble and stiffly gelled hair, who looked far too young to have any useful knowledge about carpets, started approaching her with that hopeful look of a sale in prospect dancing round his manufactured smile.

Wouldn't want to run my fingers through that hair, she thought, smiling back all the same. *Wonder what he knows about the merits of shag pile or rubber backing?*

Later that night, Marianne wrote in her journal:

What will Johnny and I be like thirty years from now? Perhaps I am scribbling my memoires, with the telly on in the background, and he's still down at the pub drinking beer in a corner with the same old mates and the same old patter. He has less hair now and sports a cap when he goes outside, and his clothes have to be secretly removed from the chair (or the floor!) for washing or he'd wear the same ones every day and never notice. There's the hint of a wheeze when he limps up the stairs and that rasping cough and those rheumy eyes ... His face is distinctly purple now, especially in the evenings, and I too have slipped through that curtain between young and old. When I look in the mirror, I see a stranger staring back.

Ohmygod! No wonder we feel a sense of madness at this time. Systems that identified me as woman are closing down. I am falling apart. The child within me shouts, help me, for I am frightened of what's to come, but I cannot say this out loud because I am a grown-up now, setting an example to those who will follow. It is not for me to scare them, they will find out soon enough when the rollercoaster bob-sleigh run begins.

So really I deserve to be unhinged until I get used to it all and find another dream. Perhaps we people of a certain age need to grieve for the youth that we see fading. Perhaps grieving is necessary and good; a way to come to terms as we drift ever further from the familiar cycles and patterns that have been part of our life for so long.

The child within wants comforting arms and reassurance and someone to say it will be all right in the end. But it won't be all right, will it? One by one all those I care about will leave this earth until I leave too.

I know I should tell you, Johnny, about these things in my head. But I'm scared that you will run …

Dear Edward,

The word Pension looms, no longer a distant word only for other people; an alien race who were never young. Once the word Pension meant stick, bus pass and tight grey perm; a basket-woven shopping trolley terrorising the ankles of other pavement dwellers; sensible shoes with flat heels and a dull green mac with a plastic rain hood. Squeaking, creaking, squinting round the supermarket looking for something pre-packaged and effortless to consume in front of Coronation Street with the pre-requisite tabby cat purring by the fireside.

Please don't let Pension mean that now.

If fifty is the new thirty, then sixty must be the new forty. Life beginning time! Not time for the P word.

What brought this on Edward? A visit to college by a woman of a certain age from Teachers' Pensions in Darlington, that's what. I only went to listen because I thought I should be prepared and try to understand the complexities of it all before it becomes imminent and necessary. Finance is a foreign language to me.

Pension!!! Arggh! Ohmygod! I felt suddenly old … counting the years … not long now. Ohmygod!

Early Retirement! Even less long till that could be an option. Early retirement, I mean me, Marianne Hayward … Retired pensioner with bus pass and cat.

All kinds of things to consider that once seemed so far away …

"How long do you expect to survive?" said the woman from

Darlington with a Geordie lilt and a friendly smile, trying hard to make palatable such unpleasant thoughts. This, she said, was a question you must consider when contemplating whether you can afford to exist on a reduced pension.

How long indeed. I have been a low-fat, high-fibre woman for a long time now. But what of the student years of eating chips and takeaway kebabs? What about the stresses of being a teacher?

To: Edward Harvey
From: Marianne Hayward
Date: 27th February 2002, 20.20
Subject: The Certain Age

Hi Edward,
I think I am having a midlife crisis (or perhaps 'crisette' would be more appropriate!) Precipitated by attending a talk after work about pensions! Suddenly there seems so little time left and so much to do – except work gets in the way of doing it. What about my book? When am I going to find the time to write it?
I cannot believe we are so old and that it is nearly thirty-four years since we were at school together. The future looks predictable and bleak. Did you always know what you wanted to do? Did you have a plan to follow? Have been spending more than the usual amount of time contemplating the Meaning of Life. Is this what happens at a Certain Age?
Best wishes,
Marianne

Write to me soon Edward. Please write to me soon. Don't let me down now Edward, I need rebalancing ...

To: Marianne Hayward
From: Edward Harvey
Date: 28th February 2002, 22.43
Subject: Re: The Certain Age

Hi Marianne,

Do you psychologists do mind-reading too?!

Last night I was writing a reference for a student and I envied what they were going to; the fact that they were starting out. Wanted to play the piano, but was never any good. Didn't discover archaeology until the back end of school – thanks to our History teacher – Grimes – who responded to my question about Silbury Hill by lending me a book. After that I was hooked.

Had a plan of a sort, but the future map is clearer now and it scares the hell out of me. Following the paths of all University Lecturers, churning out the same old guff with increasing cynicism until I retire – or die. More of the same until the leaving do, the presents, the 'wasn't he wonderful' (I don't mean that I think I am, but it's what they say at these do's about everyone!) And then what? For me, most of the dreams have been fulfilled. I've done what I set out to do. Lucky, I guess. But secretly there was the hope of making a discovery of such significance that it would never be forgotten. Unless I can manage to come up with something truly memorable, it doesn't feel like it's enough to be doing the same for the next fifteen years. I need a break, a new challenge …

You must write your book!

Must dash,

Best wishes,

Edward.

Hm, thought Marianne. Not like Edward to write so much. Could this be yet another man of a certain age with an MLC coming on? There would certainly be plenty to talk about when they met … *Please let it be soon!*

"Mari … Mari!" Johnny came in late again, slammed the door, tripped on the mat and searched the kitchen for easily consumable leftovers.

She closed down the computer, turned off the light and hovered at the top of the stairs.

"Mari! Are you still up? Are you awake? For conversation, perhaps? A little chat?"

She heard him slurring his words as he rifled through the fridge. The tone was sarcastic; back in destructive mode of pub and drink and criticism. All this since she saw Charmaine touch his face; all this since she forgot her resolve and exploded.

But she quickly remembered what she must do. She must not react. Confront the negative with a positive.

So she did.

"Hi-ya, Johnny, I'm coming down. Would you like a sandwich? There's ham or turkey? I'll make it for you if you like."

Now if Johnny wanted an argument, he was arguing with himself while she spread Flora on the bread, a benign expression on her face, thinking of how she could empathise with Edward when she wrote back.

Then she dreamed of him again, a young teenage Edward, playing the piano with the virtuosity of a concert pianist. She gazed at him, entranced by the beauty of the music and the speed with which his fingers slid across the keys. She offered him a large white bucket of what looked like popcorn pieces. These he fed into the piano. He said he was playing Chopin, but she knew it wasn't.

To: Edward Harvey
From: Marianne Hayward
Date: 2nd March 2002, 21.30
Subject: Re: The Certain Age

Hi Edward,
I am sure you could do almost anything you wanted!
Marianne

Not much empathy there. But he clearly needed reassurance.

To: Marianne Hayward
From: Edward Harvey
Date: 2nd March 2002, 22.14
Subject: Re: The Certain Age

Hi Marianne,
Never that easy. Just when I am set to break away,
something interesting happens in the archaeological
world and I carry on …
Have been asked to go to St. Agnes, Isles of Scilly at
end of summer on first major excavation there since
1980s … Do I want my holiday to be one of so much
work?
Best wishes,
Edward

To: Edward Harvey
From: Marianne Hayward
Date: 4th March 2002, 20.12
Subject: Re: The Certain Age

Hi Edward,

Lucky you! Doesn't sound much like work to me! Perhaps this could be your new challenge? A bit of grubbing about in the earth with a trowel and a paintbrush might refuel your enthusiasm! I love Scilly! We went to St. Agnes in the summer of 2000 and desperately want to go back. Those rock formations! Agapanthus everywhere! Requires much advanced planning though! Have you been before? Where will you stay? We were at The Parsonage near the lighthouse …

Surely the perfect place to be inspired …

Marianne

To: Marianne Hayward
From: Edward Harvey
Date: 4th March 2002, 21.54
Subject: Re: The Certain Age

Felicity would prefer me to stay at home and decorate – as I had apparently promised.

Scilly looks ever-more inviting! If I go we will be on campsite at Troytown Farm!

Must dash – paper to write before tomorrow.

Ted

Busy again, thought Marianne. Four teenagers at home, yet a prolific producer of written material. Sounded like a paradox. One teenager to ferry around had been difficult enough and only now was Marianne finding time to write. Slowly her journal, with its soft, velvety plum cover, was beginning to accumulate her thoughts and musings as she negotiated this most difficult stage of her life. These would be the building blocks for the book that she would write; a book about meeting Edward, perhaps …

Not invisible today! The young lad on the ham counter in the supermarket, who barely made eye contact when I saw him on the fish counter a month ago, was positively helpful and even went voluntarily to the storeroom and fetched a new ham in shrink-wrapped polythene coat. The difference? Last month I was encased in a shapeless duvet-style padded jacket and he was very reluctant to go and look for some frozen, shell-on, headless tiger prawns. But I persisted; made it seem important, and eventually he shrugged and said he could check the back. Returned with a box absolutely bursting with them. Tiger prawns like tabby-cats paws … I bet he knew they were there all the time. Lazy sod. Service isn't what it used to be. (Mother again!)

But today in this rare spring sunshine, and vastly over-heated as I often am in the early morning, I was wearing a strappy summer dress, lipstick and sunglasses. Ha! The power of bare shoulders!

It is aggravating that one has to play sexy to be noticed. Perhaps one always did. Maybe a padded duvet doesn't turn heads even when you are twenty-one? Trouble is: appropriateness. The certain age brings up the question of whether it is right and proper to flounce around in girly clothes. The young man on the ham counter obviously thinks so! Nigella Lawson says you can't be too obvious to a man and she should know!

When Johnny and I were in the New Forest two summers ago, the ginger-haired man on the fish counter in a supermarket in Lymington was full of flirtatious charm and attentiveness and made me feel like a teenager again. They're not like that in London …

I make a plea to all young men on fish or ham counters: please notice those of us of a certain age, because one day it will be you.

27

Biobabble

For the next two weeks, Marianne focused on regaining her composure. She knew deep down that since her re-acquaintance with Edward, there was a permanent shift in the way she felt about the past, but she had to start believing it at a conscious level, and act on it.

Those bastard bullies, she thought, *where are they now?* And she imagined their heads shrunken to the size of hockey balls, spaced along the white line of the semi-circle surrounding the goal mouth on the big games pitch at Brocklebank. There they sat, round and shiny – Pete Glanville, Jeremy Lanigan and Barnaby Sproat – and there she stood, now ten years old again in her blue aertex shirt, navy divided skirt and red hockey socks.

Probably pillars of society now with never a thought of their past behaviour. Doting parents with tough-guy kids; like father, like son. 'He thumped you, did he, and you thumped him back? That's my boy! Gotta stand up for yourself in a cut-throat world.' But she no longer cared who or what they were; *she no longer cared.* With stick in hand, she thwacked the shrunken heads one by one into the back of the goal and heard them thud and crack against the wood. It was a distinctly pleasurable sensation and she wondered if she might be developing a taste for violence in her mature years. Standing in the background cheering her on were her good friends Abi and Susannah, and somewhere on the sidelines looking puzzled by the fuss, was the young Edward Harvey.

To: Edward Harvey
From: Marianne Hayward
Date: 17th March 2002, 21.05
Subject: The Uses of Men

Hi Edward,

I have just been listening to Radio 4 about the perilous state of the Y chromosome. It is now so short and carries so few genes that all men could be infertile in 125 years time. Indeed, presumably if the Y chromosome disappears altogether, there won't be any men, so the infertility issue will never arise. The scientists speculate that babies will be created using cloning techniques, but with eggs from two female parents. I wonder if they will eventually grow them outside the body … In metallic oval 'foetalpods' perhaps?

One of our college lecturers used to say that humans are nothing more than a 60p bag of chemicals and a rain-butt of water. One day, will we be able to synthesise a baby from a few bottles in the chemistry lab? This got me thinking that if men weren't needed to create babies, would they be missed? (Present company excepted!!)

I used to work with someone who Johnny said was the scariest woman he had ever met. She said that the three uses of men were: getting the tops off (jars, etc.); buying the wine and sex, or as she put it, 'a bit of the other'.

Presumably if there were no men, then natural selection would eventually favour stronger women, so that would solve the 'tops off' problem. But would selection also favour mathematicians and the spatially aware? Who would put the flat packs together if there were no men?

And if men weren't needed for procreation, would the
sex-drive eventually be selected out of the population,
or would there still be a case for men for purely
recreational purposes?
Best wishes,
Marianne

She clicked on *Send*, then started to panic. Did this count as a
taboo topic for discussion?

*No, it's science. Nothing more than an intellectual debate. A floating
of views.*

She needn't have worried.

To: Marianne Hayward
From: Edward Harvey
Date: 18th March 2002, 18.50
Subject: Re: The Uses of Men

Hi Marianne,
Well thank you for that cheering news!
Rachel says that if there were no men, the instructions
for flat packs would make sense, so there wouldn't be a
problem!
I think we're indispensable, but am biased!
Edward

To: Edward Harvey
From: Marianne Hayward
Date: 18th March 2002, 21.47
Subject: Survival of the Unfit

Hi Edward,
Good for Rachel!

Continuing this thought … If selection favours stronger women in the future, how will this fit in with the current medical advances allowing people with all kinds of afflictions to survive to breeding age? This cannot be good for the human condition.
Marianne

To: Marianne Hayward
From: Edward Harvey
Date: 19th March 2002, 22.31
Subject: Re: Survival of the Unfit

Hi Marianne,
Gene therapy will ultimately rectify the faults, so the problems of the future will never arise!
Edward

"Men are strange creatures," said Taryn to Marianne, sitting on a wooden seat in a local park overlooking the ornamental lake. "I have given them up for Lent – but it's a bit of a cheat 'cos it's no great loss. I feel positively liberated! Marc 'with-a-c' was a bastard, but he played a damned good game of Scrabble. That woman Brenda-what's-her-face has done me a great favour. If it hadn't been her, it would've been someone else further down the line. Best to find out now before it gets toooo deep. If you ask me, email is the best distance to keep them; meeting is bound to be a disappointment. Ooh look, is that a grebe? I love grebes."

Taryn Danielli, quintessentially gamine and with her spiky dark hair and wild brown eyes, had been Marianne's best friend for all their adult life. They had met first on the teacher training PGCE at the Institute of Education, and been workmates from the very beginning of their respective careers, both teaching in the same school. Taryn had seen Marianne fall in love with Johnny and shared her joys at having Holly and the pain of not being able to have another child. She was always there to lend an extra pair of hands, but had drawn the line at babysitting. "I don't do babysitting," she had said firmly. "Course I'd help out in a crisis, but I don't want any of this 'let's ask Taryn, she's on her own this weekend ...'"

"Johnny didn't say that!" Marianne had said.

"Maybe he didn't, but people do, do they not? They've said it to my face! Don't want to be put upon. Babysitting is a reciprocal activity, or for teenagers who need a bit of extra cash. I probably won't ever do *kids*, even if I do *husband*."

That was eighteen years ago and now Holly had flown and Taryn remained resolutely unmarried and childless. How time marches on, stealthily and with ever-quickening pace as the years go by. But Taryn had an ageless quality about her and sometimes Marianne forgot how old she was.

Taryn knew all there was to know about the foibles of men and took great delight at extolling their weaknesses whenever she met up with her married friends.

"There's no sub-text with Edward." Marianne said this somewhat wistfully, feeling the throb of the season changing as the blossoms appeared and the buds formed on the trees. A second grebe swam from behind one of the small islands and joined the first one.

"You don't know that. Much can be hidden in the written word. We self-censor emails to a far greater extent than in real conversation."

"I do know ... He seems to be a very happy bunny – at least as far as his family life is concerned – and even if he wasn't, he isn't that kind of guy. Believe me; I have antennae for anything that smacks of the untoward."

"Then he is a rare one indeed," said Taryn.

"That's why I'd hate to lose him. It's so difficult getting the balance right between mailing too much and not mailing enough. It would be so easy to stop and then never start again. We haven't yet been through enough history for a significant gap not to matter. I want to tell him things so he knows what I'm like – but I don't want to overdo it or scare him."

"He wouldn't keep replying if he didn't want to."

"Maybe he's just being polite. Ex-public school … trained in good manners …"

"You can be polite without replying as often as he does."

"Once we've met, I'm sure it will be easier, but for now … oh it's so difficult to know what to do for the best. In time I think we could be friends. Real friends … And it is useful having a male friend …"

"Why don't you stop writing and see if he mails you?"

"But what if he didn't?"

"Well you'd know you weren't that important."

"But would I know that? Men are bad at initiating emails. Most of the ones I know wait for me to mail them first. They're much swifter than most women when it comes to replying, though! In any case, I'm sure I'm not particularly important to him."

On the island in the middle of the lake, herons were courting and making a noise like the rattles spun by football fans. The grebes with their Taryn hairdos came a little closer.

Taryn and Marianne watched with the comfortable silence of friends that have known each other for a very long time.

It was some minutes before Marianne spoke again. "Taryn," she said. "As you've never been serious about wanting kids, do you think this means you use different criteria for choosing men?"

"If you mean do I prioritise them on how they rate on the bonk-scale, then probably, yes. Why do you ask?"

"I was reading that testosterone affects the facial features. Masculine looking men have more testosterone. More testosterone makes men more restless and less likely to stick around to look after the children – 'cos they have more other-women options."

"That figures."

"When women are looking for a mate to settle with, the theory goes that they are likely to select a man with more feminine features because they have less testosterone and are less likely to stray."

The grebes came close to the bank, casting their beady eyes over the two women in the hope that food was forthcoming.

"Marc-with-a-c is certainly masculine – square jaw … chiseled … and he strayed. Had a big dick too, if that's relevant!" said Taryn.

Marianne laughed. "By this reasoning, only Barbie dolls and the super beautiful can risk settling down with Mr Gorgeous … But what happens when she reaches a certain age and starts falling apart like us?" She threw broken crust for the grebes.

"Trade in time!" said Taryn.

"God, life's so unfair."

"But now there's always cosmetic surgery."

"Would you ever consider it? Money no object …"

"Thought about adding to the boob department once. D'you remember me saying?" said Taryn. "But then I met Alec – or was it Don? – who said that all most men want is a handful and a little bit more, so I decided it wasn't worth the effort – or the cost, and the bother of finding a whole load of new bras!"

"But now everyone seems to be doing it …"

"Only in the media," said Taryn.

"Everything that starts with the media, ends with the

woman next door. Where does that leave those who are too scared or who can't afford it? An under-class in the looks department …"

"But that's true already."

"Yeah, but at least there was a levelling of the playing field when past a certain age. Some of those sultry maidens from the sixties are looking quite haggard now. Tough, I say."

"There'll be a backlash one of these days," said Taryn. "Scare stories; long term effects. Look at what tanning does for you eventually? Now it's okay to be pale. I really can't understand the lengths some women go to."

"It's biologically driven … Beauty equals reproductive fitness, so evolution says, and men are wired to chase the best they can. No point in wasting sperm on someone who's past it."

"But if Ms Averagely Hideous spends a few grand turning her enormous honk into a veritable button, won't the guys fear the kids they produce may be like tapirs and keep well clear?" Taryn threw another piece of crust into the water and it was immediately besieged by Canada geese.

"Assuming they know about the nose-job."

"Would they see the woman as sex partner, then, but not marriage material?"

"Didn't stop Cilla's Bobby."

"And what if someone of fifty-five has face lift, boobs done and liposuction …" Taryn made a slurping noise. "Imagine that! Ends up looking like a startled thirty-year-old … does Mr Gorgeous's primitive brain take over and does he want to shag the pants off her, or … does he rationalise that she's not likely to be capable of bringing forth any sprogs?"

"But rationally he probably doesn't want any more kids, so it shouldn't matter that she's fifty-five."

"So why does it matter that she's had plastic-fantastic?"

"Primitive brain responds to beauty."

"Primitive brain linked to dick! Ah-ha, I see!"

"And women, traditionally," said Marianne, "are much more concerned with bread-on-table matters, so they will settle for an ageing, bloated, lump of a guy provided he's generous with the cash handouts."

"Oh look!" said Taryn. "The grebes are doing their weed dance."

Marianne looked, and across the lake the grebes were rising out of the water facing each other with beaks full of weeds, heads shaking this way and that, feet paddling furiously just under the surface.

"And how's Johnny?" continued Taryn. "Has he stopped seeing the Cow-Charmaine?"

"I think so … He says so … But I'm still cross with him …"

"Of course! It's important that you are. Be cross until July."

"Why July?"

"Summer holidays! Don't want to spoil them!"

"Holly's bringing Dylan to stay next week …"

"The wonderful Dylan! If he hasn't got a sculpted face, you'd better buy a hat!"

And so the conversation went on, flitting from this subject to that; rarely finishing one line of thought before another one interceded. This is why women needed women friends and no amount of conversations with Edwards or Johnnys, (or Patricks or Richards or Winstons or Kurts), could ever take the place of the convivial girly chat with all its unspoken understanding of the female condition. That was the crux of the matter. Women knew without having to say. At best all most men could do was to try to understand.

28

Dylan

"This is Dylan," said Holly beaming lovingly at the tall, angular, young man on the front doorstep of the house in Beechview Close.

Marianne gave Holly a big hug and held out her hand to Dylan, noticing his wild brown hair and bohemian style, not unlike Johnny as a teenager. He had big dark bush-baby eyes. Honest, vulnerable eyes that said: 'I am an open book waiting to be read.' He would have turned her head when she was at college.

"We've put you in Holly's room," she said, adding hastily, "but Holly won't be there."

Dylan's flicker of surprised joy quickly vanished and he looked embarrassed. "Hi-ya. Good to meet you, Holly has told me lots about home."

"Where will I be?" asked Holly as they stepped into the hall. They had already had the conversation about the appropriateness of separate rooms, Marianne saying that it would be best not to upset Johnny.

"In the spare room with the computer and the junk," said Marianne.

"I wouldn't've minded," said Dylan. "I'll sleep anywhere. You should see my room at home."

There was a touch of the public school about his accent and Marianne was cross with herself for being pleasantly surprised. There she was being judgmental again when she swore she wouldn't be. She ushered them into the living room where

Johnny was standing waiting to greet his precious daughter and give this 'friend of hers' as he kept saying, with emphasis on the *friend,* the once over. He was ready to be critical, but so far as first impressions went, Dylan had done nothing wrong and seemed to have impeccable manners.

Just the kind of young man my parents wanted me to bring home, thought Marianne, *once they got past the hair and the clothes, that is.* She remembered that apart from Nick, they were always hyper-critical and always disappointed. Worst was the time when she was dating a meteorologist called Max who was ten years her senior and so worldly-wise by comparison that he would never pass the test. They grilled him for a good two hours after their first supper, assessing his intentions and deducing that he was bound to be a bad influence. After he had gone, they pulled him apart piece by piece, calling him too full of himself and even criticizing the way he was dressed. After Max she gave up bringing boyfriends home until she and Johnny got together.

Marianne had been determined not to be negative, no matter what Dylan was like, but she need not have worried because almost immediately they were at ease and she began counting chickens and grand-children. Soon Johnny and Dylan were drinking beer and talking about the merits of real ale. Seeing Holly glowing beside him and noting his attentiveness towards her gave her a warm feeling that she hadn't experienced with any of the previous boyfriends that had crossed the threshold of Beechview Close.

The *'what are you going to do with your life?'* question hovered on her lips, but she kept biting it back and eventually Dylan offered the information that he was hoping to do a PhD and then eventually become a barrister.

"Either that, or go round the world doing a bit of this and a bit of that," he added with a chuckle and a disarming smile. "Quite like the idea of keeping the student-thing going for as long as poss. Thought about taking a gap year after school – but worried that getting back into study after might be tricky … And the parents weren't too keen on some of my suggestions… South America … Said they'd worry … A friend of theirs, who was kipping out in the rain forest, had his arm eaten by a snake … Slipped out from under the mosquito net while he was asleep, and when he woke up, there was this snake looking right into his eyes with its jaws around his arm and up to his shoulder."

"No way," said Holly.

"God's honest truth," said Dylan. "Course they couldn't pull it off like a sleeve because the teeth are angled backwards …"

"Gross!" said Holly.

Johnny and Marianne were listening with rapt attention.

"And it had begun to digest the arm by the time—"

"Too much information," interrupted Holly.

"And how did they get it off?" asked Johnny.

"I wouldn't like to speculate," said Dylan, grinning. "But the guy was okay in the end."

Marianne wanted to ask what his parents did, but she knew that this was yet another question that smacked of assessment and judgement. She had hated it when her parents asked. It shouldn't matter these days.

"You could forget South America but still do the gap thing with me, after we've graduated," said Holly, adding swiftly, "if we just happen still to be together after all that time."

Dylan smiled at her and squeezed her hand reassuringly.

"Young love," said Johnny later, when they were getting ready for bed. "Do you remember feeling like that? All fresh and new and hopeful?"

"Oh yes."

"It seems a long time ago – suddenly."

"Does it?" Marianne was acutely aware that this was one of those critical points in a conversation where a misplaced word could have major consequences.

"I still feel like that about you Mari. We are okay, aren't we?"

"What's brought this on?"

"Seeing them setting out at the beginning of it all. I felt old."

"You are Peter Pan. No need to feel old."

Johnny climbed under the duvet, watching Marianne undressing. "I've stopped seeing Charmaine outside of work. Keeping things more businesslike ... You were right ... She was getting too involved."

Marianne held her breath, wondering if this was going to be the apology she had long been waiting.

"I know I've said things I shouldn't ... I know I've upset you sometimes these past few months ... but I've always told you I loved you. Never stopped."

Here she could have made peace and said she loved him back, but the hormonal undulations dimmed her rationality and made her provocative. She could feel her heart beating.

"If you really loved me, you wouldn't have said such hurtful things. Wouldn't have made such a fuss of Charmaine and made me feel I was getting past it."

"You know I didn't mean it. It was just once or twice ... I'd been drinking ..."

"It only takes one bad comment ... You only remember the bad things." She turned her back on him and combed her hair slowly, pausing over a tangle, feeling the silky strands run through her fingers.

This was his opportunity – the perfect opportunity – to say sorry. But he didn't. Instead he said: "But you still love me don't you?"

Marianne was privately annoyed and unforgiving still. They could have a row about it. She could take the discussion forward, repeating that she felt hurt and making him feel guilty. But that would have been like she was extracting an apology and it would have meant little. She wanted him to apologise with sincerity and not because he thought there was no choice. Once she would have replied without hesitation that she loved him. This time she said: "What is love? I don't know any more. It's been a difficult year. You haven't been easy to live with. You're much nicer when you don't drink too much."

"It isn't the booze."

"You just said it was."

"The booze is a consequence, not a perpetrator."

Marianne was baffled. She put down her comb and turned to get into bed. "A consequence of what?"

"You don't look at me like you used to do … Like you did until just a few months ago."

"So now you're saying it's my fault?"

"I don't know when it started – or how. You don't act as if you love me any more."

Marianne was not in the mood to pacify. "It wasn't easy to feel love with Charmaine floating about in the background. I'm sure you don't want me to fake it. I've never faked anything with you!"

When Holly was alone with her mother in the kitchen next morning, Marianne sought to reassure her that Dylan met with their approval.

"He's perfectly lovely," said Marianne, creating a pile of wholemeal toast. She was about to add that both she and Johnny would have preferred to hear that he had firm career options in mind rather than swanning around doing research or travelling, but she stopped the words escaping just in time. This was her mother again, whispering in her brain. Research or travelling might have been things she would have done herself if she'd been given some encouragement. In any case, it was only his second year in college. Time enough for the future to sort itself out.

"He *is* lovely, isn't he!" said Holly. "Not a malicious bone in his body and sooo mature. We talk for hours about everything. I'm sooo lucky."

"You deserve someone nice," said Marianne. "He's lucky too."

"He's really kind. I mean *really* kind. I've never met a guy who's so thoughtful. And it's genuine – not just put on to impress. He's kind to everybody."

"Kindness is an often underrated quality," said Marianne.

"Dad's kind," said Holly, exploratively, as if waiting for a contradiction from her mother. "Or he was until this last year or so … I don't like to see him upsetting you."

"We're fine. Don't worry about us."

"I heard you arguing again …"

"Not arguing. Just discussing. It takes time to put the train back on the track, but we will."

Holly narrowed her eyes and looked closely at her mother; wanting to believe.

While they chatted Holly sat down at the little pine table in the corner and began working through the toast pile. "And what about Harry Potter? Are you still writing to him?"

Marianne felt the rush of heat rising from her knees and she went to water her pots of herbs on the window sill. "Now and then."

"But you haven't met yet?"

"No."

"I wonder when you do if he will be like you think he is."

"I doubt that anyone would be exactly as expected after thirty-odd years and a few emails."

"Does Dad mind?"

"What is there to mind? It's not as if he was ever a boyfriend."

Holly shrugged.

Then Dylan came in with the typical awkward gait of a nineteen-year-old with seemingly too many uncontrollable limbs, and hair that flopped disconcertingly over one eye and shoulders that seemed too wide to fit through the door frames.

"Hi-ya," he said, grinning and taking a seat by Holly and helping himself to a piece of toast from her plate. He began to spread it liberally with strawberry jam. "Did you know, yeah, that pigeons used to work on the production line in some jam factory? They pecked the jars and could identify the sound made by a cracked jar. If the sound was wrong, they triggered a lever and the jar was ejected from the line."

"Who on earth told you that?" said Holly.

"One of our lecturers."

"It must've been a joke," said Holly.

"I think not," said Dylan earnestly. "Even if it was a joke, it is perfectly possible to train them."

"Indeed it is," said Marianne. "Learning theory …"

"Exactly," said Dylan. "Positive reinforcement!"

Holly pulled a face.

Marianne smiled. "What are you two planning, today?"

"Dylan wants to go on the London Eye. We might go by boat from Greenwich. Why don't you and Dad come too?"

"I'm sure you don't want us cramping your style."

Dylan interjected: "Please do come. It will give us a chance to chat some more."

This guy chats! thought Marianne. *A man who chats; such a rare thing,* and she said that they would love to come and went to find Johnny to persuade him.

The Thames sparkled and glinted, bejeweled with spring

sunlight and Marianne was glad they had decided to go out together. Spontaneity had been missing in recent years and it would do them good to break from predictable routines. They were in Greenwich and they walked past the majestic Cutty Sark in its dry dock, oozing history to such an extent that one could almost hear the calls and smell the sweat of the mariners who once climbed her masts and set the sails.

Dylan was impressed. "I've never seen her in real-life before. She's cool. Much better than on the telly behind those marathon runners."

"Why do men call boats *she*?" asked Marianne.

"Don't you approve?" said Dylan.

"It smacks of oppression," said Marianne.

Holly interjected: "Dylan, don't get Mum onto her favourite subject, please."

"I think it's a compliment to women," said Dylan, adding mischievously, "and didn't Holly tell me you once had a car called Jeremy?"

Marianne laughed.

On the pier waiting for the launch to Westminster they gathered with the tourists. Marianne and Holly left Johnny standing a few yards away with Dylan, gesturing towards the wharfs on the north bank and no doubt giving his own explanations about the history. She thought he looked rugged and handsome with his grey flecked hair blowing in the breeze. *Still got a cute bum too. Must tell him sometime soon when the dust settles.*

Then, without the warning that one might hope accompanying such a surprise, and with hair tumbling in a cascade of peroxide waves, who should be in the queue in front of them but Charmaine with an insipid looking man in tow. She had on a frilly skirt that was too short and the backs of her legs were orange with fake tan and dimpled with cellulite.

Marianne was instantly irritated and, taking a deep breath, stole the initiative before Charmaine noticed her.

"If it isn't Charmaine!" she said with a touch of iciness.

Charmaine swung round, nearly overbalancing on her spiky heels. The man beside her reached for her arm to steady her.

"Johnny – John's wife. Though I'm sure you remember …"

"Oh, hullo … Gosh …"

A waft of sickly alien perfume drifted under Marianne's nose. Perfume she'd desperately tried to detect on Johnny's shirts, or on Johnny himself, and the menopausal madness crackled in her brain and unleashed her tongue.

"Gosh, indeed …" Marianne smiled, sending mixed messages, hoping to confuse.

Charmaine looked as though she wanted to escape, eyes darting this way and that under designer-framed sunglasses, while the man she was with stared open-mouthed, as if he had walked into a film halfway through and was trying to catch the plot.

"So rude of me not to introduce myself," said Marianne, extending her hand to the man in question, surprised that he wasn't more hunky. "Marianne Hayward, amazingly still married to Johnny Ingleton, despite Charmaine's best efforts … I take it you are someone else's husband?"

"Mum!" hissed Holly from behind Marianne's shoulder where she had been skulking since the beginning of the conversation.

The man shook Marianne's hand in a reflex action, closed his mouth and gulped, then opened it again and made a strangulated noise. Charmaine chipped in: "Nice to see you again, but I think we should be—"

"And where exactly might you be going on such a beautiful day? Down to Westminster, same as us? There might be time for a little chat before the boat arrives, don't you think? I would really like to know why you were trying so hard to steal my husband."

Now it was Charmaine who stared, transfixed, uncertain. "I was only being a friend; trying to help," she said. "John said you were going through a bad patch."

Holly backed away awkwardly in the direction of Johnny and Dylan.

"Coming onto him? Going for drinks with him? That was help, was it? Telling him about your love-lorn plight? Making him feel sorry for you? Calling him *John*? Flattering his middle-aged ego with your glamour-puss style? All designed to rock our boat a little more."

"I don't know what to say," said Charmaine, flustered.

"Quite so," said Marianne. "It's just as well I am not the violent type."

The man whose name was still in question said, "I say, is this really necessary?"

Marianne exhaled and smoothed her skirt. Now she had started, she felt the weeks of accumulated vitriol backing up as if behind a sluice gate that was leaking spurts at the moment, but was in danger of collapsing and spewing forth all her anger. Should she let go completely? Should she have a raving rant at this woman who had wrecked her peace of mind from the moment she appeared in her kitchen all glossy and polished; from the time Johnny had become infatuated and thoughtless? Or should she stop now, enough said?

One or two other waiting passengers were looking over their shoulders, evidently listening, but trying not to stare. Dylan too now hovered in the background, bush-baby eyes unblinking. The pause was palpable. *Press the red button now,* thought Marianne. *Option one: slap the face!*

"You endangered a perfectly happy relationship. Should I be very British and silent and let you think no harm has been done? Your little-girl-lost act took in Johnny, but not me. You're good, I'll say that."

"I was confused," said Charmaine. "I didn't mean … Really … I'm not like you think … It was a mistake …"

Suddenly Johnny was at Marianne's side, giving her warning glances, steering her away down the pier towards the river, looking apologetically at Charmaine and the nameless man.

Marianne allowed herself to be steered, because she wasn't clear what to do or say next.

Holly reappeared. "Sooo embarrassing, Mum."

"Everything's under control," said Johnny.

"You should've let me finish," said Marianne, glaring over her shoulder at Charmaine who was walking back towards the Cutty Sark, evidently no longer intent on catching the same boat.

"Wicked," said Dylan, hands in the pockets of his jeans. "Nothing like this ever happens in Rustington!"

29

Psychobabble

'Give me a child till he is seven and I will give you the man'
Jesuit motto

In Beckenham the spring blossom burst forth with sumptuous
candy-floss colours and with Easter over, Marianne once again
turned her attention to Edward.

To: Edward Harvey
From: Marianne Hayward
Date: 17th April 2002, 21.11
Subject: A Question of Understanding

Hi Edward,
Holly has been and gone. She brought her new boyfriend
home. We both approve, which is a great relief as they're
clearly madly in love!
I have been puzzling over how men and women are able
to write books from the perspective of the opposite
sex. Many men write of us as remote, manipulative and
mysterious creatures, full of sexual allure, but without
heart. Men can only really know us if they listen beyond
what their wives, daughters and women friends are
saying. And are we women any better in knowing men?
We think we do, but too often we know without any
attempt to understand. If we understood, we wouldn't
try so hard to change them.

These are idle thoughts ...
Time to sleep.
Marianne

To: Marianne Hayward
From: Edward Harvey
Date: 17th April 2002, 21.57
Subject: Re: A Question of Understanding

Hi Marianne,
Daughters and boyfriends are an unsettling combination!
We are only just entering that arena with Rachel.
What do you mean 'listening beyond'?
Edward

To: Edward Harvey
From: Marianne Hayward
Date: 18th April 2002, 19.12
Subject: Re: A Question of Understanding

Hi Edward,
I mean don't take what is said at face value. It's not that
women mean to deceive. But they think men will be
frightened by the truth unless it is unravelled slowly. So
they say something that runs parallel to the truth and
expect to be asked further questions – as their women
friends would do. Women friends are always fishing, but
men accept what's said and move on to the next thing –
often football ...
So the confusion perpetuates ...
Marianne

To: Marianne Hayward
From: Edward Harvey
Date: 18th April 2002, 23.02
Subject: Re: A Question of Understanding

Dear Marianne,
Indeed!
So that's where I've been going wrong all these years!
Edward

Dear Marianne? This was a deviation from the norm. Was it a patronising 'Dear', an acknowledgement of friendship, or a slip of the keys?

She smiled. She suspected Edward would not be impressed by her feminist principles. She wondered if Felicity kept her thoughts under wraps to keep the peace. Or maybe she was the kind of woman who was happy with a cave man. Except she didn't think Edward was a cave man.

It seemed to Marianne that Edward didn't go wrong at all. But maybe he wasn't the New Man she had suspected. She would probe further.

To: Edward Harvey
From: Marianne Hayward
Date: 19th April 2002, 17.38
Subject: Metrosexual Man

Hi Edward,
Have you heard the term metrosexual? This is the man of the 21st Century, the next evolutionary step from the New Man. Metrosexual Man is in touch with his feminine side. He is androgynous and has high emotional intelligence. He continues to challenge

traditional male stereotypes.

Holly's Dylan seems to fit this description.

Best wishes,

Marianne

To: Marianne Hayward

From: Edward Harvey

Date: 20th April 2002, 22.28

Subject: Re: Metrosexual Man

Hi Marianne,

Metrosexual Man?!! Mere psychobabble! (Sorry, no insult intended …)

Will have to hope Felicity doesn't get to hear about this or there will be even more for me to try to live up to!

Am coming to London next Thursday to lecture to the Camden History Society. You're welcome to come if you're free!

Dashing …

Edward

"Shit!" said Marianne to the computer. "Typical, typical... Shit!"

She gazed at the email from Edward in near disbelief. She shook her head and sighed. Why oh why of all days did he have to pick that one to suggest meeting? She didn't even need to ask him whether the lecture was during the day or in the evening. Either way was impossible. She was teaching from nine to four and interviewing prospective students in the evening. She would finish, shattered, at about eight – no time to freshen up and go out again. In any case, when they did finally meet, she didn't want to be a complete wreck.

To: Edward Harvey
From: Marianne Hayward
Date: 22nd April 2002, 21.12
Subject: Re: Metrosexual Man

Hi Edward,
Alas I am teaching all day on Thursday followed by an
interview evening – otherwise it would have been lovely
to come and hear your lecture – (you didn't say what it
was on?) But there will be other opportunities I'm sure.
In haste …
Best wishes,
Marianne.

"Shit." She said again. "Dammit … dammit … dammit …"

"What's the matter with you?" Johnny appeared suddenly
in the doorway, his shirt splattered with water from doing the
washing up. He looked at her searchingly, a little sadly, brow
furrowed. Since the fracas on Greenwich pier and the
subsequent arguments, he had tried to talk to her about how
she was feeling, but she had remained silent and distant,
disinclined to say more than she already had.

"Are you coming down? Do you want tea?" said Johnny.

Marianne hastily clicked *Send later*. "Yes please," she said,
smiling, feeling all hot and hoping she wasn't blushing. In any
case, what was there to feel guilty about?

★

"Cyberaffairs …" said Marianne to her students, a couple of
days after the invitation from Edward. She paused expectantly,
hoping she was adopting the kind of tone David Attenborough

might use when creating anticipation before explaining the habits of some obscure animal living in the dim dark world of the ocean's floor. "What do you think we mean by cyberaffair?"

"Straying away from home online," said Jason.

"Love on the internet," said Stanley. Today, instead of the plaits, his hair was a springy bush of tight black curls and he was dressed from head to foot in lime green, standing out from the rest of the class and their monochrome sobriety.

"Yes," acknowledged Marianne, "although the 'love' word might not always be appropriate."

Stanley grinned and exchanged a significant look with one of the girls sitting across on the opposite arm of the horseshoe.

"According to Griffiths (1999), there are three types of cyberaffair. Firstly, meeting on the internet in order to engage in erotic dialogue for sexual arousal …" She paused, watching the class scribbling furiously. "This is called 'hotchatting' and in its extreme form, 'cybersex'."

"How does that go on?" asked Sean. "I just don't understand."

Cate chipped in, knowledgeable in matters of electronic communication and not afraid to share her thoughts with others. "Basically, isn't it like dirty talk but with someone you don't know, so you can tell them your deepest fantasies without being embarrassed, 'cos you can't see their reaction."

Marianne interjected: "That's the extreme form of a cyberaffair. Erotic dialogue …"

"Like interactive porn!" said Sharna, slapping her hands on the table.

"When I go into chat rooms," said Cate, I get messages – like, dirty ones – and it's not even like *what's your name?* Sometimes when I was younger, I would encourage it."

"When you get older, you realise how dangerous it can be," said Marianne.

"Not really," continued Cate. "My Mum's started doing it as well!"

At this some of the students clapped while others laughed or looked shocked at the revelation.

Ellen said, "I didn't think people took cybersex seriously. Me and my friend – when we were at school – we used to do it … crowd round the computer and take the piss out of people."

Marianne raised a cautioning eyebrow at Ellen's choice of language, but continued: "Branwyn, (1993) says, and I quote, 'compu-sex enthusiasts say it's the ultimate safe sex for the '90s, with no exchange of bodily fluids, no loud smoke filled clubs and no morning after.' But is it safe? We'll come to that in a moment …"

"I've actually seen a programme on television," said Jason. "Late night—"

"Channel 5!" interrupted Chantelle.

"Flicking through the channels …"

"Oh, yeah, people always say that!"

"It was cybersex," continued Jason, "but they was doing it more … I dunno, more physically. You had to put electrical pads in a certain place and then the person the other end can trigger a signal to stimulate that place."

Even Marianne was surprised by this revelation. "Are you sure the technology is possible?" she asked.

"Oh yeah," chorused three of the boys.

"I think all this cyberaffair stuff is really quite sad 'cos people can't get someone for real," said Sharna. "I just don't like it."

"But this, as I mentioned, is the extreme end of such relationships," said Marianne. "There are other possibilities that are perhaps slightly less controversial. Griffiths's second type is those liaisons that are more romantic and emotional than sexual and may or may not lead to offline meeting. Or, thirdly, people may first meet offline, but then conduct their relationship online – perhaps because of geographical distance."

Now and then she glanced down over the pages of her notes, checking the spelling of a name or the accuracy of a date. These she wrote on the whiteboard behind her and by the end of the session it would be covered with spidery scrawl denoting researchers and theories relevant to this very new area of psychology. Interactive whiteboard technology was only just beginning to enter the college and hadn't yet reached her department, something for which she was extremely thankful, not because she was afraid of using it, but because she knew its presence would make her feel she ought to be presenting high-tech lessons and she didn't see how she would find time to prepare them. PowerPoint was as far as she was inclined to go, and even that had its disadvantages with students frantically scribbling everything they could see instead of listening to her and processing the information.

Today the students were squinting as the sunlight burned through the windows. She pulled a blind and threw off her cardigan.

Marianne continued: "The rules for such encounters are not yet properly established. The boundaries are fuzzy. No one knows for certain what's acceptable and what's not. What exactly is the difference between an 'emotional affair' and an innocent friendship? Bearing in mind that any friendship is sometimes going to venture into discussing personal matters."

"An affair is basically, yeah, cheating. Friendship is okay," said Chantelle, bangles jangling like a wind chime as she flicked her jet black hair.

"It's only an affair if you're married," said Obi.

"Does that mean anyone who's married shouldn't communicate with opposite sex friends by email? Are all cyber relationships wrong if you are already in a relationship?" Marianne probed the class further.

"It depends what you talk about, innit."

"How do you keep it within acceptable boundaries?" asked Marianne. "Cyberaffairs would be romantic or sexual, but where does friendship end and romance begin? Fuzzy boundaries again. Will there be unwritten rules for this in the 'rule-repertoire' of future generations? There's already a Netiquette of a sort … Can you remember what we call unwritten rules? From last year's AS course?"

"Norms," said Jason.

"And why are such relationships addictive?" asked Marianne.

"'Cos it's easy, innit."

"Email's dead quick."

"You don't have to get dressed up."

"No one can see if you're in your knickers!" added Cate.

The class laughed.

"You can also escape from them if you need to," said Stanley.

"Change your email address!" said Ellen.

"Can you think which theoretical perspective would explain the addiction? Jason?"

"Social learning theory."

"Why?"

"Reward … positive reinforcement …" said Jason.

"Classical conditioning … association with something nice …" said Naomi.

"But why do it in the first place?" asked Marianne.

"Som'ink to do … boredom …" said Sean, stretching his enormous frame.

"Some people are shy in face to face relationships, aren't they? This is a way of making contact when they would otherwise be too scared … Why else?"

"Unhappy."

"Who's unhappy? Speak in complete sentences please."

"Married people in bad relationships," said Cate.

"Yes, and it is a form of escapism from real life … and what about people who work long hours? People who don't have time for a social life? Cooper's Triple A Engine: access, affordability and anonymity; or Young's ACE: anonymity, convenience and escape." Marianne wrote these on the board.

"And what are the problems with such relationships? Three main things for you to remember: People pretending they're someone they're not. This has received headlines when it is a mature adult man pretending to be sixteen in conversation with a schoolgirl."

"That's sad," said Chantelle.

"Secondly, the internet relationship may replace a potentially more satisfying real relationship. This might be true for those who are busy and choose this form of meeting because it saves time."

"Isn't that a good thing, rather than a problem?" asked Jason.

"Real relationships are ultimately more satisfying," said Marianne.

Cate waved her hand. "Not to everyone, they're not … Like you said … there's some things – like mess – that you don't have to worry about on the internet!"

"What mess d'you mean?" asked Ellen, grinning.

Obi said: "Better to have an internet relationship than no relationship … I don't think they're always bad news …"

"So a few conflicting opinions there," continued Marianne. "Thirdly, of course, they may put at risk already existing real relationships. Much has been in the papers about Friends Reunited causing marriage break-ups when the spouse runs off with his or her lost love from way back when … But there are hundreds of happy stories as well. Perhaps when two people have each lost a partner through death or divorce and they are free agents … But it's the break-ups that hit the headlines. Mid life is when people have often been married for a long time, the kids have grown up, and then the boredom creeps in. The excitement of meeting an old flame causes people to get carried away.

"But should we blame the internet? The telephone and letters have always been used for clandestine purposes. So what's the difference between email and these other forms of communication?"

"No one need know about it."

"That's right. The phone rings and anyone might answer it. A letter drops on the mat and suspicion is aroused. But email comes and goes stealthily. Does this make it wrong?"

Marianne paused and felt a momentary anxiety. Was she therefore doing something wrong in mailing Edward? Surely not. Anyone could read their letters. It wouldn't matter if Felicity was looking over his shoulder. They were innocence itself. Mostly it was reminiscence or talk of work or other lightly philosophical matters. And it wasn't as if they were mailing every week, or complaining about their spouses behind their backs.

"It's all right if people know," said Obi.

"What people?"

"Person you're married to, right. If they know, then it's okay."

"I don't agree," said Sharna. "When you said the other time, Miss, about an imagined rival being threatening … Well it could be even worse than a real one because with a real one you can see the extent of the flirting; you can see what's going on …"

"Can see she's a dork!" said Cate and the class laughed.

"Yeah, if it's someone in cyberspace, you could imagine they're the most beautiful person on Earth," added Ellen.

The bell rang and the class stirred, their attention momentarily broken.

"Just to finish," said Marianne. "All internet relationships are potentially inflammatory and in the future there will probably be an accepted unwritten code of conduct. The boundaries will be clearer, but until then, all such relationships should be handled with extreme care."

When the lesson was over, Marianne walked in contemplative mood to her office. When she was at work, she was very feet-on-the-ground; no time for frivolity when you were dealing with the futures of these young people. In this mood she wondered about and questioned her motives.

Dear Edward,

Today I'm having serious doubts over whether I should be writing to you. I think that I am honourable and I think you are; I'm sure you are. But my students believe that all emailing between a man and a woman is dubious – even if it isn't, it could lead to a partner feeling insecure or jealous.

I know I would never have phoned you, or written to you by snail. But to stop now ... How can I? That would seem wrong too.

When she was younger she thought that people over forty lived in a passionless world. Now she knows that's not true!

The Id: the Pleasure Principle: Freud's first element of the human mind.

Marianne was hovering on the brink of fantasies. Dare she go there? What would she find if she let her imagination run wild? Should she feel guilty? After all, Johnny had fantasies. She knew he had them about all kinds of women, from the celebrities strutting on red carpets in designer dresses, to the bank clerks with their prim white blouses and the artificial nails. It was the kind of thing men did and you asked no questions if you wanted a quiet life. Foolish is the girl who thinks her dearly beloved is dreaming about her every time the S word floats through his mind – approximately once every eight minutes according to some statistics, and once every three minutes according to Robin Hamilton one lunchtime in the staffroom.

Best not to ask questions or expect anything different. It is the way it is; pre-programming from an ancient time; primary drives stuff. So why shouldn't she fantasise too? She did – occasionally, but not about people who really existed in her world. Her fantasies were sporadic and confined to sports personalities and others in the media – not too different from her *Man from UNCLE* daydreams of long ago. Her dreams were more about being indispensable, being heroic, being loved to madness; the kind of thing that was rarely the way it was in real life. Only if she liked her fantasy object for a long, long time would she consider taking off their clothes.

But she couldn't go there with Edward. The id would not win this one. Edward had originally entered her life before the time of lustful thoughts. When she was ten he had set her heart dancing with his gentle manner and extraordinary mind, and now that she was forty-six, it was exactly the same. She didn't need any more excitement than this idle dreaming; this hero-worship.

And one day; one day when they finally got round to meeting, reality would sink in and the bubbling sea would settle. They would be friends; friends without fear of rejection because they went back so long and had come so far. Friends who would be concerned for the other, and who would be there over the next few years in that hazy world of the internet to share a word or two when the going got tough as it always did. He was her intellectual consultant; her motivator, her reminder of her own capabilities that she had almost forgotten, so bound up as she was in the day to day needs of child and husband and job.

She was Androcles' lion. His presence in her cyberspace had subtly pulled the thorn of her past and stopped her hurting, and maybe one day in the far-flung distant reaches of time, he might call in the debt and she would do whatever she could to help. This was unconditional; independent of further action on his behalf. She had such belief in his integrity; such trust in this man whom she hardly knew, yet believed she knew so well.

'Give me a child till he is seven …'

30

The Big Questions

To: Edward Harvey
From Marianne Hayward
Date: 2nd May 2002, 18.04
Subject: The Big Questions

Hi Edward,

As an archaeologist, you must wonder frequently about the past and where we've come from. Do you spend your quiet hours musing about pre-historical existence, while I spend mine thinking about our current state? Do you contemplate the gender roles of long ago, seeing in every ancient arrangement of houses the answers to the question of who did what and how? Meanwhile I agonise over our inability to 'get it right' in relationships, the angst and disharmony and failure. In times gone past humans must've been so concerned with matters of survival, they wouldn't have energy to worry about compatibility matters. Men's arguments would be with their neighbours, or with the brute in the next settlement rather than with their women. And children would be leading the lives of adults as soon as they hit puberty. Not for them the molly-coddled existence of many young people of today, constantly excused their bad behaviour and immaturity because of their tender years. The role

models would be parents – no spitting, swearing, hooligan footballers to emulate then; and no time for binge drinking and purposeless closing-time brawls, because you would be trying to prove your worth as protector of the family or creator of the home. So these 'new' inappropriate behaviours are merely substitutions. I am beginning to see the advantages of National Service. Education happened through merely living. Kids were the apprentices of their parents. This is a very Vygotskian view of learning!
Hope all is well,
Best wishes,
Marianne

To: Marianne Hayward
From: Edward Harvey
Date: 12th May 2002, 20.51
Subject: Re: The Big Questions

Hi Marianne,
Sorry for delay in replying; it's been a busy week. Still busy, so this is brief …
Archaeologists do wonder about gender roles but tend to steer away from 'sociologese'.
I spend less time thinking about the past than I used to. Is this a sign that I am tired of it all?
National Service may have its merits, but it's not something I would have wanted; nor for my kids. Sport is a more civilised way of channelling the energies of the young.
Edward

To: Edward Harvey
From Marianne Hayward

Date: 16th May 2002, 22.16
Subject: Re: The Big Questions

Hi Edward,

Why do humans want to know so much? Did they always want to know, or were they quite content to exist and struggle to live in the present and propagate for the future like other animals? What is the point of us knowing what we know if we're going to lose it all? The chances are we'll all disappear in some global catastrophe soon – a mass extinction – and then who will read the books and take things onward? Some inconsequential animals will survive, but how many millions of years before intelligent life emerges again? And what will remain of us in fossil records of tomorrow?

In any case, I think archaeology is a good advertisement for cremation. Who wants to be dug up and brushed and x-rayed and scrutinised in a few thousand years from now? No doubt the techniques will be ever more sophisticated in producing a likeness from a skull. Already forensic artists bring people uncannily back from the grave. I don't want to be judged yet again; measured against the ideal of the time. RIP should mean just that. No wonder the curse of Tutankhamun …

This morning on the radio they were talking about 'flu pandemics. Like there's bound to be one sometime soon and we're so unprepared. They talked about 1918. We could all be finished off in a 'flu pandemic. "Poor sods," they'd say. "Cut off in their prime …" well, give or take a few years, "by yet another 'flu pandemic. Saw it coming a mile away, but did they do anything? No, just sat back

thinking it would cost too much, heads in the sand, ostriches all … thinking it wouldn't happen to them …"
It is incredible to think of the thousands – probably zillions – of events through history that had to occur in order for us to exist as we are. Is that why people believe in gods? Perhaps it is comforting to think that there's someone pulling the strings and that we're not just dependent on chance. The responsibility is too much.
Best wishes,
Marianne

To: Marianne Hayward
From: Edward Harvey
Date: 19th May 2002, 22.38
Subject: Re: The Big Questions

Dear Marianne,
If all history is wiped out by your global catastrophe theory, then there will be a role for the archaeologists of the future – assuming intelligent life emerges from the mess.
Sorry this is yet another brief reply to all your profound thoughts. Very hectic here at the moment, exam marking, etc.
Edward

Dear Marianne again … perhaps it was intentional … a way of assuaging his guilt because he didn't have time to have an extended discussion. Probably she should pause for a couple of weeks before she wrote to him again. But her brain was working overtime and she didn't feel like discussing her thoughts with Johnny.

To: Edward Harvey
From: Marianne Hayward
Date: 30ʰ May 2002, 18.19
Subject: Re: The Big Questions

Dear Edward,

I've been having a lot of Profound Thoughts lately. Is it an age thing? Maybe there's another stage of Cognitive Development that kicks in somewhere between forty-five and fifty; the stage of Profound Thoughts! Most researchers cover this under the category of 'Stages of Life' and although they deal with thoughts about ageing and midlife crises and changes, they don't appear to have suggested that there may be something intrinsically different about thinking itself. Hmm. Might I be onto something here, or is this another of my wild ideas?

Best wishes,

Marianne

To: Marianne Hayward
From: Edward Harvey
Date: 1ˢᵗ June 2002, 23.14
Subject: Re: The Big Questions

Hi Marianne,

The environment is my Big Question. Too much talking and not enough action ... Too many extreme events have happened weather-wise in recent years. (We are even thinking of planting a few vines and an olive tree!) Am constantly worried about the future ... Both of the Planet and – perhaps selfishly – where the career's going ... Where is there left for it to go? Supposed to be enthusiastic: used to be enthusiastic: am surrounded by enthusiasm! Archaeology's a discipline that attracts the enthusiastic ... Finding such difficult since getting back from Aus. Tired of giving the same old lectures. Tired of the conference scene; of the travelling and living out of a suitcase; of bad hotels and late trains. Have decided to take up the Scilly offer – late August/September. You are probably right that a bit of 'grubbing about'– as you put it – may revitalise my interest!

Fascinated by your embryonic theory of midlife thinking ...

Have to go and pick Harriet up from a friend's.

Best wishes,

Edward

From: Marianne Hayward

To: Edward Harvey

Date: 2nd June 2002, 20.59

Subject: Archaeology For the Soul

Hi Edward,

Talking of weather, we are very 'hot' (ha!) on recycling here, but the council don't make it easy. Plenty of places for paper and glass, but our mountain of plastic still goes in the bin. The inventions of the twentieth century may have made life easier for us, but the future generations will suffer – assuming there are future generations. (Refer back to the uses of men and the dwindling Y chromosome!! ... Or to 'flu pandemics ...)

Sorry you're still having career doubts. Do you have an alternative in mind? What about the restaurant idea that you mentioned a while back? Or counselling? You

have empathy enough for that. I have been reading *Sophie's World* in which a link is made between archaeology and psychoanalysis! Says both involve digging – one through layers of earth and the other through layers of the mind. Have never been much enamoured of Freud. One of our degree course lecturers called him one of the Twentieth Century Poets – along with Jung and Adler. We were told that we would fail our degree if we so much as mentioned him in an exam! My psychological perspective has always been cognitive-behaviourism, though with the unravelling of the human genome, the biological approach is becoming ever more seductive!
But we have to teach Freud for A level and some of his ideas regarding the unconscious are very compelling. As our re-acquaintance exorcised my Brocklebank ghosts, I am beginning to be converted! Am still dubious about his dream theory, though. When I dream about trains (which I did only a few days ago!) I know it is because I've had some irritating experience trying to book tickets, or like you, am worried about getting from A to B on time. It's nothing to do with sex!
Glad to hear you are going to Scilly, but am awfully jealous!
Rushing too,
Marianne

To: Marianne Hayward
From: Edward Harvey
Date: 2nd June 2002, 22.23
Subject: Re: Archaeology for the Soul

Hi Marianne,
Interesting links!

244

The restaurant is more Felicity's dream than mine – and a post-retirement option.
Have thought about counselling and even checked out courses. No chance of doing this full-time – too many dependents! Probably impossible anyway …
Not quite sure how you deduce I have empathy from my often hurried emails.
Bring back paper bags!
Now about these train dreams …!
Must dash,
Edward.

From: Marianne Hayward
To: Edward Harvey
Date: 13th June 2002, 21.03
Subject: Re: Archaeology For the Soul

Hi Edward,
Some supermarkets have started putting chickens in plastic or foil trays! This is a serious backward step – except for Blue Peter's creative department!
How will you feel in ten years time if you don't take the risk? We're getting to that time of life when we should do all the things we want to do.
Marianne

To: Marianne Hayward
From: Edward Harvey
Date: 14th June 2002, 22.17
Subject: Re: Archaeology for the Soul

Hi Marianne,
The packaging issue is a nightmare. Felicity has started

selling china on eBay and all our polystyrene containers
are being recycled!
Widening participation is sapping my energy for the
university life. Universities no longer populated just by
the academically able. Numbers increasing – like a
production line. We don't get to know them any more.
Atmosphere changing ... teaching challenging ... results
still expected ...
Are you doing all the things you want to do?
Edward

Marianne wondered about this. With Holly gone, the emphasis was less on others and more on herself. For eighteen years Holly's needs had been paramount, governing what they did at weekends and where they went for holidays. Now she was free to make decisions about what she wanted, she didn't know what to do. She wondered if Johnny was having the same thoughts. They must talk to each other; find out where they were going for the next twenty years.

We'll talk in the summer holidays, she thought. She thought this every year, as teachers often do. And then when the time came they didn't want to spoil the only truly relaxing time of the year with heavy discussions, and so they put it off and another twelve months went by.

To: Edward Harvey
From: Marianne Hayward
Date: 15th June 2002, 18.18
Subject: Re: Archaeology for the Soul

Dear Edward,
I am compromising as most of us do – fitting the person
I am into one of the zillions of niches in today's world.

Always wanted to live by the sea in a quiet place, and have a dog … but Johnny likes it here.
Marianne

To: Marianne Hayward
From: Edward Harvey
Date: 15th June 2002, 18.25
Subject: Re: Archaeology for the Soul

Dear Marianne,
Dogs are great! Perhaps I am lucky, but up to now I don't feel I have had to compromise.
Edward

To: Edward Harvey
From: Marianne Hayward
Date: 16th June 2002, 21.38
Subject: Re: Archaeology for the Soul

Dear Edward,
It is always the women who compromise! (Please don't be offended!)
Marianne

Then there was silence again and she wondered if the thread had run its natural course or if he was offended.

Shouldn't try to be flippant by email, she thought.

And the silence expanded as the days went by.

31

Dancing out of Time

'Is there not a something wanted, Miss Price, in our language – a something between compliments and – and love – to suit the friendly acquaintance we have had together?'

Jane Austen *Mansfield Park*

And so it was with Edward.

After eight months of mailing, best wishes seemed to be hopelessly inadequate and ridiculously formal. Marianne wanted to put 'love', but meant in a friendly way. Too old for the 'luv' of teenage years.

Colin Gottleib – a college friend from Sheffield – always wrote *love* at the end of his emails. So did Mike and Charlie. She never thought twice about doing the same in reply to them.

But after dozens of emails to Edward, signing off with love had all kinds of connotations even if it was only the lightest of casual salutations. It suggested genuine acceptance of friendship – which she didn't feel was the case just yet. How could they until they met; until they'd had a proper conversation with eyes and spoken words and gestures?

She often thought of love these days. Once she just accepted it without need for analysis. It was something that made your stomach lurch; something that made the world smile and the darkest day seem bathed in light. It was rainbows and autumn leaves; misty mornings and the first snowdrops. It made all else seem trivial, but the older she became, the more she realised it wasn't as simple as that.

The Inuit have over fifty different words for snow and ice so how is it that the multifaceted love has just the one? Some have dabbled with distinguishing between Eros and Agape: passion and unconditional love. But these words seem clumsy and archaic; inappropriate for common usage.

'D'you Agape me?'

'Nah, more Eros, darlin'.'

'We need to talk …'

So the Soap script might run; new clichés for men to dread in twenty-first century courtship.

Johnny had asked her if she still loved him when Dylan was visiting. What type of love did he mean?

And if you have to ask, can you believe the reply? Marianne had lied to Johnny and she knew he was upset.

Of course she loved him still, but she wanted him to hurt and to understand what it was like to feel unwanted after twenty years. And it was working; sort of working. He was at least staying with her in the evenings instead of chasing *her*.

Love; the many masquerades of love …

L – O – V – E. Throw it up in the air and it might come down as V – O – L – E: like a rat. Men could be rats when they followed their pants.

D'ya love me Johnny like when I was twenty-five? D'ya love this overheated woman who flies into rages, puts the sugar in the fridge and misplaces keys?

Hell no … How could he?

What did Edward Harvey know of love? She guessed he wasn't afraid of it; that he was loved and knew how to love back. But this was conjecture of a sort, a reading between the lines, for their discussions had barely brushed the surface of emotional themes. That was a dangerous place to go in cyberspace. She might have told him about Charmaine, but he would have been uneasy, wondering if her marriage was on the rocks and if she was looking to him for some sort of comfort. Had they been able to talk face to face, she could have reassured him that all she was seeking was a friend.

Edward Harvey ... Edward Harvey ... Edward Harvey ... Once she might have loved him in a childlike kind of way; the first crush of youth, the bursting bloom of the rose with all its innocence and wonder. But now? Admiration, respect; fondness, perhaps.

That was a dreadful word. *Fondness* ... Fondness was the pat on the head for the great nephew who only visited his ageing aunt twice a year, and wrote thank you notes under duress for the weird and wonderful Christmas presents that smelt of mothballs. In romantic relationships it was a woolly, mealy-mouthed kind of word, used by those about to ditch their partner to excuse a lack of passion.

She still had difficulty sometimes believing that she and Edward were actually exchanging mail. His name had tripped off her tongue occasionally over the years as one speaks of people from the past that have receded into the shadows, never to emerge again. She never thought they would have any more contact, let alone be trying to get to know each other. She often blinked a few times at his name in the Inbox. The mythical Edward Harvey ...

To: Edward Harvey
From: Marianne Hayward
Date: 5th July 2002, 23.01
Subject: Sibling Composition

Hi Edward,
I've just been reading an article on sibling composition and future relationships, and thought you might find some of the conclusions interesting. It said that if you

are a younger sister of brother(s) – moi – then the most comfortable relationship is with an older brother of sister(s). The logic being that younger sisters like to be protected and older brothers are used to doing that. Conversely an older sister of brothers pairs well with a younger brother of sisters. Older sisters are bossy and younger brothers are used to being bossed! Makes sense in a way and certainly it is true of Johnny and me.

Our term is winding down now and I am looking forward to a break. Have you finished yet?

Best wishes,

Marianne

Love Marianne ... she thought ... *love Marianne* ... *next time, maybe* ...

To: Marianne Hayward
From: Edward Harvey
Date: 6th July 2002, 08.56
Subject: Re: Sibling Composition

Hi Marianne,

My two sisters are younger than me and Felicity is an only child. Presumably she would be used to getting her own way (she does!) and I would want to boss her around – but I haven't time; I just go with the flow!

Interesting ... What about same-sex siblings?

Sorting out next year's timetable so no break yet!

Felicity has just bought two goats – Margo and Barbara!

All part of the re-cycling scheme!

Edward

To: Edward Harvey
From: Marianne Hayward
Date: 6th July 2002, 15.45
Subject: Re: Sibling Composition

Dear Edward,
Same sex siblings will be familiar with competitiveness.
Perhaps they could team up with only children, or find
partners who also have same sex siblings??
Good luck with the goats!
Best wishes,
Marianne

Yes, I'm chicken, I know … But I can't … I just can't take the risk.

Then there was silence and she was glad she had played it safe.

She was also glad of the pause. She needed to collect her thoughts. The summer was racing by and nothing was being done to bring back the passion with Johnny. She wished they had booked a holiday, but the only time they had discussed it, neither could decide where to go.

Two days later she was propped up on the pillows reading when he came to bed. It was Sunday and all day he had been roaming the house and garden, catching up on chores and looking rough and ruffled and sexy. She had nearly propositioned him when he came in from mowing the lawn, but the phone had rung and by the time she had finished talking to her mother about her annual summer visit, he had begun to clear the garden shed.

Now there were no distractions, so she took off her newly-acquired glasses and closed her book.

"Ravish me," she said, allowing the duvet to slip just enough to alert him to her nakedness.

Johnny stopped in his tracks. He stood at the end of the bed for a moment, looking at her.

"What does ravish mean? I've never really known."

"Fill me with pleasure." She ran her fingers over the quilt cover, inviting him with her eyes.

"Just like that." His tone was incredulous. He averted his gaze.

"Yes."

Johnny shook his head. "Mari this is too weird. This is not you ..."

"Love me," she said. "Love me madly ..."

"What about foreplay?" he asked, softening a little, his mouth trying very hard not to smile.

"That's my line!"

"It's work tomorrow."

"That's my line too."

He sighed. "I need to shower."

"No you don't."

"Mari ..."

She caught the hesitation in his voice. Of course she understood. It was difficult to turn it on when he was still being cranky over the Greenwich outburst. Even though it was almost three months ago, he still looked at her sideways whenever they were in company as if waiting for the madness to overcome her again.

In any case, he was the one who liked to do the seducing, not the other way around. Funny that. Men may think they want to be pursued, but according to those who claim to know a thing or two about such matters, something about their biology means that it works better if they do the chasing. Somehow you have to get their attention with the low-cut top and the high-heeled shoes, or the power suit, or the white t-shirt and jeans, or the slinky dress, or the wind-blown hair; or whatever turns him on. Then wait … She thought of Charmaine again. If anybody oozed sexuality, Charmaine oozed for England.

"Do you love me, Johnny?" And as soon as she said it she thought, *you prat!* Here she was asking the silly question, knowing that the answer was irrelevant. *Don't mention the L word to men unless they mention it to you.* This was the rule. Her mother had told her. Sasha had told her. Taryn told her. Magazines told her. Men run away from an unsolicited L word. But she had read too many Cinderella novels. *Idiot!*

"Of course."

"Then love me." She would make it sound like sex not love. "You can shower first if you like, but let me watch you like I used to do." Her voice softened flirtatiously and his shoulders relaxed. She knew he was weakening.

Now she must back off and let him take charge. She picked up her book and glasses again. "Okay … no matter … you can't blame me for trying when you look so deliciously handsome."

"Oh Mari … you are an infuriating woman these days! Just let me shower."

"No … it's okay … the moment's passed … no problem. You're not in the mood … that's fine." Back in control; applying psychology. *Attagirl!*

"I am now … I'll be two minutes," he said, smiling, disappearing from the room.

Marianne settled back into the pillows, placed the book face down and closed her eyes.

Dear Edward … love Marianne.

Three minutes later Johnny returned fresh and warm and damp, the ends of his hair wet and darkened and water splashes still glistening on his nose.

Marianne shuddered with a primeval ache and longing.

Johnny turned out the main bedroom light, then made a display of ravishing her which she felt was just pretence.

To: Marianne Hayward
From: Edward Harvey
Date: 18th July 2002, 21.29
Subject: August

Hi Marianne,
Just arranged a quick trip to Cumbria in August before the preparation for the Scilly excavations kick in. Am lecturing in Maryport at the Senhouse Museum at 7.30 on Tuesday 6th. Will you be in Allonby at that time?
Edward

To: Edward Harvey
From: Marianne Hayward
Date: 19th July 2002, 22.12
Subject: Re: August

Hi Edward,
I shall be in Allonby from the 31st July to the 8th. Are you thinking we might meet?
Marianne

To: Marianne Hayward
From: Edward Harvey
Date: 20th July 2002, 12.14
Subject: Re: August

Perhaps we could meet in Allonby late-afternoon of 6th? You're welcome to come to lecture too … Will need to eat first though!

Need address, and contact details. Will be in touch on 5th.
Ted

She gave him her parents' address, phone number and her mobile number and said how much she looked forward to meeting him. How cool and calm it looked written down, when in her heart she was overfull of nostalgic emotion at the prospect of such a reunion.

Do you ever watch the swallows dart
Above the dunes?
Do you ever sit and listen to the swooshing
Of the sea?
And the lazy call of birds,
And the shrieking of the gulls,
And the traffic humming by?

Do you ever study Scotland's shape
Beyond the mists?
Do you ever taste the tangy salted air
With hints of hay?
And hear the village wake
And drift into the day
And feel the wind caress your face?

I see this place through London eyes
Yet my soul is here.
Amid the grasses on the banks,
Between the pebbles on the shore
My past is interwoven,
But I cannot stay.

A life elsewhere is mine.
A heart elsewhere awaits.

But I will ever in my dreams see the swallows,
Hear the sea.
I will ever feel the peace and the
Raw tranquility.
And the timelessness and joy
Of a thousand yesterdays
In Allonby.

32

The End of the World

No one goes to Cumbria for their holidays, yet thousands flock to the Lake District every year; a paradox of modern life. The Lake District is elegance and refinement, picturesque and expensive; grey-slate cottages tucked cosily in the hillside next to bubbling streams; up-market, classy, well-to-do, like the Italian Lakes or the Norwegian fjords. Cumbria is sheep and farmers and rough isolation; a beauty of a different kind. Near the coast, dull back-to-back terraces line the streets of towns and villages, a relic of mining and hardship; and for the last half century, there has been the spectre of Sellafield with its metallic spherical reactor glistening benignly in the sun. Who would say they were off to Cumbria for their romantic midsummer break?

But it was the place of Marianne's roots. A place that ran through her veins; a place she loved. It was also the place where Brocklebank Hall loomed dark on a hill and where Edward inadvertently cast his spell.

In Cumbria it was often cool, even in the height of summer. And the rumours about it being the wettest place in England were true, stair-rods from the heavens slicing through the air and bouncing on the roads. But when the cities were cloaked in a stultifying and oppressive heat, and carbon monoxide and other pollutants filled the atmosphere with menace, where better to escape?

It was the end of July and Marianne was on her annual pilgrimage to stay with her parents. She called it her Retreat.

Of course she visited for a few days at Christmas time or Easter with Johnny and Holly, but this was different. It was the only time in the year that she was ever away alone, and always she savoured these moments to reflect on her life and make decisions for the year ahead.

Six years earlier, her parents had retired a dozen or so miles from Derwentbridge to a cottage by the sea in the village of Allonby a few miles up the coast from Maryport. It was a village full of memories for Marianne: bucket and spade memories, with kites and castles and fishing nets in rocky pools; squidgy sand between cold bare toes, and pretty pebble collections from the beach. She remembered being seven, running madly on the grassy banks in the ferocious wind, flapping her arms wildly, sure that she could fly. She remembered her uncle's tales of the witches that roamed the shore; Maggie Oggi and Zib-Zab who made spells for good weather and the appearance of chocolate. She remembered the tweenage years when she joined the team of pony-girls at the riding school for weeks of savoured respite between the grim Brocklebank terms.

Allonby wasn't a pretty picture-postcard village, but a wild and wind-blown narrow strip of assorted dwellings behind the dunes and marram grass that edged the north Cumbrian coast. Summer brought trippers, walking their dogs or eating ice cream cones, or pigging-out on extravagant concoctions heaped upon large slices of melon, dotted with strawberries and parasols.

There were ever-changing views across the Solway that often seemed from other lands. The Scottish hills of Galloway formed a graduated backdrop of ever decreasing size, and vast tracts of empty sands beckoned invitingly when the tide went out. But in the winter time it was like arriving at the end of the world. The wind blew with some ferocity, the banks were deserted and the residents breathed a sigh, enjoying the peace.

Marianne always used to say she was going home when she went to Cumbria. Not any more. It was different from when she used to go home to the house in Derwentbridge. Here in this cream-painted cottage, in the charming guest room with its magnolia walls and flowery curtains and none of the paraphernalia from her schooldays, she would always be a visitor. But it was good to see her parents again; to check they hadn't aged too much in her absence; that they were still coping. Seeing them again, now grey and ever slower, she felt the chill of the unknown future whispering in her ear.

"Dah-ling," her mother said on the doorstep when Marianne stepped from her father's car. "Dah-ling," with the emphasis on the second syllable, "I think you are not yourself. You have a faraway look in your eye. Are you sad?"

"Oh, not especially. Just an age thing …" They hugged and walked inside, her father, Roger, following; thick white hair, slightly hunched now, carrying her bags. She knew he still wanted to do this, despite his age, and she let him because she knew it was a matter of pride, and each time she visited, she purposely travelled lighter.

Marianne's mother Daphine was half French and had been brought up on a vineyard in the Rhone valley. She was proud of her ancestry and nowadays often wore her hair combed back in a *chignon*. She hated being called Daphne by well-meaning friends and still served *moules marinières* and *coq au vin* to her guests at dinner parties. When she was younger she even plucked her eyebrows to nothing and painted them back on in stark brown pencil a millimetre or two above their natural line. She had looked permanently startled, but it somehow suited her garrulous nature. Marianne's mother had style in bucketloads. Even now in her mid-seventies she tottered around on high heels when she was in the house, because she said once you stopped, that was it; you could never start wearing them again. She despaired of her daughter's frequently casual dress and shook her head and tutted at the sight of denim.

They went through to the quaint little kitchen with its sunny yellow walls and pine furniture.

"Ah, you have the menopausals," said her mother, knowingly, filling the kettle.

Marianne smiled. Daphine had her own vocabulary – a relic from the days when English had been her second language – and even when she knew what the correct word was, she often chose to use her own version instead.

"It happened suddenly. Not gradually like I thought it would. Thought I was too young. Seemingly not."

"In Japan, they don't have menopausals. Not like we do. They eat soy and beans and sprouting things."

"What? How can you not have a menopause? It's biological."

"They have no word for it in Japan. It is a socially manufactured concept."

"My hot-flushes are very real, I assure you."

"All in the mind, and all in the diet. However … you do look peaky."

Marianne made a face, yet she liked the way her mother pulled no punches and told it how it was. But she would never admit it, blaming this overt honesty for some of her insecurities.

"Thanks!"

Peaky … that's all I need with the meeting imminent.

Dear Edward,

In Cumbria now, breathing the air that we both once breathed, feeling the same cool breeze, seeing the same patterns of the light.

I find my parents well, but inching almost imperceptibly towards the inevitable. The future is always uncertain but none of the options is comfortable to contemplate …

Here I revert to 'daughter' mode, accepting being ordered around in a way I never would in London. Does this happen to you, Edward, or is your status sufficiently elevated for them to treat you like a king?

I am both excited and terrified of our pending reunion ... Not long now ...

Later, when she went out for her evening walk, a round orange sun was setting in a darkening sky behind the Scottish hills. The imposing and familiar hump of Criffel melted into purple-grey lines of gentle hills, stretching out behind a millpond sea. It was like a Japanese painting in the *Ukioy-e* style: a picture from the floating world; and everywhere, a silence. The weather was silent; no gusting wind or stinging rain. The waves were silent; not even the faintest 'shushing' on the sands below. And all the gulls and geese had gone home to roost on the other side of the sea, so there came no crying from the skies.

Peaky! She couldn't extinguish the thought from her mind. Three days to lose the shadows, find the glow ...

Allonby was as quiet as it could ever be. The slightest sound travelled from one end of the village to the other and all but the faintest murmurings could be heard quite clearly. Not a time for sharing secrets or speaking words of passion.

"Ant-y Jean! Look at me! Watch this!" exclaimed an enthusiastic boy of about seven as he kicked a football hard along the grass. Then he ran after the ball as fast as he could, shorts billowing in the breeze, not a care in the world, his aunt and uncle following with a black Labrador limping arthritically close by.

Marianne was reminded of the fifties or sixties – before Torremolinos and Benidorm seduced the average Cumbrian with cheap package tours and promises of wall to wall sunshine and egg and chips. Being in Allonby was a regression to a time when buckets and spades and building sand-castles were the entertainment, and bright lights and all-night discos were a distant dream.

On the sand and on the banks, a couple of dozen people lazily strolled or stood and watched this magical moment on England's doorstep, costing nothing. Some hand in hand – the young romantics. Some elderly couples, companionably quiet, and families chirruping. And then there were those like Marianne who watched alone.

Swallows dived and darted, a final feasting above the dunes like little Messerschmitts in the half-light. Dogs barked in the distance and a small gathering of teens lurked as only teens can lurk, in the bus shelter by the swings, as they had always done, sharing the latest gossip about who fancied who and what they might do if Billy or Sandra, or Chris or Trudy would only give them a chance. It was just the same thirty-five years ago. Only the ponies were missing now.

Allonby ... such an unassuming little place. Once a thriving fishing village till all the herring mysteriously went away; once a seaside resort, favoured by Dickens and Wilkie Collins, where Cumbrians came to take the waters in the Bath House and stroll along the shore in the bracing salty air. And once, not long ago, it was a place where ponies from the riding school roamed along the banks with the setting sun behind.

How things change. Now this tiny outpost seemed so inconsequential in the scheme of things – except to those who know. Those who know are not seduced by Greek islands, Italian piazzas and The Gambia. Those who know are entranced by the ever changing views and the simple timeless pleasures from a forgotten era. They look beyond the dusty cobbled lanes and empty streets and out to sea. Beyond the banks is where the magic lies. A tiny speck bobbing on the waves might be a boat or a surfacing porpoise. They watch flocks of seagulls congregating on the sands, rising in telepathic unison when dogs approach. They see the V-formations of geese that fly across the darkening Solway skies to their nesting grounds on the Scottish coast.

Still a place of space and peace; still a place to drift and dream; a haven, even heaven, and some people call it home. In another hour or so Marianne might watch the stars, twinkling brightly in the blue-black sky. City children don't see stars competing in the orange-neon nights with the lights from air traffic. City kids don't feel those moments of wonder at the vastness of the universe beyond.

Marianne watched the setting sun along with all the others, wondering whether in this idyll she would finally get to meet with Edward in three days time as they had tentatively arranged. She felt the mobile in her pocket, hoping he would get in touch as he had said. They might at last converse in sentences, first one, then the other, developing a thread rather than the sound-bites of email. Oh how she longed for a proper conversation. When they met she would hear the voice behind the words; the hidden talk of tone and gesture, and the language of the eyes. Lydia's eyes …

Next morning she sat on a large piece of washed-up tree trunk on the shore, the wood bleached a creamy brown with the hot summer sun and the salty sea. She played with fronds of hair that escaped her ponytail and were being blown across her face by the persistent breeze. She kicked at the pebbles with her sandals and slapped the flies when they landed on her bare legs.

Three oyster catchers caught her attention making an awful din of squeaky-toy noises. Up and down the sand they strutted and every now and then two would mob the third and wings would flap. The one being bullied held its ground. *This is my sand too.* Minutes passed and still it didn't give way.

Good on you, bird, thought Marianne. *That's what I should have done all those years ago.*

Allonby was a world a million miles away from the city hubbub, family angst and the day to day stresses of teaching.

It was ten o'clock and she was amazed at the numbers of people already gathered in this normally quiet stretch of the coast. They were getting practised in 'beach behaviour' as the unusually hot and settled weather conditions continued, and they had staked out territories with umbrellas, windbreaks and deck chairs; all brightly coloured and reminiscent of yesteryear. Dogs bounded with unrestrained joy, not an inflatable banana in sight.

She watched a youngish man with short dark hair, wearing only navy swimming trunks, who could have been Edward ten years ago, carefully plastering himself with sunscreen. Just when she thought he might be on his own like her, two little girls with blonde ringlets ran towards him, arms outstretched, begging him to run with them to the sea. Somewhere near the waves their mother stood and waited in turquoise swimsuit and sarong, smiling fondly, and Marianne felt a momentary but overwhelming poignant feeling drift over her.

It wasn't that she wanted to turn back time, but when she had been a young mother, she had found it so very hard, constantly questioning her role, never belonging with the other mums at the mother and toddler club, always having a mind that was contemplating bigger concerns than whether her child was sitting or crawling, or standing or walking. She had never wanted what they had. But sometimes she had wished she was like them, wished it was what she wanted. It would have been so much simpler being like everyone else. It was hard feeling out of step with the human race.

She wondered if the new Marianne, the post-Edward Marianne, the Marianne with lightness of being, would have felt differently; had an easier time. And then she thought of Johnny back in London, saying farewell to her with a bewildered expression, largely oblivious to the current crazy chatterings in her brain, as he had always been. He had never fully known the internal battles, the false confidence.

One day, you'll make me dance again, she thought, as she left her tree trunk and walked back across the pebbles, watching her step carefully, sandals slipping on the stones where the green algae glistened still wet from the tide. *It isn't all lost; it hasn't all gone; I will never give up dreaming ...*

Then she thought of Edward, dear sweet Edward whose presence in her life had meant so much.

Only two more days of waiting left. Tick ... tock, the pendulum seemed to swing so slowly. How would it be? The gateway to friendship, or disappointment, followed by decline? This was not the meeting she had planned in London amid the bustle of a busy station and the constant noise of trains and information spewing from the tannoy.

Might they walk across these firm brown sands along which she had walked since she was five? Might they watch a setting sun in all its majesty? Might they understand each other without the need for explanations; cut to the real issues without too much exchanging of peripheral information?

Oh Edward, she thought. *Here in this place that is as close to my heart as any place in England; here you will see the woman that I am and always have been; a woman without the trappings of urban pretensions and metamorphoses. Here you will know the real me and my potential. Here, Edward, you will see my soul as I once glimpsed yours.*

But later in the evening, her parents' phone rang after supper and it was Johnny as it often was. But this time the words he spoke sent a chill surging through her body from head to foot; words that would echo for the rest of her life, and she knew that the joyous summer would be cut short and that nothing would ever be the same again.

"*Darling, can you come home tomorrow; Holly's fine, I'm fine … It's Dylan … He's had an accident, been rushed into surgery and he didn't come through.*"

33

Aftermath

Back in London, the house in Beechview Close woke up with
an impenetrable atmosphere of brooding grief. Marianne had
returned home by train the previous evening, and after a restless
night, she was sound asleep when the noise of a lawn-mower
from next door filtered through to her unconscious and began
to rouse her. Where was she? What day was it? Bit by bit cold
reality dawned and a sick and heavy feeling settled in her
stomach. She struggled awake, frowning, licking her lips, her
mouth dry, and reached out a hand towards Johnny's side of
the bed. She felt the warmth of the sheet that he had just
vacated and left her hand there as she turned on her back,
wondering how she could face the day.

Dylan has been killed, she thought.

Dylan is dead.

Should one say 'dead', or 'passed away'?

Dead … dead … dead.

She played with the word until it lost its meaning. So final,
so empty. She had an aunt who was fond of euphemisms for
death. Euphemisms that had once made her laugh. *Kicked the
bucket; snapped the twig; pegged out.* So much more palatable than
'dead'.

The smell of new-mown grass filtered through the window
and tickled her nostrils. Johnny was in the bathroom and she
could hear water from the shower splashing on the tiles. He
had been very purposeful and busy since she had come back,
rarely stopping for more than an exchange of a few words, even

eating supper at a different time. She had wanted closeness and reassurance but he seemed even more remote than when she left. Keeping busy was his defence mechanism, she supposed. Perhaps she should try the same. She needed to be strong for Holly.

The previous evening, Holly had been hunched and tense, arms wrapped round her knees, curled tightly on the sofa. She had lost her characteristic sunny temperament and seemed inhabited by another's essence, all sharp and brittle and lost. Marianne had never seen her daughter so distraught. Holly's life had until now been an easy breeze. She had good health, enough money, a good brain and many friends. This tragedy was something new for her. With other members of the family at the other end of the country, the bonds were never strong and she had taken the loss of paternal grandparents in her stride.

As for the meeting with Edward, how unimportant it suddenly seemed. The candy-floss feeling had dissolved into nothing. How quickly she had reverted to sensible, mature adult with crisis to deal with and others to care for. Of course he had to be contacted and she had chastised herself for not asking him for his phone number when she had given him hers.

After Johnny's heart-stopping call, she had found Edward's parents' address in the phone book and left a message with his mother. Of course he would understand, said his mother. She sounded like an older version of the voice on the Victoria line tube trains. *'The next station is Green Park; change here for the Piccadilly and Jubilee Lines. Alight here for Buckingham Palace ...'* Velvety smooth, supremely composed, a little wary perhaps, of this woman from long ago who said she was meeting her son.

Of course Edward would understand ... But were they destined never to meet? If she had had his phone number, at least she

269

would have heard his voice. Were the fates dictating that no matter how many plans they made, there would always be something in the way? Did the fates know something that she did not: that a meeting would destroy the uncomplicated camaraderie they shared?

Tick-tock … It seemed days and days since she had been sitting on her piece of bleached tree trunk by the Solway, watching the children in the sun, full of her own excited anticipation for the imminent meeting. Yet it was less than forty-eight hours ago and her world of hopeful joy was now in tatters.

Thoughts of Dylan were never far away. She heard Holly speaking his name with love; saw him lolloping through the house, so full of life and hope, exuding charm from those prosimian eyes and grinning on the Greenwich pier when she confronted Charmaine.

She heard the shower stop hissing and the familiar clunk as Johnny stepped from the bath. She must get up. She really must, but it was excruciatingly difficult to swap the safeness of the duvet for the unappetising day that lay ahead.

Where was Holly? What would she say to her today? She felt inadequate; incapable of dealing with a grieving daughter. What would they do, filling in the empty hours before their journey to Sussex tomorrow? A wave of intense heat came over her. She could feel the perspiration creeping through the channels to the surface of her skin and she hauled herself out of bed just as Johnny came back to dress. They grunted at each other, barely exchanging eye contact.

Holly was already up when Marianne went downstairs. She was sitting in the living-room in jeans and a blue vest top, legs tucked under her like her mother so often sat. Her hair was uncombed and she was gazing into space. She turned, looking sad, as if she hadn't slept all night.

"What happens now, Mum? Where do I go from here? He was 'the one' ... The one that people say you'll know when you meet. I knew within days – within minutes – of meeting him. You and Dad knew he was special, didn't you? I could tell you were impressed." She smiled through watery eyes.

Marianne sat down beside her and took her hand, brushing the hair from her face, feeling the soft resilience of her cheek. She seemed younger and fragile and oh so precious.

Holly continued: "You didn't give him the third degree. Didn't ask what his parents did or pin him down about his future. You knew he'd sort it out in time. You trusted him. I trusted him. He wasn't like the others, all full of themselves. He was bright and funny and he made me laugh more than I've ever laughed. But he was strong and sensible inside, and he loved me back. He really loved me back, Mum. Not like pretending just so he could get what he wanted. He didn't play games or try to be something he wasn't. He was the Prince after all the frogs and I thought that I was so, so lucky to have found him so soon."

"You were lucky, love. You will always be lucky to have known such a man and to have him love you."

"He was my Antony; my Romeo. We were so happy together. Is that not allowed? What happens now, Mum? There can't be another 'one' for me. That wouldn't be fair. I won't get a second chance. I shall be alone forever; I shall never love anyone like I loved Dylan ..." And the tears fell freely again as they had done ever since she heard the news.

Marianne just shook her head. The pain in her daughter's heart cut at her own sensibilities until she felt them raw and bleeding, but she was at a loss what to say or do. What, indeed, happens now?

De-cluttering: that was the thing. Keep active; stop the brain from whirring and she padded back upstairs to the bathroom, bleary-eyed with her own unshed tears.

Throw away ten things, she said to herself after breakfast, because that's what the Feng Shui experts recommend. *Then throw away ten more.* She started with clothes, searching her wardrobe and chest of drawers for anything that could go to the charity shop. She began with the mini skirts. *Getting too old for these … Or am I? Wouldn't wear them on a night out with friends any more … Wouldn't wear them to work … Wouldn't wear a mini skirt for a meeting with Edward. (Hell, no!)* And she began to fold them up and place them in the charity bag.

But Johnny likes me to wear minis. He thinks they're sexy … maybe I should keep just one for special occasions behind closed doors … Ha! If we ever have such occasions again … And she took from the bag his favourite black lacy one and put it back on a hanger.

She found jumpers and tops that had long since been out of fashion. Enormous, shapeless, grunge-style tops that would fit someone twice the size. *Only keep it if it fits, if it suits you, if it's the right colour, if you really loved it; only keep it if it's in good condition …* She heard the words of the Feng Shui experts and piled them in the bag.

After this she tackled the stack of books in the spare bedroom-cum-office; paperbacks that would never be read again. In among them were a couple of old sex manuals. She hesitated. Would these be accepted at a charity shop? She wasn't sure. There was no point in keeping them; they hadn't been looked at for years. She and Johnny had their routines – not that they were unadventurous, but they knew what worked and what was best left alone. Didn't want to bin them either after all the stories of people rifling through the rubbish. She could see the headlines: *'Psychology Teacher in Kama Sutra Scandal.'* She idly flicked through one of them. Photographs of a toned, tanned and attractive couple in acrobatic positions. *Never did try half of these!* Getting too old now. Too stiff; too creaky! She wondered if she should start doing Pilates or Yoga. She dropped one of the books in the bag, *(give the grey-permed, elderly volunteers something to laugh about!)* and took the other back to her bedside cabinet, just in case.

To: Marianne Hayward
From: Edward Harvey
Date: 6th August 2002, 14.15
Subject: Sad News

Dear Marianne,
So very sorry to hear your sad news. Sounds like the rest of the holidays will be difficult.
Leaving for Maryport shortly.
More anon.
Best wishes,
Edward

So that was it. Yes, he understood, but there was no expression of disappointment that they hadn't met. *Heigh-ho!*

To: Marianne Hayward
From: Abigail Ross
Date: 6th August 2002, 18.06
Subject: Brocklebank Reunion

Dear Marianne,
I've just heard there's an informal Brocklebank reunion on the Sunday of Bank Holiday Weekend. It's up at Brocklebank. Eightish. Susannah Colquhoun phoned me. She and Willie have organised it with Barnaby Sproat of all people. They bumped into him in Whitehaven apparently. I know it's short notice, but it would be great to see you.

Maybe you'll get to meet Edward at last!!
love
Abi

To: Abigail Ross
From: Marianne Hayward
Date: 7ᵗʰ August 2002, 19.22
Subject: Re: Brocklebank Reunion

Dear Abi,
Wow! A reunion after all these years! Thanks for letting
me know. I am not sure whether I will be able to make it
as Holly's boyfriend has just been killed in an accident
and you can imagine things are a little difficult here at
present. Had to cut short my stay in Allonby – which
was why I didn't phone you. We are all devastated. I'll let
you know about the reunion nearer the time.
Unfortunately Edward is doing a major piece of
excavating in the Scilly Isles from the end of August until
late-September. But it would be interesting to see what
has happened to some of the others – and I'd love to
see Susannah again.
Will be in touch in a week or two.
love
Marianne

She clicked the *Send* button and sat back in her chair,
remembering what she had been doing when the phone rang to
deliver the dreadful news. She had been listening half heartedly
to *Top of the Pops 2*. Donovan was singing 'Jennifer Juniper' –
black and white footage from the late sixties. Her father had
answered the phone and handed it straight over. No pleasantries
first. She should have known there was something wrong.

"Hello, love."

Then the news; straight to the point. Best way.

Donovan's gentle voice had lilted in the background about dappled mares and young love and being pretty. She would now always associate the song with Dylan's death.

That night she dreamed again of Edward and that they met in somebody's house. It was a cold, dark house with bare brickwork walls and tiny windows through which occasional rays of sun managed to sneak through, casting a dusty beam down to the rustic table and the bare floor. They were children again and Edward wouldn't speak to her. She followed him round like a dog, waiting, hoping, but he brushed her aside because he was busy making breakfast; frying bacon and eggs in such quantity that he might be feeding an army.

When she woke she was momentarily thoughtful, experiencing something strangely familiar; a subtle echo of loss from all those years ago; from that September when she went into the fifth form room expecting him to be there, and that horrible feeling of dread and emptiness when his desk remained unfilled and a realisation that he was gone forever spread throughout her being. She was left to face the world of Sproat et al without an intellectual ally; someone that even then she felt could have been her friend.

She thought of the reunion and of the possibility of going, of facing them again and of settling scores.

The funeral was a bleak affair as they always are when a young person goes before their time; parents faced with sorrows they never thought they'd have to bear. In Rustington Parish Church with its imposing square tower, mourners crammed inside and spilled outside onto the pathways, paying their respects. The whole of the village seemed to have turned out, together with a vast representation from the local schools and the university.

Marianne noticed that nearly all the young people were wearing black. She prayed for Holly's safety and knew that there were no words that would comfort Dylan's family, for such a loss produces grief beyond the grief when other loved ones go. A grief that would pummel their hearts and leave a void that could not be filled. The grief would lead to guilt, to madness, to certain knowledge that life would never be the same again; that though there may be joy, it would be a hollow joy with the catch of breath when memories impinged upon the present.

"I want to know what happened, Mum," Holly had said in the car on the way to Rustington. "But how do I ask? *Who* do I ask? I want details. I want to know whose fault it was and if he suffered. I want to know how long he took to die?" She sniffed and began to sob again.

"Remember, love, that they will be heartbroken too. They might not want to talk about such things."

"Then I'll never know. We may not meet again."

"Let's wait and see how the land lies," said Johnny without averting his eyes from the road ahead. "They may want to tell you. You might not need to ask."

"I wish today was over," said Holly. "Why is it that time can go so slow?"

When they stood round the grave in churchyard, Marianne was struck by the total lack of siblings and how lonely Dylan's parents looked with their arms around each other. *That's what it would be like if we lost Holly. The whole investment gone in an ill-conceived second.* She shuddered at the thought.

The immediate family and close friends went back to Dylan's parents' house on the edge of Rustington. Marianne was surprised at the number of similarities with Beechview

Close. All the questions that she had refrained from asking Dylan were answered in a moment. But she wished it hadn't been this way.

"Oscar Hellebaut," said Dylan's father, holding out his hand to Marianne then Johnny.

Marianne knew from asking Holly earlier that he was Principal of a local FE college. This was a time when talking shop would be a preferable option to the topic that was foremost in everybody's mind.

"Hellebaut is an unusual name," she said, realising that she hadn't known his name until now.

"It's Belgian. There's only one other family in England as far as we know. In Nottingham. The Hellebauts come from a long line of organ builders … but somehow the musical genes seem to have passed me by. Tried to play piano and guitar, each without success." He smiled weakly.

"The music in the church was lovely, though," said Marianne, struggling at first for words, then almost without her brain engaging, she found herself talking about Dylan and how much she had liked him during their brief meeting.

Oscar Hellebaut nodded. "Everyone loved Dylan. He had charm and charisma and you don't see much of that among lads of his age."

All around there were respectful voices and sympathetic eyes.

It was during a quiet moment when many people had gone that Carmen Hellebaut, Dylan's mother, came up to Marianne and Holly.

She was a tall, thin woman with Dylan's eyes and curly brown hair reluctantly subdued by two large black slides. "So good of you all to come," she said, shaking hands. Then she kissed Holly on both cheeks and smiled, sadly. "I expect you would like to know what happened, dear."

Holly nodded.

"You know what the young are like … always in a rush … We always told him to be careful who he got in a car with. Not to be a passenger with anyone who'd been drinking … you know …

"Anyway, it seems that it wasn't Danny – the boy who was driving – who was over the limit, but the fellow driving the Porsche. Lost control and veered across the carriageway. Sent Danny and Dylan ploughing into a tree. Passenger side completely crumpled. He didn't have a chance, love.

"He was barely alive when the fire brigade cut him out. Probably unconscious from the start. He wouldn't have known much about it."

"But Danny walked away, unhurt. How?"

"Just the way things happen sometimes, dear. Danny feels terrible; says he wishes it had been him. It wasn't his fault. He is not to blame."

"I don't know what to say to him," said Holly. But later she did a very brave thing: Marianne watched her go over to Danny and give him a hug.

"Johnny, there's a Brocklebank reunion at the end of the month," broached Marianne later in the day when they had returned home and changed from funereal black into something more comfortable. "At the hotel that it is now."

"Are you going?"

"Don't know if I should leave Holly."

"It's three weeks away … We'll be okay. You could visit your parents again – as you cut your holiday short."

"Oh, I don't know." She tried to gauge his tone. Did he want her to go, or did he want her to stay? Would he use her going to make her feel guilty at a future date? He was sitting with the newspaper folded on his knee and a pen in his hand. He had been doing the crossword, an excuse not to speak.

"Do you want to go?"

"Yeah … I think so …"

"You don't mind meeting up with those awful boys you never told me about?"

She ignored the dig. "I think I'd like to meet them now."

"You wouldn't embarrass yourself like you did on the Greenwich pier!"

Marianne's eyes flashed. "That was 'embarrassing myself', was it? Is that what you thought? Your wife lost her trolley?"

"I'm teasing. Don't be so touchy."

She didn't believe him. "Dylan approved." She stopped short. Suddenly aware of what she had said.

"Dylan, poor lad, was just a kid. You can hardly take his approval as justification."

"There you go again … defending her."

"Mari …"

"She needed to be told … and so do the bullies of the world."

"Kids don't know what they do. They don't realise the pain they cause."

"'Scuse me, but they do. That's the whole point. If they weren't causing grief, they wouldn't do it. They want to see their victims squirm. They soon get tired of baiting those who laugh it off."

"What I mean is that they don't realise the full consequences. You can't blame them now."

"No, I guess not, but I can make them feel just a little bit guilty."

"How will you do that?"

"I have my ways." She hadn't yet, but she had three weeks to think of some.

"They've probably forgotten anyway."

"How dare they forget! It's time they were reminded!"

"Oh Mari … What's happened to the compassionate person that I married?"

She walked away, eyes brimming. Did he really believe she'd lost her compassion?

The long summer days can be so relaxing and carefree and beautiful when all is well, but in times of stress and without the distraction of work, they drag. Later, she sat in the garden under the apple tree and the afternoon turned to evening and the August air began to chill as the sky darkened. Still summer, but with a gentle warning that it was on the wane; that the long hot days would soon be gone and the balmy nights, just a pleasant memory. Still she sat, pulling her cardigan around her shoulders, unable to go inside and greet the reality of her life – her grieving daughter and a husband baffled by her moods and sudden apparent lack of care, for him and for the bullies of the world.

Cottage garden flowers lined the borders in a mass of blues and creams and pinks. The hollyhocks, planted soon after they bought the house, were the backdrop to the rest. The celebrity gardeners would call it 'loose planting' or 'blousy', but it was just a matter of scattering seeds and watering and letting nature do the rest.

"Your flowers are here," Marianne had said every year when the hollyhocks began to stretch their vibrant fairy blossoms to the sky. "These are for you, Holly." The plants had self-seeded and now there were hollyhocks everywhere, against the hedge on one side and the fence on the other; in the front garden too, often admired by passers-by despite their tendency to be blown obliquely by the wind.

She hadn't stopped caring for Johnny. He was and always would be the closest thing to the perfect man for her, and this tragedy had just reminded her of the fragility of life. It reminded her of the things that we don't say to people that we probably should say before it's too late.

Joy has gone from this house. It went the day that woman was invited across the threshold. How can I bring it back? I'm lost in the bramble tangles and I don't know how to get out.

34

Theobabble and Geobabble

Dylan's death plunged Marianne into a state of pessimistic gloom. She brooded on the end of life and what it may be like, and all her dreams seemed pointless. How many more autumns might she see? Would there be grandchildren before she returned to dust? What about the book that she was going to write? Oh it was all so awful! Only three and a bit more years and she would be fifty. Images of Auntie Gladys floated into her mind. Great-Auntie Gladys, grey-haired and wizened, shuffling along in her slippers to her rocking-chair where she spent the day knitting and sleeping, meals fetched on a tray.

"Why does she walk so slow?" She heard herself asking her mother at the age of six.

"Nobody ever says," her mother had said. *"A prolapse, perhaps."*

"What's a prolapse?"

It was something that might happen after you were fifty along with all kinds of other unimaginably horrible things.

To: Edward Harvey
From: Marianne Hayward
Date: 21st August 2002, 20.34
Subject: Heaven

Hi Edward,
The past ten days have been ones of sad contemplation of the meaning of life and addressing my ever fluid beliefs. Things are very difficult here. Holly is in pieces.

We don't know what to say, so say nothing for fear it is the wrong thing. We creep around the house silently, frightened to be normal in case normality offends her. I want to tell her that there is a heaven and there is a God and that Dylan is in a better place; that there's some great plan that makes sense of the nonsense. But I don't know what I believe and it would feel fraudulent – like telling her about Santa when she was three …

She says that if there was a heaven, then Dylan would have given her a sign. He hasn't yet.

It's very comforting to think of meeting up again with those we've lost. But has mankind just manufactured the idea of an afterlife as a way of coping with the terrible thought of nothing? How can we all be together again as we are on Earth? We surely can't. If there is an afterlife, it's not going to be anything like our perception of it. How can we recognise another person's soul? If we reunite again with loved-ones, what about those who have married again having lost their partner? Is there no jealousy in heaven? Are we naïve to believe in such a thing?

Yet the idea of consciousness evaporating into nothing as the last breath is taken is equally unsatisfactory. I tell myself that a nothing after death can't be any worse than the nothing from which we emerged, but what about all that acquired knowledge and wisdom? All that feeling and emotion cannot surely die. What a waste that would be.

For a long time I was attracted to the idea of reincarnation and although it still seems logical, I am left with questions of where the souls started from in the first place and how they keep up with the population explosion. Perhaps there is a soul-factory in heaven!

Perhaps one of the reasons for current World problems is the quantity of new souls that are in the system! Maybe with an ever-increasing quantity, we sacrifice quality! And maybe this is where God fits in. At some point in evolution, did God say, "okay World, you're evolved enough for a few souls now." Then the soul-machine was started and a few precious, floating amorphous shapes spewed forth, eventually to make their way into the bodies of man's earliest ancestors. And that, of course, is assuming that other animals don't have souls.

At the moment the idea of living again does not appeal. I am very attached to my own life, but I'm used to being me. The thought of starting out again as someone else is very unappealing – exhausting even. We are all imperfect, but I know how to cope with my imperfections now. Imagine what it would be like to wake up one day with someone else's parents and someone else's dreams ...

Enough! I am rambling ... A product of lack of sleep, stress and fears for the future that I don't want to burden the rest of the family with. (The computer doesn't like this sentence!)

I am sorry I missed our meeting. I hope your lecture went well and that you had a good time in Cumbria. Did anyone tell you there's going to be a Brocklebank reunion at the end of the month? Pity you'll be away. I am probably going to go. (With some reservations and much trepidation!)

Have a safe and successful trip to Scilly. Hope you find something wonderful!

Best wishes,

Marianne

As soon as she had sent this email, she had immediate regrets. He would think she was unhinged; he would wonder why she was taking up his time with the speculative theorising of a student. She was a grown woman. She should have done with all that years ago.

There was also the problem in that she had invited a discussion on one of the three taboo subjects. *But theology is not the same as religion,* she thought. *And this is surely theology.*

To: Marianne Hayward
From: Edward Harvey
Date: 21st August 2002, 22.55
Subject: Re: Heaven

Dear Marianne,
Holly will be okay in time. The young are very resilient. The content of your email suggests an extended reply, but birthday celebrations yesterday (mine!) mean lack of sleep and time, and am off to Scilly next week and family require much attention before I leave! Hope there's no fog for the crossing! Need every available day!
Will contemplate your interesting thoughts on the islands (where better place to think of heaven?!) and get back to you in due course.
Perhaps the Burgess Shale holds the key?
Enjoy the reunion!!
Ted

Burgess Shale, thought Marianne. *Sounds familiar, but yet another deficiency in my education. Too much time spent listening to Radio 1 in my youth; too much time reading trash.*

"What is the Burgess Shale?" she asked Johnny after supper,

flitting between the kitchen and the living room, tidying up, putting things away.

He peered over *The Times* and took a deep breath. "It's a small quarry in the Canadian Rockies. Why do you ask?"

"Something Edward mentioned." She hovered for a second before disappearing.

"Still mailing him then." It was more of a statement than a question and seemed not to require a response.

"Tell me about the Burgess Shale." She came back carrying two mugs of tea and a plate of rock buns and she didn't look at Johnny while she set his mug down on the table beside him.

"Some people believe it's evidence for the leap from simple to complex organisms in a very short period of time called the Cambrian Explosion. It shows the sudden appearance of shelly invertebrates – and no transitional fossils, like you would expect. It's as if they were planted – but of course they weren't. Creationists say this unexplained gap disproves Darwin's theory of evolution and gives evidence for Genesis: that God created this complex life very rapidly – perhaps in the Biblical one week period."

So that explains why Edward thought it might be relevant.

"Do they have any ideas about how it happened?"

"There are several theories. There was a lot of controversy about whether it's just an artefact of preservation, or evolution at a very dramatic pace. Most people believe it's real … I favour the idea of snowball Earth – that is Earth covered in ice. The evidence for this is glacial till all over the world … And then global warming occurring – but very suddenly. So we went from igloo to greenhouse in a relatively quick timescale. This could lead to rapid developmental change of the type shown by the Burgess Shale."

Marianne was unsure whether this would help her to understand Edward's reference, but she listened attentively all the same. It had been a long time since she had heard Johnny talking about his subject and a little voice within whispered that this was something they used to do all the time, and that there was no reason why she couldn't be having the same discussions with him as she was currently having with Edward.

Johnny continued: "The 'Intelligent Design' theory might also be an explanation – although not one that I favour."

Marianne put her head on one side. "And that is?"

"It's a scientific way of looking at the God explanation. Darwin said chance mutations lead to evolution, but some say that's a mathematical impossibility. Anyway … if any organism can't be put together in step by step changes, then Darwin's theory wobbles."

"I thought Darwin was accepted as fact?"

"Some bloke discovered that the flagella of bacteria are each made of lots of interactive parts – and if any were missing, the whole thing wouldn't work. So it must have been created as a whole. This would require a creator, i.e., God. But a creator from a scientific rather than a religious perspective."

"How do you know all this?"

"Newspaper, mostly. There's a lot of heated debate in the States about what should be taught in schools. I'm surprised you haven't come across it."

Marianne detected the disapproval in his voice. Detected an *'if you didn't read so much rubbish, you'd be better informed.'*

Johnny continued: "What prompted Edward to mention the Burgess Shale?"

Marianne noted the slight sarcasm as he spoke Edward's name. "I was writing about heaven …"

"A bit deep for email?"

"Mine are – sometimes. He hasn't much time to be deep back."

"Glad to hear it! Do you remember when we used to talk about deep things?"

"I do."

"Why were you writing about heaven?"

"Because of Dylan."

"You could've talked to me." He sounded hurt.

"It never seemed the right time."

There was a pause. Marianne looked away, conscious that the conversation was heading into difficult areas.

"We could talk now."

"I don't want to go through it all again."

"What's happened to us?"

"*She* happened." Marianne said this quietly, but again, as soon as the words escaped, she wanted to suck them back like a vacuum cleaner. Her temperature rose suddenly and she panicked.

Johnny responded equally quietly. "But *she* – as you put it – was just your overactive imagination playing tricks."

"You're blaming me again."

"I'm not. You're being irrational."

Green eyes flashed.

"No … No … Not irrational … Oh Johnny, you just don't get it, do you? It's hard just now … Being hot … being so old."

"And you think it's not hard for me too?" Johnny rose from his chair. "I'm going out for a walk … Need to clear my head … May go for a drink … Don't wait up …"

"But your tea …"

He didn't turn back and was gone before she had time to protest. She knew he was upset. Perhaps he needed time on his own. Even with Holly almost permanently holed up in her bedroom, the past two weeks had been claustrophobic; getting under each other's feet; nowhere to go.

For the next two hours Marianne sat in an almost catatonic

trance, brooding and wondering how she kept making things worse when in her heart all she wanted was the opposite. Before she went to bed, she wrote one last email to Edward before he went away.

To: Edward Harvey
From: Marianne Hayward
Date: 22nd August 2002, 23.17
Subject: Re: Heaven

Hi Edward,
Johnny told me about the Burgess Shale, so I understand the reference!
If you're worried about fog, I guess you're going by helicopter. We went on the boat – which is great if you don't get sick!
Happy belated birthday (a Leo!!) and all the best for a safe and productive trip.
Marianne

Johnny still wasn't back from wherever he had gone. She clicked *Send* and sat back in her swivel chair. That was it. Soon Edward would be gone too and her cyberspace – even her world – would go colourless again.

35

Chaos

It must have been about two in the morning when a noise downstairs woke Marianne. She had been dreaming again about Edward. This time he was giving a talk in a rambling lecture theatre, to a scattered audience who gazed at him with rapt attention. The seating was steeply banked and the lights were low; a PowerPoint presentation flashed on a large screen on the wall. Marianne sat towards the back and in the middle, next to a woman called Gloria Awaratife. They had worked together once, about five years earlier, but hadn't seen each other since Gloria had moved to a job with the Qualifications and Curriculum Authority in charge of trialling specifications for the new vocational courses in Health and Social Care. Large, and flamboyant in dress, with a personality to match, a husband who worked in African war zones for BBC News, five daughters and a Jack Russell called Banjo, she was ever telling stories about one or other of her family and always full of warmth and support for the then much younger Marianne.

"He only looks about twenty," mouthed Gloria, grinning broadly, exposing what seemed to be more than the required number of teeth.

He did look young. A bespectacled and slightly taller version of the boy of eleven at Brocklebank Hall; dark hair still short and groomed, and a brisk efficiency about his presentation style as he clicked a remote mouse and eloquently described the photograph of an archaeological site of crumbling walls with ancient stones scattered on the ground.

"He's the same age as me," whispered Marianne, pondering in the dream that they would meet soon when the lecture was over, and that she would feel old and careworn by comparison.

It was with this thought that she was brought to wakefulness by the noise. What was it? A door opening or closing? She squirmed under the duvet, stretching slightly, still with a comfortable feeling left over from the dream. Then sudden anxiety when she heard another noise; then calm as she realised Johnny was still not in bed and assumed it to be him, fumbling around downstairs after a late night in the pub. She began to drift into sleep again, but something kept pulling her back as the noises stopped and still there was no sign of Johnny.

After about half an hour of semi-wakefulness, she got out of bed and grabbed her dressing-gown. *It must be Johnny, but what is he doing?* It was years and years since he had slept on the couch.

She crept downstairs silently, not wanting to disturb Holly, using the glow from the bedroom light to show the way. Her body cooled quickly and sleepiness fell away to be replaced by concern. The living room door was half open and Johnny was sprawling in his armchair, legs stretched out in front of him, arms dangling over the sides. At first she thought he was asleep, but then she heard what sounded like a faint gurgle with intermittent sniffs. He was crying quietly. She had never seen him cry before – not properly. Of course he had been upset and watery-eyed like when Holly left, but he had never cried in front of her with sound effects and tears.

She stood rooted to the spot, engulfed by indecision. Should she offer comfort, or go back to bed; pretend she hadn't seen; leave his pride intact?

She hated seeing people cry. She hadn't become the hard-hearted woman that Johnny thought. She wanted to know what was wrong. Was it her? Them? Dylan? Or something else – his own demons wreaking havoc?

Still she hovered, just out of sight, listening, transfixed, disturbed.

She couldn't decide what to do for the best and her thoughts flew around her head haphazardly like vegetables in a food processor. She seemed unable to focus and feared making things worse. She could hear the rhythmic ticking of the clock in the kitchen and her own heartbeat pulsated with the same audibility as the womb-chamber in the Natural History Museum's old Human Biology section. A voice within said that the middle of the night was not a time to be rational and that doing nothing was safer than doing something she might regret.

At length she turned away and crept silently back to bed.

In the morning she woke to find Johnny fast asleep beside her, his face buried in the pillow. She saw that just like her, he was vulnerable and her heart began to thaw a little. As she lay looking at the ceiling she wondered what she would say to him. She would not apologise, but nor would she ask what time he got home or where he had been. He would expect her to; expect castigation from the nagging wife she had become. It would throw him off balance. She would try to pretend that everything was normal, no matter what he said. She would remember the strategy she had employed soon after first meeting Edward on the internet. She might even offer to cook him breakfast or suggest they went out for lunch.

She was in the kitchen making carrot and coriander soup and giving a very good impression of not-a-care-in-the-world, humming the 'Harry Lime Theme', not very tunefully when Johnny appeared in the doorway, mid-morning after a very long lie in. He looked guilty and expectant of the third degree.

"What you said last night about the Burgess Shale was very interesting," she said, stirring her soup and giving him a casual look over her shoulder. "Would you like a cooked breakfast? A brunch? We have sausages and bacon …"

"No ta, I feel shit," he replied, then he looked at her expectantly as if waiting for '*serves you right for drinking so much*'; for what had these days become her usual parental-style telling-off.

Instead she carried on stirring the soup with a nonchalance that belied what she was feeling inside. "There's apple juice in the fridge … D'you fancy going out for a picnic lunch? Or somewhere for a bar meal?"

"I told you, I feel shit … That soup'll be fine." And he poured himself a large glass of juice and sloped off. Soon she heard the front door close and she was aware of the knot in her stomach tightening and a burning feeling in her eyes.

She sighed. Why was it suddenly so difficult holding everything together? Time was becoming increasingly precious. Dylan's death made her feel guilty about not making the best of the time she had left. Maybe Johnny felt the same. Over a year had been spent in this unsettled state. How much more? She had always believed that things would sort themselves out as they always seemed to in the past. But with each passing month, the flotsam and jetsam were accumulating into an untidy heap of detritus lying in wait to create mayhem during unsuspected moments of weakness.

She was reminded of a student she had once taught called Zibi. In the middle of a lesson, Marianne had remarked that she had never come across a Zibi before.

"Nor have I," Zibi had said with a smile that reached from ear to ear.

"Does it mean anything in particular?" Marianne had asked casually.

"It means Rubbish," said Zibi, grinning as if in anticipation of the effect that this revelation would have on her teacher and the rest of the class.

Marianne was naturally curious and probed further.

"My grandmother was called Zibi," said Zibi. "This was in South Africa ... And her mother – my great-grandmother – had children and they died. All of them. When they were babies, yeah. When my grandmother was born, her mum also expected her to die too, so she called her Zibi ... It's short for 'Zibi Can' the place where the rubbish goes. I was called Zibi after her, so the name lives on," she added proudly.

Later Marianne had looked up zibi on the internet and discovered it had come from the Zulu word 'izibi' meaning rubbish. She also discovered that Zibi wasn't the only Zibi in the world. There was a zebra called Zibi, and a cross-eyed ostrich. There had also been an anti-litter campaign called 'Zap it in the Zibi'. When she told Zibi these things, Zibi said "Oh my God, Miss. My name is famous!"

Izibi ... Rubbish ... Life ...

Dear Edward,

A madness is enveloping me like an octopus. As soon as I remove one tentacle, another swirls around my neck and the suckers hold fast, choking the breath out of me. This madness is a multi-limbed monster with evil eyes. I want to be free of it, but it is there all the time making me do things against my nature.

I thought when I found you I was free. And I was in a way: free from the terrible legacy from schooldays. If only I'd found you earlier I might have had a few years enjoying that freedom – before the M word and this new type of madness.

I read about Chaos Theory once. How there are sometimes enormous consequences from the tiniest action. The Butterfly Effect, they call it: where the smallest beat of a butterfly's wing in one part of the world may lead to some adverse weather conditions in another. How many wing-beats has it taken to create my current chaos?

Two days later she went shopping in Bromley with Taryn. With all the Dylan stuff, they hadn't met up or talked properly for ages.

Taryn wanted a news update and a hat for her cousin's wedding.

Marianne said a hat would squash Taryn's microfilament hair.

Marianne wanted a dress for the reunion.

Taryn said it mustn't be any old dress, but a dress that might launch a thousand ships like Helen of Troy.

They wandered in and out of shops and stores in the High Street and The Glades shopping centre, dodging rain showers and market researchers with clipboards; feeling fabrics, occasionally lifting a garment off the rail and holding it against Marianne before grimacing or shaking a head. They giggled like schoolgirls; they stood in doorways and scanned the merchandise with practised eyes, often walking straight out again.

Too young; too frumpy; too frilly; too silly; too black. Too long; too short; too shapeless; too revealing; too demure; too glitzy; too pink.

"All I want is a simple, summer frock. Pretty and understated; just right for a summer evening. Is that too much to ask? Something that looks great without looking like I've tried too hard."

Eventually they found just the thing in a little boutique down a side street. It was strappy and floaty and dip-dyed cotton with a handkerchief hem; it was glorious shades of deep dusky rose through to magenta, sparsely dotted with small embroidered flowers and leaves in the same colour as the fabric.

"Drop-dead gorgeous," said Taryn when Marianne emerged from out of the changing cubicle.

"Hardly," said Marianne.

"You will be … Without the white bra-straps, and with some slap!"

After acquiring a cream fascinator of net and feathers to sit among Taryn's hair spikes, they sat drinking coffee in Debenhams.

"So dish the dirt on the latest from the Scheming Cow," said Taryn.

"Charmaine? She still lurks in the background – in my mind anyway. She's devious," said Marianne. "She convinced Johnny that she had honourable intentions – including a load of blaa about the problems she's having with the guy she's seeing. How could he be so fooled? I was right all along. And Johnny is such an idiot when it comes to women."

"You're generalising. This is the first time he's been like this, is it not?" Taryn took a long drink from her cup, leaving bright red lipstick on the rim.

"I s'pose so. But with her he sees what he wants to see; hears what he wants to hear. He was completely taken in by her sob story (and her pneumatic chest) – little knowing that this was a ploy to create sympathy; to get closer. She seemed to be trying all the tricks in the book to seduce him and I'm not altogether sure whether she's been successful in her enterprise."

"Johnny's not stupid."

"How often have you told me that all men lose their common sense in the face of someone like her?"

"Not Johnny … Johnny would even resist a honey trap."

"He's been so weird lately. I don't know … Things were just beginning to get better too, but when we bumped into her and this drippy bloke in Greenwich, I just lost it; told her what I thought."

"Imagine that!" said Taryn.

"So Johnny thinks I'm a nutcase."

"I think you were wonderful to do such a thing. I also think it's time to apply the dog-training principle," said Taryn.

"Which is what?" said Marianne.

Taryn paused and scanned the cafeteria as if checking to see whether anyone might be listening. "Basically, men are like puppies … Are you quite sure I haven't told you about this? After a while you think you trust them not to run off. So you let them off the lead and they scamper around here and there, relishing their freedom. And then they find something interesting – probably other dogs' pee or poo – and they stop and sniff and are suddenly deaf to the calling. And what do owners typically do? They stand and wait for the puppy to finish checking out the interesting tree – or whatever, e.g., the likes of the Cow-Charmaine … and in desperation they retrace their steps and drag the puppy away. So next time, the puppy carries on ignoring the calls, knowing that mistress will always be waiting – and if she gets really fed up, then she'll come and fetch them. Message received that it's okay to go wandering."

"I should know all this," said Marianne. "I *do* know all this. It's basic psychology. But I'm too close to the problem to know what to do."

"The solution? You should run. Run in the opposite direction, shouting their name loudly; shouting 'follow me!' If you do this when they're young enough – while they're still insecure and scared – they'll see you disappearing over the hill and the deafness vanishes and they come rushing towards you, terrified of being abandoned."

"Johnny isn't all that young now."

"Don't let him hear you say that!"

"He's set in his ways. I am too. We follow scripts."

"Didn't you say that you were breaking the pattern? If you can do it, so can he."

Marianne grinned. "Did I tell you I'm trying to persuade him that we need a digital TV? Then I can watch News 24 and lust over Matthew Amroliwala! Of course I didn't tell him that was the reason. But if your theory's correct, maybe I should."

"Matthew Amroliwala?"

"Yes, I know he's not my type, but he's got the most amazing come-to-bed eyes!"

"At least you haven't lost your sense of humour."

"It's all a façade, and I'm good at those. Inside I'm a complete wreck and I don't know if this reunion will make me feel better or worse. Johnny seems to think Holly and he will cope without me for a few days. She's still in a terrible state, poor love. Not eating; hiding in her room. But we've talked until there's nothing left to say. It won't make much difference whether I'm here or not, and it won't be for long."

"And what about 'Lydia'?"

"He's in Scilly on some major excavation." Marianne began to fiddle with her hair.

"That's a drag."

"Well, it is a bit, but I wouldn't really like to meet under those circumstances. Too many other distractions! Maybe it's best we don't meet at all – though I desperately want to. It could be a disaster. Just imagine if he turned out to be a complete geek – or if he thought I was too far past my prime to be worth corresponding with."

"Oh for goodness-sakes! What kind of relationship is this?"

"Yeah, I know, but men are so looksist. Even friendship requires an element of attraction – not necessarily physical. Okay, I'm contradicting myself, but you know what I mean. Even if he's not looksist, I am – up to a point! There are certain packages that I wouldn't want to share cyberspace with. A bearded Yeti, for example. You know what some archaeologists are like. They look as if they might be harbouring wildlife or last week's dinner in their beards."

"You just have to meet," said Taryn. "I can't bear the suspense!"

"Enough about me," said Marianne. "What about you?"

"Oh, you know …" said Taryn, looking down. "My life is dull-dull, compared to yours." She smiled and refused to be drawn further, though Marianne suspected there was something she was not being told.

Later she wrote in the journal: *Only a few more days to go and I will be in Brocklebank again; in the place once I dreaded going to more than any other. The place that hatched the ghosts that walked with me for over thirty years; the place where hundreds of beats of butterfly wings led to a trail of chaos.*

What will I do to the ghosts from the past? What will I say to make them remember the hurt they once caused? I don't want revenge; I just want them to know. And when they know, perhaps I'll forgive them.

36

Reunion

On the edge of Derwentbridge, perched alone on a hill, Brocklebank still stood grim, grey and imposing, a testament to a bygone era when children played chase around the grounds and the conflicting sounds of laughter and tears reverberated under the Cumbrian sky. It was so long ago, but the echoes would linger on in the hearts and minds of those who struggled with their first hesitant steps on the ladder of education.

In the evening August sunlight Marianne tentatively turned her father's car between the cream concrete pillars by the lodge at the bottom of the drive. She remembered that Jenky and his wife lived at the lodge. Jenky, whose teaching amused and inspired; who understood the ways that children think and feel. A fleeting vision of his checked sports jacket with leather elbow patches floated through her mind. She wondered if he had known how hard it was for her being the lone girl in the third form. Maybe that was why he always encouraged her. *Attagirl!*

She drove slowly over the tiny bridge that spanned the beck, near to where the dreaded swimming pool lay with its icy waters, dead mice and noisy splashing. Everything seemed much smaller now. Even the driveway seemed shorter.

She parked on the asphalt by the rhododendron bushes opposite the house. Already the area was filling up with cars. It had been twenty years since she had made the journey with her friend Abi and over thirty-three years since she had been there as a child. Now the house had been turned into a hotel and conference centre and the ancient woods had been partially cleared and landscaped to provide scenic pitches for a few chalets. Here and there she caught sight of one glinting between the trees.

She sat in the car, breathing deeply, her thoughts travelling back to when she was small and frightened and the house had been so big and dark and threatening. For her there was menace in the grey walls. Did she really want to put herself through this? She recalled the smells of the different rooms: the polish in the entrance hall; the stale sweat in the boys' locker room; the scent of pine from the tables in the dining room; the dusty classrooms in the Hut, and the chilly corridor at the side of the house with its bare concrete floor, leading to the food store and the tuck room where sometimes they could buy sweets and lollipops. If each of these smells had been bottled, she would be able to place every one.

She swapped her trainers for a pair of sandals and stepped out of the car, taking her mother's pink pashmina from the back seat and draping it round her shoulders. She paused for a moment, tasting the air, savouring her emotions, wondering if coming back might be a mistake, yet already recognising with triumph that the house didn't hold the same fears any more. She looked all around her, wanting to feel something mind-blowingly huge; something to tell Edward about when he came back from Scilly.

Did it matter if the worst of the bullies were there? Did she want to see what had happened to Pete Glanville, Jeremy Lanigan, Timothy Hopkins and Barnaby Sproat? Of course she did! They couldn't harm her now.

Edward would be missing, but at least she was forewarned. How awful it would have been to circulate among those gathered, hoping he would step through the door, eyes constantly scanning lest she missed him and that dull disappointment as the minutes ticked by and he failed to show.

No, it was best this way. When they finally met, she didn't want to share him with a couple of dozen others; didn't want to vie for his time, or avoid him lest he thought she was paying him an inappropriate amount of attention.

Dear Edward … He would be far away in the Scillies among the late summer heather and the clear, turquoise waters lapping at the shoreline. How she hoped he would find his enthusiasm again.

She walked up the two shallow concrete steps, rang the bell and waited.

A middle-aged man, in a navy golfing sweater with a red and yellow diamond pattern, opened the door, releasing the sound of seventies rock music from somewhere within. He was slightly hunched and hollow-cheeked, with a bushy black beard and straggly black hair. At first she wondered if he could be a Brocklebank classmate, changed beyond any recognition and she hesitated, not wanting to appear rude.

"Reunion?" he enquired gruffly.

Marianne nodded.

She followed the man across the hall and down the little passage to what had been the Headmaster's drawing room. Already she could see bunches of purple and silver balloons within and a few bodies standing around and chatting. She was immediately reminded of old grammar school discos with their feeble attempts at festivity, and the second-rate music system playing to an overly lit and almost empty room. She entered, blinking, eyes getting used to the lighting, glancing left and right, assessing the threat.

There was a small bar in the corner with a group of men chatting close by. Two were dressed formally in suits, one was in jeans and a shirt and the other two in trousers and sports jackets. They could have been anyone, but they were men of a certain age and she knew that there was every chance that among them were the ghosts of the past, now palpable.

She went over to buy a drink, peering around the room, no longer the drawing room of old with its sofa and armchairs and portrait of a beautiful woman on the wall. Now it was furnished like a typical northern pub with dark wooden tables and stools. On some tables at the side there were plates of sandwiches and pastries, covered with cling-film.

There were only about a dozen people present and yet again she was the only female – a similar ratio to when she was in the third form, but hopefully not for long. Abi and Susannah were both expected. Soon … *please*!!

The man with the beard and the golfing pullover had seamlessly slunk behind the bar and she asked for a glass of white wine. She needed courage. She was just fishing in her bag for her purse, when there was a light tapping on her shoulder.

"Remember me? Barnaby Sproat … Bas …" said a large figure coming out from the huddle of men with a brandy in hand. "Let me get that. It is Marianne, isn't it?"

"Oh, thank you!" Marianne was surprised at his friendliness, suddenly hot, and she began to take off the pashmina, looking for somewhere to put it.

She smiled and draped the pashmina over a nearby chair. "I was going to say that you hadn't changed, but of course that would have been ridiculous after all this time." Her words were intentionally ambiguous, all part of the plan. The once athletic King Cockerel was looking distinctly bedraggled despite the flattering lighting. He was now the size and shape of someone who was overly fond of fish and chip suppers washed down with a gallon or so of beer. His face was big and round and she noticed the beginnings of a purple hue around the nose and jowls and made a mental note to warn Johnny. He was wearing a blue shirt and oversized jeans with the crotch fashionably, but unintentionally, low. His buttons looked as though they might pop at any moment and she noted the perspiration on his forehead and the beginnings of damp patches under the arms.

"It's been a long time," he said. "A frighteningly long time … Quite a few here from our class, and a few more expected." He shook his head just like he used to do, but the dark fringe was long gone for although still remarkably thick, his hair was cropped to about a centimetre and was peppered with grey. "Willie and Susannah Colquhoun have put all of this together – with the on-site caterers. They'll be back soon."

Then there were the predictable exchanges about each other's jobs and families. Barnaby Sproat said he was managing director of Coverdale's, one of the factories along the coast between Maryport and Workington. They made some crucial component for a well-known type of vacuum cleaner. Marianne wondered if there was any connection between the words corporate and corpulent. Certainly one seemed to lead to the other. He said he was married to Glynis who had been Miss Slypt Disc at the local night club in the early 1970s, and that they had two girls and a boy. The boy, evidently, took after his father and was very good at sport. He was currently at university and they hoped he might one day play rugby for England.

Marianne then told him about Holly and Dylan and noted how he didn't listen properly to what she was saying and kept scanning the room and shifting from one foot to the other.

"I don't recognise anyone," said Marianne apologetically. "Quite embarrassing!"

"That's thirty-three years for you! Or is it thirty-four?"

"Boys change such a lot from eleven."

Barnaby Sproat panned the room again, pointing out those who were present. He still used only surnames. Glanville,

Lanigan and Hopkins; combined they were her nemesis. Now she had a chance to make them squirm.

"Thought Harvey might have shown face," continued Barnaby, scratching his purple nose and sniffing, but Grossett said he was off digging things up in the Scillies. Always knew he'd do something requiring Brain. Always was a shade exotic. You and him always top of this and that. Rest of us poor buggers never got a look in. Remember him looking pretty in a pink dress in that play we did. Still got the photo." He tried to affect a more refined accent, but the west Cumbrian tones were the dominant rhythm in his speech and she was reminded of John Prescott's efforts when confronted with a microphone for a news interview.

Marianne merely smiled, not wishing to divulge the nature of her re-acquaintance with Edward. If Barnaby Sproat knew how many emails had been sent between them, questions would be asked and he would want to know more.

"Did you hear what happened to Wally?"

Before she could answer, Waverly Grossett came and introduced himself. He was a tall man, well over six feet and with enormous hands and feet. His jacket sleeves were a shade too short and an inch or two of hairy wrist protruded from the ends of each.

"Marianne," he said warmly, gazing through his glasses with the expression of a well-meaning horse.

Barnaby Sproat nodded, mouthed to Marianne, '*see you later,*' then winked at her and returned to the group by the bar.

Marianne nodded back, but inside her brain was racing and she was plotting and calculating.

Waverley continued: "Pity Ted isn't here. He said you'd been in touch. Gave him quite a surprise, I think."

"Friends Reunited has a lot to answer for," said Marianne. "In a good way."

"We've always sent Christmas cards. Ted has little time for anything else. Always on the move. Don't know where he finds the energy. He said you were teaching … Don't know how you teachers cope. My wife did it for a while … Not any more."

"Edward did tell me what you were up to, but I'm afraid I can't remember."

"An accountant, for my sins. He did say you remembered who I was, though, on the photograph, and that can't be bad. I wasn't here very long."

"You used to come and talk to me and Abi and Susannah when we were in the fourth form, and the other boys used to hang back uncertainly as if they weren't sure what to say."

"I have sisters," said Waverley by way of explanation.

Marianne exchanged pleasantries with ease, part of her mind on a different plane, logging information, emotion and little snippets that she thought might be of interest to Edward when they resumed communication. She was also vaguely aware of other people arriving, older people that she hadn't known well, and of back slapping and exclamations.

Then the person who Barnaby Sproat said was Pete Glanville, began coming over towards them, swaggering a little. He was still incredibly tall, but trimmer now than he had been all those years ago; quite good-looking too and didn't he know it. He patted his thick brown hair, felt his tie and curled his lip Elvis-style as he entered their space.

Somebody's been at the Grecian 2000, she thought. Then, *friends reuniting brings out the bitch …*

Remember me … Nostalgic sensations fluttered moth-like within during those milliseconds of time when she knew he was approaching and knew he would speak to her. *I was the girl whose bag you stole, whose books you threw across the room, whose homework you splattered with a fountain of inky droplets and whose blazer you scuffed with your muddy shoes. I was the girl who was never part of your games with marbles or conkers or paper planes. You called me swot when I did well in tests; called me everything but Marianne; never Marianne; usually that name that had me crying at home when the day was done and the lights went out. The name that under the surface was always me until I met Lydia again. What are you going to call me now, Pete Glanville? I could call you Bastard, but I won't.*

"Marianne?" His tone was soft; hypnotic; seductive. He fixed his brown eyes on her face, then for an instant looked her up and down, like some men can't seem to help. She knew she was sexy tonight in her long strappy dip-dyed dress, with her dark brown hair shining with magenta henna highlights and loose on her shoulders; that she passed the test even if she was forty-six; but still she despised him for it.

In her mind's-eye she saw herself mouthing *fuck you Pete Glanville,* and throwing her wine in his face. But she just smiled girlishly and held out her hand.

"Pete … it's been a long time … What are you up to these days?"

"If you want a new Audi, then I'm your man," he said. "Living in Whitehaven with my second wife Joanne. Two boys at University, one potential lawyer and the other looks like getting a first in chemistry but hasn't the foggiest what to do with it. Don't know where they get their brains from!" He laughed loudly.

"No," said Marianne, purposely, delighting in his look of surprise when she didn't contradict him. She spotted a couple of gold crowns at the back and a slightly mismatched white canine.

"And don't you look good," he said. "Am I allowed to say that? I heard you were teaching psychology in London-town … Rather you than me."

Typical Salesman patter. But still she smiled as if she was lapping-up the compliment.

Then a pair of sneaky eyes caught her gaze: Jeremy Lanigan, Pete's sidekick; he of the hockey stick around the ankles; the sitting in the mud. He wandered over with beer in hand, still the same rosy cheeks and lop-sided smile, still suiting the nickname Titch.

"You two still mates?" She offered, nodding at Jeremy.

"Haven't seen each other for more than twenty years until tonight," said Pete, squeezing his erstwhile friend's shoulder and re-asserting his superiority. "We had a lot of catching up to do. Tell Marianne here what you've been up to. Quite the star is Jerry!"

Jeremy Lanigan flushed and the rosy cheeks became one with the rest of his face. "Just finished a summer season in Skegness."

"Doing what, exactly?" asked Marianne.

"Bit of stand up; continuity … you know."

"Didn't know you had comic inclinations," said Marianne.

"Oh he was always playing the fool," said Pete.

Yes, at my expense, thought Marianne, but she nodded.

"So how's life treating you?" Jeremy also looked at her intently. She wondered if he was assessing the skin-damage, the crows' feet, the wrinkles. It was unnerving to be scrutinised like this, but she was guilty of the same, noting every detail. So much information could be absorbed and processed while the mouth smiled benignly and the voice made engaging small-talk.

"Very well," said Marianne, disinclined to tell the whole truth and quickly disseminating the Johnny, Holly, uni, teacher, information rather as a parrot might, a touch of boredom in her voice. Then she remembered Dylan saying *'Wicked'* when she gave Charmaine a piece of her mind. Time to put the plan into action. "And I'm on the verges of writing a book …" she added sparkily and with emphasis, nodding at Pete and Jeremy in turn.

"What kind of book?" asked Pete.

"A psychology book?" asked Jeremy.

"Oh nothing academic. Just a novel," said Marianne.

"Ahhh …" said Jeremy.

"What about?" Pete looked impressed and expectant.

"Inspired by my Brocklebank memories … You know … Being in a boys' prep school; being the only girl in the class for a while … Thought there might be some mileage in it." She tried to sound casual. Like it was the kind of thing that anyone might write.

"When you say *inspired* … how inspired?" asked Jeremy, rubbing his eye.

"I have been told my memory for life events is unusually clear … and most fiction is rooted in fact."

"I remember nothing," said Pete, rather too quickly.

"Well that's a shame," said Marianne. "Because the past shapes the present. We are all victims of our past."

Pete and Jeremy took a gulp from their pints in unison, eyes roaming around the room over the rims of their glasses as if looking for a suitable reason to escape.

Before they could move, Barnaby Sproat re-joined them, looking hotter than ever.

"Listen to this Bas … Marianne's telling us she's writing a novel," said Pete, heavy with meaning.

"A book eh? Aga saga? Chic lit? Corset-ripping pot-boiler?" Barnaby Sproat guffawed again and his face lit up like a giant pumpkin at Halloween. "My wife Glynis likes those."

Marianne looked sternly at him. "I hope your wife would enjoy it … but my intention is that it won't be trivial."

"It's about Brocklebank," said Jeremy, and Marianne thought she detected a faint tremor in his voice.

"Am I in it?" asked Barnaby, jutting his chin like Del-Boy.

"I'm going to explore the themes of bullying … and midlife

crises – associated and otherwise. Things like self-esteem … body-image … the relationship between the two. I thought it would be topical … And interesting to explore how little things in the past can damage the rest of your life."

"Don't forget I've got a would-be lawyer in the family," said Pete with a hollow laugh.

"My brother is a lawyer and you can't sue for libel if it's true," said Marianne brightly.

There was an uncomfortable silence.

"I know about midlife crises," said Jeremy, and Marianne wondered if he was trying to steer the conversation to the lesser of the evils.

"In any case, the characters will be largely fictitious …" she persisted.

She noticed them shifting their weight, looking at the floor, not wanting to be the next one to speak.

"Largely …" she said again with emphasis, giving them each a meaningful glance.

"Have you had to do a lot of research?" asked Jeremy, a little awkwardly.

"There's nothing like personal experience!" She grinned broadly … teasingly. "They say there's a novel in each of us. They say you should write about what you know. And bullying … Well there was plenty of that, wasn't there?"

"Are you being serious, or having us on?" said Barnaby.

"Deadly serious." She stressed the *deadly*, half smiling, a glint in her eye. *Got them worried, and how little effort it took. Guilty consciences oozing out of every pore.*

"I can't remember much about being here," continued Barnaby.

"Yes, that's what Pete said. Selective amnesia, I expect," said Marianne. "But now you're back in this environment, it's sure to spark a memory or two."

Over Pete's shoulder Marianne saw Abi coming in with, she presumed, Susannah and her brother Willie. She decided this would be an opportune moment to leave the conversation, while there were still unanswered questions. With any luck they would talk about her and rake up the past; blame each other and proclaim innocence. *'It wasn't me'*, they would say. *'Bully? Me? Surely not? She can't mean us.'* And all the while their hearts would beat the faster rhythm of uncertainty, and they would wonder what she might say next and whether they ought to apologise.

"Ooh, Abi Ross and Susannah Colquhoun," she said. "'Scuse me a moment."

Then she turned to greet her one-time bodyguards and there were smiles and air kisses all round.

"Look at you!" said Susannah, in the way that people do when they feel they have to say something vaguely complimentary, but can't think of words that sound sincere without being patronising.

"And before you ask," said Willie Colquhoun, with his familiarly disarming grin, and whose hand she shook because he hadn't been too much of a pest once his sister had arrived in the school, "I work for the Forestry Commission. Pa spent thousands on my education and wanted me to be a brain surgeon. What he got was a tree surgeon instead. Haw-haw."

Marianne wondered how many times he had made this quip before and how many times she might hear it this evening. She laughed politely.

"Susannah's the success story in our family," he continued, much to his sister's embarrassment. "Trains racehorses in the Pennines. Got a possible National hope in the yard at the moment, haven't you Soos. Hawaiian Dream Girl … Might be worth a few bob each way ante-post."

"Don't take any notice," said Susannah. "It's very early days and mares haven't the best record at Aintree."

311

Yet again Marianne found herself outlining the job, husband, kids aspects of her life that seemed a prerequisite to any further communication. She wondered whether an information sheet of such basic history should have been circulated prior to the event.

Of course Abi knew all this and stood by politely.

Susannah was wearing a black trouser suit and had her brown hair fixed on top of her head in a bun radiating sculpted fronds and speared with a couple of what looked like red chop sticks. "Is that Timothy Hopkins over there looking like a turkey? I wonder who dressed him this evening. He should be encouraged to take that suit off for a start."

Marianne giggled. "Do you remember when he attempted the Deer Leap and nearly fell in? Clinging onto the edge and having to be hauled up by Mr Russell?"

The Deer Leap was a fearsome chasm; a jump across a wide expanse where a stream had carved a deep gorge and the banks were constantly eroding.

Susannah nodded and the sculpted fronds vibrated.

"I remember that you were the first girl ever to attempt it!"

"Marianne remembers everything," said Abi.

"Is that good, or bad?" said Susannah. "I remember very little – probably just as well! Even last week seems hazy – but that's age … or too many G & Ts!"

"You too," said Marianne, knowingly.

"And me," said Abi.

Susannah continued: "I went to a fancy dress party a couple of weeks ago – nineteen-twenties jazz – done up to the hilt and with feathers in my hair … Walked in to this hall in Broughton and it's all bright lights and kids everywhere – not a flapper dress in sight. Hadn't I just gone on the wrong night! Party was the day before … Felt such a fool! … It's either Alzheimer's or hormones. I'm banking on the latter!"

"Just pretend I'm not here," said Willie.

"I've told *them* I'm writing a novel inspired by my memoirs," said Marianne, nodding in the general direction of the gang of three.

"They keep looking over here," said Abi.

"Perhaps I should appear a little mad … that would really get them going! Ask them if they keep rabbits!"

"Rabbits?" said Willie, puzzled.

Abi and Susannah were laughing.

"Never mind, Bro'," said Susannah.

"No Edward, then. Pity," said Abi.

"Edward's in Scilly. Probably just as well. I couldn't play the madwoman if he was around."

Abi went to the bar to get a drink and was soon in animated conversation with Barnaby Sproat. Marianne and Susannah caught up with the essentials of each other's lives and it wasn't long before Susannah had Marianne laughing until her face hurt.

Then the guy who Barnaby had said was Timothy Hopkins approached them and Marianne remembered Susannah's comment about the turkey and stifled a giggle.

Ask me who I am, not what I do … Yes I am married. Yes I have a daughter, but that tells you nothing of me. It is mere ribbons and bows along with the packaging that you see. Of course we like to know these things because we are curious. These things allow us to make stereotypical judgements, but they are no indicator of whether we could pass an enjoyable hour conversing, or even be friends.

Ask me what I like to eat and whether I am a morning person or am better in the afternoons. Or ask me if being left-handed has made life difficult in a right-handed world; or what it was like being a girl in a world full of boys. There are so many things you could ask me that would make me remember our conversation, but you won't, will you? You will prattle on and on about how wonderful you are, trying to convince

*yourself that you haven't wasted the last twenty-five years, and I will
wonder why I travelled all the way from London to hear about nothing.*

She now understood perfectly why she preferred small
gatherings to parties; one to one conversations rather than
groups. It was only then that you could get beyond the weather-
talk, the vying for position, the points scoring, the second-
hand opinions on world events and politics.

Timothy Hopkins was already in the middle of his life story
and she realised she hadn't been listening. *Better give a few nods
and a few 'aha's',* she thought, hoping he would carry on talking
until she picked up the thread of what he was saying.

" … So there I was pretending to be a very good motorcyclist,
and all the time I had been frightening her witless."

"Gosh," said Marianne, awkwardly, struggling. "And what
happened next?"

"Took her to see *Madame Butterfly* at the Coliseum and the
next day she agreed to marry me!"

"Marianne," said a rare familiar voice from behind her. A
voice that she had heard often since its teenage breaking; a
voice from grammar school days and later. She turned and
beamed. *Oh my,* she thought. No more the Blond Adonis, but
a genial face nonetheless; still the beard, though shorter than it
was, and rather less hair. He had been Johnny's best man at
their wedding, but although Johnny had met up with him a
few times after that, she hadn't seen him for years.

"Sam," she said, allowing him to give her a hug and
mouthing '*rescue me*' with wide eyes while her back was turned
on Timothy Hopkins. "It's been ages. What have you been up
to lately? No, don't answer that. No more inane pleasantries,
I've had a bellyful tonight. Tell me how you are, how you really
feel about your life."

And Sam Rycroft also looked at her now in a way he never
had when she was fifteen and so infatuated she would have

given anything to see him gaze as he was doing now.

"You sure you want to know? Not pretty. Just about to get divorced," he said. "I feel bloody awful. Been a rough few years … Would've happened sooner, but there were the children … You know how it is … Poor blighters … Not their fault, but they suffer and you can see it in their eyes. Hoping Mummy and Daddy will get back together; trying every trick to make it happen. Breaks your heart … We kept trying again for their sake, but once it's gone, it's very hard to get it back."

Marianne felt a tremor go through her body. *But it hasn't gone with me and Johnny. It's just lost … temporarily misplaced.*

"D'you hear from Sasha at all?" continued Sam.

Oh yes, Sasha had been in touch by email only a week ago, and when she heard that Marianne was going to a Brocklebank reunion, she wrote straight back and said if Sam was there, to give him her love.

"Sasha is in Bath. She married Graham Simpkins – but you must know that. Did you ever meet him? Some type of specialist lawyer, but I forget what, exactly. I always thought he was rather odd – fearsomely intelligent and scathing of those who weren't. Three kids, all girls, all grown up now." Marianne paused. Sam was listening intently, really wanting to know. Now she had got over the initial shock of his transformation, she saw how when he smiled, his blue eyes still twinkled, and the boy from long ago was somewhere under the surface. "She sends her love," she added, as neutrally as possible, noting that for an instant Sam looked into the depths of his pint and for a fleeting moment a wistful glance flickered across his face, like a remembered pleasant memory, and she thought he was going to ask something more.

Instead he asked about Johnny and recounted some of the times they'd had when young.

She would never tell him that Johnny had been drinking

too much; that their perfect marriage was going through the type of patch that had previously been only for others. That was for Johnny himself to say when they met again as no doubt they would. Sam and Johnny once told each other everything; pals from primary school; old friends.

Marianne said: "Didn't think you'd be here. Thought it probably wasn't your scene."

"It isn't, really. I was at a loose end and curious. Thought some of the Waterside crowd might be here. Susannah's still the same Susannah. Just had a chat with Bas Sproat. Too full of himself, as always."

"Well if it's any consolation, you look in much better shape than him."

"Thanks! D'you fancy having a nose around – as far as we can?"

She had only had one glass of wine, but that and the nostalgia were making her light headed. It was so easy talking to Sam since she and Johnny had been together; far removed from the blushes and hesitations of teenage years.

As they sneaked out of the room, Marianne giggled. "I feel like a naughty school kid going out of bounds."

The parquet floor of the hall was still the same, but all the books and magazines and school photographs had gone. Instead there was a hat stand, a reception desk and a few plush chairs. Up the wooden stairs they went. Opposite the top had been one of the dormitories. *I wonder if that was where Edward slept.* Now it would be a conference room or sleeping accommodation. She turned to her left, marvelling at the smallness of the spaces that had once seemed so large.

"Are you still teaching?" she asked.

"Yes, in Workington. But I want out before it kills me. I make wrought iron gates at the weekends and plan to turn it into a business."

They stood for a moment at the top of the stairs, leaning on the banister rail looking down into the hall.

"I used to think you were wonderful when you were here," said Marianne. "You were so charismatic; such a show-off! Brilliant at football."

"Not any more," said Sam reflectively. "Did my knee in playing squash about five years ago. Now yet another of the walking wounded."

The girls' bathroom had been on the left with its green cast iron bath and green tiles. It said 'Bathroom' on the door so Marianne pushed it open and looked inside. Incredibly, the tiles seemed still the same, but along the wall where the lockers had been, were radiators and towel rails and the bathroom suite was new and luxurious. Sam sat on the edge of the bath.

"I don't think I ever came in here," he said.

Marianne bent down by the skirting board near the door.

"One of these tiles used to be loose," she said. "I remember writing 'I love Sam Rycroft' on the back. Probably the first time I had ever written such a thing. It seemed so daring at the time." She ran her fingers over the tiles, almost wishing that she could find this evidence of her past, but they were all stuck fast.

Sam laughed. "I guess you got over it pretty quick. Does Johnny know?"

"Doubt it … I never talked to him much about Brocklebank … Never talked to anyone about it … I wonder why *we* never mentioned it when you were going out with Sasha?"

Sam paused, leaning on the towel rail, looking down. "Didn't want to draw attention to having gone to a posh school?"

"Probably … I was always getting stick about my accent – or lack of … From you as well! So I learnt to drop my aitches and shorten my 'a's. And then I went to London and had the mickey taken out of me all over again."

Sam smiled and his eyes crinkled.

Marianne continued: "I couldn't bear to think about this place and the older I was, the more I only remembered the bad things and the less I felt like telling anyone about it. Then I found Edward Harvey on Friends Reunited last year …"

"I knew Ted at Waterside …"

"We wrote a few emails … Reminisced a bit … Suddenly I was able to face the past."

"I remember he was always so enthusiastic about everything. A decent chap. Did I hear he is in Scilly?"

When she and Sam rejoined the gathering, she looked around the room at the rag-bag collection of people, once her classmates, once full of joy and hope and now resigned to their lot. She could tell by their expressions that most had forgotten how to dream, and as the last cobweb traces of hostility evaporated into the heady atmosphere, she felt that her own life in many ways had only just begun.

A wave of emotion came from nowhere, making her tingle. The back of her neck was hot and she knew she was in the midst of a hormonal rush. It had been so difficult being that child in the third form; being a girl; being scared; being different. Then Edward had come with his sparkling intelligence; then Abi and Susannah had come and she had discovered friendship and joy; then *The Rivals* had been performed and she made people laugh and knew the power of the stage. It was all flooding back, not just vague dissociated happenings, but a myriad of vivid memories, and the girl she once was began to smile. Now she knew that those dark days were but a transient shadow in her life and it was time to move on.

37

Ambition

Marianne went up to her daughter's bedroom to announce that she was home. She hesitated after tapping on the door, waiting for Holly to invite her in. A muffled voice croaked permission to enter and she turned the handle with mixed feelings.

Inside was typical teenage mess. Notes for the half finished holiday essays were scattered on the desk among nail varnish and eye shadow, brushes and lotions and creams. Books lay open on the floor at the same pages as when the news about Dylan came through. Posters that had started to peel from the wall in the summer heat remained unstuck and flopped dejectedly.

"I'm glad you're back," said Holly raising herself up from the bed where she had apparently been lying. She was still wearing pyjamas, despite the lateness of the afternoon, and a curled embryonic shape was deeply indented on the duvet.

Marianne rushed over to her and wrapped her in the warmest of lingering hugs that needed no words. It was a proper hug, not one of the pitiful and fleeting clasps that she had offered before the reunion. Her sense of self, of her role as mother, had altered.

"Look at all this," said Holly, gesturing with a wide arc of her arm. "Can't seem to do anything; thoughts keep going round and round."

Marianne sat on the bed. "Maybe you shouldn't go back. You could have a year out: a gap year."

"It wouldn't be the same without Dylan. We had so planned it all."

"You don't have to do the same things. But you need to do something to keep yourself occupied. A gap year would give you time to readjust."

"No." Holly shook her head and her tousled hair became caught in itself and stuck out at the side. She smoothed it with her hands. "Dylan would want me to carry on. I've made friends in my classes. Don't want to start again with another load of freshers. Uggh! I will get sorted. Tomorrow … Promise."

Marianne was doubtful. "You could get a job locally for a few months – until you feel better."

"I've thought and thought. If only … If only he hadn't gone with Danny. Those kinda thoughts. It's doing my head in. I've got to stop. I'm sick of crying. Dylan would say I was such a woos."

Marianne gave her daughter's hand a squeeze.

"Mum, I'm sorry you missed your meeting with Harry Potter."

"There'll be another day for Harry, love."

True to her word, the next day Holly was a bundle of energy, cleaning her room, phoning her friend Thalia to arrange a weekend boat trip with her parents, circulating again in Beckenham. Perhaps Edward was right about the resilience of the young.

Marianne mused on the fact that it was a year since the M word had begun to be a factor; a year since she had started looking for Edward Harvey on Friends Reunited. How quickly time travelled these days. Soon she would be fifty.

Only other people were fifty and they had tight perms like Mrs Swift. But although her hair was still untouched by anything other than the occasional semi-permanent colour, she was beginning to prefer to wear sensible shoes; opting for comfort rather than crippling pain during the long days of treading the corridors at college. Bad sign! It was a surfeit of the Nearly Fifties that she had encountered at the reunion and it frightened her.

We all seemed so old. It was as if they had aged while I had stood still. Then the awful realisation that I, like them, had aged too. They were mirrors reflecting back what I refuse to see.

Time to get out those stilettos and see if she could still balance and strut like a catwalk model. Johnny once told her after following her down the road, that he quite understood why women wore high heels; that they forced the hips to sway seductively, like it or not. And for a while when they were in flirtatious mood, he would hang back and let her walk in front of him while he admired her exaggerated gait.

Fifty! For God's sake! Only three years left before the F word. Now she knew what her mother always said was true – that you felt more or less the same inside even though the casing looked older. Certainly she didn't feel like the reflection that stared at her every day, but she was more inclined to laugh at it now; far less insecure.

With Holly more settled, she should have been able to pay more attention to her own life; the book, perhaps. Now that she had told Sproat et al., that a novel was in the pipeline, there was no ducking out. She would have to start writing in earnest.

And there was Johnny too ...

But almost immediately she was propelled into the new academic year at college and all thoughts of reconciliation strategies evaporated. It was a week of enrolment forms and course team meetings; of strategic planning (how she hated that word: *the S word!*) and briefings about the forthcoming Ofsted inspection. Then it was new classes, new tutor group, new names to learn and the beginnings of a cycle that was being played out in educational establishments up and down the land.

And just as the term was embedding itself and she was beginning to refocus on home life again, her Head of Department announced she was pregnant and would be off on maternity leave from January until the following September.

Pandrea Kinnear was a vast Scottish woman with wavy black curls who walked with her feet apart and resembled an oil-rig. She preferred to be called Pan and said that her full name was a compromise between Andrea and Pandora, favoured by each of her parents.

Marianne greeted the news of the forthcoming child with mixed emotions, one of which was a twinge of jealousy. Pan was forty-two and already had twin teenage girls. She opened her mouth to say something diplomatic but Pan interjected.

"We were grossed out at first," continued Pan. Since she had been in the States the previous summer, she had become fond of Americanisms. "It's a mistake as you might have guessed. Hey! Too much red wine! Och I know, I should know better! I always did want another one. It was Austen who couldn't face the nappies and the sick again. I told him he didn't have to, but he said that's what I'd said last time. But that was because last time was twins. Anyway he's got used to it and the girls rather like the idea of having someone to boss around just now. Of course this means we need an acting HOD. There'll be a notice going up in the staffroom next week, so if you're interested ..." she nodded at Marianne and Howakhan Gadhok, the third member of the department, a young man of twenty-four who gelled his black hair into porcupine spines and was looking distinctly uncomfortable with the baby talk. "If not, we'll advertise the HOD responsibility with the maternity leave post. Not ideal," she added, giving Marianne a significant look.

Ambition was something Marianne had always lacked.

Climbing ladders in education or anywhere was not for her. Unlike Johnny, she couldn't see the point of making the significantly increased effort for very little extra money. But something had changed. Howakhan Gadhok was wet-behind-the-ears and in only his second year of teaching. He certainly had ambition, but he didn't yet have experience. Marianne didn't fancy the prospect of working under him even if he was from a branch line of the Sioux.

If Edward can do it, so can I, she thought, and she sent her letter of application to the Principal without telling Johnny.

To: Marianne Hayward
From: Sasha Clement
Date: 12th September 2002, 17.51
Subject: Happenings at Home

Marianne,
Just a note to let you know that Graham and I are splitting up. Been on the cards for some time. Didn't say anything before 'cos thought we might sort it out. He's been seeing someone else. A floosy of thirty-five called Debbi. Hardly young, I know, but relative to us ... She's a completely dense Bimbo – typical trophy girlfriend – and now, wouldyoubelieveit, she's pregnant! This has escalated the inevitable. I'm fine now, so don't worry. Didn't want to stay in Bath where I might bump into them. New job in the City so moving back to London soon. Girls cross with Graham and on my side. Ring me when you have time.
Hugs,
Sasha
xxx

Marianne's first thought was of a Charmaine-style woman dangling on Graham's arm and lapping up his pontificating and intellectualising that most other people seemed to find tedious. Then she remembered Sam Rycroft at the reunion, gazing thoughtfully into his beer at the mention of Sasha's name. Sam with his sad blue eyes … A plan began to unfold in her mind.

"Johnny, Sam seems a bit out of sorts. Do you feel like inviting him down for a weekend after Holly's gone back?"

Then she wrote to Edward about the reunion while the memory was fresh. Edward was still in Scilly and she knew when he returned he would have a monumental mail-bag to deal with. He wouldn't respond for at least a couple of weeks. Once again, as when he went to Australia, his emails began to feel like a distant memory.

She remembered what Barnaby Sproat had said.

'*Always was a shade exotic.*'

An interesting choice of words, but she'd known it too; that underneath Edward's quietly charming exterior, there lay a heart with a fanciful rhythm of its own and a mind that buzzed like a hot summer hive.

She wondered if the breezy normality of his emails was just a veneer. Did mysterious forces lurk within? Did the shadows of his past chase each other as hers once had?

Dear Edward,

A hundred conversations are stacking up in my head. Conversations that we could've had when we were ten and conversations that we could have now that are just too difficult by email. And then there are all the ones from the years in between. I'm scared I'll forget what they are when we meet. I'm scared there may never be time for them all. I want to ask you more about your work and what you plan to do. Those are the easy ones. But I'd like to know who you really are – the man behind the writing in my mailbox – and that could take a thousand years.

Later that night she stood by her bedroom window looking at the moon shining through the trees. She smiled: another transformation had most definitely occurred. Since the reunion, the sands had shifted again and her tormentors were figments of the past now ground into dust.

It seemed she had forgiven at last.

38

Gastrobabble

In fact it was October before Edward Harvey's now-familiar name graced her inbox once again, by which time Marianne had secured the Acting Head of Psychology job with effect from January. But she still hadn't told Johnny.

To: Marianne Hayward
From: Edward Harvey
Date: 2nd October 2002, 21.52
Subject: Re: Reunion

Dear Marianne,
Apologies for taking so long to write but since Scilly I have been busier than ever. Quieter now, but not for long!
Intrigued by your story of the reunion. In some ways I wish I could've been there … But not sure if I would like to be under such merciless, microscopic scrutiny! Is this what Psychologists do all the time?
Am in doghouse with Felicity as have just invited two visiting Japanese archaeologists from Okayama University for impromptu supper tomorrow. Brought home a salmon, but forgot she has evening class!!
Best wishes,
Edward

To: Edward Harvey
From: Marianne Hayward
Date: 2nd October 2002, 22.13
Subject: Food for Thought

Dear Edward,

Psychologists only notice the odd and strange. Normality passes them by!

I am sure Felicity is a much more accomplished caterer than I am, but perhaps you might like to offer this recipe as a quick way of making salmon interesting (and escaping doghouse!).

It is a simplified version of one of Catherine Waldegrave's.

Peel and slice tomatoes into a pan (remove seeds too if you can be bothered). Add salt, black pepper and sugar (more if sour tomatoes) and simmer the pulp until reduced and thickened. Put each salmon fillet or steak in own foil parcel, with tomato mixture to cover and torn basil leaves over the top. Bake for about 15 mins (depending on thickness of salmon) at 190°C. Serve still in foil, but unwrap and sprinkle sliced spring onions on top. Good with new potatoes and a couple of green vegetables. The tomato sauce can be made the day before and the whole meal takes half an hour to cook so is excellent if short of time.

Holly has just gone back to Uni. She is coping admirably now; showing amazing resilience, as you suggested she might.

How was Scilly?

Best wishes,

Marianne

To: Marianne Hayward
From: Edward Harvey
Date: 4th October 2002, 23.21
Subject: Re: Food for Thought

Dear Delia,
Glad to hear Holly is back on track.
Who is Catherine Waldegrave? Should I know her?! I
was very surprised you suggested that I give the
recipe to Felicity (in view of your thoughts about
Metrosexual Man!) In fact I cooked the meal myself
and Felicity and the Japanese were suitably impressed
– though I did wonder afterwards if they would have
preferred it raw!
Thank you!
Edward

To: Edward Harvey
From: Marianne Hayward
Date: 5th October 2002, 20.06
Subject: Re: Food for Thought

Dear Edward,
Johnny calls me Delia sometimes too, but it is not merited
at all. I just tinker with other people's recipes and rarely
create anything original. Have limited repertoire!
It was you who implied that you didn't fit the MM mould,
so I just assumed. It is reassuring to know that you are
domesticated in addition to all your other talents. Felicity
must be pleased!
You still haven't told me about Scilly.
Delia

To: Marianne Hayward
From: Edward Harvey
Date: 7th October 2002, 21.45
Subject: Re: Food for Thought

Dear Marianne,
Felicity says to tell you that I am more Metrosexual than
I think – whatever that means – and she is pleased!
Scilly was marvellous. Long story … Article in next
month's Antiquity magazine will tell all!!
Edward

Two weeks later in a local restaurant, Johnny, Marianne and
Holly sat munching through starters of spicy pork spare ribs,
chicken satay and crispy duck. Holly had come home for the
weekend to celebrate her twentieth birthday, preferring to keep
her celebrations low key as a mark of respect for Dylan.
Marianne would have chosen to go somewhere more exclusive,
but Chinese was Holly's favourite so they had walked down
the road to The Lotus Blossom.

"You know it was on my birthday last year when me and
Dylan got together for the first time," said Holly. She was
simply dressed in a long black skirt and vest-style black beaded
top. Round her neck she wore a Y-shaped necklace of various
coloured gemstones that Dylan had given her at Easter. "Course
we'd spoken before at lectures. He used to borrow paper from
me! Told me later it was just an excuse to get to know me
better. He had stacks of A4 in his room." She paused to gnaw a
spare rib. "On my birthday a few of us went to the union bar
and he and his mates joined us. We got talking properly. He was
so, sooo, cool."

I wonder what Edward was like at twenty, thought Marianne.
Studious and energetic, or young-man wild?

"He asked me my star sign and when I said I was a Libran, he said we were compatible. He's Aquarius. Was ... But he said that the Sun signs weren't as important as Moon signs in relationships, and for that, he'd have to consult his ephemeris."

"More original than the etchings trick," said Johnny.

"He knew what he was talking about," said Holly. "His mother taught him how to do charts. He said incompatible Sun signs were less of an obstacle to happiness than incompatible moons. I can't remember exactly why."

Marianne swallowed a piece of chicken and cleared her throat. "It's because the Sun represents the external person, so any differences are clear and can often be sorted out. Moon signs rule the emotions and because these are often hidden, any differences are difficult to deal with. Compatible moons mean people are in tune emotionally."

Holly looked impressed. "I didn't know you knew so much about astrology, Mum."

"I can draw up charts," said Marianne. "At least I could when I was at college. It was a popular pastime every time one of us found a new man."

"You never did mine," said Johnny.

"You were never interested. You don't believe in it."

"I'm open minded."

"Since when?" Marianne remembered overhearing the phone conversation with Charmaine.

"Dylan said only if we had compatible moons, would he ask me out! He was serious too. So we went to his room and looked up the details, found we had harmonious moons in fire signs and that was that. I'd secretly fancied him anyway, but didn't have the guts to tell anyone."

I wonder if Edward and I have compatible moons?

Marianne scanned the room, dimly aware of the wooden pagoda carvings in the panelling on the walls, the sculpted metallic Buddhas, the tank of koi carp at the end of the room and the gentle trickling sound from the open-mouthed fish fountain in its centre.

Compatible moons are important for friendships too.

"How did you and Dad meet?" asked Holly.

"We were at the same school," said Marianne, clicking back into the moment.

"Yeah, I know, but when did the romance happen? Who made the first move?"

Marianne shifted in her seat and helped herself to some more duck.

"I first spoke to your mother on her own when she was walking home from school one sunny day in summer, and I caught up with her on the hill. For some reason our usual friends weren't with us. We carried on walking together and talking about Pink Floyd and I thought she was really sweet."

"You remembered that?" said Marianne.

"Of course ... Don't you?"

Marianne nodded and adjusted the straps of her dip-dyed reunion dress.

"Later that evening I taped an album of theirs for her – *Obscured by Clouds* ... Some of the discs had been badly produced and she didn't want to buy it, just in case she got a dodgy one. I had one of the good ones ... She came up to my room to show me how her tape recorder worked, and when she leaned close I could smell her perfume ... I wondered if she'd put it on 'specially for me."

"Houbigant's Musk Oil, probably." said Marianne, blushing.

"Probably Houbigant's Musk, or probably put on for me?" said Johnny, taking a sip of wine and looking at her over the rim of the glass.

"Probably both!"

"Her one-liners made me laugh even then, and I loved the

way she didn't know how pretty she was becoming. I was very tempted to kiss her," said Johnny. "But I didn't, even though I knew she fancied me."

"Too much information, Dad!" said Holly.

"Well you did ask!"

A young Chinese waitress whisked around their table clearing plates, followed by a second older girl who may have been her sister, delivering the main courses to the centre of the table. Dishes of fried rice, chicken chop suey, prawns and tomatoes, lamb and cashew nuts; each to share, each in white rectangular dishes.

"So what happened then?" continued Holly.

"Nothing much," said Marianne. "Dad was going steady with the gorgeous Cassie. I was just a kid in the fourth form."

"You were never just a kid to me," said Johnny.

Marianne was aware he was trying to catch her eye, and for a brief moment, she allowed it to be caught.

"But I wouldn't have admitted it to Sam and the others."

"Dad!" Holly waved a spoon reproachfully at him and helped herself to some rice.

"We used to say hello when we passed each other at school and because her mate Sasha was going out with my mate Sam, we were often in the same places. Sometimes we'd chat at parties. She made me sick once when I had too much to drink!"

Holly made a face.

"But I was too young ... and Cassie was stunning ..." said Marianne.

"Cassie was nice, but she didn't have your mother's wit."

"What happened to her?" asked Holly.

Marianne looked at Johnny.

"We split up when we went to different colleges. She met some sophisticated bloke with money. A couple of years later I met your mum again in London at a party at Sasha's. She was a grown up woman by then and I thought she was lovely. We got talking and everything fell into place. I moved jobs down to London, we got married, and the rest, you know."

Marianne felt a hot flush rising from her knees and she took off her cardigan.

"What were you like when you were twenty, Dad?"

"Masses of long hair and incredibly sexy," said Marianne.

"I mean as a person," said Holly.

Marianne realised she didn't know the answer.

"A bit purposeless after Cassie. Didn't have a steady girlfriend. Drank too much – much more than now. A lost soul. Used to see Mum sometimes in the holidays in Derwentbridge, but I was never there for long and we rarely spoke."

"I still fancied you, though," said Marianne. "You made me laugh and every time you smiled at me, I melted. My friends thought I was crazy … Unrequited love."

"Had I known, darling, we might have got together much sooner."

Holly grinned. "Mum – what were you like when you were twenty?"

"Full of romantic nonsense that nobody lived up to. Kept meeting the wrong guys, and being let down. They didn't understand me."

Marianne began to wonder if Holly was deliberately trying to make them remember the good times. If she was, it was working. She was feeling benevolent towards Johnny and wondering what the rest of the night might have in store.

The conversation shifted to Holly's month back at college; to the merits and otherwise of self-catering and to her criminal law lecturer who looked like a conservative version of David Bowie. Then three portions of pineapple fritters later, they left the restaurant in buoyant mood.

It was raining and the three of them tried to huddle under one umbrella. It was impossible so Johnny stood to the side and pulled up the collar of his jacket. He jumped with both feet in a puddle as a child might do and swung round a lamp post with one arm.

Holly grabbed his free arm and pulled him forward. "Get a grip Dad! What if someone sees? You're so embarrassing!"

Marianne laughed and the three of them made unsteady progress towards Beechview Close. "Did you know that Pam Shriver is marrying George Lazenby," she said.

"Yes," said Johnny. "But they're already married. In summer, I think."

"Who's George Lazenby?" said Holly.

"The Bond between Connery and Moore." Johnny jumped in another puddle. "*On Her Majesty's Secret Service.*"

"Hey, you're splashing my tights!" said Marianne.

"Did you ask Harry Potter if he looks like Pierce Brosnan?"

"As if," said Marianne, mimicking Holly.

"Who's Harry Potter?" asked Johnny.

"A young wizard," said Holly, hurriedly. "Surely you know that?

Still laughing, they rounded the corner that led to the house and Marianne stopped in her tracks. There, sitting on the low wall by the doorstep, looking wet and bedraggled, her long hair in darkened ropes down her back, was Charmaine.

Marianne hurried forward and was first to speak. "What the hell are you doing here?"

Holly's face collapsed. "Mum …"

Charmaine turned to Johnny, her cheeks streaked with mascara tears. "I need to talk to you. I've got a problem. I don't know who else—"

"You've got a nerve coming here again," said Marianne. "Which part of 'fuck off' don't you understand?"

"Mum!"

Johnny put his key in the lock and opened the front door, ushering Holly and Marianne inside in front of him.

"Go upstairs with your mother," he said to Holly, rather too sharply.

Marianne thought about protesting, but it seemed like a good idea. Johnny clearly didn't trust her not to make a scene after the Greenwich outburst. She would speak her mind to him in due course. At the top of the stairs, she and Holly each went into their own rooms. How quickly the mood of optimism disintegrated.

Trollop!

Her eyes began to sting and she paced around the bedroom.

She's got a problem, she says … And what might that be? Why does she need to see Johnny? … Maybe she's pregnant like Sasha's Graham's Debbi! They have had an affair! It's his baby! Arghh!

Two and two make seventeen …

She went to Holly's room. "Go downstairs and make sure they're not getting up to any funny business."

Holly was lounging on the bed with a book. "Dad wouldn't …"

"Please."

Holly padded off reluctantly. Marianne listened to her progress downstairs and into the living room. Through the opened door, she heard Johnny mumble something and Holly returned.

"He asked me to leave them alone."

"Were those his exact words?"

"He said: '*Leave it, Holly. Can't you see she's upset? Vamoose*'."

"Was he touching her?"

Holly hesitated. "N-no."

"You mean 'yes'?"

"Sort of."

"How 'sort of'?"

"Just on her arm ... Reassuring ... like this ..." Holly placed her hand on Marianne's forearm. It was an innocent enough gesture.

"I don't want that woman in my house," said Marianne, going back into her bedroom, sitting on the bed and slapping the duvet cover. "Why did she have to spoil such a lovely evening?"

Holly hovered. "It doesn't have to be spoiled, Mum. Please. Don't blame Dad. There must be an explanation. It'll be okay."

How trusting the young were. She knew it wouldn't be okay. Whatever he said, the fact remained that Charmaine had sought him out when she needed help. What did that say about their relationship?

Marianne went to the bathroom and got ready for bed. *No sexy lingerie tonight, Johnny, my dear.*

About forty minutes later, the front door banged shut and Johnny appeared in the bedroom doorway looking sheepish. Marianne was in bed reading, but she put her book down and gave him an expectant stare.

"What could I do?" he said. "She was in a right old state."

"About what, exactly."

"Oh, man problems. Stuff ..."

"You're not going to tell me?"

"I'd rather not. She asked me not to."

"I'm your wife."

"This is her business."

"You said you'd stopped seeing her."

"I have. Out of school. But we work together. I can't not listen when she tells me things. Please Mari ... Don't be like this. We've had a lovely evening. Let's not spoil it."

"You just did," said Marianne, turning away from him and onto her side, flipping the off switch on the bedside lamp and plunging the room into semi-darkness.

39

Archaeobabble

Towards the end of October Marianne was sitting on the sofa writing up her journal with some enthusiasm. A smile flickered now and then as she scribbled and paused, then scribbled some more. She was dressed in a summer skirt and camisole but the evening air was cool, so she had wrapped a warm cardigan around her shoulders.

Johnny was in the office-bedroom and hadn't been seen for over an hour. He said he was preparing a worksheet for the following day, but he may have been surfing eBay, or buying early Christmas presents, or ordering champagne and flowers as a romantic gesture, or (surely not!) gazing upon some enterprising luscious-lipped student with a loan to pay, a web-cam and wearing not many clothes. She wasn't sure; today she didn't care.

Beside her was a copy of the archaeological magazine *Antiquity*, and on the front of this in large white type and superimposed over a photograph of an impressive rock formation with turquoise sea beyond, it said 'Edward Harvey Uncovers Scilly Mystery'.

She had been reading the article describing Edward's excavation of the Troy Town Maze on Castella Down at the western edge of the island of St. Agnes. This had been part of his recent digging on the Isles of Scilly, and was the first significant archaeological work on that island since the *Isles of Scilly Survey* by Vivien Russell in 1980. Edward had discovered the much talked of, but never previously confirmed existence of a maze far predating the 1795 one, supposedly built by a lighthouse keeper searching for something to do to while away the daylight hours.

The fascination with mazes in general, and now the Troy Town maze in particular, meant Edward Harvey's name was appearing in all the serious newspapers and he had been given an early morning grilling on the *Today* programme. Indeed it was surprising he hadn't yet appeared on the national news. Marianne was delighted at his recognition, but it also served to remind her of her own lack of achievement and the notes she was making in her journal were now very much concerned with the book. Since the reunion there was a new urgency to developing a plotline.

Maya and Adam … Friends Reunited … Lucy and Lydia …

To: Edward Harvey
From: Marianne Hayward
Date: 29th October 2002, 20.05
Subject: A-mazing!

Hi Edward,
I have been reading about your work on the Troy Town Maze. Interesting!! It is written with such enthusiasm, I find it hard to believe you have ever thought of giving up the job. I was under the impression that the maze had been irretrievably ruined by supposedly well-meaning dowsers in 1988. Most of the guide books I've read say that the archaeology was destroyed, and many regular St. Agnes visitors report that the new maze does not give the same 'feeling' as the old maze. When we were there, we didn't know what we were supposed to feel, but I remember sitting on the grass close by and Johnny saying how peaceful he felt. For me there was something

other-worldly about it. I mean all of St. Agnes is peaceful, but the maze area was like peace in another dimension.

It's the symbolism that I find interesting. You write: 'the spiral is a journey towards the very centre of our being and then back again into the world …' Was that tongue-in-cheek? Do you believe it, or are you just pandering to the likes of me – witchcraft for the modern masses?

Having made this discovery, what are the plans? Will there be any chance of moving the current maze back to where it once was, or will this further disrupt the archaeology? If there is any possibility of restoration, then it will make a lot of people very happy.

Having said this though, I still sometimes wonder what archaeology is for. I mean does it serve any purpose other than increasing our understanding of our forebears – knowledge for the sake of knowledge?

Best wishes,

Marianne

For a few moments after she sent this email, she was mentally transported back to Scilly; to the boats and the silvery sands; to the the sculpted granite outcrops and the heady scent of agapanthus blooms; to a time when she and Johnny rolled on the grass like adolescents, revelling in their first holiday alone since Holly had been born.

To: Marianne Hayward
From: Edward Harvey
Date: 31st October 2002, 21.16
Subject: Re: A-mazing!

Hi Marianne,

Thanks for your feedback on the article. Perhaps the 'grubbing about' worked its magic on me!

You ask the purpose of archaeology. Shall not take this as an insult! Most of my non-archaeological friends soon adopt a glazed look when I try to explain my subject area. It is simply to understand how people of the past interacted with their environment and to preserve such history for present and future generations. But then you know that, anyway. Once archaeology is destroyed, it is lost forever.

What we found was not the lighthouse keeper's labyrinth, or indeed the one that supposedly existed before that. Our discovery was of a much, much earlier one lying below and beside the area damaged by the dowsers. Acted on a hunch and for once it was fruitful! Always very sceptical about the spiritual aspect until St. Agnes. You could say I had a transforming experience on Castella Down ... Feeling at peace with the world; knowing this was what I was supposed to be doing. All great stuff! It is not archaeology that I would like to give up, but teaching and all its annual predictability of admissions and interviews and exams and marking ...

We also had some success in discovering yet more burial cists on Wingletang Down – but these have not been so newsworthy.

Best wishes,

Edward

To: Edward Harvey
From: Marianne Hayward
Date: 2nd November 2002, 22.15
Subject: Re: A-mazing!

Hi Edward,

Do you realise it is a year since I found you on FR?!
Is there a difference between a labyrinth and a maze and
d'you think the more recent copycat mazes – sorry,
labyrinths – exert the same effect? Never having had
dealings with an archaeologist before, I am ashamedly
ignorant of the discipline – hence silly questions…
Here's another one… Would there be a place for
archaeology once all pre-historical sites had been
excavated? In other words, could you have new
archaeology (neo-archaeology??) being created in
historical times?
As for giving up teaching, could you not revert to
grubbing about on a more permanent basis?
Marianne

To: Marianne Hayward
From: Edward Harvey
Date: 8th November 2002, 22.42
Subject: Re: A-mazing!

Hi Marianne,

Have been asked far sillier questions!
If the historical record of people and their lives is
complete and accurate, then there should be little need
for archaeology. However, such is the curiosity of people
that one can imagine in a few millennia, digging up some
bones buried with some artefacts and wanting to know
more about whom the bones belonged to and the life
that they led.
You have been watching too many 'Time Team'
programmes! Sadly the grubbing about doesn't generally

pay enough to support ever growing family!

A labyrinth is a unicursal maze – you just follow the path. No decisions to turn left or right; no dead ends. They say walking a labyrinth is an exploration of consciousness – hence spiritual connection. Mazes are multicursal and require an active mind for problem solving.

As for the copycat ones giving the same feeling, I can't say. Many of the original ones were built on ley lines, so the power may come from that rather than the labyrinth itself. If your copycat labyrinths have any effect then it can only be because of the meditation of walking the spiral – unless of course they are also placed on ley lines.

Am lecturing on the subject of the TTM in London at the Society of Antiquaries (Piccadilly) on 5th December at 4.30 p.m. You would be very welcome to come if you are free.

Edward

Marianne's heart quickened ever such a little and hardly daring to hope that a meeting might finally occur, she gingerly leafed through the pages of her college calendar.

To: Edward Harvey
From: Marianne Hayward
Date: 12th November 2002, 18.01
Subject: Re: A-mazing!

Hi Edward,

Do you never have qualms about digging up bones? I know they are treated gently, but is that not more in the interests of preservation than compassion?

As far as I can see, there is nothing to stop me coming
to your lecture this time!
Marianne

Surely this time there would be no hitches …

To: Marianne Hayward
From: Edward Harvey
Date: 13th November 2002, 22.11
Subject: Re: A-mazing!

Hi Marianne,
It is believed by many archaeologists that we do the
dead a great favour by discovering them and bringing
them to the notice of the world. The Egyptians, for
example, practised mummification with the intention of
preservation for eternity. What better way to live
forever than to be discovered by archaeologists?
However, there is also a trend towards repatriation of
bones that have been removed from their country of
origin, and also, following excavation, towards re-burial.
Edward.

To: Edward Harvey
From: Marianne Hayward
Date: 15th November 2002, 20.43
Subject: Re: A-mazing!

Edward,
I am not convinced that the original owners of most
bones necessarily feel the same way as the Egyptians!
Many people propagate for continuity; others write
books. Skeletons don't exactly show one in the best light

– not compatible with our looksist world! I suppose the Egyptians believed that mummification would preserve them as they were. The way cosmetic surgery is going, suggests perhaps one day we will all be buried looking about forty-five and full of non biodegradable fillers and implants. Future excavations might then discover zillions of startled Anne Robinsons!
Marianne.

To: Marianne Hayward
From: Edward Harvey
Date: 15ʰ November 2002, 22.45
Subject: Re: A-mazing!

God forbid!!
Ted

40

Meeting Lydia

When the snow came and turned south-east London winter white, it was like being in another land. Marianne was conscious of the feel of it squashing beneath her feet, each step silent until the final compacted crunch against the pavement. It wasn't crisp and icy but as soft as cotton-wool, almost melting, but not quite. How often are there days like this when the snow falls during the daylight hours instead of making its stealthy appearance with the foxes under cover of darkness?

She looked up at the trees and the branches carrying their fragile load – a breath of wind and they would be shaken clean. The air was still and cold, and the virgin whiteness on the path tempted her to be the first to leave a trail.

To: Edward Harvey
From: Marianne Hayward
Date: 2nd December 2002, 15.43
Subject: Meeting Lydia

Hi Edward,
The promised snow has come and there was grid-lock from early morning and through the rush hour. Buses were stranded, lorries jack-knifed and cars abandoned. Forgotten to grit it seemed.
I didn't have to go to college because we were having a Reading Day and it was oh so beautiful. Do hope these conditions don't get in the way of our meeting next week.

Looking forward to your lecture.
Best wishes,
Marianne

Marianne wondered again if life after meeting Edward would be the same as before. Would the bubbles all burst and leave her lost once again in a midlife wilderness of predictability? Would he make her feel safe like he did all those years ago within the dark grey walls of Brocklebank Hall? Perhaps it would be better not to know and to stay forever with her dreams that somewhere out there was a man without the human frailties of most of the people she knew.

But she had to take the risk. Their tenuous link would not sustain unless there was opportunity for growth, and moving on could only happen if they each knew who they were talking to. *You can't be proper friends with a disembodied voice,* she thought, puzzling over the paradox of this, together with the knowledge that dozens of people left their life partners on a whim to see what lay at the end of the rainbow of emails from someone first encountered in cyberspace.

There would be no dubious agenda with Edward. Logic said there would be no need to worry about who she was or what she said. But this was all speculation and she did worry. She was repeatedly worried that she had said the wrong thing in email. The 'I could tell him everything' feeling might be appropriate if they met, but she probably couldn't or shouldn't tell him everything in cyberspace.

When she returned from her walk, she unearthed her planetary ephemeris from a pile of books on one of the shelves in the office. She kept thinking about Holly's comments in the restaurant about astrology – specifically about moon compatibility. Once she believed such things without question and in this current state of uncertainty, any information would be useful.

August 20th 1956.

She leafed through the pages and placed a ruler under the numbers that were relevant for that date. Then she glanced down the column with the crescent moon symbol at the top. She saw two wavy lines, one above the other.

Moon in Aquarius!

They had harmonious moons in air signs, signifying understanding at an emotional level. *Of course they had.* Her eyes scanned the rest of the line of numbers and she thought she spotted other potential contacts with her chart; trining Mercuries for one. But she couldn't remember her own details exactly and she felt it would be intrusive to probe any further without his permission. Compatible moons were enough, at least for now.

To: Marianne Hayward
From: Edward Harvey
Date: 3rd December 2002, 22.45
Subject: Re: Meeting Lydia

Hi Marianne,
Very busy time of year teaching. No snow here. Think positive!
See you Thursday!
Best wishes,
Ted

She thought positive.

The snow began to melt a little when the sun came out, but it was so very cold and banks of ominous grey clouds were never far away.

When the day arrived, she was a complete bundle of anxiety and neuroses, made worse by the fact that she had half a day at college to complete. Her eyes shone, she taught with extra passion; her breathing was a shade faster and mounting excitement was evident in the tone of her voice.

All day she had been visualising a parking space at Beckenham Junction station. One of her friends said it always worked for her. Marianne was sceptical; it couldn't work – especially not at this station at three o'clock in the afternoon. So she left early in case she needed to walk from the town car park.

But there was a space! *Thank you.* Now she was far too early. Twenty minutes to while away before her train was due. Twenty minutes in the freezing cold. She would wait in the car where the sun shining on the windows made it seem deceptively warm. Oh this was good being able to park so close. There was a chance her shoes would get to the point of hurting if she had to walk very far.

'*Shoes maketh the woman,*' her mother used to say from a three-inch stiletto elevation when Marianne was in her teens. Today she had brought ones with medium heels to change into; a compromise between comfort and crippling pain, and more respectable than the flat ones she wore in college.

Then there was the question of whether she needed to wear a cardigan. Clouds kept scudding across the sun and in seconds the air was full of tiny stinging sleety rain like pins against the skin. There would be bound to be somewhere she could leave her coat at the venue, and she could stuff her cardigan and scarf down the sleeves and emerge a picture of elegance and composure. *Ha!*

What about a hat and umbrella? Hats squashed hair and umbrellas required shepherding like children. Hats and umbrellas were anathema to 'cool' on a day of such significance when 'cool' was everything. Would she take a risk that the worst of the wet stuff had passed and leave them in the boot?

Finally she set out wearing the cardigan and scarf but minus hat and umbrella. Only one and a half hours to go and they would meet and thirty-four long years would be over …

This is madness, feeling like this; like a schoolgirl going to a party, knowing that a special someone might be there. Unbalanced, crazy woman! Get a grip! You cannot arrive in a state. You cannot give yourself away. He cannot ever know that once you thought he was so wonderful.

She clomped across the bridge over the railway tracks, listening to the echo, then down the stairs – dodging a grey-haired man who was in her way, but she didn't scowl. This was a good day for her and everyone would be treated to a smile. Then she heard the announcer say that the train on the platform was just about to depart for London Victoria. If she hadn't been faffing around with her hat, she could have caught this one. But she didn't want to be too early, and she didn't have her ticket yet; couldn't risk travelling without that.

Past the departing train she walked and into the ticket hall with ten minutes to spare. Up on the computer screen the two trains that she had thought of as possibilities were listed, one on time, the other due five minutes late.

She bought a travel card and decided to wait in the ticket hall out of the wind, sitting down next to a woman with a massive patchwork bag on her knee. She looked around, scanning, wondering whether anyone else was about to undertake a journey to a meeting as momentous as hers. People drifted in and out of the station: old and young, smart and shabby, mostly alone with fixed expressions, fighting the elements, fighting the world.

She calmed herself. She was here, the car was parked, she was warm enough and she was sorted.

Then the announcer said: "There are no trains from London

to Kent due to problems with the line. We apologise for any inconvenience caused."

Marianne thought she was hearing things. *Surely a mistake?* She had just missed one to Victoria. It was the first slight hint that all was not well and a tremor ran through her stomach. As if she wasn't scared enough already!

But London to Kent isn't the same as Kent to London!

Then she heard the man at the ticket office telling someone that there were no trains to Victoria, "for the time being". But that couldn't be right. The computer screen said otherwise, still showing her two alternatives: the one on time and the other five minutes late. Surely if there was a problem it would show on the screen?

She was dimly aware of the woman next to her giving helpful directions to someone who wanted to go to Peckham, and of a trail of passengers, one by one, buying their tickets and being told that there were no trains to Victoria. The potential for not getting there in time suddenly seemed very real and she was immobilised by panic and indecision.

Then the announcer said: "Passengers awaiting the service to Victoria are advised to take the London Bridge train on Platform 1 and change at Crystal Palace."

That train went all round the houses and took an age – and what if no train came to Crystal Palace? *Where do they come from to get to Crystal Palace?* What if they were affected by snow too? *Oh please* … She wouldn't get there in time. She would miss it all. Unable to tell anyone too, for she still hadn't asked Edward for his mobile number. *Idiot!* Tick-tock. *Oh my* …

Her brain started searching through all the options. No point in staying put. Staying put was guaranteed disaster. She had to try something. With spirits now plummeting and her buoyant mood deflating rapidly, she went and boarded the London Bridge train. It was her only hope.

She heard a woman shouting at some boys. "Am I gonna get someone or are you gonna stop?"

What was going on? Marianne couldn't face any trouble and went into the next carriage, but she could still hear the woman: "I said, are you gonna stop, or am I gonna get someone?" A determined voice. Someone not phased by wayward youth.

Marianne wondered if she should go and lend moral support. Often she did jump in and play the teacher. Sometimes the well-practised tone was enough to stop the problem, but times were changing. All sorts of horror stories made the news these days. Even little children answered back and swore; and the bigger ones carried knives. No point in being heroic if there was a price to pay. She weighed up the options. She was already stressed to pieces and couldn't take the risk of losing her cool even more. The woman repeated her request again … and again. Then, "Yeah, that's better. You have got a brain after all." More abuse followed and she came into the carriage where Marianne was sitting, fair hair scraped back into a ponytail and a floppy fringe, similar age to Marianne and dressed in jeans with a pale blue quilted jacket. She didn't look the type to take on a group of naughty school kids. Marianne had instant respect for her and wished she had gone to her aid.

Pathetic wimp! She thought of herself.

"Are you trying to get to Victoria?" Marianne asked. They were the only two people in the carriage.

"Yes," said the woman arranging herself on a seat. "What is it with some kids? They are so rude."

Marianne agreed and explained her plight. "I have to get to a lecture in Piccadilly for four fifteen. Not sure if I should go all the way to London Bridge? Do you know where it is in relation to Green Park?"

The woman produced a diary from out of a denim bag that

clearly had Mary Poppins aspirations and seemed to contain everything. She leafed through it until she found a map of the underground.

"Four stops. Not far. That might be your best bet."

Marianne thanked the woman and sank once more into the depths of her scarf.

Breathe ... Breathe ... You will get there ... There is time ... Thirty-four years ... Edward Harvey ... Who are you now? What will you look like? What will you sound like? How will you greet me? What will we say?

It seemed to take forever to get to London Bridge. When she arrived it was loads of platforms and stairs innumerable, and time ticking by relentlessly – she hardly dare look at her watch. Where was the tube station? She asked a station cleaner with vacant eyes that sprang to life as soon as she spoke to him. No point in wasting precious time going down blind alleys. Even so it was a long, long walk down the platform, through a concourse and then to the escalators.

As she stepped on the one leading down to the Jubilee line, she relaxed her shoulders ever so slightly. It would be all right. She would make it. And her mood lifted and she began to look forward again to this oh so special meeting.

"Passengers for the Jubilee line please note there are delays in both directions. We apologise for any inconvenience caused."

The tannoy again, and she wasn't even half way down the escalator.

Arghhhh! She howled within. It was surely all over. Any more delays and she would be late. Too late to meet up before the lecture; too embarrassed to turn up in the middle of it; but she carried on down the escalator and followed the signs that would take her westbound to Green Park, just in case.

There were no trains on the platform and the waiting crowds looked uneasy. The electronic information boards were completely blank and no welcoming noises could be heard from down the tunnel; no roaring wind heralding the imminent arrival of a train. Just an eerie silence. Some of the passengers were turning back, looking for alternatives. In twenty minutes the lecture would start. Alternatives would be too late. By the time she emerged from the underground, another five minutes would be lost and she didn't know how far away she was from Piccadilly. She could no longer think straight. Even a cab would probably take too long or be ridiculously expensive.

Half formulated thoughts tumbled over themselves in her head, each one evaporating before she could turn it into something workable. She had already missed the chance to talk to Edward before the lecture started, and when it was over he would be besieged by others, all keen to congratulate and ask questions.

She waited another ten minutes, frozen by indecision, transfixed by the silence from the tunnel and the slowly emptying platform as passengers drifted away. The voice on the tannoy kept repeating the words: *"Passengers for the Jubilee line please note there are delays in both directions. We apologise for any inconvenience caused."*

For Marianne, they were the worst words in the world and eventually she too gave up and began a lonely trip back up the escalators. What would he think of her now?

Later, after a very difficult return journey with much hanging about in the cold, she arrived back home tired and numb. Johnny was already busy in the kitchen, preparing potatoes to go with the lamb stew that was simmering in the oven.

"So how was the lecture then?"

Marianne took off her coat and scarf and glanced at herself in the hall mirror. She looked bedraggled and damp and sad. *How, indeed?*

"Didn't manage to get there," she said. "Snow and train problems … and more train problems. And I'm freezing cold."

Johnny emerged from the kitchen and gave her a gentle hug. "Your nose is red too!"

She sniffed and smiled weakly, the adrenaline from the day all lost with her dreams on the rail network of London.

When later she sat by the computer in the room upstairs, she allowed herself to cry a little. But it was a cry of frustration more than sadness, for a fruitless journey, for wasted energy, for questions that still remained unanswered, for a soul from long ago.

To: Edward Harvey
From Marianne Hayward
Date: 7th December 2002, 21.15
Subject: Re: Meeting Lydia

Dear Edward,
I am so sorry I didn't make it for your lecture. I did try!
Train cancellations in south London due to snow and then even though I managed to get as far as London Bridge, there were no trains on the Jubilee line. No chance to get there in time, so came home.
I hope all went well for you.
I am sure we'll manage to meet one day!
Marianne.

41

Two Thousand Years Hence

"So here we have a woman of probably forty-something, Marianne Hayward, hormonally unbalanced, perhaps even mentally deranged; married to Johnny Ingleton according to the community records, and possibly having an affair or some sort of illicit liaison with eminent archaeologist Edward Harvey when she was taken so untimely from the world."

"I wonder why she was called Hayward and her husband was called Ingleton?"

"Oh, that's how it often was in the twenty-first century. Women went through a phase of keeping their maiden names, before the feminist backlash really took hold."

"And they had a child?"

"Yes, Holly Ingleton."

Marianne was idly contemplating the far distant future, when the worst of her doom-and-gloom scenarios had been and gone and the world population – decimated due to the 'flu pandemic, global warming and the resultant raised sea levels, and then the 2095 meteorite impact and subsequent cooling – had re-established itself and begun a series of new civilisations around the planet.

Life would be very different in two thousand years: unimaginably so. The oil reserves would likely be gone and alternative and renewable sources of energy must surely prevail. There might be wind turbines in every desert-planted back garden and solar panels on every roof. Perhaps they would fly around on personal airborne scooters like characters from *Thunderbirds*, or maybe there would be a return to horsepower, camels and yaks.

She was lounging in a chair with both her legs over the arm. She had a pencil in her hand and was making notes in her journal. Following her recent immersion in archaeology, she was still contemplating the unsavoury possibility of being dug up at some far future time. She couldn't erase the images of skulls and bones from her mind and sometimes when she looked in the mirror, she imagined the flesh falling from her cheeks and her eye sockets empty; soul-windows gone. Despite Edward's assurances, there were no guarantees that the archaeologists of the future would be similarly respectful. Marianne did not relish the prospect of her bones being dusted, dated, analysed and preserved and then turning up in a glass case in some architecturally futuristic museum to be gawped at by the swarms of curious schoolchildren in a couple of millennia.

But why would anyone want to see her anyway? What had she done to change the world? What would the museum guide book say to warrant the admission charge? What fascinating inscription would be on the plaque by the exhibit?

She was slightly depressed. This might be just another menopausal fluctuation, or her home situation, or it could be because thoughts of archaeology naturally led her to thoughts of Edward and where they were in their respective lives. She and Edward had started out at a very similar academic level and now, relative to her, he was in another continent. Of course it was partly his motivation and opportunity that served to bring about the current gulf between them, but that was no consolation when the remainder of life seemed to be contracting at an exponential rate and there seemed so little time to redress the balance.

And he has a wife, thought Marianne. *If I had a wife instead of a demanding husband, then maybe I would be written about in magazines; maybe I would have had time to develop some ambition. If more women had 'wives' then their achievements would be so much more.*

Another problem was that she hadn't heard a word from

Edward since their failed meeting. It was so unlike him not to acknowledge an email – however briefly – that she was more than a little concerned.

She began scribbling in her journal again. She was trying to sharpen her literary style. Soon she would begin her book in earnest, but she was having trouble with the plot; trouble with the way it should end. Should Maya and Adam meet, or should they not? Would a meeting make a more sellable story? And if they met, how would it be?

"She didn't do much of significance for most of her life … Taught kids in a sixth form college … That was just before the time when everyone went to university … when the children had to stay in education until they were twenty one …"

"I remember … then they ran out of electricians and plumbers and builders and it was another sixty years before society re-stabilised."

"But she had always liked to write."

"Wasn't she the one who wrote a half finished novel about bullying?"

"That's her! That's when her life took on some impetus. She found a classmate on that Internet thing and they wrote to each other for months. But the 'flu got her before the book was finished."

"And that guy she wrote to was Edward Harvey?"

"That's the fellow! Renowned for his survey of St. Agnes, Scilly in 2002 and considered a world authority on labyrinth mazes."

"Is there any evidence to suppose that he and Marianne Hayward were anything other than friends?"

"None at all, although people like to speculate about these things."

"Huntley Shorthouse, for one."

"The Affair theory doesn't wash with me. It is the notion of scandalmongers and busybodies. Tabloid-trash, out for a quick buck. Anyone with half a brain can deduce that Edward Harvey was too busy to have an affair – least of all with someone who lived two hundred miles away."

"Shorthouse would say that distance was irrelevant in 2002 and

that busy people are the ones who manage to fit most in."

"But if Marianne Hayward's opinion of Edward Harvey is the same as her character Maya's opinion of Adam, then Edward Harvey wasn't the type of person to have an affair."

Marianne knew that people were unpredictable and that it was impossible to be certain about anything, particularly the sexual proclivities of men. Readers of books wanted passion; readers of books often suspended their morality …

'In this futuristic world two thousand years from now, it is the growing absence of heterosexual relationships that is increasing interest in the love affairs of the past, and neo-archaeologists have looked to literature for clues as to how such relationships were manifest.

'Recent interest has focused on the unfinished novel by Marianne Hayward, not least because of her acquaintance with Edward Harvey and their suspected connection with the soon-to-be restored Brocklebank Hall in the north of England.

'In trying to select the most appropriate ending for Ms Hayward's book, several eminent scholars have attempted to find evidence of what really happened between her and Edward Harvey. A visitors' book from The Society of Antiquaries in Piccadilly, London holds a record of signatures of guests attending society meetings. It is known that Edward Harvey lectured occasionally at this venue and in view of Adam's written invitation to Maya in Chapter 27 and Maya's subsequent acceptance, scholars believe that a meeting may well have occurred. However, there is no record of Marianne Hayward's signature in the guest book on the date for which the invitation was made. Also, it should be noted that there are significant differences between the lives of Marianne and Edward and the fictitious lives of Maya and Adam. Although it is clear that her novel is in some respects autobiographical, that is true of many novels – particularly first novels – and it is always difficult to be sure where the fact ends and the fiction begins.

'The debate is centuries old, but has taken on a new momentum since the discovery and excavation of Marianne Hayward's burial site.

'Archaeologists have also in recent months found what they believe to be the site of the Oakleigh House of Ms Hayward's book. This would have been the Brocklebank Hotel and Conference Centre, formerly Brocklebank Hall which was indeed once a boys' prep school. But again, this is a speculative link, based on the assumption that Ms Hayward attended such a school, and shared a class with Edward Harvey.

'Records show that Edward Harvey's great-great-granddaughter, Candrina Atwell-Harvey – one of the last surviving descendents of the Harvey family before the cataclysmic events of 2095 – kept a scrap book with a photograph of her great-great grandfather aged eleven and dressed in a frock and clearly involved in some dramatic production. It could well be that this was his appearance as Lydia Languish, but there were no notes to confirm or disprove.'

Marianne paused and nibbled the end of her pencil.

'Stacy Greetham's version of the end of the book continues the picture of Adam-as-Enigma as he and Maya never meet. On the other hand, Imogen Cartwright predictably sees a passionate dénouement as the two protagonists reunite at Victoria Station, become enchanted with each other on a launch to Greenwich and seal their fate with a lingering kiss among the figureheads on the lower decks of the Cutty Sark, followed by a somewhat explicit encounter in the grounds of Greenwich Observatory. There the novel ends, Cartwright failing to deal with the undoubted aftershocks.

'It is difficult to ascertain which, if either, of these endings Marianne would have preferred, and in any case, would she go for truth or fiction? That was the question that occupied biographers for much of the twenty-first century. Kendal writes that she had a puritanical streak which suggests she may have favoured the former option, but a tattered Christmas card from Waverly Grossett to Edward Harvey in 2002 warns him against any form of Internet Liaison with the Other Species – by which we assume he means women – predicting all manner of dire events should Edward ignore his advice.

'Armytage – the Oxford Armytage – believes that Marianne did meet Edward at the Antiquarian Society, but that this so shattered their *respective images of each other that their relationship was never the same again.'*

Marianne paused again, thinking that perhaps the train problems had been a fateful intervention to avert disappointment – not just hers, but Edward's.

'The dual endings of the fifth edition of her novel – a failure to meet on the one hand and a passionate encounter on the other – have led to much reader dissatisfaction and it is hoped that by establishing the truth of Marianne Hayward's relationship with Edward Harvey, it may be possible to select the most likely option for Maya and Adam in the book. Who will make this decision is yet to be decided. British Heritage has expressed an interest purely on the grounds that they have recently proposed to restore Brocklebank Hall as a typical example of a mid twentieth century preparatory school, and they believe funding to be largely dependent on the continued interest in the Hayward-Harvey relationship. However, Shaynee Postlethwaite of the Ancient Literature Society said that selecting the wrong ending – that is the ending that Marianne would not have approved – would be a disaster on a par with the removal of the sex scenes from Lady Chatterley's Lover, as carried out at the beginning of 3956 as part of the demonising of all physical relations between males and females.'

Marianne paused. It was getting late and dark and she had to get up early for work the following morning. The clock on the wall was approaching midnight and Johnny – if still awake – would wonder where she was. She had been carried away by a single thought about life in the distant future. Yes, this was certainly a justification for cremation and a good reason to start writing her book.

But how would she break the news of such a book to Edward?

42

Cybersilence

To: Edward Harvey
From: Marianne Hayward
Date: 12st December 2002, 20.55
Subject: Re: Meeting Lydia

Hi Edward,
I am increasingly becoming an archaeological junkie!
Reading about all this stuff you have discovered on Scilly
has inspired me. I also think it is about time I tried to
leave something for posterity! Perhaps I should follow
my dream of writing a novel based on my Brocklebank
experiences. Have been making preliminary notes for a
while and the plot is beginning to take shape. Our
'Friends Reunited' has given me an idea. (Don't be
alarmed!)
Holly is back next week after staying a few days with the
Hellebaut's. (Dylan's parents.) It's nice that they want to
keep in touch.
We will be here for Christmas, but may go to Cumbria
for New Year.
Best wishes,
Marianne

Marianne sent this email with some consternation. She still
hadn't heard from Edward since their failed meeting and didn't
know what to think. Emails went astray. People thought they'd
replied when they hadn't. The cyber world was a world that

was riddled with uncertainty. She would wait and see if and how he responded to this one before she told him any more about the book. Subtle tactics would have to be employed so he didn't take fright: the drip, drip approach. She imagined he would be fascinated and would want to know more. If he asked her questions, it would somehow legitimise her telling him the details – as far as she knew them.

But days went by and her inbox was curiously lacking in a reply from Edward Harvey. Marianne began to wonder if all was well. It just wasn't like him to be so silent. Now she had two reasons to think she may have caused offence. Was it the lecture or the book? Either he thought her failure to attend was because she didn't want to meet him, or perhaps he didn't like the idea of her writing a novel with some inevitable autobiographical components (but surely he would say?); or he was ill; or something untoward had happened to him in the snow; or he was merely busy. But he was always busy, and that didn't usually stop him from responding. In any case, from what she knew of Edward Harvey, he would have contacted her soon after the failed meeting as a matter or courtesy. The puzzle continued.

Christmas came and Holly returned with some of the bounce of old.

"It isn't that I've stopped being sad, Mum," she said. "But I know Dylan wouldn't want me to spend months and months moping around when the uni opportunity flies by so fast."

Marianne was proud to see her daughter being so pragmatic. It made her think about her own life. It wasn't just uni that raced by, but everything. The time it took to complete the typical degree was the time until she was fifty. No time at all!

Johnny was being more considerate, but there was a tension about their communications that masked the joy of old. They were trying too hard to say the right thing; frightened of making mistakes.

Even after New Year, there was still no mail from Edward. After much weighing up of pros and cons, Marianne decided it was time she wrote again. She would appear unconcerned and adopt her usual breezy style.

To: Edward Harvey
From: Marianne Hayward
Date: 7th January 2003, 20.09
Subject: How to Make an Arrowhead that Pierces a Boar

Hi Edward,
Happy New Year!
Christmas was uneventful and New Year in Cumbria was cold.
Today I was watching an archaeology programme and expected you to appear at any moment! I now know how to kill wild boar should any appear in Beckenham! Have you ever thought of doing work for TV?
I heard someone on the radio earlier this week saying that ninety-six per cent of the universe is missing. This is the amount needed to create enough gravity to stop everything falling apart. Apparently they've been looking for this 'Dark Matter' for about fourteen years. It sounds incredible to me … Unless the stuff that we can't see is like another dimension that is alien to humans … I wonder if this fits in with String Theory which predicts we are surrounded by hidden dimensions and that there are worlds next to us that are invisible?
Enough!
Best wishes,
Marianne

Surely if he was there on the other end of cyberspace he

couldn't fail to respond to this.

But he didn't.

And by the end of January there was still no reply and she became seriously concerned. Had she written the wrong thing? Had she been misinterpreted? Had the programme *The Curse of Friends Reunited* scared him? But why should it? They lived two hundred miles apart; each was content with their life. So was he okay?

She wondered that she was so upset by his distance. He had been but idle distraction. It wasn't a relationship of sex or romance, but with their acquaintanceship rooted in childhood, and the trust she had in his integrity, it was so much more than most of the e-contacts she had with men. And he had saved her from the Brocklebank ghosts, which in turn was helping her to find a less self-destructive strategy in dealing with the Johnny problem. Perhaps she was scared that without him, the ghosts and the lack of confidence would return.

She re-read her recently sent emails, looking for the key that could cause offence. There was nothing tangible. Nothing to warrant a severing of contact. So what was it? Was her paranoia finally getting the better of her? Or was he in crisis. The thought lurked in the background and made her unsettled.

She knew she was doing what the psychologists called 'catastrophising'. Playing the 'what if' game until driven to distraction from worry. Her mother would have said she was *going to pot*. Many things went there according to her mother. Usually people – particularly adolescents and the over-fifties, alcoholics, criminals, the country and the government. When she looked it up in the dictionary, it said *ruined, gone to the bad*. Catastrophising was definitely a way of going to pot. Marianne knew it was a futile gesture. It was time she learned to leave it alone.

The spring term was underway, Pandrea had gone on

maternity leave and Marianne was now in charge of the Psychology Department. She told Johnny at the end of the second week.

"By the way Johnny, did I tell you Pandrea's having a baby and I'm covering her leave?" She chose to tell him when they were about to drive off together to get the weekend shopping.

"When did all this happen?" said Johnny over the top of the car.

"Sometime last term," said Marianne, getting into the passenger side.

"And you didn't think I'd be interested?"

"Too many other things going on," she said lightly. "I've been in denial about it happening until now. It's not so bad … And it's only until the end of the year."

"I think we should celebrate," said Johnny, reversing out of the drive. "Shall we buy something special to eat or would you prefer to go out for a meal?"

Marianne considered the options. If they went out, they would have to make small talk for the duration of the meal. If they stayed at home, the cooking would provide distraction if there were any awkward moments. "Let's buy a duck and some langoustines," she said.

"And some champagne," added Johnny. "I think you deserve that."

It was gratifying that he was making an effort, but later as they sat watching TV, when he moved beside her on the sofa and made a hopeful gesture of affection, Marianne began doubting his motives over the celebration and her response was less than enthusiastic.

Days went by and still no news from Edward. If it had been anyone else, she wouldn't have been concerned, but he was always so reliable …

He must be away. Must have just missed her last letter and be off on one of his lengthier jaunts in a far-off place doing exciting things …

Round and round went the negative thoughts until she thought she was going mad. There was nothing rational about this. Should she write to him yet again?

To: Edward Harvey
From: Marianne Hayward
Date: 18th January 2003, 21.37
Subject: Cybersilence

Dear Edward,
You have been so uncharacteristically silent lately I fear something is amiss. I know you might be horrendously busy, but then you always have been. I cannot help but wonder if all is well with you.
Or have I said something wrong? Didn't think so, but email seems to be prone to misinterpretation. If I have, please say and I will try to put things right.
I cannot imagine you would disappear from our renewed acquaintance without some explanation. Which brings me back to something being wrong. And after so much communication over the past year, of course I am a little concerned.
Hope to hear from you soon.
Marianne

But she didn't send it. She dreaded making things worse. To be seen as paranoid or just too involved. So what was going on? Surely she could make a mistake – if such she had – and not be judged?

God … I am going mad. I just want you to be there Edward, on the

*other end of cyberspace for sharing things when no one else will listen …
Be there again Edward … Write to me! Don't let me down. Please!*

She heard an echo from the past: *'A woman should never plead.'* Words from a man with a camel embroidered on the back pocket of his jeans in a pub in Worcester; a man ranting about his ex-wife and subsequent stormy divorce. He was a creep and had pestered her one evening when she was on holiday with a friend. She had never forgotten his words.

How she wished she could unwrite her last few emails to Edward. He must've read something in a different tone to what was meant. Perhaps it was the book. He must've thought she wasn't to be trusted any more; that she was far too fey for his feet-on-the-ground persona to cope. Or had he told Felicity about the book, and did her alarm bells ring? She tried to put herself in Felicity's shoes. She knew she wasn't Charmaine. But Felicity didn't know that.

Or maybe he was dead.

Edward,

Ours is an example of a 'new' type of relationship. That's the problem. Not yet friends, yet more than just mere acquaintances. You could disappear and I would never know what had happened to you.

Edward?

Have you disappeared?

Johnny came in and Marianne stopped her reverie.

"Charmaine has done a runner," he announced, looking cross. "Buggered off with that bloke from the Greenwich pier."

43

Voices of Reason

After all the failed communications, Marianne tried very hard to dismiss Edward from her thoughts. *It's never going to happen,* she thought, *we're never going to meet. I must stop hoping, wishing, wanting to be friends. Time to forget him; time to pull away from this crazy phase of life.* But she arranged to have lunch with Taryn all the same, to talk about it, to analyse and look for clues as to where she should go from here. Taryn would talk some sense into her.

"The problem is, I haven't heard from him since we didn't meet."

They were eating Italian, and while Taryn was an expert in dealing with spaghetti, Marianne kept losing it off the end of her fork.

"I'd be more concerned if you hadn't heard from him and you had met."

"I did apologise … there was nothing I could've done, short of turning up late… but then they probably wouldn't have let me in … and I'd have been so embarrassed."

"I don't think you should read anything into it. You say he's always so busy."

Marianne nodded.

"There you go then. He'll be off wooing the archaeological masses with his brilliance!" There was a touch of irony in her tone. "Then there's Christmas, his family and all this writing you say he does. I hate to say it, but you're probably way down the list of priorities. Stop fretting. Tell me again if you haven't heard from him in a couple of months."

"I know you're right. I'd just hate to lose him."

"Are you sure your obsession isn't getting in the way of sorting things out with Johnny?"

Marianne took a deep breath. This is what she had wondered herself; many times. But always she came to the same conclusion. "No way. Absolutely the reverse. I know things aren't exactly great. But we've stopped rowing. He hasn't properly acknowledged that I was right to be upset. He thinks I over-reacted to the whole Charmaine business and so he hasn't apologised. But he can't make me feel bad about myself any more – not in the way that he did – and that is indirectly down to Edward. Thanks to mailing Edward, I've left behind the past. Edward's also distracted me. He gives me something else to think about – even worry about. And he's my hero from when I was eleven!"

"Does he know all this? Does he know you're a batty middle-aged woman with a suspected errant husband who's got the hots for him?"

Marianne shook her head vigorously. "Not the hots! No! It's not like that at all. Just admiration … Liking … Wanting to be friends."

"Honestly?"

"Hand on heart honestly."

Taryn raised her eyebrows skywards and shook her head and her microfilament hair shimmered.

"You don't believe me," said Marianne. "I hardly believe it myself. I am constantly analysing my motives – searching for anything dubious – but they're nothing but innocent."

"Imagine that!"

"Indeed!"

"And what is the latest on the Cow-Charmaine?"

"Would you believe she's done a runner with her fancy-man! Didn't turn up for school one morning and when Johnny phoned her flat, he was given some tale from some squeaky-voiced woman called Leanne, that the man had turned up on Charmaine's doorstep with a suitcase. Wife had been shredding his clothes and he was worried about his precious Jag apparently! Took passports and haven't been seen since. Johnny's furious."

"You must be pleased!"

"Of course I pretended to be sympathetic. Adopted a suitably concerned face. But it was the best news. And frankly I don't care if it causes Johnny a few administrative problems. Serves him right!"

"By the way," added Taryn, just as they were parting. "Marc and I are moving in together next week."

"Marc-the-bastard?" said Marianne, incredulously. "Marc who you said you were glad to see the back of not that long ago?"

"But there's the Scrabble factor," Taryn added, "and winter nights are long!"

The following weekend, Marianne was watching Johnny clearing up the garden in preparation for spring. The autumn was getting later every year and with adverse weather conditions in December, a busy Christmas, a New Year up in Cumbria and a frenetic beginning of term, the usual end of season jobs had been left over and clumps of soggy brown leaves had welded themselves to the fence, the hedge and the shrubbery.

Johnny worked quickly and energetically, piling the offending vegetation into a black bin liner. He looked very fit for his almost fifty years. She cast her mind back to Holly's birthday meal when he had said that between Cassie and meeting her again, he was a lost soul and had drunk too much. She hadn't known this; he never told her.

Does that mean he feels like a lost soul now?

She couldn't imagine life without him, yet knew that one day it was inevitable that one would leave the other behind; the awful truth that awaits all couples. She felt it as a pain that she could scarcely bear to acknowledge.

In February Sam Rycroft, came to stay at Beechview Close for a few days over the half term holiday. He arrived by train on the Monday afternoon with the intention of staying only until Wednesday. However, the way things panned out, it was Saturday before he left. Poor Sam. He was full of woe about his divorce, his failed relationships and the fact that his two girls were used by his wife for scoring points. He was in a rut; in a downward spiral. It was good for him to get away.

"I'm too soft," he said when they sat drinking wine before supper on the first evening. "I always was soft. Too easy-going. Never noticed that things were going arse-over until it was too late. When the rows started, there was no going back." He had shaved off his beard since the reunion. He looked younger.

After supper, Marianne suggested Johnny take him down to the local so they could catch up on some male bonding. They stayed out until half past eleven and had clearly had a good time. Marianne heard them trying to stifle laughter downstairs and she smiled to herself and waited for Johnny to tell her the news.

Johnny said that it had been like old times in the pub. They had reminisced, reverted to their old form of childish humour, rediscovered that you could say almost anything to old friends and know that it wouldn't be taken wrongly; wouldn't cause a rift.

Sam said he hadn't been to London since 1978 and he wanted to make up for lost time. On Tuesday Johnny and he went ice skating in the morning, to Borough Market in the afternoon and then in the evening, the three of them went to see Queen's *We Will Rock You*.

When they walked out of the theatre and into the evening bustle of London's West End, with all its lights and glamour and people going somewhere, they had big smiles on their faces and felt truly alive.

And on the third evening, Wednesday, Sasha came for supper.

Johnny hadn't been too sure about the arrangement. Said it smacked of match-making; of interference. Marianne said if it hadn't been for Sasha, then she and Johnny would never have got together in the first place. Had he regretted that? (A comment which she wished she hadn't made as soon as she said it, but he let it pass.) In any case, Sam and Sasha both knew the score and they wanted to meet up for old time's sake. No strings; no need to feel awkward. And not much chance of anything more when one considered how their lives had diverged.

Marianne called upon all her *Delia* skills for this meal, dimmed the lighting, found the candles and even did some fancy origami with some cream paper napkins. She cooked three courses from her specially adapted repertoire for guests. They started with a Rick Stein inspired spicy concoction of smashed crab claws with soy sauce, ginger, garlic and chilli, which required the hands-on approach and lots of finger licking and trails of hot sauce around the mouth. It broke the ice, relaxed the atmosphere.

Marianne looked at each of them as they sat round the table. It was over twenty years since they'd all been in the same room at the Castle Inn, Bassenthwaite, when she and Johnny were married – and never had the four of them sat like this, two couples across a table. Sasha and Sam had long since finished when Johnny and Marianne had got together at her party. Now Sasha sat as composed as always, hair still long and straight but now a golden corn colour with fashionable ash blonde streaks. She was wearing a simple long black dress with short sleeves and a plunging neckline, and she exuded an effortless sexuality, her subtle gestures full of a grace that melted hearts.

Sam watched her every move and listened intently while she spoke. Once they had been a couple from the A-list of Derwentbridge; fashionable in a Bohemian seventies way. Beautiful people invited to any party that was worth going to and wooed by young men and women alike; popular, charismatic; a couple to know. Johnny too had been part of that crowd along with his girlfriend Cassie. Cassie who had legs to die for, wore her school uniform skirts so short it was a miracle you couldn't see her knickers, and bore a distinct resemblance to the young Jackie Bouvier-Kennedy-Onassis. The two-years-younger Marianne knew she was in the relegation zone by comparison and she had looked on in awe and resigned herself to being B-list; being second best along with most of her friends.

Sasha, on her own now for the first time in decades, seemed vulnerable. "I was attracted by what Graham stood for," she said in response to a question from Sam, before sucking crab meat from a piece of shell and licking her teeth. "He knew people. Helped with my career. Call it mercenary if you like. It's what women do to get the best for their kids. If you just happen to like the guy too, then it's a bonus."

Sam looked worried. "I hope that's not why you went out with me."

Sasha shook her head. "When you're young, it's all about experimentation and testing the water. Getting the best looking guy you can ..."

Sam's blue eyes twinkled as he appreciated the compliment, and he laughed the same laugh from grammar school days.

"Women often choose a different type of man to settle down with," said Marianne, remembering her conversation with Taryn. "They want him to stick around so they opt for something that looks more reliable than the Playboy."

"D'you think that's what happened to me with Gayle? Was I targeted because by that time I'd given up playing the field and had a stable career and good prospects?"

"Very likely," said Sasha.

"Surely not in this day and age," said Johnny.

"Not consciously," added Sasha. "But the old programming is there."

"So Mari, did you select me on those grounds?" asked Johnny, looking hurt.

"Course not … in any case I always fancied you. But then having kids wasn't my prime motivation at the time."

"It wasn't?"

"No. I've never been the maternal type."

"What?"

"Sasha will tell you. Couldn't abide babies when we were growing up." Marianne sipped her white wine thoughtfully. It was time for Johnny to know exactly who he had married.

"It's true," acknowledged Sasha.

"But you never told me."

"It was never relevant. I knew if I met the right man, I would want to have his child eventually."

Johnny seemed satisfied with this and the conversation moved on through the main course, to talk of the stresses of teaching and of alternative careers that might be pursued before the job took a significant toll on physical health. Sam told Johnny about his wrought iron gates which were becoming so popular he was considering teaching part-time the following year.

"I don't think there's anything I could do apart from teach," said Johnny.

"There's always Marianne's book," said Sam.

"What book?" asked Johnny.

"Just a rumour at the reunion," said Sam.

Johnny looked at Marianne and she blushed.

"Oh, you know, I've always wanted to write, but there's no guarantee it can be turned into a retirement option."

After the pudding of blackcurrant pie, raspberry sauce and ice cream, Sasha went through to the kitchen with Marianne, carrying plates. "That was delish. A long way from the packet soup, the MSG, and the tins of mince. But I can't believe you haven't got a dishwasher."

"Never seemed to need one with only the three of us … So tell me, how do you find Sam?"

"As sweet as ever!"

"And?"

"Shaggable still …"

"D'you want to stay the night? Drive home tomorrow?" said Marianne.

"Thanks, but I have work tomorrow. And even if I stayed, it wouldn't be for that. We've moved on. I wouldn't want to hurt him by playing games."

"Poor Sam …" Marianne put the kettle on and reached for the teapot.

Sasha opened and shut the kitchen cupboard doors in an absent kind of way while they waited for the kettle to boil. "So this Edward whose name you have been dropping …"

"God! Is that what it sounds like?"

"Just a tad! Who is he? I don't remember a *you* and Edward."

"There never was a 'me and Edward'. Not in that sense. Edward Harvey and I were at Brocklebank Hall together. Before I knew you. Did I never mention him? He was the only one of the boys who I am sure was never, ever, horrible to me. And he had an interesting brain. He went to Waterside. Sam knew him there. Don't you remember me trying to find him when we were on that science course?"

Sasha shook her head and her blonde streaked hair gleamed

under the strip lighting. "I can't even remember the course, never mind an Edward!"

"We've been mailing for a while, that's all."

"And he's a famous archaeologist?"

"Not exactly 'famous', but increasingly known in his field."

"Don't you think you might be making a bit much of this e-relationship?"

Marianne reddened and went hot. "Course not."

"You sure you're not trying to get your own back after Charmaine?"

"It isn't that kind of relationship. In any case, what if I was?"

"It rattles Johnny obviously. Haven't you noticed his eyes when you mention his name? And two wrongs don't make a right. You do go on about him."

"Do I?"

"How many times have you said 'Edward said …'? How many times have you written about him to me in emails? … Not that I had a clue who you were talking about then. I mean in the scheme of things, he's worth piss-all."

Marianne shuddered. "I hope – I hoped we'd meet … be friends. Though that looks increasingly unlikely as I haven't heard from him since early December."

"But does it matter if he never writes to you again? What matters is this." She made a wide sweep with her arm. "This is real. Johnny is real. Johnny isn't some fantasy from way back. Well, actually he is, if you remember."

"Of course I remember."

"This guy won't be a bit like you imagine."

"I know that."

"He won't be Mr Perfect. And whatever he is, he'll be past his prime. You won't think 'phwoar' when you do meet."

"I never thought I would. And he won't either. Hey what is this?"

"I'm just telling it like it is. Trying to keep your feet on the ground before you do something crazy."

When Johnny and Sam adjourned for a quick drink at the pub, Marianne decided to tell Sasha some truths; to justify her relationship with Edward.

"When we were young, I never had any confidence."

"I knew that … Always told you it was ridiculous."

"But did you ever wonder why? What lay behind it? Why it didn't matter what you or anyone said, I always felt like second best. Remember Nick and Phil? How surprised Lana was that I had landed the best looking one?

"When I was at Brocklebank, I felt like a second class citizen; like I'd always be worthless in the eyes of men. When Sam came to the grammar school and I started fancying him again, I knew I would never have a chance with him. Most of us wouldn't … When he started making overtures towards you, my best friend, can you imagine what it felt like? I didn't want to spoil things for you, so I tried to hide the hurt. It was horrible. And even when I moved my affections to Johnny, I still knew nothing could come of it because I wasn't beautiful enough for their crowd."

"It was more because you were young," said Sasha. "They had the pick of girls their own age."

"Maybe so … but I really liked Johnny and when we used to meet occasionally by accident and walk home from school together, we got on well. It didn't seem fair …"

"If you'd had more confidence, it could've happened for you then. You didn't believe you had a chance, so you shrank into the background."

"I started to shrink again when Charmaine came onto the scene. But revisiting the past with Edward has changed all that. For the first time in my life, I feel like I should always have felt. Like you thought I should feel … Like you probably felt. That

377

means much more than 'piss-all'."

"Sorry … I shouldn't have said that. It just makes me mad to see you risking messing up like I did. You and Johnny are good together. Still are. Don't throw it all away on some midlife daydream."

Later, in bed, Johnny said, "I never knew you had any reservations about children, Mari."

"I didn't, once we got round to it."

"These past few months you've kept coming out with all kinds of things I didn't know. Like this book … I thought I knew you so well …"

Marianne was silent. She could hear him waiting for her to say *you do,* but she didn't.

"Will you let me get to know you again? Properly."

"You might not like what you see."

"Don't be daft, woman!" He laughed. "Nothing you could tell me would make me feel any different about you." He reached over the duvet and hugged her body through the padding.

Marianne allowed herself to be drawn towards him and they lay close, a healing warmth between them.

Sam wanted to go on the London Eye, like every other visitor since the millennium. After breakfast next morning, Marianne and Johnny took him into town. From the highest point of the wheel, the city was shrouded in mist, but in the distance tower blocks loomed as if floating on water, and nearby the dome of St Paul's rose in architectural splendour. Marianne was reminded of the last time, when they had been there with Dylan, and how when they were circling on their way back down, he had stood at her shoulder and said, "That was really cool what you said to that blonde woman on the pier." He had said it loud enough for Johnny to hear, as if he was aware that the incident had put further strain on their relationship. *Poor*

Dylan, she thought, momentarily sad.

Sam had been much perkier since the previous evening and Marianne wondered if Sasha had set his heart racing again. She wouldn't be surprised.

"It was good to see Sasha again," he volunteered. "Made me realise that we would never have suited each other. She's far too political for me. Too sharp, too much of a feminist. We wouldn't have lasted five minutes once we grew up … To think I've been chasing her shadow all these years; nobody ever quite measuring up. Now I know I was looking for all the wrong things. Should've been content with someone sensible, normal and averagely bright. Like Gayle, in fact."

"So is Gayle with anyone now?"

"No. There was someone for a while, but it didn't last. Said he didn't like having someone else's kids to look after. Shame!"

"So what about you and her then? Any hope of a reconciliation?"

"Nooo," he paused. "I know it sounds terrible, but I'm not far off fifty and so's she. If I did settle down again, I had in mind someone of about thirty-five."

"Sam!" Marianne was cross.

"Yeah, I know …"

Johnny interrupted. "Do you want more youngsters then?"

"God, no!"

"Chances are she'll either have two or three in tow from some failed relationship, or she'll want to start a family with you."

"Hadn't thought of that."

"And," continued Johnny, "there are distinct advantages in growing old with someone. Facing the same age-challenges at the same time."

Marianne raised an eyebrow, pleasantly reassured.

Before Sam left, he found a moment to speak with Marianne

alone. "I have had a great break," he said. We shouldn't've left it this long. But before I go – and this is not meant as criticism – Johnny's worried about you. About you both. Says he doesn't want you going the same way as Sasha and Graham ... or for him to end up like me ... You didn't tell me things were rocky at the reunion."

"I felt it was up to Johnny to tell you."

"Well he has."

"I don't suppose he told you about Charmaine?"

"Yes, he did. All the gory details. But he also said that nothing happened between them, that he was a fool and that she's gone."

"Did he tell you I'm a madwoman ... hormones up the creek?"

"No ... he's just worried."

"Then he should say sorry ... like he means it and not trying to put the blame on me. It all went wrong from the moment she appeared."

"He did mention Edward. I presume that's Edward Harvey?"

"So?"

"He thinks you tell him stuff ... personal stuff."

"Not really. Edward has been my salvation. If it wasn't for Edward, I'd still be feeling the negative pull of the past. Johnny should thank Edward, not denigrate him."

"He wasn't."

"Look, Sam. When Johnny brought that woman home, I was just on the threshold of my midlife crisis. You know, when you look in the mirror and realise that things have moved on without you noticing. Even when he knew how bad she'd made me feel; even when I told him how it raked up all kinds of ghosts from the past, he never said sorry. Not properly. Not like he meant it. Not like I'd know it wouldn't happen again.

You know what he said to me one night when we were sniping at each other? He said: 'Mari, mentally you're the perfect woman for me.' He said if I'd had long blonde hair and boobs out here, then I'd be perfect. What woman wants to hear that when she's going menopausal and feeling over the hill? And I hear those words over and over. Whenever it's just him and me, I hear him say I'm not perfect."

"But he thinks you're wonderful? What about all the times he tells you you're great?"

"It's the bad things you remember. Even a thousand compliments don't make up for being told you're not perfect."

"Johnny doesn't like blonde and boobs. We never went for the same kind of women. You know that. You know you're his type. He probably only said it 'cos he was hurt."

"Then he needs to unsay it along with all the other stuff that's been wearing us down."

Sam sighed and shook his head. "You have to get this sorted before it festers. I'll have another word with John before I go. You need to talk to each other. Tell each other how you really feel. Get to the bottom of it – not snatched moments when one of you gets mad."

"Have you thought of marriage guidance – as an alternative career, Sam?" asked Marianne, teasingly.

"Plenty of practice, but so far poor results! You two could change all that!"

I wish, thought Marianne …

44

Farewell

Sasha had provoked Marianne into thinking about Edward in a different way. Sasha was wise; Sasha didn't have a head full of fluff, and just like in the old days, she had touched a nerve. It was all midlife madness. Of course Edward wasn't important compared to Johnny. In any case it was now nearly three months since she had heard from him, so it looked like their re-acquaintance was already dimming. But before she gave up on him completely, there were loose ends to be tied and she wanted to tell him what he had done for her.

She was making vegetable soup in the kitchen and a pile of diced carrots and swede was accumulating on the chopping board. The smell of sautéed leek and onion filled the air and made her eyes water.

Of course she couldn't tell Edward exactly like it was because he didn't know how it had all started when she was five, and it would be too much angst to drop in an email inbox to be found, perhaps at the end of a long day at work when all he would want to do would be to eat, to go to bed and sleep.

But she couldn't say nothing, because what had happened was, to her, incredible. She couldn't avoid the angst altogether.

Until she met Lydia again it was as if the child Marianne, the Marianne who cried alone in the woods under the canopy of rhododendron bushes and who faced a barrage of insults every day, still inhabited her being. It was the baggage just under the surface, an ancient seam of fossilised remains that the presence of Charmaine, like a landslide, had exposed once again; it was the snapping Moray eel lurking under a rock on the ocean floor.

Meeting Lydia again had changed all that, and the child in the woods was now a distant memory. She was a fragile flower in a far-off land. She was somebody else past with somebody else's pain. Edward had given her a gift so precious and priceless. He had given her back the good times and strength to face the bullies at the reunion. This time she wanted a real good bye and not the slipping away that had happened when he left Brocklebank without her saying a word.

She waited for a time when she was alone in the house so she could think clearly and write candidly.

To: Edward Harvey
From: Marianne Hayward
Date: 22nd February 2002, 21.12.
Subject: Is there anybody out there?

Let me end as I began ...
Dear Lydia,
It seems we have come to the end of the line.
Unexpectedly sudden from this perspective, and I hope this doesn't mean something awful has happened to you. Perhaps my cyber-chatter just got too much? Or my efforts at trying to present the multifaceted 'me' possibly backfiring with the misinterpretation of email. But c'est la vie! Some people, they say, meet for a reason, some for a season, and some for a lifetime. Hard to know which category we fall into. It smacks of carelessness that I should lose you twice. The first time excusable, but this time?
I shall ever be grateful that I found you again; that you took the time to meet me in cyberspace for that

extended and precious exchange of memories that was to change my life. That may sound as if I am being overly dramatic, but it's true. For thirty-three years I had carried a burden that I could never face; the burden of Brocklebank Hall. When full of self-doubt, I would look over my shoulder and it was there, this dark shadow, bouncing along behind me, the size of a planet, engulfing all my hopes of moving on. Now I sometimes expect it to be there – those feelings of hurt from yesteryear – but no, there's something very different: an emptiness; it has gone.

I found you by chance and expected nothing more than the polite exchange of a couple of emails that is so typical of most of the Friends Reunited contacts. Your zealous replying suggested some enthusiasm. You didn't have to. I have been entertained by your contributions, inspired and motivated by the fact that you do so much, and I hoped one day we'd meet; that we would finally get to know whom we were talking to, whether we had things to say and whether we could be friends.

More than any of the Brocklebank boys, I had never forgotten you. Your intellect, your lack of hostility when all around were giving me a hard time, your wonderful portrayal of Lydia, all left an impression that meant your name occasionally floated through my mind when thinking about the past.

Farewell Edward, I am glad you have found happiness in your work and with your family. I think you are one of the good guys in this world. I always knew that email relationships were ephemeral – and one of the reasons I wanted to meet you, was to try to make it more secure. Indeed a meeting is worth a million words as far as understanding a person is concerned. If we had met, I

doubt I would have felt compelled to write so much –
and perhaps this misunderstanding (if such it is) would
never have occurred!
I hope that the rest of your life brings you your dreams,
and I will never forget that you helped to set me free.
Best wishes, and love,
Lucy

She read it through a couple of times, paused for the briefest moment, took a deep breath, connected to the phoneline and clicked on *Send*.

Then she lay down on the floor in a foetal position and cried, clawing at the carpet with her fingers, feeling the roughness of the pile against her cheek, wishing that it didn't matter, knowing that it did. *I just wanted to meet you so badly. To see ... to hear ... to find out if all this emotion and expectation was justified. And now I'll never, never know. I can't bear it.*

Her curiosity was overflowing. Would it never be relieved? Would it carry on expanding like the universe? And the future stretched moonscape bleak as she resigned herself to the only possible conclusion.

Edward Harvey was lost.

45

Dear Mari

"Mari ... Oh Mari, love ... Where to start?" said Johnny, running his hands through his hair in the familiar way that he always did.

It was late on Friday evening, the day after she sent the farewell email to Edward, and Johnny was in his favourite armchair, poised on the edge, elbows on knees, a white envelope in one hand. Mostly he looked down, searching, struggling it seemed for the right words, every now and then flashing a glance to Marianne who sat on the sofa to the side, arms folded, waiting ...

The living room was dimly lit with the uplighter casting shadows in which to hide.

Johnny continued: "I remembered you saying a few months back, it had been good ... No, perhaps 'good' is the wrong word ... 'therapeutic' was what you said ... You said it was therapeutic writing emails about your bad times at Brocklebank to that Edward bloke from your class. It got me thinking maybe I should do the same. Not sending emails to anyone, but writing – just simply writing stuff down.

"Started scribbling, crossing out, more scribbling; more crossing out. Hell, I couldn't believe how bad I was. So out of practice. Years since I've done any personal writing – not even letter writing – except Christmas notes, or letters when somebody's died. It's just been formal stuff for work. Reports, lesson notes, planning ... Nothing with a 'feelings' agenda! I used to be good at English ... essays – even poetry. Suddenly couldn't do it any more. Hell that was a shock – a big shock. You think you'll always be able to write. When did I lose it? You don't ever imagine you will lose something like that. Thought it would still be there to draw upon whenever I needed to. I forget how much time has passed since I last constructed something with a more creative edge. No, I don't mean creative – that makes it sound false – I mean … Oh, I don't know what I mean … I mean truth from inside …" He paused and glanced at her again, looking for help, she thought, but she said nothing.

It had been another row that had prompted these revelations. Marianne had been offhand when he seemed to want her to listen to him about his 'helluva' day at school. She had turned on him big time. *"How dare you make all these demands that I should listen. Where were you when I needed to talk to you? Off drinking down the pub with Charmaine, that's where … I've had a bad day too. You don't have exclusive rights to bad days."* It was another of those M word moments when she opened her mouth and the vitriol came spewing forth without any apparent brain engagement along the way. She still hadn't forgiven him even though he was doing all the right things now and there was some pretence of normality for most of the time. It was 'sorry' that was missing. It was evidence of genuine remorse. No guarantees that it wouldn't all start again if she relented, softened, returned to her more compassionate self. So he'd had a bad day. The old Mari would have showered him with soothing words, run a bath, cooked a meal … But if she hadn't been paying attention to him before, at least now she was listening intently.

"Anyway, I carried on scribbling … I stuck at it. More crossing out … start again … Screwed up half a note pad and chucked it in the bin. And you know what? Even that began to feel good. Like I was chucking away all the bad bits; the bits that hurt; the bits where I had fucked up.

"So I thought 'hey, this has got to be helping …' so I started yet again … started telling it like I was talking to you … not that I was going to let you read it … hey, no … but it felt good telling you … Where did we lose that, Mari? We used to talk, didn't we? All the time … Anyway, bit by bit it all fell into place … the anger, the fears, the blame. The 'getting old' stuff … Realising I'm not twenty-five any more. Scared of being past it … You know … men worry about that …

"Been a shit … A fucking ace bastard … My fault! Then the drinking … All got out of hand, Mari. Drifting … purposelessness … swimming in circles. Didn't know what was going on with you … Should've asked, but didn't know what to say. Frightened of making things worse, I s'pose. Didn't know what was going on with me, either. Far too early for a midlife crisis, I thought. God how did we get to this? Us? I mean us, Mari? You and I never messed up like this before."

Marianne unfolded her arms and bit her lip. Still she said nothing.

"So I wrote and wrote and at first it was a bit pretentious. As if I was watching you listening to me and putting on a show. Watching you reading it, gauging your reactions, trying to impress, holding back – even trying to be funny… Still the cocky bastard … But after a while it began to look like truth … truth from here … from the soul …

"When I'd finished, or at least when there was no more I had to say, it felt like a great weight had gone. You know when a bunch of balloons is let go into the air and you look up and watch the wind taking them higher and higher. They look so free … That's what it was like.

"And then, only then, I wondered if it would help if you did read it. I thought *she needs to know this*. Then she'll understand. She needs to know so she may begin to forgive me …

"You've been distant these past few months. Remote. I'm

not blaming you, but it's like you've stopped caring about us. I want you to care again and maybe reading this will help because it's more articulate than I'm being. And it says things that I find hard. And you don't have to say anything at all. I'd rather you didn't say anything. Just read it and try to understand and know that I'm trying, really trying to sort it, that I am really sorry for all the things I said and did. I don't expect you to do anything. You can't do anything, can't fix it ... It's something I have to do myself. And I will. You know I will, don't you, Mari? You do know I want to make it right again?"

He handed her the envelope, still holding onto it as she grasped the other end, as if that connection was a touch begging for reassurance and that some force might be conducted along the paper from one to the other. Their eyes met briefly, registering concern, then Johnny dragged himself from the armchair and turned away. One last look over his shoulder, a pleading look, she thought, and then he left the room.

She looked at the white foolscap envelope with *Mari* written on the front. She fingered the edges and traced her thumb over her name, remembering the time way back at grammar school when she, aged fifteen, had been so excited at acquiring Johnny Ingleton's geography text book; at seeing the look and style of his writing for the first time. *John Ingleton* in black biro, and *1972*. That's how she discovered his loopy I's and continental sevens. Johnny made her knees go weak in those days, and when they used to pass on the stairs on a Wednesday – he coming down from English and she going up – he always smiled at her and said hello, and she would flush and smile back, so pleased to have been spoken to by a guy in lower sixth that she would scarcely be able to concentrate for the next half hour.

But all that girlish fancying was years before they got together. How she used to wish for him to notice her for being more than just a school kid. For two years she was besotted – until he went away to university and she discovered real boyfriends, real romantic angst and finally real passion. Even then she often wondered what he was doing and where he'd gone and if he was still involved with the glamorous Cassie with the legs up to heaven. Sometimes she would see him briefly in the holidays when her crowd and his crowd were in the same pub, and her heart would still somersault if they exchanged a few words. But they were never alone for her to find out anything personal. Then, a few years later, the chance encounter in London at Sasha's party to which she nearly hadn't gone, and the kiss that changed their lives.

Now it had come to this. A white envelope. She hesitated, just like she'd hesitated almost a year ago when the first of the emails from Edward – the reply via Friends Reunited – had appeared in her in-box. But with Edward, although there had turned out to be a lot at stake, she hadn't realised it at the time. Within this white envelope from Johnny lay words that may heal – or not. There was a debt to be paid and maybe the time had come. It had sounded like a last ditch effort; a final attempt to bring her back to him. But would it be enough?

She got up and lit the candle on the mantelpiece, knowing she must read this offering with openness and generosity of spirit. She breathed deeply, relaxing her shoulders, trying to let go of any residual anger, dimly aware of the faintly ticking clock, the lateness of the hour and an all consuming tiredness that must wait for its relief. Then she settled down on the floor to read.

Dear Darling Mari,

This is one of the hardest but most important things that I have ever written – have ever done.

So many weeks ago now I listened to you telling me about

the M word, as you call it, and I was so relieved. Here was an explanation for you being mad with me, and I forgot to look beyond. Forgot to look at me.

Perhaps I should have told you then what I was going through, but it didn't seem fair – as if I was trying to upstage your problem with mine. In any case, I couldn't find the words – needed to think things through and prepare. Your revelations came as a surprise. I was taken unawares and didn't know what to say.

You told me that you'd got help with your old school demons by writing to that bloke Edward. That hurt at the time. Knowing you were telling a virtual stranger what you could never tell me. I couldn't believe you'd kept it secret all those years. I'd never known you had all that angst inside and I felt cheated. You tried to make me feel okay about it – said it was because he was there at the school, you didn't have to put into words the half of it, you assumed he would understand, but it didn't matter if he didn't, it was the process of writing that helped you. So that's what I'm trying now. At least partly.

I know now when it started to go wrong. It wasn't with you being all hot, was it? It was months before that. It was when things were going wrong in my head and I brought Charmaine home. Why did I do that? It wasn't as if you'd been neglecting me. Never.

I wanted to break free from predictability – from knowing where I was going to be every hour of every week. Such indulgence! I felt constricted by the daily routines. Suffocated. Fed up with being 'Reliable Johnny …' Not your fault. It was like I could see the rest of my life falling into a never-changing pattern. I thought I might as well be dead. It's an old cliché, but I had this yearning for space, a desperate need to go off on a journey, walking the Cornish coast, perhaps – a quest to find myself again. My equivalent of riding off into the sunset on the old motorbike with the leathers on. And then I'd come back whole and be ready to face the rest of our life together.

Charmaine reminded me of youth and dreams. I know she's not that young, but when you get to forty-eight, thirty is 'a mere sapling', to quote Taryn! She paid me attention and I was flattered. I wondered if I still knew how to flirt! Childish I know. Pathetic. I invited her home because I wanted you to see that I could still attract women. It wasn't meant to make you mad – or insecure. It was me that was insecure. I wanted you to throw yourself at my feet and tell me I was wonderful like you used to do …

When you were mad, it was an excuse to blame you – to accuse you of being unreasonable when really it was me that was the unreasonable one. And the more you were annoyed by Charmaine, the worse I got. I enjoyed your jealousy. I hate to admit it, but it made me feel as if I mattered, and when I'd had a few beers, I played with it … used it. Stupid. Couldn't understand why this didn't make you want to have sex with me all the time. Didn't know then that you were going through all the same kind of thoughts that I was.

I never wanted to have an affair with her. Nice girl, but not my type. Too 'high maintenance' – hairdressers, beauty salons, dining out and all that stuff. Insecure too. And dangerous. She could have messed things up, but she wouldn't have wanted me long term. We were too different. All I would have been was a casual fling. But at first I wanted you to think I wanted to have an affair, because I thought that would somehow spice things up for us.

Don't get me wrong. I'm not complaining about our sex life. On the contrary. It sounds as though I am, I know, but for a while I thought I wanted something that I don't. Some late night TV programme and everybody at it with ropes and ice cream! At the time I regretted not having been more adventurous. Yet we have been. We are. Adventurous enough!

We always used to talk about everything. I wanted to provoke you into asking me if there was anything I wanted – before we got too old. Wanted to know if you had any unfulfilled fantasies too. No good trying to swing from the light fittings when we're seventy! Didn't know how to bring up the subject.

Behind all this was some kind of fear. I was – am – scared of losing it: the ability to love you properly. You remember that time after we'd been to the Cedarwood barbeque? Maybe I thought that being more adventurous would solve any problem should it arise again.

As well as all that there was the usual stuff … What have I done with my life? Where am I going? What have I left for posterity – apart from Holly – and is it enough? Is it too late now for anything else? I started wondering if we should have tried harder for more kids … Please don't be upset – I'm telling it how it was … I know it was me who gave up on the idea. Selfish reasons at the time. Didn't think how you might feel. And once I started wondering and regretting … But I've thought it through now and I wouldn't change anything. Honestly.

So that's it. The sum total of my shit-state. A man who's scared of growing old and being past it. A man who has forgotten how to hope for the future. I see the young people and want to tell them how short it all is, like people told us and we took no notice 'cos you don't when you think you've got forever and that forever is a long, long time away.

I'm so, so sorry for upsetting you – for making you feel less than the wonderful, beautiful person you are. If I could turn back time and unsay those things … I didn't mean any of it. You, Mari, are my Perfect Woman. Always.

I can't bear seeing your eyes with the love missing. Please look at me again like you used to do. Please forgive me.

I love you,

Johnny

Marianne held the letter tightly, looked up with closed eyes, hints of tears bursting between her eyelashes, she rocked on the floor, desperately trying not to cry, fearing that once she started she would never stop. Tears for Johnny found, for Edward lost, for the tiny scrap of life that hardly existed at all and that Johnny knew nothing of. Tears of relief, huge and precious relief that it was all over now and that they could put the lid on the box and move into their Indian summer years with hope again.

And still she sat on the floor, in a trance-like state with the clock ticking away, the candle burning low and calming vanilla infusing the air with a luscious exotic scent.

So this was it. The long months of craziness were coming to an end. Or perhaps not quite to an end, but at least to a point where it would end sometime soon and they would find a way to contentment again.

What would she say to him? He would want a response. Need to be reassured that this act of complete trust and faith would not be abused or thrown back in his face. She'd been throwing things back at him for months now, paying him back for all the jibes and taunts, and for his dalliance with Charmaine.

In all the twenty-three years that they had been together, they had never had a time like this. Never been cross for more than a day or two. Hadn't known what it was like to feel resentful and trapped and wondering if you were married to the right person.

She knew that every word she said now would have the potential to make the difference between unity and separation. So much power attached to the tiniest utterance; the smallest inflection. The merest glance could heal the rift or create a chasm that could never be crossed.

When, eventually, she made her way quietly to the bedroom, Johnny was fast asleep and breathing quietly. He looked so vulnerable, on his back and naked, one arm outstretched on top of the duvet. Of course she still loved him; had never stopped. But she'd stopped showing it. Had purposely withdrawn her care and affection as a punishment because she didn't feel he deserved it. Sex had become mechanical and on her terms. And it had been easy while her emotions were partially engaged with Edward.

She crept about the room, undressing silently, padding softly to and from the bathroom, fearful of disturbing him but almost pleased to have the extra time before she had to respond, react, forgive.

She was just about to put on her nightdress when she paused. *Predictability,* she thought, *predictability, according to Taryn, was the enemy and must be avoided at all costs,* so she left it on the chair. Then she slipped under the duvet and realised as she breathed in the familiar warmth of Johnny that her anger had gone.

46

Transported

In Marianne's dream the summer sky was blue with wispy clouds and a blazing sun, and on the grass idle groupings of young people chattered excitedly as students do. Edward was among them. Marianne kept catching glimpses and exchanging smiles. Again and again she tried to start a conversation, but he wouldn't go beyond the pleasantries, the weather-talk. Wouldn't let her show him how well they could get on as friends. Then he was off across the lawns until she caught up with him again.

Sometimes they were twenty-something, sometimes just as now. Except she didn't know what 'now' was as far as he was concerned, so there were even variations of that.

Then she was lying on the grass in a z-shape with head raised and supported by her hand. The grass was summer-long and vibrant green, scattered with broken daisy chains and rhododendron blossoms. Edward lay opposite in similar pose. She was trying to get his attention, but although his body was facing hers, he was talking to someone else over his shoulder. Then suddenly he moved to get out of the way of something. A swivelling movement with a final flip. His back was up against her. Touching. He seemed disinclined to move away, yet still he talked to someone else. They lay like spoons. Who else would she let so close apart from Johnny and her most intimate friends? She could feel him and she breathed in his scent – somehow familiar – evoking memories of when they were young.

But in this picture they were still young – perhaps twenty-two and still with the bloom of youth.

Where were they? She thought this in the dream. Lots of little buildings scattered haphazardly. Some residential centre perhaps. They must be on a course. And Sasha was there, roaming sexily.

Marianne was wondering why he wouldn't talk to her when there was so much to say. Surely she could interest him if only he'd give her a chance? He must like her or he wouldn't be this close. He must be going to talk to her properly sometime soon.

She could feel his heat on her hand under his back. He did not move for an age. Then without warning he was off again, disappearing among the throng and she kept catching sight of him, not little Edward anymore, but tall and lean in black open-necked shirt and black jeans, with shortish tousled dark hair and sometimes with glasses, sometimes not; confident and full of charm as he shared a word with everyone – everyone, that is, except her.

She was hungry, but couldn't find the food. She saw Sasha go into an old-fashioned refectory with high ceiling and arched glass windows, pine tables and long benches. Sasha went and sat at the same table as Edward and some other young men. Gave him the eye, she did, and Marianne watched through the open door feeling jealous. He would never look at her now. Sasha came bouncing out all blonde and glowing. "He wants to be called Benjamin," she said loudly, smiling.

"No, no! Not Benjamin! He wants to be Edward! It's Ted he doesn't want to be. He told me …"

"He said Benjamin … You call him Edward if you like, but he prefers Benjamin." She paused. "What's your astrology?"

"Leo and Capricorn. Fire and Earth," Marianne gabbled, struggling with the words as if speaking with mud in her mouth. Then more clearly: "But we have perfect trining Mercuries – within two degrees – and harmonious moons and interconnected T-squares … What about that, then? What do you know about astrology anyway? It's me who knows about astrology."

"I know much more than you think. I know that you can't make assumptions about anything until you know the Ascendant. Surely you know that? You must find out his Ascendant. Then you'll know for sure.

"You wait," Sasha continued, "he'll be over here in a flash."

And sure enough he started to approach. "But it's you he wants to see," Marianne said despairingly. "Not me. You were flirting with him. It's you he wants now."

Sasha brushed this problem aside. "I'm not free. I'm not interested. He's nice, but far too serious. Now it's your turn. You have to be less available. That's how it's done."

"But then he won't speak to me at all," Marianne wailed.

"Grab attention, then leave," she said. "Never stay too long. Leave them wanting more. Run away, they'll follow."

Deep down she knew Sasha was right. She had never listened before; always tried too hard. Was it too late to change? Game playing wasn't her thing. Especially not with friends ... Or prospective friends.

He looked first at Sasha, she thought, adoringly, but Sasha smiled and was gone. He looked at Marianne.

"Tell me about archaeology," she said. "I want to know, honestly."

He was on a dusty floor unfolding maps for them both to pore over. Enormous maps ... Maps from the pens of old cartographers, now worn and torn and faded.

She slipped onto the floor opposite him, hoping not to startle him, hoping he wouldn't run away again. She held her breath. At last he looked up and for the first time met her gaze with those beautiful brown eyes she remembered noticing first as Lydia's. Seconds passed. Wordlessly they embraced in a hug that understood all the hurt and pain of long ago.

She thought she heard him say, *"What do you want from me?"* A muffled sound lost in her hair. She wondered if she had imagined it; that it was what she wanted him to say so she could answer and put his mind at rest.

"Just friends. That's all …"

He hugged her even tighter and for a precious instant she felt so safe.

But then the floor seemed to slide and a wind whipped up and ruffled the edges of the maps under their knees. Now it was Marianne who was pulling away; pulling back from the closeness she'd been chasing, it seemed, for hours.

No, she thought, *please no. Let me stay a while with this gentle man whom I need to know. Let us talk a while …*

But it was not to be, she was mercilessly dragged back to wakefulness, aching awake, with beating heart and gasps of breath, dripping in sweat and with feelings of oh such overwhelming sadness at not being close to him anymore.

She blinked away the tears and sighed a long and quiet sigh of resignation. She lay till she was quite composed again and then turned on her side.

A pair of bright blue eyes stared back at her.

"Hello. Where were you?" whispered Johnny, with furrowed brow. "What was it? Tell me."

She shook her head against the pillow and smiled. "Nothing … Nothing important … Hey …" She reached for him under the duvet to distract his attention.

"Where've you been?" he brushed the tears from her eyes and folded her up in the warmest of embraces. "These past few months … where have you been?"

Where had she been? Away on a voyage of middle-aged madness. Thankfully all in her head. No harm done. On the contrary.

"I'm back now," she whispered, looking at him like she used to do.

47

Renaissance

To: Marianne Hayward
From: Edward Harvey
Date: 25th February 2003, 22.43
Subject: Re: Is there anybody out there?

Dear Lucy,
Many apologies for long silence. Guilty for not being in touch …
Felicity's mother died, so back and forth to Surrey every weekend. An emotional time; impossibly busy and very distracted. Long story.
Then computer problems: hard-drive failure, lost email addresses … Still catching up.
I'm sure I don't deserve all you say. But thanks, anyway. Intrigued by the sound of your book!
Lots happening as a result of maze discovery. Exhibition at BM … Lectures too. Should start next month. Will write with details soon in case you're free …
Packing for Norway tomorrow!
love,
Lydia.